Pirate V

Published by CLC Publishing, LLC, Mustang, OK.

ISBN: 9781092737739

Fiction

Pirate V

Kirkston United

S.C. Lauren

AC Publishing

This book is dedicated to my earliest pirate posse –
although I have lost touch with many of you over the years,
this series would not have ever come to fruition without
your relentless encouragement…

Kendel Sorrel – Once in a while you will find a friend who
will be a friend forever. Thanks for putting up with me for
all of these years

Paige Boyer – The first person to have ever laid eyes on a
Pirate manuscript. My first, unofficial "editor"

Julia Carnes – My first and greatest fan. Thank you for all
of those wonderful memories in math class talking about
my dreams of becoming an author and for truly listening to
me tell my story for the first time

Kirkston

Akito Berry
Island

Danger
Shallow Waters

F

Caldara

☆
Caldara City

BEWARE
Annihilators make
bay here

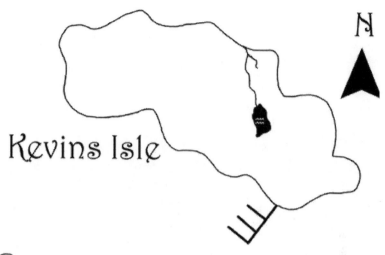

Kevins Isle

Skull Island

Black Dragons Hideout

Property of Captain Smith

Part I
Sea's Ghost

Chapter 1

Her eyes were blue crystals as elegant as the ocean itself, and her hair was black as night and combed neatly – stretching as far as her lower back. The undeniably familiar features of her face sent a shiver up and down Smith's spine. His throat felt as though it had closed up as his eyes fell upon her. The amber colored dress was not something he had ever thought he would see her wearing, but like anything, it made her look stunning. After the intense trauma from the past few days, Smith's first assumption was that he was having some sort of hallucination, that it was merely his mind desperately creating an illusion, as a way to cope with everything that had happened.

"My God –it's her!" a voice from behind called, and Smith glanced over his shoulder, for just a moment, to see Yin exiting Mrs. Barons home.

The woman smiled. It was a smile he had not seen in many years.

"Hello, Peter," she said to him as she turned away from the grave – her grave – that she had been examining in order to face them.

Smith gasped, sucking in enough air to clear his throat so that he could question what it was he was seeing.

"Courtney?" he asked, glancing at the grave she had been standing by that read Courtney "Sea" Livingston. His eyes immediately darted back to the woman standing before them.

"Oh, God," Yin said. His entire body shook beside Smith as the two stood in the doorway.

"Oh, my," the woman said as she came closer. Smith's bottom lip quivered. He wanted to dart to her, wrap his arms around her, and kiss her lips, but his current state of shock made it impossible to lift his feet off the ground.

"Courtney?" she questioned. "Oh, no, no." Her voice was like music. "I think you two are mistaken."

A delightful young voice called out from the woods, "Is that Peter?"

Upon hearing his name, Smith turned his head to his right to see a young boy playing amongst a cluster of trees. The boy seemed to be about eleven years old, and he looked so much like the woman in the amber colored dress. Smith had tears in his eyes now as he turned back to the woman.

"Courtney," he said again.

"No," she said, and Smith could sense her pity for them.

Yin gave Smith a gentle nudge, and the two of them stepped out of the doorway and towards the woman standing in front of them.

"Who are you?" Yin asked because Smith was unable to speak.

"Carissa," she said, smiling sadly. "Carissa Livingston."

"Livingston?" Yin questioned.

"Courtney – Sea – she was my cousin," she said.

Carissa turned her head towards the young boy standing in the woods. "And, this is my son, Pierson." Smith glanced over at the child. The boy blushed to have so many eyes on him so suddenly and hid himself behind a tree.

Smith immediately looked back at the woman. It was like seeing a ghost. "Carissa?" he questioned as though he did not believe her.

"Yes." She smiled at them.

Smith grunted slightly, attempting to clear the knot that had formed in his throat. "And, you say you are Sea's cousin? You look as though you could have been her twin."

The woman nodded slightly. "Yes. My father used to say that." She touched her cheeks that had become flushed from the uncomfortable encounter. Her eyes darted over towards Yin.

"And who are you?"

"Mathew," Yin said. "Sea would have called me –"

"Yin!" Carissa said excitedly and reached out a hand to shake. They shook with their left hands since Yin's right arm was tied up in a sling. "Yes, I've read all about you in her letters."

Smith's head continued to spin. "How is it you came to be here, Miss Carissa? Why have we never met you before?"

"I have lived in Balla my entire life," she said.

"The family Sea went to visit after Mr. Keg died?" Yin questioned.

"Yes, that would be us. She came to my father's home after the Black Dragon's first pillage did not go well. She stayed with us for many months. The poor girl, so young, was so devastated by the death of her guardian. She blamed herself something terrible." Carissa frowned.

Every gesture she made seemed to remind the two men of their former captain, but there was a hint of elegance about her that Sea had lacked. The woman continued speaking. "I came here to seek help from the Black Dragons, my dear cousin's old friends. But the moment the ship came into port, we were raided by government men then interviewed and questioned before being allowed into the country. I now know the capital has been taken over by a foreign enemy. They are quite hostile."

"They let a ship into harbor?" Yin questioned.

"Yes," she said. "But it was quite a rigorous process, and they raided much of the ships supplies."

"Do you think they are allowing ships out?" Yin asked, looking at Smith. "Perhaps Harold could send a letter to England after all?"

"If Harold is alive, that is," Smith said with a solemn expression. He looked at Carissa and wondered if she could sense the feeling of longing he had for her, in the pit of his stomach, simply because of her face. He attempted to shake the feeling away.

"Pardon me for staring, Miss Carissa," he said.

"I have not seen my dear cousin since she was fourteen. And, we only communicated through letters after that. Mrs. Keg had written me after my dear cousin had perished. I went by Mrs. Keg's home before coming here and saw that she too has since passed. All I mean to say is that it has been a long time since I last laid eyes on dear Courtney, but if she had grown in the same manner as I, I assume I am her double, as we had been as young girls. My own father had a hard time telling us apart the one time she did visit, so I understand your anxious behavior."

Smith thanked her for her sympathy. He rubbed the back of his head, his eyes drifting back towards the boy who was still hiding.

"We won't bite you, lad," Smith called out to the boy who slowly came out from behind the trees and over to Carissa. Smith smiled at him, and the boy smiled back. The child gripped onto Carissa's dress and buried his face in her side.

"You say you came here to seek our help?" Yin asked.

"I did," she said sadly. "I did not expect to get myself trapped in a country at war by doing so, though."

Smith sighed. "Unfortunately, we cannot stay here. We must travel south. The rebellion camp, the Black

Dragon lair, was ambushed a few days ago. We do not know who is alive or dead."

Carissa's eyes drew towards the fresh graves in the garden. "I believe you know of two that you have lost?"

Yin lowered his head. "My brother and my best mate."

"Yang and Cannonball?" she asked.

Yin looked up. "How did you –"

"Letters," she said. "Courtney wrote me quite often before her passing. She told me much about each of the Black Dragons. I had hoped to meet each of them." She looked back towards the graves. "It seems I have waited too late."

"What sort of trouble are you in, Miss. Carissa, that you would need our help?" Smith asked.

She shook her head and nodded down at the boy. "A conversation that should be saved for later when young ears are not listening in."

"As you wish," Smith said. "But we must travel south to find our friends and learn who managed to escape Stevenson's attack. Please, if you will, accompany us, and perhaps we may find time to have that conversation."

Smith helped Carissa and her son, Pierson, up onto the horse that he had stolen from John Stevenson a few days before. He and Yin walked. It would take several days before they would arrive at the gulf where the rebellion had fled. During their travels, Carissa kept fairly quiet. Smith and Yin remained unsure as to why she had decided to come to Kirkston so suddenly, and they learned very little about her and her son on their journey. Both men, Smith especially, found themselves unable to look away from her for too long. It was like the ghost of Sea had returned to them.

Chapter 2

One Day Earlier

Snake wiped tears from his eyes as Sky wrapped her arms around him, placing her head on his chest. "Ignore them," she said softly, referring to the taunts coming from the other side of the iron door. Snake, along with his wife Sky and her brother Hethusaka, were locked away in a prison cell. The Spanish guards on the other side had just informed Snake that Yang, who had been taken from them many hours ago, had been hanged and that his body would be placed in an iron cage, to rot along the Eastern docks, as a warning to all who dared to oppose John. The thought of his friend not being able to have a proper burial sickened him.

Hethuska stood a short distance away from the two of them. He spoke in his native tongue to his sister for a moment, and when she responded, she then offered Snake a sad expression.

"He wanted to know what the men were saying to you," she said.

Snake rested his chin on top of her head. The voices had dispersed, and they could hear footsteps leading away from their cell. The three of them sat down against the far wall in silence. Sky kissed his cheek, and he could see that she too had tears streaming down her face.

Without warning, the iron door suddenly screeched open. Snake gripped his wife tight, but the guards were on them in a matter of seconds. "Leave her alone!" Snake screamed, mistakenly believing that they were after his wife. The men grabbed him, and Sky gripped onto his arms. One of the men kicked her in the face to get her to let go.

"Let go of me! Let go of me!" Snake roared as he was yanked to his feet. He glanced over at his wife. "Mapiya!" he cried, reaching towards her as the men dragged him out of the cell.

"I'll kill you! I'll kill all of you!" he screamed as he was forcibly removed from the prison chambers, away from his wife and her brother. The door was shut behind them.

Snake fought the entire stretch of hall they dragged him through. Eventually they arrived outside of the royal chambers; two men held Snake by his arms, while a third gently knocked on the door. The door opened, and John was standing before them. Snake cringed and instinctively yanked his arms in an attempt to free himself from the men who had taken him there.

"It's been a while, Johnny," John said to him, and Snake gritted his teeth. He contemplated kicking the man's cane out from under him.

John Stevenson had become a mere shadow of the man Snake had known as a child. His once warm smile and handsome face had long ago been replaced by a permanent scowl covered in disfiguring scars. A glass ball rested where his right eye had once been – the deepest, most hideous scar on his face – which cut through his eyelid from forehead to cheekbone. He was Kirkston's current conqueror and traitor to the royal Caldara family – Snake's godfather.

"Send me back to the prison cells. I'd rather be there than standing here with you."

John shook his head then looked over at the men. "You can let him go. He won't cause any trouble." He waved his hand. "Come inside, Johnny."

The men released Snake and departed, leaving him standing in the hallway. "I should kill you," Snake snarled. John shrugged his shoulders, as though the threat to his life had come from a mere child throwing a tantrum.

"Come in. I have someone I would like for you to meet."

John entered into the royal chambers. Snake's first instinct was to run, but he knew the guards would catch him before he got too far – and he certainly would not try to escape with his wife still in a prison chamber. He reluctantly followed John inside.

Maria, John's wife, was asleep in the bed. There were dark circles under her eyes. "Hey, Johnny!" a young voice called out, and before Snake knew it a young boy had his arms wrapped around his legs. Snake glanced down to see Robbie, John's son, smiling up at him.

Anxiously, Snake patted the boy on the head. "Yes, hello, Robbie. It's been a while."

"Keep quiet, Robbie," John said. "Your mother is exhausted. Don't wake her."

"Is she ill?" Snake asked, finding himself being pulled into the strange world he always got trapped in whenever John managed to get him away from the other Black Dragons. It was a world in which John, playing make-believe, acted as though they were old friends catching up.

John chuckled slightly. "No, she's not ill. She's doing quite well actually. Come here, Johnny." John knelt down in a corner after propping his cane up against the wall. Snake watched as John leaned over into a bassinet and lifted up a small baby wrapped in a white, knitted quilt. The baby started to fuss, and John carefully bounced the baby in his arms.

Snake approached cautiously. "Yours?" Snake asked.

"Of course," John said. "Her name is Amy."

Snake cringed. "I wish you hadn't named your children after my parents, John."

John frowned. "I see." The baby girl began to cry, and Maria's head popped up. John and Snake both looked her way. Maria had as sour look on her face.

"¿Por qué él está aquí?" she snarled. John approached the bed and handed the crying baby over to his wife.

"Sé amable con él," John seemed to warn her, and she put on a smile. Snake watched the woman carefully cradle her newborn baby.

"She's lovely," Snake managed to say, still playing make-believe.

"Thank you," Maria said, clearly uncomfortable with Snake in the room. She certainly was not the only one; Snake wanted to bolt, but he knew John was not going to give him any option for true escape.

"I'd like to return to my friends," Snake said.

"They're not going anywhere anytime soon," John said as he pulled up a chair beside Maria.

"Not like Yang, then?" Snake questioned, his voice full of hurt.

John sighed. "It had to be done."

"No, John, it didn't," Snake retorted. "You had him hung."

"This is a war, Johnny. You and your friends should have never gotten involved," John said. "I am sorry about your friend."

"*This is war*, you say? A war *you* started, you dog! Have someone escort me back to the prison chambers, John. I won't stay here and play house with you," Snake said.

John started to argue, but Maria intervened. "John, you are making him upset, and there is no reason for it. If he wants to stay with his friends, let him. You just had his friend hung, and now he is worried about the two left in the prison chamber. He's angry, and there's no sense in forcing him to be here with us so soon. Let him mourn for his friend how he wishes to." Snake actually appreciated the sentiment and offered Maria a slight nod of approval.

After a moment of contemplating, John rose from his seat, gripping his cane. "I'll take you back to your friends," he said, grumbling slightly as he spoke, knowing his wife was correct in her thinking.

"Thank you," Snake said, looking at Maria as he said it. She just nodded, avoiding eye contact.

"You're leaving?" Robbie questioned.

"Go sit with Mamá, Robbie," John said. John walked past Snake and opened the door. Snake was held back by Robbie for a moment; the boy wanted him to play.

"Antonio?" Snake heard John question, and Snake glanced over his shoulder to see John and whispering to the man known as Antonio at the door. "I don't think…" John mumbled, but whatever he was about to say was cut off by Antonio's angry grunts.

"Very well," John said and turned back towards them. "Robbie, I said go sit with your madre. Come, Johnny, and we will take you back to your friends."

Snake followed John, who seemed to merely be following the Spaniard. Instead of heading towards the prison cells, they exited the castle and stood out in the courtyard just inside the exterior walls.

"John," Snake said sternly. "Are you not taking me to my friends?" Before John could answer, Snake heard ruckus coming from one of the outer buildings. Looking up, he spotted Hethuska and Sky being dragged across the courtyard towards them.

"Mapiya!" Snake wailed and started after them, but two guards grabbed hold of his arms.

"Watch how you handle him!" John snapped at the men.

Sky was thrown to the ground a few yards away, and one of the many guards surrounding them hit her in the head with the back of his musket. Hethuska fought viciously to escape the grasps of his captors; four men had to hold him back. Snake glanced over his shoulder at John.

"What is this? What are you doing?" he shrieked. John said nothing, but the man named Antonio stepped forward.

"We need to know which way the ships headed. Surely your little rebellion had some sort of contingency plan?"

"Harold must have made it out, then?" Snake sneered.

"Just tell them what they want to know," John said softly. The older man was looking down at his feet, gripping the top of his cane as though he was in physical pain.

Upon hearing Sky's cries, Snake turned his head back towards her and her brother. He could see that the man with the musket had struck her again, and her face was coated in a layer of fresh blood.

"Stop!" Snake screamed, and his knees wobbled.

"He's not going to break over a couple of slaves," one of the guards grumbled.

Snake managed to slip his arms out of the grasps of the two guards holding him back, and he instantly darted to Sky, throwing himself over her and holding up a hand in defense in the event the guard beating her struck at her again.

"Leave her alone!" Snake roared.

"Johnny," John called out to him. "Tell Antonio what he needs to know, and they will leave your servants alone. Do not get yourself so worked up over your slave girl."

"Slave girl?" Snake roared. "She's my wife, you cad!" He held her close to him as the two of them sat on the ground. In surprise at this new revelation, the guards released Hethuska, who knelt down near them to check on his sister. She nodded in reassurance, as if the say that she was as well as she could be after such a blow.

John gritted his teeth as he turned towards Antonio. "Call your men off, Antonio. I won't have you beating my godson's wife. We agreed he was off limits, and that means his wife too."

Antonio huffed and waved his men off. He pointed a finger at Hethuska. "And who is this man to you, Mr. Lee?"

"He is my wife's brother," Snake said, still gripping onto Sky.

Antonio nodded. "I see. Well then listen to me, boy. You tell us where those ships were headed, and we'll spare your brother-in-law. Otherwise, we'll have him quartered and make that pretty wife of yours watch."

Sky sobbed, and Hethusaka spoke to her calmly in their native tongue. Snake guessed that she was translating for him based on the way his face contorted slightly at the news.

John spoke on Hethuska's behalf. "If you think I am going to let you harm them —"

Antonio interrupted him. "This is war, John, or have you forgotten? We still have not managed to kill Harold. I agreed to leave your godson alone, and I'll leave the man's other half be as well, but I won't make any more exceptions for you. Your boy will talk, or he'll watch that savage man be torn apart." Antonio looked to his men.

"Bind him!" he ordered, waving his hand towards Hethuska who was still knelt down on the ground by Snake and Sky.

"Don't!" Snake screamed as the men approached.

One man reached down, touching Hethuska's shoulder. In one swift movement, Hethuska yanked the man's dagger from his belt and gutted him without the slightest hint of hesitation. Before the men could react, Hethuska grabbed Snake by his hair and pulled him to his feet. Snake felt himself being squeezed in the man's arms, and Hethuska pressed the blade against his throat.

"Clever bastard," Antonio grumbled under his breath.

"Hethuska!" Snake shrieked. "What are you doing?"

Sky began to sob as she stood up and attempted to pull her brother off Snake, but doing so only caused him to press the blade into Snake's throat, and a bit of blood trickled down onto his shirt. Snake hollered out in pain as Hethuska slid the blade to the side of his neck. Hethuska glared at John as he spoke. Sky, in loud sobs, translated her brother's threats.

"He says to open the gates or he will kill him!" she pleaded, her hands gripping her brother's wrists. "Hethuska, let him go! Let him go!" She attempted to pull her brother's hand back, and he kicked her in the leg.

"Hethuska!" Snake shrieked. Hethuska made a quick motion, moving the dagger from Snake's neck to Snake's back while wrapping his free arm around Snake's neck – causing the guards and John to all shift uncomfortably.

Hethuska screamed his threats in John's direction, and Sky translated each threat of violence between sobs. Snake felt the blade being pressed into his back, and he screamed out in agony.

"Open the gates!" John roared.

"Are you mad?" Antonio questioned, and John jolted his head towards the man.

"Open the gates," John said in such a cold firm tone that even Antonio winced slightly.

Snake could hear the castle gates opening behind him, and slowly Hethuska walked them both backwards. Sky sobbed and pleaded with her brother as they made their way backward, but Hethuska never once flinched. His cold stare cut through Stevenson, and he occasionally gave Snake a forceful enough jab to make him shout in pain but not enough to cause major damage. Snake felt blood drip down his pant leg, and he knew that John could see the blood on his shirt now from where his neck had been cut. John looked horrified, and before Snake knew it, they were standing outside the gates.

Sky gave yet another translation for her brother. "He says to close the gates behind us, or he will drown my husband in the river."

John gave the orders, and Hethuska did not relent. Snake continued to be pulled back towards the woods, east of the castle, while John's guards watched from the lookout towers. As they were approaching the woods, Snake could hear John's voice shout, "Don't!"

A string of bullets rang out from the guard towers, and Hethuska threw Snake down at his feet, forcing Sky down as well. Snake felt Hethuska encircle himself around them both as a slew of bullets shot in their direction before they could get out of range.

"Get up!" Snake shouted. "Run! Run for the woods!"

The three of them bolted, heading southeast as quickly as possible – putting a tremendous amount of distance between themselves and the castle. They did not stop until they were south of Caldara City when Hethuska abruptly collapsed behind them. Sky shrieked and ran back towards her brother, kneeling down beside him. Snake followed closely behind, and he could see that Hethuska had been shot by the men at the top of the guard towers.

Sky looked up at Snake with her eyes full of tears and said, "He says he cannot go any further. He says he is going to die."

Snake knelt down beside him, and he and Sky managed to help him sit up against a tree in the midst of the woods. He had been shot twice in the back and once in the chest, and he had never mentioned it during their escape.

"We can try to stop the bleeding," Snake said, and Sky translated just as Snake pressed his hand against the mans bloodied chest.

Hethuska, upon hearing his sister's translation, grabbed Snake's wrist. Snake looked the man in the eyes – something he often avoided doing. Hethuska's eyes looked tired, and there was a sadness in them Snake had never seen before. When the man spoke, he did so looking directly into Snake's eyes, trusting that his sister would translate for him. "He says he would not have killed you – that he only hurt you to make the bad men think that he would kill you. He says he would not have killed his brother."

Snake felt Hethuska squeeze his wrist. Snake's heart began to ache. He and Hethuska had not exactly gotten along; they mostly had just tolerated one another, but to see this strong man – his wife's brother – withering away before him, it made him sick.

"He asks that you give our first child a name of our people for him, and that you let me teach our children about their ancestors and the Great Spirits he worships, even if you wish to raise them Christian."

"Tell him I promise to," Snake said, and when Sky spoke to her brother, Snake again felt the man squeeze his wrist.

"Mapiya," Hethuska groaned as he closed his eyes. Sky reached out and wrapped her arms around her brother's neck.

"I will take care of your sister," Snake said. "I promise you I will."

Sky managed to translate what Snake had to say between quiet cries. Snake felt Hethuska's grasp loosen around his wrist, and slowly the man lowered his arms. Hethuska was dead.

Snake gave his wife a moment – but only a moment. He touched her shoulders. "Love, we have to go," he said. "They'll be on us soon if we don't. We have to leave him."

"No," she said, wiping a mixture of blood and tears from her cheeks. "Not here."

"I'm sorry," he said and gripped her under her arm to pull her to her feet.

"Hethuska... deserves... better," she sobbed.

"He does," Snake said and clasped her hands in his. "But he did not just die for us to get caught again. I'm so sorry, but we have to go."

They fled south, crossing the river near the waterfall – unaware that Smith and Yin were just awakening at Mrs. Barons' home only a few miles west of them.

Chapter 3

Several Days Later

Smith watched Yin slowly drift off to sleep near the fire. He threw a blanket over his friend and felt a sigh of relief escape his lips.

"The poor man has not slept during this entire journey." Carissa spoke softly from across the fire. Her son, Pierson, was asleep beside her. John Stevenson's horse was tied to a tree nearby; they were in the middle of the woods, only a few miles from their desired destination. They would reach the gulf in the morning.

"He lost his brother and his closest friend," Smith said. "And, only God knows who else we have lost. We will not know until tomorrow, and the thought troubles me terribly. Everyone I love was at that camp when it was attacked. My mother, my uncle and cousin, my friends, and so many whom I have come to know during this war are victims."

Carissa started to speak when she suddenly broke out into a coughing fit. She pulled out a handkerchief to cover her mouth, and she abruptly stood and walked away so as to not be too loud near their sleeping companions.

Smith followed her. "Carissa?" he questioned once they were a good distance from the fire, but not so far that they did not have a bit of light. Her coughing became heavy, and once she managed to get a hold of herself, he saw that her handkerchief was covered in blood.

"Carissa!" He hurried right next to her, and she shooed him away.

"It's all right. I'm fine," she said harshly.

Smith frowned. His shoulders slumped. "You're dying," he said.

"Yes."

"Is this why you came to Kirkston?" he asked.

The woman put away her handkerchief. She looked nearly ready to cry, but she fought off the temptation. "Pierson is why I came."

"You do not have anyone to look after the boy?" Smith asked.

"No," she said. "We are all each other has left. My cousin spoke very highly of you and your crew. There is no one in this world I would trust with Pierson, but I believe Courtney would have told me to put my trust in you."

"I assure you, miss, that if you are truly kin to our beloved Sea, and by your face I do not doubt it for a moment, that the boy will be cared for and loved by both myself and my crew."

Carissa forced a smile. "Thank you."

During their conversing, Smith had come nearer. He placed a hand on her arm and returned her sad expression.

"Is there anything I can do for you now?" he asked. "If he survived the attack, there is a wonderful doctor amongst the rebellion soldiers. Perhaps he-"

She placed her palm against his chest. "I do not believe your doctor will tell me anything that others have not already. Anything that I do not feel myself. Anything that sweet Pierson does not already suspect. I am dying. My only concern is for the boy's well-being now – not my own." She looked up into Smith's eyes, studying him.

"Something more than news of a stranger dying is troubling you. Is it about your friends? Are you worried about them still?"

"Yes, certainly," he said. "But that is not all that is bothering me."

"What is it, then?"

Smith realized he still had his hand on her arm. He lowered his hand, but he let it linger for a moment. "I'm sorry," he said. "But, it's quite uncanny how much you look like your cousin. I thought I had seen a ghost when I first saw you."

"I believe you did see a ghost," she said. "I am halfway there." He continued gazing into her eyes. She broke eye contact after a moment, looking down at her feet to avoid his intense gaze. "Is there something I can do for you, Smith?"

Smith hesitated, but he caved after a moment of contemplating. "I know it is a peculiar thing to ask, but might I kiss you?"

"You just caught me coughing up blood, and now you wish now to kiss me?" she questioned.

"Yes," he said.

"You truly loved my cousin, didn't you?" she asked, and he nodded. "You realize I am not her, yes?" she asked, and he again nodded. She leaned towards him somewhat reluctantly, and Smith pulled her into his arms so that he could have her close when he kissed her lips. It felt familiar to him, but he knew that it was merely a temporary supplementation. They walked back to the campfire and pretended that the kiss had never happened.

***

Smith and Yin exited the wood line from where they could see five ships in the harbor – only one ship short of what had been back at the Black Dragon camp prior to the attack. The Black Dragon was one of the surviving ships in the gulf. There were tents pitched all along the shoreline and firepits scattered about. A small pile of bodies lined the beach – the majority of the dead, Smith assumed, were back at the Black Dragon lair, and these were merely those who had died from injuries on the route to the new campsite.

"Smith! Yin! We thought you were both dead!" Snake was the first to see them. Ace walked behind Snake, and both men jolted when they spotted Carissa.

"My God!" Ace wailed, and Carissa embarrassingly covered her face.

Smith could see tears in Ace and Snake's eyes as they came closer; their eyes were puffy and their cheeks red. Smith knew instantly that the loss from the attack must have been great.

"She is Sea's cousin," Smith said quickly. "And, I believe that is a conversation that can be had later."

Ace nodded, and his pained gaze fell back on Smith and Yin. "You two look quite broken," Yin said. "How great was the loss here?"

Ace and Snake exchanged glances; they seemed to be silently arguing who had to break bad news to them both. Snake lowered his head, and he seemed to shake slightly as he reached his hand out and placed it on Smith's shoulders. "You need to come with me right now, mate," he said.

"Snake?" Smith beckoned, feeling his stomach twist into knots at the look of sorrow on his friend's face.

"It's your mother," Snake said, forcing the words out of his mouth. "Please, come with me... now."

Smith felt a horrid pain in his chest. Snake walked quickly, and Smith followed close on his heels.

"What's wrong? What's wrong?" Smith questioned franticly. As they made their way through camp, he caught glimpses of some of his friends – all of whom looked at him with equally teary eyes, much like those Snake and Ace had greeted him with, and it sent a wave of terror up his spine.

They arrived outside of a small tent that was pitched in the sand, and Snake went to bend down to open up the flaps. Smith grabbed him by the arm, and Snake spun around to face Smith – tears streamed down his face. "Tell me," Smith said. "Tell me what to expect."

Snake shook his head. "The rest of the crew have already said their goodbyes. I suggest you do the same."

"No," Smith wailed, keeping his voice down the best that he could. "This is some sort of horrid jest."

Snake stepped forward and put his arms around Smith's neck. "I'm sorry, mate. She took a bullet to her stomach." Snake pulled away. "Do not waste any more time with me, Smith. Go see your mother."

Smith took a breath and crawled into the poorly pitched tent. The scene before him broke his heart. Jackson White was seated up by Smith's mother's head; her head rested in the man's lap. The woman had lost all color in her face, and her eyes were closed. To her left was her brother Andrew, and beside him was his son Thaddeus.

When Smith entered into the tent, Jackson looked directly at him through a pair of watery eyes. "Smith," Jackson said his name in such a way that it almost felt fatherly – as though the relief at seeing him alive was enough to help pull the man through this tragedy. Jackson lowered his head, looking down at Mrs. Barons. "Ellen, your son is here. He's alive, Ellen."

Her eyes opened slowly, and she raised her head slightly. A look of absolute joy passed over the dying woman's face. "I had hoped at least one of my children would not go in the ground before me," she said.

Smith crawled into the tent and sat to her right; he could not bring himself to speak. He feared that uttering a single sound would unleash more emotion than he could handle. He grabbed her hand and held it tight. The flaps of the tent flung open, and Yin popped his head inside. Tears covered his face as well.

"Mrs. Barons," Yin said with a sob. "Snake told me. I just had to come see you once more for a moment." He seemed to be asking Smith permission before he entered into the already crowded tent with the slight glance he made in Smith's direction.

Smith scooted closer to Jackson so that Yin could enter. The other crew-members it seemed had already each shared a final farewell to the woman, so Smith thought it would be cruel not to allow Yin the same.

. "Mathew, thank heavens," Mrs. Barons said as she smiled at him. She released Smith's hand for a moment to reach out and touch Yin's. "Your brother? Is he alive?"

"No," Yin said, his voice shaky. "He and Cannonball did not make it."

Mrs. Barons looked very saddened by this news; she squeezed Yin's hand tight. "Don't let this break you, Mathew."

"You have been like a mother to me," Yin said. "To all of us. I love you, Mrs. Barons."

"I love you, Mathew," she said, and Yin slowly released her hand.

Yin placed his hand on Smith's shoulder, giving him a saddened yet somehow reassuring look before departing the tent. Smith grabbed hold of his mother's now free hand and kissed her fingers. She smiled again, but this time her smile seemed weak. "I am so glad you're here," she said to Smith.

"You should have never been at that camp. None of this had anything to do with you." Smith sobbed. "This was not your war. My crew should not have been involved. I should have left the Caldara's to fight their own war."

She shook her head. "Peter, no. This is our war as much as theirs. Kirkston is our home. It always has been. Don't let them take it."

Thaddeus looked across Mrs. Barons at Smith, his little face red and splotchy from having cried for his aunt. Smith could see that Andrew, his uncle, was trying hard to fight off his onset of tears as well. Jackson perhaps looked the most pathetic; he was a loud, pitiful crier –something Smith had never seen the man do before. Smith's heart was still racing as he desperately hung onto a fictitious hope that his mother could somehow be saved.

"Dr. Conal, has he been in to –"

"He's done all he can," she said weakly. The woman started to close her eyes again, and Smith squeezed her hand and touched her face.

"Mama, don't," Smith whispered. She forced her eyes open again and looked at him hazily. Smith felt Jackson put his hand on his shoulder.

"She kept saying she knew you were alive. She's been holding out for you."

Smith clenched his jaw shut to keep his lip from quivering. He could see that her blood had already stained the blankets she was wrapped in. She had been undressed and was covered merely by a few sheets so that Dr. Conal could easily access her wound, it was still being cared for, but it seemed that the man had been forced to give up on staunching the bleeding. The blood had seeped through her new bandages long ago.

Smith tried not to look at the crimson stains as she squeezed his hand again. "I love you, Peter."

"I love you," Smith said. Slowly, Jackson helped Mrs. Barons to sit up a bit upon her request. She leaned back against Jackson and reached out for her son. Smith wrapped his arms around her and rested his chin on her shoulder. Her long black and silver hair fell into Smith's face, but he did not mind. He held her close, and he could feel her becoming still.

"Please, don't leave me," he pleaded. "I still need you."

"William," he heard her say, and almost as soon as she did her arms became limp. He knew instantly that she was gone, but he held onto her anyway and let the tears flow freely. He opened his mouth; he thought he would scream, but no sound emerged from his throat.

After a moment, he felt Jackson forcing him to release her. As a first instinct, he wanted to slug Jackson for pulling him apart from her, but before he could even think to react to the gesture, Jackson had pulled Smith into a tight embrace. Smith's cries become more vocal, and he screamed – although the sound was slightly muffled under Jackson's tight encirclement. Thaddeus began sobbing, and the boy fell into his father's lap in a fit. Andrew stared down at his sister, his hand moved to cover his mouth as if to keep himself from falling apart as Smith was allowing himself to do.

Several minutes went by before Smith allowed himself to pull away from Jackson. He attempted to catch his breath. Thoroughly shaken, and while hyperventilating, Smith managed to ask, "How did this happen?"

Jackson had since calmed himself down, but upon hearing Smith's question he began to sob all over again.

"She took a bullet for me," he said. "It should have been me. It should have been me!"

Before Smith could react to this claim, Andrew reached across Mrs. Barons' body and gripped Jackson by his elbow. He pointed a finger in the man's face. "Don't say that. Just don't. My sister loved you, and she'd do it again if given the chance."

Jackson took a calming breath before returning his gaze to Smith. "One of John's soldiers got her. He was aiming at me, and your mother grabbed me as we were running down the beach. She got between the two of us."

Smith gritted his teeth. "Tell me you killed the bastard."

"I did not have a chance to," Jackson said. "Your mother shot at him with her own pistol and brought him down before I even knew she had taken a bullet herself."

A sad chuckle emerged from Smith's throat. His mother was a fighter; she always had been. He wiped his face and took several breaths before he could speak somewhat calmly and without an overwhelming amount of anger in his tone. "I know a lot has taken place these past few days. But I intend to take her home, to bury her beside my father and sisters. I have a duty here, I know, but I have a duty to my mother as well."

"There is not a person at this camp who was not graced by her presence," Andrew said. "Everyone will understand, and the journey back to the river will not take many days. Your duties here can wait."

Smith took another breath and again wiped his face to be sure no more tears had escaped onto his cheeks. "I'm going to let the others know that she has passed."

"Do you want a moment alone with her?" Jackson asked.

"I suspect I will have time for that before my journey north," Smith said and then exited the tent. He still knew very little of what sort of horrors had befallen those who had not escaped by land. Looking out into the gulf, he could see that one of the ships from the Silver Queen fleet was not among the rebellions grouping of vessels.

He headed towards one of the few campfires that had been set up, not daring to venture near the place designated for the bodies being laid out, in fear of unexpectedly seeing someone he cared for. By the campfire, he could see a number of his friends all gathered around Carissa and her boy, staring in awe; Yin had clearly filled them all in on the mysterious woman from Balla who was related to their beloved Sea.

When Smith approached the fire, all was quiet. "She's passed," he said, and a moment of silence overtook his friends. He could hear Squirt beginning to sob as the young boy sat himself on a log; the older crewmembers were quiet – all having already mourned her loss after having given up on her having any chance of survival.

Before any uncomfortable conversation about Mrs. Barons could begin, Smith averted his attention elsewhere for a moment. "Who have we lost?" He looked around, and in each passing second, as he counted heads, he became slightly reassured.

Smith looked at Cassidy who was under Ace's arm. "Where is Nicole?"

"She was on the ship," Cassidy sobbed, and Smith felt horrid for having gotten the woman worked up. "The ship that those wretched devils sunk." Ace squeezed her tight in his arms. Cassidy's sister, Clara, stood nearby and rested her head against Ace as well, and he wrapped his big arms around both of the women.

"Hethuska?" Smith questioned, looking over at Snake and Sky. Sky looked away.

"The three of us and Yang had been captured by John's men. Yin tells me you know already what happened to his brother. Hethuska helped Sky and I to escape the castle, but he was shot while we were fleeing. We had to leave him in the woods lest we be caught again." Snake kissed his wife's forehead. Gomda covered his face in anguish over his lost brethren.

As far as Black Dragons' numbers went, Cannonball, Yang, Hethuska, and Nicole were all that they had lost, as well as Smith's mother, Mrs. Barons.

Smith's eyes were drawn towards Knot and Anna, who were seated by the fire. Anna was mourning for more than just her husband's fallen comrades; he could see that on the woman's face.

"Anna?" Smith coaxed.

"Susan and Tim are dead," she said, and tears started to fall down her cheeks. "They were on the same ship with Nicole. Thank God young Jake ran with his stepfather and mother." Her eyes drew towards Mouth and Abigail who were seated with Jake on the ground. Anna continued. "My mother… She was on that ship too. Jimmy and Hannah, thank God in heaven, were both with Maxi. John's men sunk the first ship that came out of the hideout. Whoever was captaining the ship rammed into one of John's ships before they could sink. They sacrificed themselves so that the rest of the ships could escape."

"Who all were on that ship that sunk? Do we know?" Smith asked.

"Only a small handful," Ace said, his voice quivering slightly. "Susan, Tim, Mrs. Cook, and Nicole. Neela and four of her men were on the ship. She was the one who captained it during the assault. All of them pulled the ship away with the intention of clearing room for the rest of us. Even Tim, blind as could be, worked to help sail that ship straight into John's little armada. They all knew they were going to die in order to get the rest of us free, and they did not hesitate for even a moment when Neela called out the order."

"My daughter helped Neela at the wheel. I could see her from where I stood on the Silver Queen Two," Cassidy said and wiped her tears, but a small smile appeared across her face. "My daughter helped to save the entire rebellion. I am devastated, but I have never been so proud of her."

"She and the others are heroes," Smith said. "Bless them all. What can you all tell me of the Caldara's?"

"They all made it out," Ace said. "They were on the Black Dragon, and she was a faithful ship even after taking on cannon fire. General Alex Ashley did not survive the journey here aboard our ship – he had been by the cannons when we started taking on fire, and a cannon came loose and rolled on him. He was crushed."

"Blimey!" Smith exclaimed.

"Stewart found him before he passed," Ace said. "Didn't have to die by himself down there. May he rest in peace."

"How bad were the losses at the hideout?" Smith asked.

"The Silver Queen's and the African's lost the most because many remained back to fight off the on-slaughter from the woods," Blade said. "And, Jeremiah and Helena are all that are left of the Annihilators. The Skull Island gang took a number of losses because many of them were working the cannons below deck on Maxi's ship when the armada started to fire on us."

"This isn't the end," Smith said, his voice becoming harsh. "We will rain fire down on John. This does not end until John ends."

"Believe me," Ace sneered. "We are all with you on that one, mate."

Snake scowled when he said, "For Mrs. Barons, for Nicole, for Hethuska, for the Cooks, for Alex, and for Neela. This will not be forgotten."

***

Smith re-entered the rebellion camp at the gulf for the second time that week; he and his crew were just arriving back from his mother's home after having buried her next to his father. Jackson was particularly pale. The man had hardly spoken a word during their journey. Smith had elected to bury his mother with the ring Jackson had gotten her along with the ring Smith's father had given her, and the gesture had touched the man tremendously.

The camp had done little in their absence apart from burying the dead and attempting to scavenge what they could. Smith, after the death of his mother, had not had a chance to speak with Kathleen. While his mother's death had devastated him beyond his capacity to think of much else, he had felt a tremendous sense of relief to see that Kathleen was among those who had survived. Now that he had properly buried his mother and had given her a fitting farewell, he felt that he was well enough put together that he could speak to Her Majesty.

He took Kathleen by the hand shortly after entering into camp and took her for a walk away from the beach and not far from the marsh land they were stationed near. They found themselves a seat near a dry patch of grass, and they began to converse – both of them treading lightly in the conversation at first before Kathleen placed her hand on his knee and looked sadly into his eyes.

"Your mother was a good woman who did not deserve this fate," she said. "Are you going to be well?"

"In time," he said and took a breath to keep his head steady. "I am glad you are well. I suppose my denial about my mother is the only thing keeping me from breaking down. I have to push it to the back of my mind lest I lose my head. I do not know what I would have done if I had lost you as well, Kathleen."

"I thought I did lose you," she said. "I was overwhelmed when you returned to camp."

"Stewart did a prayer at my mother's graveside," Smith said. "And, I spoke with him about God, and he told me that all things are done in accordance to His plan. At first, that made me angry. But today when we returned to camp and I saw this..." he glanced back over his shoulder towards the line of abled-bodied men heading towards the large tent that King Harold and Kyo were currently stationed at. Now that the location of the rebellion camp was no longer a secret, and now that a Black Dragon had been hung in the capital – striking a revengeful heart in the people of Kirkston – new groups of volunteers had been arriving in the masses.

"You believe that God wanted John to attack the camp?" Kathleen asked.

"In only a week since the attack, our numbers have doubled," Smith said. "And, they are still growing. If God is on our side, and I pray that He is, then perhaps so. It is a sad thought, but it is a reassuring one too. Stewart says nothing happens that God does not oversee and permit. My mother, God bless her, perhaps she was taken so early so that she would be spared future heartache that will likely come from this war."

"My father is looking this way," Kathleen said. "I believe he needs your assistance with the new recruits."

Smith nodded and stood before holding out his hand to help her stand. He smiled at her. "I am truly thankful that you are safe, Kathleen. Seeing you here is all that is keeping me sane right now."

Chapter 4

Yin sat far off from the beach where the rebels had
gathered. With the surplus of new recruits coming in, the
camp was becoming a bit crowded. He needed room to
breathe. His brother and his best mate were still on the
forefront of his mind. He was so far from their graves, and
they had not been given much of a proper funeral. His
fellow Black Dragons had given them grace when they had
all gone with Smith to bury Mrs. Barons, so it made the
sting a little more bearable. They had also created wooden
crosses for Nicole and Hethuska despite not having bodies
to burry.

As he was sitting down near the wood line, he
spotted Clara coming his way. He cringed slightly. He felt
a tremendous amount of animosity towards her, and he had
felt it ever since losing Cannonball and Yang. She offered
him a sad smile as she knelt down beside him. "We have
not spoken much since the attack on camp," she said.

"Yes, you must have been quite relieved to see that
one of your men made it back to you," Yin practically
snarled his response.

She frowned. "What do you mean by that?"

He lowered his head to keep from having to look at her. She had been a part of the crew for almost three years now, and ever since her arrival, he and his brother and his best mate, Cannonball, had been at each other's throats. Clara had enjoyed pinning the three of them against one another. Now that they were gone, Yin realized just how cruel they had been to one another all because of her. "I only mean that without me you would have to find someone else to torment since Cannonball and Yang are gone."

"What a horrid thing to say," she said. "I know you are heartbroken about your brother and about Cannonball, but you realize I have lost my niece? Do not be cruel to me." She reached out and touched his hand, and he instantly yanked it back. Her face flushed. "Why are you so cold towards me, Yin?"

"I had been close to my brother and to Cannonball before you joined the crew," he said and gritted his teeth slightly. "Our last years together were spent quarrelling over a former working girl!"

She popped him in the jaw. "You know I was never such a thing!" She stood, her eyes blazing. "Do not take your heartbreak out on me. I came over here to you hoping for some comfort and to offer some myself. I will not sit here and listen to you speak to me in such a way. Enjoy sulking here alone, you rogue!" With those parting words, Clara stormed back into camp.

***

Jeremiah White took his share of food from the man passing out the bit of cooked meat in the center of camp. He brought his and Helena's food over to one of the fresh fire pits that had been started. She took her share from him and began casually nibbling as he sat down beside her. He felt sick. The two of them were all that was left of the Annihilators apart from his brother, but he did not feel as though that counted for much. There was also Bud; Jeremiah, along with many others, had seen Bud captaining one of the ships that had attacked them. Between the loss of the crew and the sinking of his ship, he knew his and Helena's life of piracy was likely behind them. The chances of him being able to get another ship with no money to his name was unlikely. All of a sudden, the life he once knew was off the table.

A group of children who had arrived at the camp with the new recruits were playing not far from the fire where he and his wife were seated. He was surprised when a slight smile appeared on his face from watching them play. Jeremiah had never thought much about a future outside of his future as a captain. With the promise of a royal pardon for his work at the rebellion, Jeremiah's future was open to a number of possibilities he had never entertained before.

"Helena," he said, and she glanced up from her food. "Have you thought much on what we are to do once this war is over?"

"Well, if we lose the war, we will likely be dead," she said.

Jeremiah shook his head slightly. "I meant if we win the war."

"I do not know how with a foot soldier's salary we could possibly get ourselves a ship," she said. "Perhaps if

John does not wipe Skull Island off the map, we could attempt a new life there."

"Or," Jeremiah said, gently testing the waters. "Or, we could make use of those pardons."

Helena laughed. "Are you telling me you wish to be an honest man, Jeremiah?"

Jeremiah again treaded lightly and spoke as though he was merely jesting. "Is there anything of a woman's heart in you, Helena? Would you not want to one day have a little one call you mother?"

Helena laughed loudly. "Oh, surely you are jesting! Never would I ever fancy myself in such a position. I hope you are jesting. You are jesting, yes?"

Jeremiah tried not to show his disappointment. "Yes," he said. "Of course, I am jesting."

***

Yin approached Clara cautiously. He had seen her wander away from camp, and he had become worried about her. When he found her, she was sulking in the woods alone, seated under a large oak. When she spotted him, she started to scurry to her feet with a huff, but he stopped her. "Clara, wait, please," he said softly and fell to the ground beside her on his knees.

She remained on the ground, and he could see that the woman's eyes were red. It had been a difficult time for all of them, and Clara was no exception to that. "I do hope you did not follow me out here just to continue with your verbal lashing!"

"Never," he said. "I owe you an apology. I am upset, and I took it out on you. There's no sense in that."

"You are not the only one who has lost someone, Yin," she said. "My niece is dead after having saved us all. My sister… I do not think will ever be herself again after losing Nicole. And poor Sky and Gomda lost the last surviving members of their entire culture, outside of themselves. And, if you think my heart not has not broken, for your brother and for Cannonball as well, you are wrong. Neela too is dead, so the entire group of Africans' who came here under her guidance are mourning for her as well. The Cooks too have lost loved ones. It is all so much to take in. And, sweet, sweet Mrs. Barons. I do not know if my heart can handle all of this alone. Say what you will about me and the way I was towards you three, but do not dare say I did not care about them or the others we have lost."

"I would never think it," Yin said.

"You are right, though. I tormented you three and had you all fighting like a handful of loons. I'm sorry." She gazed at him sadly, and he could see true remorse in her eyes.

"The three of us were being childish," Yin said. "And, it was childish of me to suggest it was in some way your doings. In the end, my brother died for me. And, I mourn Cannonball no differently than I would have whether we were at odds about you or not. We loved one another, and nothing – not even someone as lovely as you – could possibly have changed that. I am sorry for suggesting otherwise."

He took a breath and made a confession.
"Truthfully, I have always been intimidated by them both. I had hoped you would love me first and stop tormenting all three of us eventually. What bothers me now is wondering if you would have chosen me at all if they had not been killed. Will you love me Clara, because I am the only one left of the men you chased after, or did you truly love me to begin with?"

"What a horrible thing for you to have to ponder," she said and reached out and touched his chest. "I enjoyed the attention, and perhaps that was wrong of me. But you are so different from Cannonball and Yang because of this."

"Of what?"

"Your heart," she said. "You've always been jealous of those two – and that was not my doing. From the way your friends spoke of it, it has always been that way. But, it should not have been. Your heart is what I love. Your brother and Cannonball were strong men, yes, but you are just as strong as they. I am done toying with you. Life is too short for me to continue on behaving like that. I love you, Mathew, and I pray you feel the same towards me."

"You know that I do," he said and leaned towards her to kiss her lips. He helped her stand and walked with her arm in arm back to camp.

Chapter 5

Smith smiled as the day came to a close. The sun had set, and all the light they had was from the moon and the firepits. They had doubled their army in size as people all around the peninsula had arrived. John was going to pay for the attack at the hideout.

While it had been a tremendous tragedy, Smith knew now more than ever it was part of a divine plan to rescue his beloved country. With that knowledge, he somehow managed to find peace. Had it not been for the attack, they never would have come out of hiding, and the rebellion's numbers would have remained stagnant.

He was getting ready to retire to bed, heading towards the tent he had finally pitched for himself, when he was stopped by Carissa. He smiled at her. He enjoyed having her around, although the sight of her often brought him as much pain as it did joy. He felt he could truly see what Sea would have looked like now had her life not been cut so short.

"Evening, Ms. Carissa," Smith said politely as the woman approached him. "Where is your boy?"

"Off to sleep," she said. "I don't believe he has ever seen this much excitement in his life. The poor lad is exhausted."

"He is not the only one," Smith said and offered her a smile. "Is there something I can do for you?"

"With everything going on after the attack, I thought it best to wait. But, it cannot wait much longer. I have something for you, Mr. Barons." She pulled an envelope out of her bosom and handed it to him.

"What is this?" he asked, squinting slightly at the sealed envelope. He saw his name Peter Barons scribbled in a painfully familiar handwriting. He looked up at Carissa with sad eyes. "Did... did Courtney write this?"

"Yes," Carissa said. "She was only thirteen when she wrote it. It was while she was staying with my family in Balla for a few months after Mr. Keg's passing."

"That was years ago," Smith said. "You held onto a letter that was never sent?"

"I did," she said. "Although, I am aware of its contents. I should have sent it to you long ago after Courtney died, but I did not. Take time to read it tonight by yourself. For now, I am retiring to bed, and we can speak on its contents in the morning."

Smith nodded and bid her goodnight before heading into his tent. He lit several candles before breaking the wax seal on the envelope.

***

Snake sat by the fire early in the morning enjoying his breakfast. Today they would be discussing with Harold their next course of action. He wanted to be well fed and rested because the meeting, in the large tent that was acting as their war room, would likely last a while. He was looking forward to it. After the devastation at the hideout and the murder of his brother-in-law, Snake was ready to launch their counter-attack on John's men.

Ace, as well as a number of other Black Dragons, sat with them at breakfast, all discussing what little had been said about Harold's intentions for a counter-strike.

"I know I'll be on the front lines," Mouth snarled. "For Mrs. Barons and the others. Truthfully, mates, my heart was only partially in this before. But, now… John will get what's coming to him, if I have to drive a dagger into the man's heart myself." He glanced awkwardly over to Snake, but Snake gave a reassuring nod.

They all still tip-toed around the subject of John near him, but after holding Mrs. Barons hand and crying, as he bid her farewell, he too was ready. Snake doubted how well his mind would handle it if he was the one to come face to face with John, but he did not doubt what he would do. John had to pay.

Squirt came running up to them, sliding in the dirt slightly to stop his quick pace. "Snake, um, and Ace," he said awkwardly to get their attention.

"Everything all right, mate?" Snake asked because the lad looked rather distressed.

"Yes, everything is fine," Squirt said, although by his tone Snake was not so sure how truthful he was being. "Smith asked me to come fetch you two. He wants to speak with you two privately."

Snake and Ace rose from their seats and followed Squirt away from the firepit. Squirt walked a short distance with them before pointing off into the woods. "He's out there somewhere. You two should know, though, I think he's drunk."

"Drunk?" Ace questioned.

Drinking was something Smith rarely did. He was almost as sober of a fellow as Stewart. "It's nearly eight in the morning!" Snake exclaimed. "And, you're telling me he's drunk when we have a meeting with Harold this morning?"

"Yes… very drunk," Squirt said and shifted his stance uncomfortably. "He was really angry. I don't know what about, but he told me to fetch you two. He grabbed me by my hair and yelled at me to hurry up. I've never seen Smith so upset."

Snake and Ace exchanged glances. They could not imagine Smith yelling at Squirt of all people. Smith had a soft spot for Squirt –they all did.

"Run along," Snake said. "We'll handle it." Squirt nodded and hurried back into camp as the two of them started towards the woods.

They walked for several minutes but were unable to find Smith, but they did find two empty bottles of liquor, of gin. "Gin?" Ace questioned. "Smith's never touched gin before. Something really must have him up and arms this morning!"

"He did just lose his mother," Snake reminded Ace as they continued walking. "Smith!" Snake shouted. "Mate, where are you?"

"If he drank both of those bottles, he's probably passed out somewhere," Ace said.

"I don't like this. Smith never drinks," Snake said, and before the words could finish leaving his lips a bullet went flying past their heads. They both ducked behind trees, and Ace let out a loud curse.

"It's Smith!" Ace shrieked as the two of them hid themselves. "He's firing at us!"

Snake peered around the tree and could see Smith hobbling towards them with his gun drawn. "Smith, damn you, it's us!" Snake shouted and started to step out from behind the tree, but as soon as he did, Smith fired in their direction a second time.

"I know it's you!" Smith shouted, his words slurring. "Now, both of you come out so I can put a bullet in yer heads!"

Ace glanced over at Snake with wide eyes. "What?" he mouthed as they both tried to piece together what could possibly have Smith so angry with the two of them.

"Smith, put down your blasted gun!" Ace shouted as the man came closer.

Snake saw Smith coming up near the tree where Ace was hidden; Smith took a swig from a bottle and threw it violently at the same tree. The glass shattered, and a bit got Ace in his arm. Ace shouted in surprise, and Snake hurried behind Smith and grabbed the drunk man by his arm, twisting it back until he dropped the gun. Ace gave them both a push, and Snake was able to pull Smith to the ground.

"Get off me! I'll kill you! I'll kill you both!" Smith roared.

Smith was intoxicated enough that he could not put up much of a fight against Snake. Snake shook and shouted down at him, "You had Squirt send us into the woods so that you could use us as target practice! What ails ya... you drunken fool?" Snake yelled. As he shouted, Smith grabbed Snake's wrist and bit his hand, causing Snake to jolt back with a shriek.

"Enough of this!" Ace shouted and yanked Smith up to his feet, ramming him into a tree. He held Smith's arms down at his side, and the man squirmed. "What's wrong with you?" Ace demanded.

"I'm going to kill you, Ace," Smith said with a frightening amount of confidence, conviction, and sincerity. "The letter," he snarled. "Look at the letter in my pocket, and you two rats will know what ails me!"

Ace squeezed Smith tight. "Check his pocket," Ace said to Snake, and Snake obliged.

He found the letter Smith was referring to and unfolded it. Smith snarled at them all while trying to pull away from Ace. "You two were my closest mates, but I see you're nothing but vermin! Vile traitors! Backstabbing bastards! Both of you!"

Snake was reading the letter that was written in Sea's hand. His arms shook. "Oh, God..." he muttered.

"What?" Ace asked, glancing back at Snake. "What is it?"

"A letter from Sea. Dated ten years ago," Snake said. "Is this real?"

"It's real!" Smith roared. "And, it tells all, doesn't it, mate?"

"What is in the letter, Snake?" Ace snapped, still holding onto Smith's arms.

"Courtney had a son," Snake said, his voice airy and almost unrecognizable. He glanced over at Ace who was now staring back at him with a horrified look in his eye. "You too, Ace?" Snake asked.

Ace abruptly released Smith, and Smith was unable to keep his balance. He fell to his knees and began shouting and screaming up at the both of them with angry tears streaming down his face. "All these years and neither of you ever told me you took my Sea to bed with you? That you loved her? She was everything to me. Everything! Everything she did after Mr. Keg died was a lie. She did not leave us because she needed time apart! She was pregnant!"

Ace seemed to be struggling for a breath. Snake went to hand Ace the letter, but he refused it, he seemed almost dizzy. Ace muttered, "The boy... whose son –"

"She didn't know!" Smith roared. "That's why she left. She left so I wouldn't find out. She left because she was worried you two would question whether or not one of you were the father and unveil her dirty secret to me!"

Ace took the letter, but his hands were too shaky. "I can't read it," he said and handed the letter back to Snake.

"Read it," Smith hissed. "Read it to him."

Snake hesitated, but after a moment of debate, he began to read:

Dearest Peter,

I have written a hundred letters like this one. I do not know if I will ever send them to you because I am afraid. The truth is, I fled to Balla to visit my family, not because of Mr. Keg, but because I was with child. His death was merely a convenient excuse for my melancholy. I would have told you of my child sooner, but I am fearful to tell you the entire truth. I do not know if you are the father. Here is the truth, love.

Before our relation was known to the rest of the crew, your dear mate Snake came to me and professed his love to me. I turned him away initially, but he became angry when I told him of you, and he pleaded with me to leave you. I became enraged by this, and I harmed him terribly and cut his forehead with a piece of jewelry he had offered me. We laid together that evening, and I became distraught the next morning and threw him out and threatened him if he ever spoke a word of it to you.

Being young and foolish, I became fearful that I could become pregnant from my evening with Snake and sought out Ace. It was a cruel trick I played on him. You see, though I have sworn to myself I would keep it secret, I know Ace is truly Prince James Lincoln Caldara. I know that must be surprising to you, but it is the truth. he does not know that I, as well as our darling companion Benny, are aware of this. I encouraged Ace to drink and brought him back to the captain's chambers for foul play, so that if I was already pregnant, I could claim the child as his if we ever found ourselves in a dangerous predicament with the Caldara's. He too confessed his love for me after the interaction, and I fear I broke his heart as well when I denied him. For all I know, it was that evening that impregnated me.

And then there is you, my love. We, as you know, had regular relations. We are both so young and so foolish! Myself especially because now I do not know whose child I now carry. Every day, I pray to God, that when my child is born, his or her face will undeniably resemble yours so that there is no question. I will continue this letter once the child is born.

My child has come, and I am devastated to say my son resembles me rather than his father – whoever that may be. I feel blessed to see how healthy and fat the little boy is, and I have named him Pierson – a fitting name, I believe, for my child.

My uncle's family has agreed to take him in. A life of piracy is not what I want for my boy, and I do not intend to leave my mission behind now, for it is a noble cause that is just beginning. I am but a fourteen-year-old fool who knows nothing of child raising. He will have a safe and happy home with my uncle and my aunt and my cousin whom already he has grown attached to.

I grow weary and fear that I will never tell you the truth, but it is a truth you deserve to know. I have told my uncle and his family that on Pierson's fifteenth birthday, when he is a man by Kirkston law, if I have not told you the truth, to send this letter to you, regardless of how I feel about it at the time. Pierson will one day, regardless of his true heritage, call you father. That much I can pray for. Forgive me, love, for this dastardly deceit. May God bless you and may God bless our son. All my love,

-Courtney "Sea" Livingston

By the time Snake had finished reading the letter, Ace had made his way over to a tree. He stood with his back to them both, his hand holding him up by a branch. Smith was on the ground, stewing in his growing hatred for his closest friends. After a moment of quiet, Snake spoke.

"It seems this letter has come early," he said. "Why?"

"Carissa, her cousin, is all the family the boy has left. She is dying, so she has come here in hopes of finding out who the boy's father is." Smith pulled himself up to stand, struggling significantly to do so, for his legs wobbled from all of the drink he had had. He took several calming breaths and wiped his eyes dry. "I warn you both to stay away from Carissa and from Pierson for now, or I will wait for a time when I am sober and will not miss my mark." With those parting words, Smith snatched the letter from Snake and marched back into camp to locate Carissa and Pierson, leaving Snake and Ace behind.

Ace turned and looked at Snake, and Snake shook his head. "I did not know you fancied her," Snake said.

"Didn't we all?" Ace questioned.

"I believe we all did, but you and I are the terrible friends who actually pursued it." Snake stared off in the direction that Smith had headed. "He should have shot us dead."

"He should have," Ace agreed. They were quiet for a while longer before Ace spoke again. "Have you gotten a good look at Pierson? I only spoke to Carissa once. Does he look like –"

"He looks like Sea," Snake snapped. "And, even if he looked like mine or yours and it was undeniable, I'd lie and say I believe him to be Smith's double because I've already broken my dear friends' heart enough."

"This will ruin him," Ace said.

"Oh, Ace, I fear it already has."

Chapter 6

Jackson followed rapidly on Andrew and Thaddeus's heels as they hurried towards the wagon that Smith had loaded. Word about the boy Carissa had brought from Balla travelled fast, and Smith was nearly ready to do something foolish. The boy, Pierson, was playing in the back of the carriage while Carissa was quietly seated up front, avoiding eye contact with anyone who dared to look their way.

Andrew and Jackson and Thaddeus reached Smith before anyone else, and Andrew grabbed him by his arm before he had a chance to load up onto the wagon himself.

"A word, Peter?" Andrew snapped in such a way it let Smith know he had no choice. Andrew yanked Smith a short distance away from the carriage. Jackson and Thaddeus stood quietly aside to let Andrew do the talking.

Smith jerked his arm away. "Be quick," he demanded.

"You're going to abandon this rebellion over a letter a dead girl wrote you ten years ago," Andrew hissed, and Jackson's stomach twisted slightly.

"I am leaving, Andrew," Smith practically snarled. "This is not my war. It never was."

"But, your crew is still here! Still fighting!"

"Let them if they so choose, but I am gone. I am taking my son back to Balla," he said.

"You will never make it out of port," Andrew said. "And you do not even know if that is your boy. You are abandoning your friends for utter nonsense!"

"I have nothing left," Smith said. "And, those vermin are no friends of mine. Ace and Snake were my closest mates aboard the Black Dragon, and they're nothing but backstabbing fiends! This boy is all I have left."

"What of me?" Andrew asked. "What of Thaddeus? I am your uncle. Your mother's brother. Are you to leave us too? We're your family!"

"Family?" Smith's tone was cruel. "Go to hell, Andrew. You, your father and your brothers abandoned us long ago. My family died off one by one while you and your pompous family lived in wealth in Balla. You're no family of mine."

"Cousin Peter," Thaddeus whined slightly. "Don't say that."

Smith turned his nose up. He glared over at Jackson. "And, why are you here? Come to bid me farewell?"

"I am twice your family now, Smith. I would consider your father my own father, and I was to marry your mother. We did not see eye to eye for a long time, but I am begging you not to do this to me or to your crew who all care about you. You are only leaving to keep that boy away from Ace and Snake, and it is cruel! You are reacting on emotion only, son –"

"Son!" Smith yelled. "Don't you dare call me that! Don't you dare!"

"Peter!" Kathleen's voice called out, and they all turned to see her fleeing in their direction. Clearly, word had already gotten to her that Smith was about to attempt an escape out of Kirkston. There was a horrified look about her as she approached. "Peter, don't do this! You're liable to get yourself killed!" She reached out for him, and he slapped her hand away.

"Do not beg me to stay," he said to her. "In another lifetime, Kathleen, I could have loved you. But, every time I start to allow myself to feel anything towards you, some jest of God gets in the way. I have a son that I am to worry for now. Find a man of your status to pester – one more deserving than I."

"Smith, I won't allow you to do this," she said.

"I am leaving," he said and turned his back on them all. "I feel nearly naught towards this cause now. I am numb to it all. I will pray for you all that you can take Kirkston back because I would be a liar if I said I do not care at all – but, that is all the help you will get from me. I am a Black Dragon no longer. I am just a father. That is all." He loaded up and whipped the reins of the horse, disappearing from sight.

Kathleen began to cry, so Jackson took her by the arm and led her back into camp. A distraught Andrew and Thaddeus followed close behind. By one of the campfires, Jackson could see both Ace and Snake seated with Sky and

Cassidy; both men had red eyes and shaky hands. Ace leaned forward, covering his face with his hand while Cassidy gently tried to coax him into speaking to her. Snake stared at the fire with a mixture of hate and despair on his face. Jackson shook his head as he gazed out across the camp at the other Black Dragons who all seemed at a loss of what to do. Smith, their lifelong captain, was gone.

Interlude

John sat in the war room of Caldara Castle, fiddling with his fingers, as he waited for Antonio and Juan to enter. A soldier had informed him, nearly an hour before, that the two men had wanted to meet him there. They were making him wait in order to make him nervous; he knew that was what they were doing, but that did not mean it was not working.

The doors opened, and the two brothers entered. "Sorry to keep you waiting," Antonio sneered as he sat himself down across from John, a slight scowl on his face. "We know where they are. Harold and his men are camped out along the peninsula."

"Excellent," John said. "We will send our armies."

"Not going to work," Juan moaned as he plopped himself down beside his brother. "He's got scouts watching for us all over the place. We go anywhere near there, and they'll flee."

"Scouts? So, his men are scattered now? This is good, isn't it?" John questioned.

"If his numbers were low, yes. Ever since the attack on their camp, it seems Harold has managed to gather more soldiers now that he has come out of hiding." Antonio angrily crossed his arms and leaned back. "Cruz is furious. He has no intentions of leaving his home until we take out Harold. He writes that he will remain in Spain for the time being, but he stresses that we had better handle this pest problem."

"How many soldiers has Harold gathered?" John asked.

"Hundreds, and the numbers are growing every day," Antonio said. "What are you going to do, John?"

"I don't know," John said. "If his numbers are truly growing as quickly as you say, this has become a lot more than a mere pest problem. This will become a real war – not a chase. I have no way of seeing a predictable end in sight. This could take months or even years, if Harold continues to gain support."

Antonio leaned forward on the table; his eyes focused entirely on John as though he was intending to kill him with his stare. "Handle this, John. Cruz will not be walking into a death trap. You may have married the man's daughter, but he will not put up with this for much longer. I know I won't. Handle this, or soon Harold will not be the only one La Cofradía is hunting."

Antonio stood, and his brother followed – the same wicked grin painted on Juan's face that he so often wore. John tapped his fingers against the table, his nerves growing with each passing second. He knew that Cruz was running out of patience.

Part II
Journey to London

Chapter 7

Two Years Later

Kathleen stepped back, keeping her legs steady as she practiced her footing. She crossed to the side, her sword held up, and then swung in front of her, moving her feet carefully forward in the proper motion of an experienced swordsman. *Watch your breathing*, she reminded herself, just as Blade would often tell her during their training sessions. She had become an excellent swordsman – not that she expected she would ever actually put it to use outside of sparring with Black Dragons. She had, much to her surprise as well as everyone else's, (and on two separate occasions), bested Blade in a sword match.

Blade was not the only one she had learned from since Smith's departure two years before. Ace, her brother, had taught her to fight. During one of their first sparring matches, he had busted her lip, and due to his own discomfort, he had tried to opt out of being her teacher, but she had refused to allow him to cower and step down because of it. Eventually, he had taught her to use her small stature to her advantage, and she could even hold her own in a fight with Ace. She had never won in a sparring match with him – no one had, but she could keep up with him.

From Knot she had learned all about the ships. She knew every position the crew held aboard a ship now and could handle taking on any job given to her. Yin had pulled his knowledge of weaponry, he had learned from Cannonball, and had taught her well. Snake, Mouth, Jackson, the Irish sisters, and even Abigail had all taught her their expertise, and she had done her best to be an excellent student.

The rebellion was dying. Their numbers, while they had started to flourish for a while, had been gradually dwindling as John continuously managed to outnumber them in brutal attacks. It was clear John would not stop until the Caldara's, herself included, were dead and buried.

Kathleen stepped left and raised the sword, attempting to get used to its weight. She had broken her old sword during a spar with Blade, and Ron had been kind enough to create a new one for her. Her stomach growled, and she attempted to ignore the noise. There would be no food tonight; she had already eaten her rations for the day.

Two years ago, after the attack on the original rebellion campsite, the surplus of soldiers had made her and everyone else hopeful, but things had changed. They had been hit and hit hard time and time again. Now, they felt like they were constantly on the run; it had been months since they had last gone on the offensive. Soon, she could feel it in her heart, John would take them all one by one. She had made up her mind, though; she was not going down without a fight.

***

King Harold sat near one of the campfires, poking the dwindling flames with a stick. He was tired, and he had been tired for a long time. Smith leaving was perhaps the worst thing that could have happened; the Black Dragon's had always been a beacon of hope for the people of Kirkston, but now it was as though the Black Dragon's no longer existed. True, most of the crew was still present and fighting in the war, but without Smith they were just fellow foot soldiers.

Movement from across the fire caught his attention, and he spotted his son, Ace, sitting down with a pitiful amount of food on his plate. Ace's hair was full of silver patches, and it saddened Harold deeply. His son looked even older than himself now. Smith's departure had affected Ace and Snake the most, that much Harold was certain of. Both men seemed to have aged quicker than the rest, and they rarely spoke to anyone, especially each other. Snake had his wife who always did her best to pull him out of his melancholy, and Ace had Cassidy –although after the loss of her daughter, she was truly the one who needed the support that Ace simply could not give.

Harold could not imagine. The boy, Pierson, for all Smith knew, could be Ace's or Snake's, but that had not mattered to him in the least. He had fled, letting his anger guide his actions. They had never received word from Smith; they did not even know for certain if he had made it out of Kirkston, though the rumors said that he did.

Harold had finally managed to get a letter out to England, but they had not offered their assistance. Not yet. There was a growing favoritism towards John by the English, so his friends in the old country were waiting it out a bit longer before sending assistance. Harold's lack of interest with helping to fund the colonies was surely something affecting his former allies decision to wait; he believed that England was hoping they could convince John to do what Harold would not.

Dave, Harold's nephew, approached Ace. Harold pretended not to notice, but he witnessed Dave throw his rations down onto Ace's plate. Ace glanced up at his younger cousin; the two had somewhat made amends after the attack on the Black Dragon hideout two years prior, but they certainly were not friends.

"What are you doing?" Ace asked weakly.

"I know you've been giving some of your rations to your lady's sick sister. Eat a bit today, would you? Yin is splitting his rations with the woman today, so there's no need for you to do it too. I know she needs it to keep herself well, but there are others willing to help. Eat." Dave walked off before Ace could argue.

Harold locked eyes with Ace when his son glanced up in his direction. Ace's eyes were full of sorrow. He had told Harold in private that he had had every intention of adopting Cassidy's daughter, and the loss of the girl had pained him even more so than the loss of Smith and the bastard child of Sea, at least there was hope that Smith and Pierson were alive. It was a lot for Ace to handle, and Harold could feel his son's pain. Uninvited, he stood and walked around the fire, sitting himself down beside him.

"You cannot take care of Cassidy and Clara if you do not take care of yourself first," Harold said to him.

Ace nodded and ate the dry food he had been given by his cousin. "Today makes two years since Smith left with the boy."

Harold knew this. Everyone around camp knew this. "I know," he said. "What Smith did was not fair to you or to Snake. He had no way of knowing if that was his boy or not."

"What *I* did was not fair to Smith," Ace said. "What Snake and I did. You were not there. Smith was so in love with her…with Sea. And, even after she died, the man could not let her go. I had so many chances I could have told him and perhaps spared this heartache, but I never did. I loved Sea once, and now I feel so betrayed, realizing how she used me. I love Cassidy now, but this madness is making me cold towards everyone, Cassidy included. What if Pierson was mine or Snakes?"

Harold put a hand on his son's shoulder. "You have to let go. Smith, despite the anger he held when he left here, is a good man. That boy, even if he was yours, I know is well looked after and is away from this war. Find peace in that."

Ace nodded. "Thank you," he said.

Harold removed is hand and positioned himself to look directly at the fire. The mended bond between father and son was perhaps the only good thing that had come from the past two miserable years. John did not have much more work to do to take them out. Harold could feel it in his bones that he would be facing a hangman's noose soon, but at least now he knew that he had the affection of his children.

***

Prince Richard tried to ignore the words of the three soldiers who had pulled him aside late that evening. The sun was setting, and they stood a short distance from camp.

His stomach growled, and he was sure the men could hear it. "You've been giving your rations to your wife and son, aye?" One of the men asked and Richard nodded, but he did not say a word.

"We need new recruits," the second man said. "But we have run out of luck. We have not gotten new recruits in nearly a year. People cannot take your father seriously, Prince Richard. Besides, he is getting old. Even if by some miracle we manage to take this country back, he would be retiring from his throne soon thereafter. And, we all know what that means, don't we?"

"Her Majesty, Queen Kathleen," the third man snarled. "That's why we are not getting new recruits. Your spinster of a sister is not what the people of Kirkston want. You, however, should have been given your birthright since your brother has refused his throne. You are the son, and you have already provided a proper heir in your son."

Richard nibbled on the inside of his lips. He shook his head. "My sister is not what is keeping people back."

"What then?" the first man asked. "Because the way it seems to me is that people would prefer stability, and stability is far from what your sister represents. They'd rather have John Stevenson than to have that woman on the throne. You and I both know that John is not what this country needs. He's tearing it apart, but if Harold were to surrender the right as heir over to you… well… then perhaps this rebellion would be taken more seriously."

Richard shook his head. "I doubt that."

"Don't doubt it!" the man shouted back. "Your sister is preventing us from getting new soldiers. We are all going to die at John Stevenson's hand if we do not get more recruits. And, by we, I do mean *we*. You, me, your wife, your son – all of us are going to die running from John. He's not going to stop until the Caldara's are dead. Aren't you tired of running?"

"Of course, I am," Richard said, and he began to ponder if what the men were staying was true. Perhaps Kirkston was not ready for a female ruler? If his sister had married, it might have been a different story, but the thought of a single woman suddenly taking the throne might just be what was holding people back from joining the rebellion. "What is it you three are supposing that we do?"

The first man who had spoken to him grabbed him by the wrist; Richard felt him place something into his hand, and when he looked down he saw that he was now holding a dagger.

"No Kathleen means there is no one left but yourself to take the throne since Prince James has refused it."

Richard jolted back. "You must be mad if you think for one second that I would harm my sister!" He clutched the dagger tight in his hand and glared at each of them. His stomach growled again, and it pained him.

"It's for the greater good of this camp," the man said. "Your father will not see reason. He still believes Kathleen to be the best option, but things have changed. Women are not meant to rule a country on their own."

The third man nodded and spoke angrily. "Idiotic – women are, that is. If I was given but one word to describe them, that is what I would say. And, your sister, though she is perhaps the most intelligent of her breed, she is still only a woman."

"I would say *fragile* if given only one word," said the second man.

"Nay," said the first man. "*Deceitful.*"

"*Lesser*," Richard said, suddenly being pulled into the game that these men were playing. His hunger was dictating his thoughts. He clenched the dagger tight in his hand, and for a brief moment he played with the thought of following through with the request the men had made of him.

"I would say *capable*," Kathleen's voice echoed around them, and they all turned to see that the princess was standing nearby with her sword drawn. "If I were given but one word to describe *all* women, I would say *capable*. We're quite capable of anything if given the opportunity." Her eyes darted straight towards Richard. "Put that dagger down, or you will taste my sword, *little* brother."

Richard dropped the dagger, and Kathleen came forward, the sword pointed towards the man who had handed Richard the dagger. "You'd dare try to turn my brother against me? You must be mad. I shared a womb with him, and I know better than anyone that he is a weak fellow."

"Weak!" Richard yelped. "You think I am weak?"

"You let three buffoons toy with your head like this? Yes, Richard, I think you are weak," she said with anger, and Richard stepped forward with his fists at the ready, and suddenly he was staring down the barrel of her pistol.

"I think there has clearly been a misunderstanding!" one of the men said quickly, but Kathleen laughed at them, pistol in one hand, sword in the other.

"A misunderstanding? So, I did not just overhear you four discussing my assassination?" She gritted her teeth. "You three sit down in the ground, or I will scream loud enough that soldiers come running and have all of you hung here tonight."

The men obeyed, holding their hands up to show that they were unarmed. Kathleen turned to face Richard, her eyes full of hurt.

"I would never have done it, Kathleen," Richard said. "I love you, and you know that, yes?"

She pointed the tip of her sword in his face and returned the pistol to her side. "Draw your sword," she said.

"Pardon?" He questioned.

"You heard me, Richard. Draw your sword!"

He drew his sword. "I do not want to fight you, Kathleen. I have years of experience on you, and it would be unfair. And, you cannot move so well in that dress, now can you?"

"Perhaps I am at a disadvantage," she said. "Then this should be easy for you. I just want to spar with you, brother. Let me show you what I have learned from our friends. If you can strike me with your sword before I do you, I will go to Father and refuse the crown and tell him that you are the better party. I will even threaten to leave the rebellion camp if he refuses my suggestion."

Richard glanced down at the men who were eagerly nodding for him to go along with her childish game. He was certain they were just worried what Kathleen would do to them once the charade was over; they had, after all, been caught plotting her murder.

They touched swords, and Richard immediately went in for a strike, but Kathleen moved her feet gracefully, and her sword danced about in such a way that it seemed as though it was merely an extension of herself. The only other person he had ever seen appear so natural with a sword was Blade. Richard knew she had been training under him, but he had no idea that she had become so accomplished.

Their swords made contact several times, and it did not take Richard long to realize that she was only toying with him. Her sword struck his hand, and he screamed and dropped his weapon, a tiny bit of blood trickling down his sleeve. He closed his eyes – would his sister kill him? Had she seen the maddening look on his face when he had contemplating following through with the men's horrid suggestion? He would deserve it, he felt.

Richard heard two swift swooshing sounds of her blade, and he opened his eyes and looked down at his chest to see that she had sliced open his shirt. She returned her sword to her sheath that was strapped at her side by a belt that hung loosely around her dress. Kathleen stepped forward and held open his shirt, eyeing his visible ribs.

"When was the last time you ate?" she hissed. Richard did not answer. She grabbed him by the one ear he had left and squeezed it. "When was the last time you ate your rations without splitting them with your wife and child?"

"I do not even remember," he said, and he felt his sister slowly release his ear and come forward, wrapping her arms around his neck.

"You will take my rations tomorrow, and do not even try to protest. I will not try to tell you to not give your wife and child your rations because I know you will not listen. You must eat, Richard. Your hunger is making you mad. I know you would never hurt me, but do not let these horrid men tempt you." She pulled away and removed her pistol, waving it towards the three soldiers who were still sitting on their knees. "Stand up."

They stood. The man who had given Richard the dagger spoke nervously. "Princess Kathleen, please, forgive us –" Kathleen shot her pistol, hitting him in his right knee. He screamed and cussed before falling to the ground.

"Oh, what a silly girl am I!" Kathleen called out in a dramatic fashion. "Honestly, what are they doing giving ladies swords and pistols? I clearly don't know what I'm doing. Shame on me."

"Don't shoot us!" the second man pleaded, holding out his arms in a defensive manner.

"You three should leave, and if you're lucky I won't shoot you in yours backs on the way out. Consider this mercy because I ought to have all three of you hung for treason!" Her voice boomed, and the three men ran off into the woods, the man she had shot hobbling the entire way.

Richard smiled slightly at her as he picked up his sword and returned it to his side. "Well done," he told her.

"You thought about killing me," she said coldly, her eyes piercing through him.

"Kathleen, I would not have done it. I hope you know that."

"But, you thought about it," she said, facing him head on.

"Desperate thoughts," he said, but he did not deny what had gone through his mind. "I love you, Kathleen. Please believe that. If there is anything, I can do to show you that this is true and that I am truly sorry –"

"There is," she said. She placed her pistol back at her side. She looked at him with a serious expression.

"Anything," he said, his guilt outweighing all common sense.

"I need you to help me convince Father to allow me to do something very, very... *very* stupid."

Chapter 8

"No, no, no," Harold said, shaking his head. "This is not going to work. Kathleen, my dear, you look too much like Richard!"

"This is madness!" Queen Rachel snarled, shaking as she held her daughter's chopped hair in one hand and a knife in the other.

Kathleen was dressed in one of her brothers more casual justaucorps', his jacket, and his breeches. The fabric was mostly a cheap silk, so it would not attract too much attention. "I do!" she shrieked as she looked in the mirror Richard was holding up for her. "I have my brother's face!"

The four of them were hidden away in one of the larger tents meant for meetings, and they were attempting something rather desperate. They had dressed Kathleen in men's clothing, and her own mother had cut off her daughters beautiful, long black hair.

"She looks like a twelve-year-old boy," Queen Rachel said, a bit faint after having been the one to saw her daughter's hair off. She slammed the wad of hair on a nearby table. "You can't let her do this, Harold."

Harold ignored his wife and studied Kathleen carefully. "They will recognize you," he said and shook his head. "That, or they will just think you are Richard."

"Perhaps not," Richard said. "It is not exactly a secret that I have lost an ear. They portray it in the wanted posters."

"Well, then someone could mistake her for a Caldara nonetheless. This won't work – especially with those!" Harold pointed to her cheek where three little freckles sat – the same as her twin. "I never realized how much you two truly resemble until we cut off that beautiful hair of yours." The door to the large tent opened, and Ace entered. He jumped back in surprise. "Close those flaps!" Harold snapped, and Ace did as he was told.

"Now, just what is it exactly that I'm looking at?" Ace questioned as his eyes went back and forth between Richard and Kathleen.

"I am going to England," Kathleen said. "I will negotiate terms face to face with the fools who are ignoring our father's pleas for help."

"You're mad," Ace said. "You will never make it out of port. Two years, and John's men still inspect every passenger and bag before a ship is permitted to leave the country. And, whose bright idea was it to cut off your hair? All that did was make you look like Richard, and they're looking for him too!" Then Ace paused. He glanced over at the table where his mother had laid Kathleen's hair and the knife she had used to cut it.

"You know… you could use that to make a beard."

"A beard! Yes, Ace, wonderful idea!" Kathleen called out. "One thing the Caldara men are certainly not known for is their ability to grow good fascial hair."

The three men looked at her with offended glances – all three of them instinctually touching their faces, and Queen Rachel laughed. "With a large enough and convincing enough beard, those guards at the ports would not even notice you."

"I can grow a beard," Ace said.

"You grow stubble just like our father," she said and waved him off.

Harold grunted, but she did have a point. "Can we make a good beard out of that? A convincing one?"

Queen Rachel sighed. "We're not really going to let her do this, are we?"

"Mother, someone has to," Kathleen said. "They'd spot you or Father in an instant, and Richard is too recognizable with his missing ear. A Caldara must go to England. It's the only way we can convince parliament to help us."

"I do hope you intend to address them as yourself and not as a cross dresser?" Ace questioned.

"Of course. I'm not a fool," she said.

Harold shook his head. "I'm still trying to figure out how you managed to convince me that this is a good idea."

"It's not," Queen Rachel said. "If she gets caught, John will have her hung, Harold. Our daughter –"

"Is capable," Richard said. "She can do this, Mother. I know she can."

Harold watched as Kathleen smiled at her brother, and he felt that perhaps there was some sort of secret between them. He watched as Ace stepped forward and put his arms around Kathleen. Yes, this was the only good thing that had come out of all of this madness. Watching Ace with his younger siblings was perhaps the most rewarding thing he had ever experienced.

"All right," Ace said. "Let's see what we can do about making you into a man, sister."

***

Kathleen took a deep breath. The eastern docks were always busy and full of people; while those docks had more guards, the immense amount of people coming in and out of the ports would be a lot for the invaders to handle. Her hope was that by taking the busier docks, she would be overlooked. She wore her disguise, the black beard and all, and walked confidently in her steps. She dragged a small chest behind her with a change of clothes and a few other belongings to appear as though she was merely travelling and was not on a secret mission.

She paid the gentleman at the dock some money so that she could board his ship bound for England. The Spanish guards stood all along the docks in front of each ship, digging through everyone's belongings. Kathleen got in line for the ship destined for England.

"Rebellion!" one of the Spanish men shouted, and Kathleen froze. She tried not to look, but with her peripherals she saw a man being assaulted by Spanish soldiers, for they had found some old parchment that had come from one of the Protestant churches John's men had burned down.

"I'm not with the rebellion!" the man pleaded. "It's just some old parchment I had at my home from before the war!"

The man was instantly arrested and dragged away from the docks. *This was a terrible idea*, she thought and started to slowly back out of the line. "Next," the guards in front of her snarled and waved her on.

Two of the men opened up her chest and began digging through it. "Where are you going and why?" the one guard not busying himself with her belongings asked.

"England. To visit my sister who is ill," she said, attempting to make her voice sound deep.

One of the men pulled out a dress from the chest. "What is this?" he snarled.

"It was my mothers," she said, having already worked up a story for the men. "I thought it would mean something to my sister, so I am bringing it with me on my visit."

"Are you English?" the man in front of her asked.

She was not sure what answer he was wanting, so she simply spoke with confidence in her tone. "My mother was English. My father was a Spaniard, though he died when I was a boy, and I know little of him."

"Speak some Spanish," the man said.

"I don't know any Spanish," Kathleen said.

One of the men who was now repacking her chest snapped at the man in charge. "He said his father died when he was a boy. Pay attention so we can move this along."

The man eyed her cautiously. He reached forward and began searching her pockets. Kathleen felt a nervous lump form in her throat – would he notice her figure and question her? He did not, and he merely grunted and waved her on. She took a relaxing breath and continued to drag the chest behind her. Behind her she could hear that he was giving the next gentleman in line an equally troubling time.

She had made it, and within the next hour the ship was leaving Kirkston. Kathleen stood out on the deck of the ship, hardly able to believe she was leaving. Her heart raced from fear and excitement as she watched her homeland disappear in the distance.

Chapter 9

During the long journey to England, Kathleen did her best to keep to herself. There were some Spaniards aboard the ship, and she did not want to find out that they were working for John. Most of the people on board were either families fleeing Kirkston to avoid the war or were Englishmen returning home. When the captain finally announced that they had arrived in England, she felt as though she could breathe again. She had never spent so much time on a ship, and she certainly had never spent so much time pretending to be a man. Thankfully, since she had done her best to remain unnoticed by her fellow passengers, she had not had to do much pretending and had merely stayed away from everyone.

The ship docked in Liverpool, and soon Kathleen managed to procure herself a means of travel to London. She travelled for nearly forty-eight hours without much of a break before finding refuge just outside of the city of London at a privately-owned tavern and inn. She had since removed the beard, but she remained dressed as a man during her travels. A lady travelling on her own through back roads and questionable towns was not an enticing idea; she did not know the area at all having never ventured outside of Kirkston on her own.

The barkeep was incredibly friendly and found a room for her. She asked the gentleman if she could get a letter sent to His Majesty, King George I. The man laughed. "He's in Germany, sir. Has been for some time now. And, who are you, lad, to request to send word to the king?"

Kathleen rolled her eyes slightly. "I need to get a hearing with the Regency Council if His Majesty is away."

The barkeep looked at her curiously. "Who are you exactly?"

Kathleen hesitated for a moment. "Prince Richard Caldara," she said.

The man looked surprised. "My apologies, Your Majesty."

"Keep this between us, yes?" she said. "I need your assistance, sir."

"I have heard of what it is like in Kirkston now," the barkeep said. "How did you manage to get out at all?"

"Never mind that," Kathleen said. "Can you help me or no?"

"I will fetch you some parchment and have my boy deliver your letter, Prince Richard," he said and disappeared.

The barkeep had seemed like a trustworthy fellow, so Kathleen hoped he would keep his mouth shut. She locked herself away in her room and waited for the man to return. There was a knock on her door, and she answered it to see a woman standing before her. The woman stared at her curiously and held up some parchment.

"Who are you?" Kathleen questioned.

"I am the barkeeps wife," she said, still staring. "Are you truly Prince Richard Caldara? I've never met a royal before."

Kathleen snatched the parchment from the woman. "I am. And, how dare your husband! I demanded he keep quiet, and he blabbers to the first person he sees."

"My husband keeps nothing from me, sir… madam?"

Kathleen frowned; not one other person had noticed, but this woman somehow had seen right through her. She grabbed the woman by the arm and pulled her into the room, slamming the door behind. "How?" she asked.

The woman blushed. "I guessed. You looked too young to be Prince Richard, but you have those freckles they say he has that make him seem so youthful, but even so you could not possibly be a man of that age. Your femininity gave you away trying to pretend to be a man your own age. Are you Princess Kathleen? Why are you dressed as a man?"

"It was my only way out of Kirkston," she said. "And, I had hoped to speak with King George or someone from parliament, but now that I am here, I am not quite sure whom to go to. My father's pleas for help have already been ignored for two years."

The woman smiled. "I have an unusual suggestion, Your Majesty, if you care to listen to a poor woman whose ideas are only as good as the knowledge she's gathered from gossip in a bar."

"Anyone can be useful if in the right place at the right time. What say you, madam?" Kathleen asked.

"Do not write to parliament. Send a letter to Isleworth instead and request to speak with the duchess of Kendal."

Kathleen turned up her nose. "You must be mad to suggest such a thing. I do not wish to speak with that scarecrow."

"Do listen to what I have to say, I pray you," the woman said, practically whispering. "I know you must have a sour taste in your mouth for George's mistress, but I know the mistress fancies sweet Princess Kathleen of Kirkston."

"And, why would the duchess of Kendal fancy me?"

"She speaks highly of you, so they say. I only hear whispers from courtiers and others who visit the bar. The duchess has a bit of pull in London, and if your father's letters have been ignored by parliament, then perhaps a new approach is necessary. I am but the wife of a barkeep, but that is my thought." The woman curtsied and promised to keep her secret before departing.

Kathleen frowned. She did not care for Melusine Von Der Schulenbur, duchess of Kendal and Munster, but to hear that this sophisticated woman had an interest in her as a ruler somewhat made Kathleen proud. She debated for several minutes before deciding to try the advice of the barkeeps wife; she wrote a letter to the duchess and signed it proudly, *Princess Kathleen of Kirkston.* The barkeeps son took the letter to Isleworth, and Kathleen retired to bed, completely exhausted after her travels.

***

A small part of Kathleen enjoyed the barkeeps confusion when, instead of Prince Richard, Princess Kathleen emerged from the room she had rented that following morning. Now that she was in England and far from Kirkston, there was little need for her disguise, though a part of her had enjoyed it. She blushed slightly when she looked at herself in the mirror with her short, choppy hair. It lacked the elegance it had once had, and it made her look like a boy in a dress or a silly girl who had ruined her hair.

The barkeeps wife was kind enough to help her tie up her corset. Kathleen had hidden her petite crown within the dress, and thankfully the Spaniards at the docks had not located it. If she was to be speaking with royalty, parliament, or any person of political persuasion, she felt the need to bring it to appear serious. She tied her short hair back because it was terribly uneven – sloppy like that of a peasant man's hair, and if she was going to be in the presence of the duchess, she was going to do her best to look presentable.

"I was unaware you were here, Your Majesty," the barkeep said as she made her way down into the bar.

His wife, who was behind the bar with him, laughed and popped him in his arm. "Don't be so daft, Eric. She was the boy you spoke with last night."

The couple spoke with Kathleen in whispers so as not to alert their patrons. Kathleen smiled. "Forgive me for my inappropriate attire," Kathleen said to the man. "But, my escape out of Kirkston required it. Otherwise, I would have been caught and hung at the docks, I'm sure."

"A princess dressing as a man is perhaps the strangest thing I have ever heard of," the barkeep, Eric, said and wiped his brow with a handkerchief. "A letter from the duchess has arrived for you, Your Majesty." He handed her the letter that he had carefully placed in his coat pocket. "My son brought it back just this morning after his journey."

"Bless you, kind sir," Kathleen said and took the letter. She breathed a sigh of relief as she read the letter signed by the duchess that told her to come to her home in Isleworth within the city of London at her earliest convenience. "It seems I will need a coach," she said and looked up at the barkeep. "Sir, I do hope it would not be too much of a burden to ask that you acquire for me –"

"I will acquire a coach for Her Majesty," he said. "And, there is no need to pay me for it. My son will escort you to Isleworth in our carriage. It is perhaps not a suiting ride for you, but –"

Kathleen cut him off. "For the past two years, sir, I have been sleeping on the ground in a tent ever since my country has been overrun. Any carriage, I promise you, will be most comfortable for me."

The man smiled and soon was calling for his son, a young boy of twelve, named for his father. Young Eric blushed to see that he would be escorting a princess, and Kathleen could tell there was a slight excitement in the boy's uncomfortable gaze. He loaded up the horse and the open carriage, and soon they were on their way to meet the duchess. It took only an hour before they arrived outside of the duchess's home. Kathleen handed Eric Junior a bit of money and told him to go buy himself something sweet in town as a thank you for waiting on her. He thanked her, and she escorted herself in through the front gates.

She was asked to wait in the garden by a serving maid for the duchess, so Kathleen found herself a seat by the rose bushes. She twiddled her fingers as her anxiety grew, but only a few minutes passed before she saw the tall, thin woman that was Melusine Von Der Schulenbur. Kathleen stood as the woman entered the garden and curtsied to her, and the woman returned the gesture. Upon closer examination, Kathleen saw that the woman was wearing the royal blue – a much more significant statement in England than in Kirkston – and she found it to be almost provocative considering she was the mistress to the already married king. This was a powerful woman, and Kathleen desperately needed her assistance.

"Princess Kathleen of Kirkston," the duchess said in a slight Germanic accent.

Kathleen decided to be as formal as she could manage to be with her greeting. "Duchess of Munster and Kendal, Marchioness and Countess of Dungannon and Baroness Dundalk, Countess of Feversham and Baroness Glastonbury, Melusine Von Der Schulenbur, it is a pleasure to meet your acquaintance at last."

The woman laughed at Kathleen's over-done greeting. She came close, and Kathleen could see why the people of England called her the *Maypole*. She was frightfully tall and thin, and Kathleen, who was a rather short woman, felt child-like standing beside her.

"I'm having some tea brought out," the woman said and waved Kathleen towards the seat near the rose bushes. "I am quite eager to hear about your travels."

Kathleen sat; she was nervous. It was in that moment that she realized this was truly her first diplomatic act as heir – the first one that mattered. She was not just a little princess running about Caldara Castle any longer. She had come to make a deal on behalf of her father.

"Duchess –" Kathleen began, and the woman waved her hand.

"No need for that. You may call me Melusine. I do hope you'd allow me to call you Kathleen?"

"Of course," Kathleen said, feeling slightly more relaxed since the woman was willing to be less formal.

A serving girl brought them some tea, and Melusine thanked her. Kathleen took a sip as the serving girl disappeared back inside the house. The woman took a long sip of her tea before placing the teacup on the small table beside them. She seemed to be studying Kathleen's face. "I am very impressed with you," Melusine began. "I have wanted to meet you for some time. Kirkston is but a small nation, but it is not unlike ours. Here you are, one elder brother and a twin brother as well, and yet your father grants you the throne. Dare I ask if you know why that was?"

"It is a question I ask myself every day," Kathleen said.

"No doubt he saw something in you," the Duchess said. "How is it you managed to get out of Kirkston? From what I have read, it would be a nearly impossible feat for a Caldara."

"I'm quite embarrassed at how I did it," Kathleen said. "I dressed as a man to avoid detection."

Melusine pressed her lips together to keep from laughing. "Oh, did you?"

Kathleen removed her crown, sitting it on her lap. She undid her hair and let the poorly cut waves fall. "What do you think?"

Melusine laughed. "My word, what a handsome boy you would have made! That twin brother of yours must be stunning."

Kathleen caught herself giggling. She had had her reservations about this woman; she knew that she and the king had three daughters together. And, rumors were that George's wife was locked up in some sort of tower or prison somewhere while his mistress was running half the country, but Kathleen had to admit to herself that she knew very little of King George's personal life. It was so difficult to differentiate rumor from truth.

"I believe so," Kathleen said. "Though since the war in my country has begun, he has been shot in the head twice."

"My word!"

"By the grace of God, both bullets merely grazed him –although now he is missing an ear. His face, still handsome, but I believe he is paranoid that he has lost his former charm."

"Well," Melusine said and shook her head. "I am truly sorry to hear that. I imagine that you all have suffered great loss these past two years."

"Sadly, yes, and we would have hoped to have gotten aid from our ties here by now," she said in a firm tone, eyeing Melusine with care in order to read her the best she could.

"Believe me, I have wondered the same thing. There is a lot taking place in England right now. I am to be leaving soon to be with George, and parliament will be handling much of the politics until our return. Truthfully, I am surprised you asked for an audience with me. Why?"

Kathleen spoke cautiously. "I know you have pull in London, and I thought perhaps you would take me seriously. I am not my father, after all, but I thought a woman such as yourself could sympathize with me and my travels. All I ask of you is to speak on my behalf – on behalf of all of Kirkston – to plead with His Majesty to send us aid."

Melusine paused, her carefully painted lips seemed to poke out as though she was pondering something. "Very well," she said. "But, I ask for two things in return for this favor."

Kathleen nodded. "And, what would you like from me?"

Melusine smiled at her. "First, I wish for you to attend a soiree as my guest this evening here at my home. Then tomorrow I will venture into the city to speak on your behalf as well as write to George for you."

"And, the second thing you ask of me?"

Melusine again smiled. "Only to be among those invited to your coronation ceremony. I do believe I would enjoy seeing Kirkston's first queen being crowed."

Kathleen smiled back. "I do believe I can certainly arrange that."

Chapter 10

Kathleen, after spending several days in London, packed up her dress and belongings into the chest she had brought with her. She dressed in her disguise and looked at herself in the mirror; she really did make a convincing young man. The beard had fallen apart, and she had been unable to fix it, so she would have to go it again with a bare face. The guards in Kirkston were much more concerned with rebellion members escaping than what was coming into Kirkston, so she hoped that the missing beard would not be what got her caught.

Melusine was still making deals on her behalf, but it seemed as though parliament would arrive at a decision very soon. Melusine had told her to expect aid to arrive within a month or so. Kathleen paid the barkeep and his wife handsomely for their hospitality before travelling back to Liverpool. Much to her dismay, there were no ships bound for Kirkston, and it did not sound as though there would be one anytime soon.

Eventually, she found a captain who would be travelling to Balla, and Kathleen knew she could find a ship heading to Kirkston from there. She offered the captain money and her service, and he agreed to let the "strapping young lad," aboard. The thought of going to Balla made her cringe slightly. Smith was in Balla, or at least, that was what his plan had been two years before.

She had many days aboard the ship to contemplate whether or not to spend time looking for Smith, but in her heart, she knew what she wanted to do. When she thought of Snake and of her brother, Ace, her heart ached for them – they needed Smith. *She* needed him. She decided that once she got to Balla she would not take the first ship bound for Kirkston, but instead she would seek out Smith. The thought weighed heavy on her mind, but she knew that it was for the best, as she felt she deserved some sort of closure, even if he broke her heart all over again.

***

If Kirkston was the little sister of England, then Balla was England and Spain's love child. Nearly every person, rich or poor, was bilingual and of mixed heritage in Balla. Along with the Spanish and English, there was also a surplus of Romanian dialects as well. The culture and the music and the clothing were a unique blend of such lovely cultures. Kathleen had been to Balla with her family many times, but she had always been escorted in a carriage and had not been able to enjoy the busy streets of the port city from a citizen's perspective. There were street performers all around dancing, playing music, and doing tricks for coins. The gypsy life was a popular one in Balla, so she kept an eye on her pockets.

"Pardon, sir!" a young woman said, grabbing Kathleen by her sleeve. She was a gypsy – or a prostitute – Kathleen could not really tell. The woman smiled and held out her hand. "Care to see a show?"

"Um, well, I –" Kathleen stammered, and she was almost instantly yanked into a circle.

"Behold!" the woman shouted, and a few people watching clapped. "My handsome volunteer!" The next thing Kathleen knew she was holding up a large hoop that the maddening woman caught ablaze. The woman performed a few incredible feats all to the sound of a lute that a young boy behind her played. Kathleen laughed at the spectacle of it all. The woman bowed and took the hoop and in a single breath extinguished the entire thing. People clapped. The woman waved a hand towards Kathleen. "And, please, a round of applause for the young man!"

Kathleen pulled a coin from her pocket and gave it to the woman. The boy on the lute went around with a hat collecting coins from the onlookers who had enjoyed the performance. Kathleen went to grab her chest, and then frowned to see that it had been stolen during the show. She gritted her teeth and turned back towards the woman. Kathleen had been the only one standing around with luggage – which was probably why she had been pulled to be the woman's volunteer. It had been a distraction. She marched up to the woman who was now counting coins. "All right, where is it? I'm sure you had some third-party swiping pockets during that charade. Where is my chest?"

The woman laughed. "I do not know what you are talking about."

Kathleen rolled her eyes; apart from her crown, there was really nothing in the chest worth getting into a fight over. She double checked her pockets to make sure her money had not been swiped. She still had her money, so she decided not to cause a scene. "You best hope you do not run into me again," she warned the woman before storming away from the ports to distance herself from the street performers.

Soon she located a bar. This was the port city; if Smith had come to Balla two years ago as planned, he would have had to have come through here. It was the only bar in the area, so perhaps Smith, Carissa, and Pierson had stopped to get something to eat? It was a long shot that the barkeep would still remember those faces from two years before, but she figured it was worth the gamble. Plus, Carissa was a Balla native, so there was a chance someone there knew of her location.

Kathleen entered into the bar and found herself a seat. A bar wench came over to offer her assistance, and Kathleen requested that she fetch the barkeep. The woman disappeared, and Kathleen sunk down into her seat. It had been a long day. She heard giggling and then glanced over to a corner where she spotted three young women looking her way. One of the women waved shyly, and Kathleen offered her a smile but looked away so the girl would not think she could come over. *What are they so flustered over*, she wondered.

Suddenly, the bar wench plopped a glass in front of her. "I did not order anything to drink," Kathleen said.

"The ladies in the corner bought you a drink," she said and trotted off.

Kathleen blushed, and the women in the corner giggled. She looked down. *So that's what they're flustered over*, she thought. A moment later, the barkeep appeared. "You asked to speak to me?" he asked and sat himself down in the seat across from her.

"I'm looking for someone," she said. "I'm a bit desperate, and I was hoping you could help. My guess is just about anyone who comes through the main ports probably stop here. How are you with faces and names?"

"Pretty exceptional, lad," he said. "Who are you looking for?"

"A woman by the name of Carissa Livingston with her boy, Pierson, came through here about two years ago with a young gentleman near the ladies age," she said.

"Ah," he said with a laugh. "They won't be difficult to find, but I'm afraid if it is Ms. Livingston you are looking for, she passed away about a year ago."

Kathleen frowned. She did not care for the way Carissa's appearance had taken Smith away, but to hear that the woman was dead made her sad. "I don't see how that is funny, sir," she said.

"Oh, no, not that Ms. Livingston passed, forgive me, you misunderstand. I just find it funny how serious you are about finding Mr. Barons. Everyone in Balla knows him. You could have asked a street gypsy, and even she could have pointed you in the right direction."

"Mr. Barons?" Kathleen questioned.

"Peter Barons," he said. "Pierson's father, yes? That's who you're looking for?"

Kathleen sat upright. "That's exactly who I am looking for." She was shocked to learn that Smith was going by his actual name.

"Mr. Barons lives in Lupei less than a mile from the capital. You can walk there from here in less than an hour.

Just stay along the beach and head east." The man rose from his seat and stretched his back. "Tell me, lad, how do you know Mr. Barons?"

"An old friend," she said.

"Well, any friend of his is a friend of mine. He's a good man." The barkeep headed back behind the bar.

Kathleen took a sip of the drink the women had bought her and cringed; it was terrible. Either way, she smiled and thanked them on her way out, making them giggle. A small part of her was enjoying playing the part of a strapping young lad from Kirkston. She walked along the beach due east as the man had instructed until she came to the town of Lupei. Lupei was a short walk from the country's capital; it was a district for the wealthy. The homes were all large, and beautiful cobble streets made up the roadways. She smiled as she entered into the little town. Children were playing in the street, all laughing and chasing their friends about.

Smith has certainly done well for himself if he lives here, she thought. "Excuse me, young miss," she said as she approached a young woman who was attempting to gather up the young ones and shoo them away from her front yard.

The woman blushed and smiled at her. "A Kirkston man," she said. "Like Mr. Barons."

Kathleen raised a brow. Clearly, Smith was well known in this area. "Yes, exactly like Mr. Barons. I am an old friend of his. Do you know where I could find him?"

"Of course," she said and pointed down the road. "He lives at the end of the street in the large white home with the red door."

"Thank you, miss," Kathleen said and tipped her hat to the woman like a proper gentleman.

She took a breath. She had not seen Smith in two years. Would he even want to see her? She made her way to the end of the street where she spotted the large, white house the woman had mentioned with the red door. Her heart started to race.

"Pierson!" she heard Smith's familiar voice calling out.

"Papa, catch me!"

Kathleen approached the white picket fence surrounding the property. She saw a young boy, Pierson, leaping off the front porch into a man's arms. She felt her heart flutter to see Smith spin the boy around and put him back down on his feet. Smith was dressed in a fine suit like a proper gentleman. He removed his hat and placed it on the boy's head and laughed. Smith looked up the stairs of the porch, and Kathleen followed his stare to see an older woman in fine clothes making her way towards Smith and the boy. Smith held out his hand to her, and she took his. When she reached the bottom of the porch, Smith put his arm around her waist.

"Are you ready to go?" the woman asked.

"Of course. You look lovely as ever," he said and kissed the woman's lips.

Kathleen felt sickly. She could hardly breathe; Smith looked so perfectly happy. Who was this woman?

Smith took the woman by the hand, and the two of them began heading down the walkway towards the gate; Pierson ran in front of them, laughing in his excitement. As Smith reached to open the gate, he glanced up in her direction. At first, he did not seem to recognize her. He probably just assumed she was some out of town boy. But, he made a second glance her way, and his face became pale, and his mouth hung open slightly. She heard him speak directly to her for the first time in two years.

"Kathleen?"

Chapter 11

Two Years Earlier

Smith held his breath, his heart racing. He had never felt so incredibly claustrophobic, feeling as though the box would close in around him. He could hear Carissa's voice as she spoke with one of the guards at Kirkston's eastern ports.

"Yes, my poor brother," her voice went. "We're taking him home to be buried."

"Name?" the Spanish guard asked.

"His name is Reginald Livingston," she said.

"Open that casket and make sure she's not smuggling something out," another guard's voice boomed.

"Oh, please, don't do that," she said, but the men were already opening the casket.

Smith remained perfectly still – would they notice? The top of the casket opened. Carissa shrieked. "Oh, do close that, please!"

The men did not leave the casket open long enough to notice he still had color to his face; he had kept his eyes closed. The casket was almost immediately shut. "All right, leave the woman alone. There's nothing but a body in there."

Smith felt the casket being moved. He pressed his hands against the side to keep from being jolted around too much. He remained in the box for several hours. He could feel the ship rocking, and he was certain they were moving. Another hour or so went by before the casket door flung open. He felt as though he could finally breathe. Carissa smiled at him. "That was quite clever," she said and offered her hand to help him out.

"Where is Pierson?" he asked.

"He is running about the ship. This is only his second time on a ship, you know? He loves it." She smiled. "The captain has been informed of your presence here, and he found the incident to be quite entertaining. He hates those Spaniards as well, so I do not think you will need to hide any longer while on this journey."

"Wonderful," he said and followed her up the stairwell to the main deck. A number of people were running about the ship; Pierson was looking out at the ocean, standing near the bow. "He looks just like his mother," Smith said sadly.

"I know Courtney would have wanted you to raise him," Carissa said. "But, should we have taken him from your friends Ace and Snake so suddenly?"

"Friends?" Smith hissed. "I do not believe we were as such."

"You're angry," Carissa said. "And, it is keeping you from thinking straight. Will you regret leaving them all behind?"

"I don't know," Smith admitted. "But, that is Courtney's son. I will make sure he has the best life I can provide him with." Pierson turned and waved at them before turning his attention back to the sea. "How much does the boy know?"

"He knows all. He knows that I am not his mother. He knows his mother died at John Stevenson's hand. He knows his mother was unsure who is father was, and he knows how desperately she prayed that it was you. He calls me his mother, but he knows it's not true. He has read many of the letters Courtney wrote from the time she had him up until her death two years later. He reads them often, so he knows much about you. On our way here, all he could talk about was meeting his Papa."

"You really think I'm awful for this, don't you?" Smith asked.

"I think you are hurt. And, it is not as though I have time to let you sort through it. I don't know how much time I have left, Smith."

"Peter," Smith said. "Just call me Peter. There's no sense in going by *Smith* anymore. I'm done with that life." He looked at her with a sympathetic gaze. "You are very certain that there is nothing I can do for you, Carissa?"

"I am dying. Believe me – desperation is what brought me to a war-torn country to find my cousins old lover. I have no one. Your company is enough. Knowing that Pierson will be taken care of is enough for me to leave this world in peace. That boy has been in my home since I was a girl of thirteen. He started calling me *mother* when he was still a wee little thing. He is my son in my eyes. I think he knows that my time is up as hard as I've tried to keep it hidden from him. I just want him to feel loved and to feel safe. Bless you for taking him in so willingly." Carissa touched his arm. "To hear she was unfaithful, I'm sure, was heartbreaking. Will you be all right?"

"I will," Smith said and gazed across the ship. He walked towards Pierson. "What are you doing?" he asked and propped his elbows up against the side of the ship and gazed out across the ocean as the boy was doing.

"I love the ocean," Pierson said. "My mother wrote about it a lot. I think it's amazing you all lived on a ship. I wish I could have lived on a ship. Before I was born, she was the captain, right? But, then you became the captain when she came back to Kirkston, right?"

"That's right," Smith said.

Pierson smiled at him. "Can I call you *Papa*?"

Smith smiled back. "I would love for you to call me that."

"Will you tell me stories about my mother?" he asked. "Mama, um, Carissa, she did not know my mother very well. She only has so many stories she can tell me."

Smith felt a warm feeling pass over him. His eyes watered, but he smiled. "Pierson, there is nothing I would love more than to tell you all about your mother."

***

Smith had moved into the quaint little home that had belonged to Carissa's father. It was a small two-bedroom shack. He was given Pierson's room; Pierson, with his adoptive mother growing worse in health each day, wanted to stay by her side at all times. Smith, before leaving Kirkston, had swiped all of the savings he and Sea had put aside for the crew's dowries. They had had a significant amount of money set aside for each crewmember in the event they chose to leave – Smith had already given Knot his dowry. With the hurt he was feeling after Ace and Snake's betrayal, he had not thought twice about taking the money he and Sea had put aside that had been stored in the basement of Benny's Inn. Thankfully, despite the inn being burned down, he had managed to locate the crate the funds had been stored in.

With some of that money, he had hired a doctor to attend to Carissa regularly; the doctor had told him the same thing she had, though. She was dying, and all the doctor could do was make her more comfortable. A majority of the money he had, upon realizing money would not save the woman, he then began investing it in the local shipping businesses, and within a few months of living in Balla, he had managed to turn a major profit.

Approximately four months after arriving in Balla, Smith purchased several merchant ships and purchased land along a shipping dock. He treated his employees with such unheard-of generosity that soon new captains were arriving at his doors in the masses looking for additional work. Eight months into living in Balla, and Smith was a thriving businessman. He could hardly believe it himself. *Maxi Cook would be proud*, he thought one day while working at the small desk he had gotten for his room. He frowned when the thought crossed through his mind. He certainly had not thought about anyone back home in some time, and Maxi Cook of all people! He shuttered, thinking about how Maxi had lost his mother, his sister Susan, and his brother-in-law eight months prior. Smith had just left, offering no comfort to his friend.

Smith laid his paperwork down and shook his head. It took a lot of energy to keep thoughts of Kirkston out of his mind. All it took was one little thing that reminded him of home and then memories and guilt would come flooding in.

How dangerous would it be to try to send a letter to the rebellion? He shook away the thought. It would be dangerous. It would lead John to him if one of his guards at port caught the messenger. John was also someone he had not thought of in a while.

Eight months was a long time to be away from people he had spent every day of his life with. His friend's faces appeared in his mind's eye, Ace and Snake in particular. His throat ached. What had brought this on all of a sudden?

"Papa," a soft voice whispered behind him.

He turned around in his seat and saw Pierson standing in the doorway with tears in his eyes. Smith jumped out of his chair and scurried to the doorway; he knelt down and put his hands on the boy's shoulders.

"Pierson, son, what's wrong?" he asked.

"Mama won't wake up," he said.

Smith had known that this day was coming. He lifted the boy up; he was heavy, but he carried him nonetheless on their way back to Carissa's room. The woman was lying down on her back, her face frightfully pale. Smith sat Pierson up in a small chair in the corner, his heart breaking to see the boy wiping his eyes. He knelt down by Carissa and stroked her cheek. She was warm. He watched carefully and saw her chest rise and fall. He turned to look at Pierson. "Do you think you can run down the street to fetch Dr. Jargon?" Smith asked; Pierson nodded, and the boy ran out the door.

Dr. Jargon lived only a few houses down, and he was the doctor who had been treating Carissa. Smith touched the woman's cheek again, and she moved slightly. Her eyes opened. "Pierson?" she questioned, her voice hoarse.

"He's fetching Dr. Jargon," Smith said. "I would have gone and let him stay here instead, but I was worried he would be alone with you when…" He shook his head. She nodded her head slightly to let him know she understood his decision. Smith took her hand and squeezed. The woman died before Pierson arrived back with Dr. Jargon, and Pierson was irate.

Smith dragged a struggling Pierson out of the room. The boy clawed and bit him. Smith eventually was able to calm him down, but Pierson was more than simply devastated. Carissa was, to him, his entire world. She had been his adopted mother and the only link he had left to his true mother outside of Smith. Smith, he had only known for eight months, and suddenly the boy found himself completely in Smith's care.

For Carissa, Smith spared no expense in putting her to rest, to the point of drawing the attention of the local community to his wealth. Shortly after her death, after giving Pierson an appropriate amount of time to mourn,

Smith sold the small property and bought a home within a nicer district where he could get Pierson a proper education. The home was within walking distance of the local church as well as the beach and the market.

It took some time, but soon Smith and Pierson became incredibly close. Only a few months after Carissa's death, he and Pierson met a gypsy woman who would inadvertently complete their broken family.

Chapter 12

"I would appreciate it if you would consider my offer," Smith said with his charming smile plastered on his face. He sat in his home office behind his desk and across from a nervous older gentleman whom Smith was attempting to persuade into allowing him to buy out his shipping business. The man's small business was certainly no competition with Smith's now incredibly intricate operation, but the loading dock the man owned would certainly make for a great addition.

"I don't know, Mr. Barons," the man, Mark, said nervously, scratching the back of his head. The fisherman had been offered far more than what his dock would ever be worth; Smith would never try to cheat such a kind-hearted man, but selling a dock that had been in his family for three generations was a hefty decision.

"I understand your hesitancy," Smith said and leaned back in his seat. "The dock is sentimental. And, you can't really put a price on that – though I would like to try." Smith scribbled down some numbers on a piece of parchment and handed it to the man. "This is my last offer. Do think it over, won't you?"

The man looked at the numbers and turned pale. He tugged at his shirt collar. "I'll sell it," he said. "But, I have one condition."

"And, what is that?"

"I want to work for you on the docks. My sons too," he said.

"Now, Mark," Smith said with a grin. "Who in the world did you think I was intending to work the docks? I had hoped you would stay. That was never a question."

Mark smiled, and Smith knew he had him. Before they could make the deal official, the door to his study flung open. "Papa!" Pierson shouted. There was an alarmed tone in his voice.

Smith looked up. "What's wrong, Pierson?" Before Pierson had a chance to answer, a loud shattering noise could be heard outside his window. "What in the world?" Smith hissed and jumped out of his seat. He flung open his window and gazed out into his front lawn where he spotted a small crowd of people stomping around in his flowers. "Honestly!" Smith shouted and hurried out of the study, followed closely by Mark and Pierson.

Smith darted out onto his front porch where he came face to face with a number of angry looking men stomping around in his yard. One of the men had a gypsy woman by her hair; she had clearly fled from the small mob onto Smith's property. "Pardon us, Mr. Barons," one of the men said, realizing they had stampeded through his yard in an attempt to get the gypsy.

Smith knew the group of men – they were known for enforcing societal expectations on those uninterested in maintaining them. The new town Smith and Pierson had moved to was not crawling with gypsies in the way that much of Balla was, and men like this preferred to keep it that way. They had chased off the nomads a number of times under false accusations of various crimes.

"Let go of that poor woman's hair!" Smith snapped and gripped the man's arm who had a hold of her.

The older woman, when her hair was released, fell into a small bush that made up part of Smith's garden. The man Smith had grabbed yanked his arm back. "She's not a woman to be pitied," he sneered. "She was attempting to whore herself off to a married man."

"I'm no whore!" the woman shouted from her place on the ground. "That man assaulted *me*!"

"Go inside," Smith hissed down at her as he yanked her up by her arm, giving her a slight shove towards the house. The woman did not hesitate to obey Smith's command. She'd do just about anything to get away from the angry mob.

One of the men pointed a finger at Smith's chest as the woman scurried past Pierson and Mark. "You'd let that harlot in your home? You know you cannot trust her type. They're nothing but pick-pocketing thieves. They don't belong here."

"You say she was a prostitute? She says she was assaulted? Rather than act like a crowd of foolish vigilantes, let's go get that man she is accusing and hold a proper trial. And, while we are doing that, I'm sure the local courts will have a thing or two to say about you ruffians attacking a woman in the streets."

"Honestly, Mr. Barons, what good are you doing trying to defend the honor of some common street walker?"

"Get off my property," Smith snarled. He glanced around the small group, catching eyes with one face he knew particularly well. One of the men worked at one of Smith's docks. Smith did not need to say a word; he just stared his employee down with a hateful glare until he straightened up.

"We should go," the employee said. "I am quite sorry, Mr. Barons, for the trouble." He gripped another one of the men's arms, and the small crowd quickly dispersed.

As the men left, Mark tapped Smith on his shoulder. "Perhaps I will come back tomorrow, and we can sign the necessary paperwork. It seems you have another ordeal to deal with apart from myself. I know you were merely trying to help the woman… but do check her pockets before sending her on her way."

"Believe me, I will," Smith said before shaking hands with Mark on his way off. He hoped that Mark would not go home and reconsider.

Pierson was still standing on the porch when Smith headed up the small flight of stairs. "Why did you let a gypsy in our house?" Pierson asked.

"She needed help," Smith said and patted the boy on the head. He entered into the house, Pierson on his heels. Smith quickly found the woman standing in a corner in the family room. She wore a long, loosely fitted dress dyed colorfully like the Romanian gypsies that made up a large portion of the nomadic groups in Balla. Her hair was long and chestnut brown with streaks of silver to show off her age. It was tightly curled and pulled up with colorful scarves. There were bells tied to her waists, likely meant for dancing performances. She looked to be about Smith's mothers age. He did not smile at her, but instead he studied her face for a moment.

The woman spoke. "Thank you for helping me," she said in what he detected to be a fake Romanian accent.

Her features were undeniable. "You're a Kirkston woman," he said.

She blushed slightly. "I lived there when I was a girl," she said, dropping her fake accent.

"What is your name?" Smith asked.

"Agatha," she said.

"She's lying," Pierson said. "I can tell."

"Why won't you tell me your name?" Smith asked, and the woman crossed her arms and looked down. "Fine," he said. "*Agatha* it is then. What happened? Will you tell me that much?"

"Only that all men think that because I wear colorful clothes, I must be a working girl," she said. "A man grabbed me and told me to go home with him, and I scratched at his face and ran. His friends asked what happened to him, and he told them that I was harassing him and attempting to sell myself to him. He claimed that when he said 'no' I attacked him."

The woman's lip was busted; she had clearly suffered some abuse from the men. "Pierson, go get some water from the well."

"Okay," Pierson said and trotted off.

"Are you hungry?" Smith asked.

"Please, you don't have to –"

Smith reached a hand out to her like a proper gentleman. Clearly, she was not used to being treated like a lady because she stared at his outstretched hand for an uncomfortable amount of time before taking it. He led her into his dining room and had her take a seat. He had a bit of pork hanging in the kitchen, so he chopped it up for her along with some vegetables he had prepared earlier that day for his and Pierson's lunch. He brought her the plate, and when Pierson returned with water he poured her a glass.

"Go up to your room, Pierson," Smith said, but the boy did not listen.

"Are you really a gypsy?" Pierson asked as the woman nervously ate her food.

"I am," she said.

"So, do you know magic?" he asked. "Mama Carissa used to take me to see the gypsies performing magic in the streets. Her papa used to hate it; he said it was black magic."

The woman giggled slightly and smiled at him. "No, it's just tricks is all." And, with that, the woman performed a small feat for the child's enjoyment. She snapped her fingers, and a card seemed to appear out of nowhere in her hand. Smith watched with hidden enthusiasm as she fiddled with the card, making it seem as though it was floating and twirling on its own between her fingers and across her knuckles. It was a rather impressive looking trick, and she smacked her hands together, and when she opened her palms the card was gone, but a small silver coin appeared in its place. She handed the coin to Pierson, and he was starry eyed at the bit of magic he had witnessed.

"And, at that point your confidant would swipe two coins from the mother's purse, I'm sure," Smith said with a slight amusement in his voice.

"But, of course," she said. "If I had a companion, I'm sure they would."

She ate her dinner, and Smith sent Pierson to his room to give the woman some air and so that the boy would stop demanding to see more tricks. He sat across the table from her while she ate.

"You are welcome to stay here for the night," Smith said. "And, I will tell you now if you promise not to steal from me in the night that I will send you on your way in the morning with your pockets full."

"Do I look like a thief to you, then?" she asked.

"Perhaps a bit," he admitted. "I apologize if I am coming off a bit strong, but I do not know you. And, you will not even give me your real name."

"I told you my name was Annabelle," she said.

"No, you told me it was Agatha," he said.

"Did I?" she smirked.

"You did," he said, and she laughed slightly. Smith shook his head. "I'll have a guestroom made up for you." He rose from his seat and prepared a spare room for Agatha to sleep in.

Smith did not rest well that night with a stranger in his home, so he did not fall asleep until early the next morning. When he awoke, the sun was shining bright into his room, and he realized he had probably slept until noon. He jumped out of bed, worried about Pierson. To think that he had slept in so terribly late with a stranger in their house! He hurried down the stairwell, and he found Agatha with Pierson in the kitchen. Pierson was seated on a stool beside her, and she was stirring a pot that was hanging in the oven. Something smelled incredible.

He watched as Pierson fiddled with a playing card. He flipped the card, and then dropped it, sending it soaring across the room to Smith's feet. "Almost," he heard Agatha say with a slight laugh.

The two of them followed the card with their eyes, and they spotted Smith standing in the doorway. "You're still here, I see," he said.

"You did promise to send me away with full pockets, and I thought it would be rude to wake up my host," she said with a grin as Pierson hurried over to pick up the card.

"Papa, Mary is showing me how to make the card fly like what she did yesterday," Pierson said.

"*Mary?*" Smith questioned. "I thought it was *Agatha.*"

"Was it?" she questioned. "I can't remember what I told you."

Smith rolled his eyes at the woman. Pierson laughed, though. "I like Agatha better because there are far too many Mary's in our town. There are four on our street alone."

"Agatha it is then," she said.

"I'm sorry I slept in," Smith said as Pierson bent down to pick up the card. He patted the boy's head.

"It's all right. Agatha made me breakfast, and now she's making us lunch too," he said.

Smith nodded approvingly. His stomach growled at the pleasant aroma that was filling their kitchen. Agatha poured all three of them a bowl of stew, and they sat down together for lunch. Smith said grace, and when he was looking up after having his head bowed he noticed a crucifix hanging from the woman's neck.

"Are you Catholic, madam?" Smith asked curiously.

"I grew up Catholic before I married my Protestant husband," she said. "This was a gift from a mutual friend of ours. He was fine with me keeping it, and he would let me hang my father's crucifix above our door in our home."

"And where is your husband now?" Smith asked.

"Dead," she said.

"I'm sorry," Smith said.

"It's been many, many years. I am alone now, but I am well. Mostly well, I should say. I suppose days like yesterday are a true test to my faith."

"Not many Catholics in Kirkston," Smith said. "Well, there weren't until the Cruz's took over."

The next thing Smith knew, it was late in the evening, and Agatha was still with them. Truthfully, she had proven to be excellent company. She stayed another night, and the next morning Smith awoke to a hardy breakfast and a clean kitchen and living area. Another day went by, and he noticed his home becoming tidier. Nothing seemed to go missing as he would have expected from any other gypsy.

He learned that, prior to joining the gypsy community, Agatha had been a rather educated woman. Truthfully, it seemed rather fitting to have a woman like herself around. She could cook, she cleaned, and she could teach. By the end of the first week of her staying in his home, he made it official and offered to pay her to be a live-in nanny. He bought her some appropriate serving woman's clothes to get her out of her tattered gypsy attire, and she looked like a regular housemaid. She certainly looked more like a Kirkston woman. She wore her long, curly hair pulled back on most days so that it did not get in the way of her chores. He paid her well, and she became less frightfully skinny with a good diet. Once the color from good nutrition returned to her face, Smith could not help but to notice how lovely she looked, but the loveliest thing about her, to Smith, was her care and adoration for Pierson and the boy's mutual feelings towards the older woman.

Soon Smith was taking Agatha to church with them every Sunday as though they were one big family, and he walked her into church on his arm. He could not help but to feel as though he was turning into Maxi Cook with the way people scoffed at him for seemingly being with a woman of lower status. He laughed at the thought – if they had only known that their wealthy neighbor, Peter Barons, had once been a rogue pirate!

Several months after introducing Agatha into their home, Smith worked up the courage to give the woman a quick kiss after the three of them had taken a walk down the strip of beach near their home. The woman had blushed and laughed slightly, shaking her finger in his face and saying, "get a pretty girl your own age, boy," but Smith had kissed her again, and she had not protested at all.

Chapter 13

Several Months Later

Smith slowly turned to his side, his eyes still closed after a late night. He reached his arm out only to realize he was alone in bed and that Agatha was gone. He blinked his eyes open and frowned as the sun blinded him. He had slept in a bit, it seemed. Smith blushed when he realized he was nude, and he hurried to get himself dressed. The thought of Pierson catching him in his current state embarrassed him terribly. Once he was dressed, he headed down the stairwell. He had expected to get a whiff of a freshly cooked meal, but upon checking his pocket watch he realized he had probably missed breakfast, and it was far too early for lunch. He shook his head, disappointed that he was to be missing one of Agatha's wonderful breakfasts'.

He stood in the entryway of the large family room, and he saw Agatha and Pierson seated around the coffee table with one of the boys' study books open. She was a wonderful tutor, and ever since hiring her not quite a year before, Pierson had become the head of his class. Smith smiled as he watched Agatha and Pierson laugh and giggle at whatever it was they were studying; she always managed to make his study time fun for him, which was probably why he had learned so much since she had joined their household.

Smith felt his heart swell slightly to see the two of them seated on the floor deep in studies. Pierson loved Agatha very much, and Smith was starting to feel whole again. He had left everything behind in Kirkston, and while thoughts of his friends and of the rebellion returned on occasion, he felt with Agatha he could push the memories aside.

"All right, that's enough for today," Agatha said and patted the boys head. "Return your books to your bookshelf and hurry back down so that you can help me with lunch. I'm going to make a little cook out of you yet. A man shouldn't starve just because a woman's not in the house."

Pierson laughed and collected his studies. He grabbed all his books in his arms and almost ran by Smith in his hurry. He smiled. "Good morning, Papa!"

"Good morning, Pierson," Smith said with a smile as the boy ran past him and up the stairs.

Agatha stood up slowly from her seat in the floor, and she smiled and blushed slightly at Smith. "Good morning, Mr. Barons."

"Good morning, Ms. Agatha," he said and came over to kiss her. He felt the woman melt into his arms. "Let's get married," he said abruptly, and she pulled away slightly, keeping one of her hands on his chest.

"Pardon?"

"You heard me," he said. "I've known you for almost a year now, and you are good to me and to my son. You and I have been bedmates for a while now as well. I think I should make an honest woman out of you. I love you, and I –"

"No," she said, cutting him off and pulling away completely.

"No?" he questioned, a bit hurt by her swift refusal.

"Peter," she said softly. "I would love to marry such an undeniable gentleman as yourself, but you do not love me. You may say the words and do what you think you should towards a woman you love, but you certainly do not love me."

"Why do you say that?" he asked, starting to wonder if she way playing some sort of game with him or if she was truly serious.

She hesitated slightly before answering his question. "You talk in your sleep."

Smith blushed. "Oh?"

"And, you are always saying another woman's name – and you seem quite upset by it all," she says. "Sometimes I think I should wake you when you get that way. You cry her name out in your nightmares."

Smith felt his ears grow warm; he had no idea he had been talking in his sleep, and he was quite embarrassed by this revelation. "Courtney has been dead since I was practically a boy. I think it is time I moved on. I am sorry if I upset you by saying another woman's name in my sleep, but I do – I did… love Courtney dearly. She was my first love. I hope you can forgive me if I have made you jealous, but she is dead. Are you going to hold me accountable because someone I loved was taken from me and that it sometimes gives me nightmares?"

"Perhaps I would not hold you accountable if the name you were uttering was *Courtney*," she said with a confused look about her. "Peter, you cry out for a woman you call *Kathleen*."

Smith felt sick to his stomach. He said nothing more to Agatha, and instead he left the room and headed back up to his bedroom, locking himself away. He had never told Agatha about Kathleen – in fact, she knew very little about his life in Kirkston –so he knew she could not possibly be making up some story about him crying out Kathleen's name in his sleep. Was he having nightmares because he was constantly refusing to think of Kathleen and of the others? He was not sure. Now, hearing her name for the first time in nearly two years, he could not get her face out of his mind, and it made him sad. He felt almost sickly.

He curled up into bed and called for Pierson to send a letter to one of his employees that he was supposed to be having a meeting with that day. "Tell him I'm not well," Smith grumbled, and Pierson trotted off – happy that his father was entrusting him with such an important task and eager to put his new-found writing ability to the test. Smith curled up into bed and remained there, and Agatha slept in the guest room that night.

***

When Smith awoke the next morning, he felt a little better. Plus, the house smelled wonderful with whatever it was Agatha was making for breakfast. He headed downstairs; it was Sunday, so they would be heading to church soon. Pierson had already eaten, so Agatha shooed him upstairs to go get dressed. Smith sat across the table from Agatha and scarfed down his food, starving after not having eaten a thing the day before.

Nervously, she said to him, "I'm sorry if I upset you yesterday."

Smith frowned and lowered his utensils. "I overreacted, and I perhaps pushed you into a direction you were not ready to go."

"I was flattered by your proposal, Peter, but you do not need to marry an old woman like me. Especially not if your heart is still longing for someone else." She spoke with her head down, not wanting to make eye contact.

"I understand," he hesitated. "And, thank you. I feel that you are merely looking out for my well-being, are you not?"

"That was my intention."

"Well, thank you. You're right. Kathleen was someone quite special to me, but there is no chance of that ever becoming anything. I would like to move past it if I can," he said and then stood, finished with his breakfast.

"I think you and I need to have an honest conversation about our pasts. To ask you to marry me, not even sure if you're real name is Agatha is quite foolish. I have not been very honest with you either, my dear. We have known one another for a long time now, but we do not truly know each other at all. Perhaps today after church we should spend some time speaking on the matter?"

She nodded. "Very well."

They both cleaned up the mess left behind from breakfast and hurried to get ready for church. Soon the family was ready to head out. Smith started out the door first and down the small stairs of the front porch. Pierson was still inside when Agatha exited the building.

"Pierson!" Smith called out for his son to hurry up, and the boy came bolting out of the home.

"Papa, catch me!" he heard Pierson shout as the boy jumped from the top step.

Smith laughed and grabbed the boy under the arms, spinning him around before putting him down on the ground. Smith removed his hat and put it on the boy's head, laughing slightly as he did so. He held his hand out to help Agatha down the steps; she was wearing her large, Sunday dress. He put his arm around her waist.

"Are you ready to go?" she asked, smiling at him. She was glad to see that he was still affectionate after her refusal.

"Of course. You look lovely as ever," he said to her and kissed her lips.

As they approached the white gate that surrounded his front yard, he reached out to open it. Glancing up, he spotted a young man that he could swear looked exactly like a young Prince Richard. *Honestly,* he thought, *it's like I cannot shake them from my mind.* The young man had looked frightfully familiar, and he could not help but to look back at him again. The boy's eyes were fixed in Smith's direction, and a horrible, sinking feeling replaced the rather chipper mood he'd developed after Pierson's playful antics.

"Kathleen?" he said as he beckoned, and the young man, or perhaps woman… spun around and took off towards the beach. "Kathleen!" Smith shouted and darted out of the yard and down the road. The youth kept a quick pace.

"Peter, what on Earth are you doing?" He could vaguely hear Agatha calling after him as she and Pierson were left behind in the yard.

The familiar figure had made its way down to the beach, and Smith practically sprinted to catch up. "Stop!" Smith called out desperately. The figure stopped suddenly and stood a few yards away from where the low tide was sweeping up onto the sand.

"Turn around," Smith said in a fierce, commanding tone. The figure turned, and Smith knew it was her, despite her unusual choice in attire. His heart swelled, and he bit the side of his cheeks to prevent himself from crying at the sight of her. She looked so sad, but she remained fairly stoic in her demeanor as she crossed her arms and pouted slightly.

"I have missed you," he said to her, and she rolled her eyes.

"Have you?" she questioned. "You have certainly made no effort to alleviate that pain, now have you? Two years, you coward!"

"You came here for me?" he questioned softly, hoping to move the conversation away from his abrupt departure.

She laughed at him. "Come for you? You think I chopped off my hair, dressed as a man, and snuck out of

Kirkston – risking my life – for *you*? You're a fool if you think that. I went to England to negotiate a deal on behalf of my father – for my country! For our country. You do remember the place you abandoned when it needed you most. When *I* needed you most! And, you think I came here for *you*? I am only in Balla in hopes of finding a ship to take me home!"

Smith felt slightly hurt by her claim, but at the same time he felt a bit of pride towards her.

"You did all that on your own?"

"Yes," she said.

Seeing her after a two-year absence was almost too much for him. He had not realized how relieved he would feel just by seeing her face. A pang of guilt twisted his stomach into knots. She was right. He had abandoned them all. He stepped forward.

"Kathleen, I'm so sorry," he said as he reached his arms around her waist, hoping to pull her into a tight embrace. He thought that perhaps he would kiss her; he had never kissed her lips before. He leaned in, but instead of his lips being met with a kiss, his face exploded with pain. She had elbowed him in his nose and knocked him clear on his back in a swift, unexpected motion. He landed on his back in the sand and clutched his now bloodied nose. Truthfully, he was more impressed than upset. *Where did she learn that*, he wondered as he sat up, his trousers now soaked from the wet sand.

"You think I would let you kiss me?" she shrieked. "You must be out of your mind! Honestly, Smith, if I had not loved you once, I would blow your brains out into the sand!" she said this as she pulled a pistol from her hip and pointed it directly at him.

"Kathleen!" Smith cried and held up one of his hands in defense while gripping his nose with the other.

"Papa!" Smith heard Pierson cry out, and he glanced over to see Agatha grabbing onto Pierson's arm when she saw that Smith was being held at gunpoint. They had followed him.

Kathleen glanced over at them, and it seemed that she was getting her first good look at them both. The angry expression on her face faded as she gazed upon Pierson. "He looks different now that he's older," she said softly and then turned her gaze back towards Smith. Her voice shook slightly, and she spoke in the saddest tone Smith had ever heard. "He's not yours, Peter. And, you know it, don't you? He looks just like –"

Smith looked down and felt a few tears escape him. "Please, don't say anything. Not in front of him."

Kathleen returned her pistol to her side and reached a hand out to help him stand. As he stood upright, he felt Kathleen's arms wrap around his waist, and she laid her head on his chest for a moment, causing her hat to fall back into the sand. He rested his head on top of hers for a moment, and he felt a sense of calm wash over him that he had not felt in a long time. Slowly, Agatha and Pierson made their way over now that they could see Kathleen had put away her pistol.

"What was that about?" Agatha shrieked as Pierson wrapped his arms around Smith. Kathleen took a step back.

Smith blushed slightly, and he made an uncomfortable introduction. "Agatha, this is Kathleen."

"What an odd name for a boy," she said and then blushed. "Your lover is a boy?"

"Oh for crying out loud, woman!" Smith shook his head. "She's a lady! She's just in men's clothes!"

"Lover?" Kathleen questioned, and Smith's cheeks turned red.

Agatha laughed. "I know she is a lady. I am only jesting with you, Peter." Agatha smiled at Kathleen. "Perhaps we should venture back to the house? I think we may be missing church this morning."

"Yes, I think so," Smith said and led the group back to his home.

Chapter 14

Kathleen eyed the woman, Agatha, with a hint of jealousy as the four of them sat in the family room. Pierson had become a rather precious lad under Smith's care. Despite her anger towards Smith for leaving, she was quite saddened for him and for the boy for their loss of Carissa.

"How is it you came to be here in Balla, Ms. Kathleen?" Agatha asked as she sat a tray on the coffee table; she had taken it upon herself to make a fresh pot of tea and was just arriving back with it.

"Yes," she heard Smith say, and she glanced his way to see him holding a rag to his bloodied nose. "I'd like to hear all about it."

"There is not all that much to tell," Kathleen said. "The rebellion has been getting desperate. It has been shrinking quite steadily, and our rations have been getting low. England knows of our turmoil, but they have yet to intervene despite a number of letters we've managed to sneak out. Our desperation pushed me into action. My parents and my brothers helped me to disguise myself so that I could escape the ports and head to England. His

Majesty was in Germany, of course, so I spoke with a woman of… influence… who could vouch for us with Parliament. They are still negotiating amongst themselves what sort of help they are to send us, but they tell me to expect aid within the month. There was no ship heading to Kirkston, so I took a ship here to Balla knowing there would be one bound for my homeland long before a ship from England could take me home."

"And, what position in your homeland do you hold, Miss, that you would be trusted with such a daunting task?" Agatha questioned.

Kathleen huffed slightly. "I am the king's daughter, of course."

The woman became quite pale. "Oh!" she shrieked. "Your Majesty, I had no idea! Peter, why didn't you tell me this? I've made quite a fool of myself!"

"It's quite all right," Kathleen said.

Agatha seemed to be studying her face. The older woman smiled. "Oh, how much you look like your parents!"

"You know them?" she asked.

Agatha's response was quick. "Yes, but it was long ago. I was once a maid at Caldara Castle."

"I did not know that," Smith said, and Agatha shrugged. Smith waved a hand towards Pierson. "Son, why don't you go up to your room and play?"

"Okay, Papa," Pierson said and obediently scurried out of the room.

Once she was certain that the boy was out of ear-shot, Kathleen's eyes darted towards Smith. "How long ago did you figure it out, Smith? You and I both know he's not you son!"

Smith removed the rag from his face and slammed the bloodied thing down on the coffee table. "A while," he hissed slightly. "But, what would you have me do, Kathleen?"

"You know good and well what you should do! Take him to his father! You are just awful for keeping him here, Smith." Kathleen gritted her teeth as she spoke.

Smith took a deep breath. She watched as he sunk back into his seat. "I wanted him to be mine," he said, and his voice was full of sorrow.

"I know," she said. "And, it does not bring me any pleasure to say that he's not, but you know it by that face of his. And, keeping him here is just cruel. You're playing house is all you're doing."

"I know."

"It's time to stop playing. I can tell you now that the rebellion fell apart after you left. Our numbers dwindled. John is hitting us with everything he's got. I did not leave Kirkston to come looking for you, Smith, but I am glad to have found you. Come home," she said the command with such tenacity that it clearly struck a nerve with Smith.

He sat upright and stared at her. "Is that an order coming from my dear princess?"

She took a breath to calm her tone. "No. A request from an old friend. One I hope you will take seriously."

There was a long silence. Agatha stirred uncomfortably in her seat. "Peter, are you telling me you took another man's boy away from him?"

"It's not quite that simple," Kathleen said in his defense.

"You were part of the rebellion before you came here?" Agatha questioned, and again Kathleen spoke before Smith could.

"How long have you two lived together, and dare I say bedded together, that you know so little about one another?" Kathleen questioned.

Agatha's face turned red, and she excused herself. Smith glared at Kathleen. "There's no sense in speaking harshly to her. She's done nothing wrong? Be angry at me. I certainly deserve it. I know that I should never have left. I know that. I've missed you, Kathleen."

Kathleen stood from her seat. "Then come home," she said and began walking out of the room.

"Where are you going?" Smith asked from his seat.

"To apologize to your little housewife," she said and departed from the room.

She found Agatha hiding out in the kitchen. Kathleen removed the gentleman's hat that she had been wearing and sat it down on the counter. "Ms. Agatha, I am sorry for being so hostile towards you. I am upset with Smith. Not you."

"You are quite right about me, though. When Peter... Smith... found me, he was saving me from a mob, I was a gypsy accused falsely of a crime. When Smith was kind to me, I did all I could to stay here and assure myself the comfort of living with a man of his status. I tried to make him love me, and I dare say he even thought for a while that he did, but I knew that it was a lie he was telling himself. And, what a fool I was to think he ever could!

I could not even love him. He is a mere child compared to me! If I had known my competition for his heart was someone as lovely as the Princess Kathleen, I would have considered myself a fool."

"He spoke about me, then?" Kathleen asked.

"In his sleep, he would call out for you," she said.

Kathleen blushed. "I do not know what to do now," she admitted. "A ship will be leaving for Kirkston in a few days. I believe I should be on that ship."

"I believe Smith should be too," Agatha whispered.

"I will be." Smith's voice jolted Kathleen. She spun around to see a very broken looking man standing in the doorway. He looked sad, and he did not dare meet either woman's gaze. "I cannot keep running, and Pierson deserves to know the truth. Agatha, would you be so kind as to help Pierson pack some luggage?"

"Of course," she said.

"Your face is still on many wanted posters around the ports," Kathleen said. "If you are to come back, they will kill you on the spot. And John knows how you escaped. They will search caskets."

"How did *you* know I escaped in a casket?" Smith asked.

"Rumors spread quickly," she said. "I see by your response the story is true. I thought it mad, but it was quite an ingenious idea. They stabbed a man last month who was alive trying to leave the country in a casket, so that won't do. They stab corpses in the heart now, and they check luggage for stowaways coming in and coming out."

"Then how in the world am I supposed to go back?" Smith questioned.

They all pondered this in silence for a moment. Agatha suddenly smiled. Her cheeks turned red as she examined Kathleen. "Oh dear," she said with a slight giggle. "I believe I have an idea."

***

"How do you women even breathe?" Smith snarled as Agatha strung up the last loop of the corset.

Pierson let lose a loud fit of laughter and rolled about the floor as though he would collapse from the circus-like spectacle taking place in his father's bedroom.

"Papa, you look like Ms. Agatha!"

Smith stared at himself in the tall mirror and shook his head. "No one is going to believe for a second that I am a woman!" The long dress and the corset did nothing to hide his broad shoulders. True, his youthful face coupled with the dress made the idea plausible, but certain attributes still needed to be hidden.

"I am nowhere near finished with you yet," Agatha said, and Kathleen fought off a snicker. Agatha added a lady's overcoat that did fairly well to hide his shoulders, and she buttoned him up as well. The overcoat along with the corset did a good job at portraying his non-existent curves.

"I really cannot breathe," he wheezed.

"I think if I could run around and play as a young girl in one of those, you will be fine for a few days resting on a ship," Kathleen said.

"It's crushing my ribs," he complained.

"Papa, this is silly!" Pierson said from the floor. He sat on his rear with his feet out in front of him, staring up at Smith with a large, ridiculous grin.

"Yes, it is very silly," Smith said. "And, it's not going to work."

"I'm still not done with you. I have my summer wig," Agatha said and began pinning a wig on top of his head. The hair looked a bit fake, so she added a lady's bonnet to hide some of the fake hair. Then she got to work adorning his face with various makeups, and soon she spun him around to face the mirror once more.

Smith's cheeks turned red when he saw himself. He looked like a rather large lady. "Oh my," he said in awe of his appearance. "This... this is just a terrible idea..."

"It's bloody brilliant," Agatha said. She pranced over to Kathleen and hooked her arm into hers. "Kathleen will play the part of the gentleman, and I will be his dear mother. Pierson, you are to be my son and Mr. Kathleen's child brother. And, Peter, you will be my charming son's fiancée! We are all headed to Kirkston for the wedding after coming to pick up Ms. Peter in Balla to escort her back to her future husband's home."

Smith shook his head and looked down at his hands. "My hands. They're a bit –"

"You have feminine hands," Kathleen said. "No one is going to believe a tad bit of hair on your thumbs means that you're a man."

Truthfully, Smith was looking for any excuse not to go through with this plan. Before he could respond to Kathleen, Agatha tossed a pair of lacey gloves his way. "I bet your wee little hands will fit in my gloves."

"I do not have little hands," he said in a hostile voice. He shoved his hands into the gloves, and they fit perfectly.

"He's awfully flat-chested. Should we stuff his bosom?" Kathleen suggested.

"No!" Smith retorted, and Pierson began laughing all over again.

"I think he's starting to look too lovely," Agatha teased. "Mustn't draw too much attention to ourselves. A full bosom will attract too much attention from the sailors."

"I'm not doing this," he said.

"Honestly, Smith, I've dressed as a man for many weeks now. I think you can stand to be a woman for a few days."

"It's not the same," Smith argued. "At least trousers are comfortable!"

"And, how is it fair that a lady must be uncomfortable every day of her life, yet you cannot go for a few days? I'm sorry, but we must hurry along. The ship will be leaving port soon." Kathleen hooked her arm with

Smith's and helped him down the stairs of the home to keep him from tripping. He grumbled the entire time all while Pierson and Agatha tried to keep straight faces.

Pierson dragged their luggage out the door, locking up the home behind them. "Papa, what are you going to do about your shipping business?"

"I sent a letter to one of my employees who will handle things in our absence," Smith said.

"How long will we be gone? Do they know?" Pierson asked.

"I'm not sure, Pierson. And, you mustn't call me *Papa* right now," Smith said.

They took a carriage to the ports, and Kathleen left them for a moment to make arrangements and procure them a spot on a ship. She returned moments later, Smith still seated in the carriage. "Ship will be leaving soon," Kathleen said. "So, we will need to get going."

Smith was rather hesitant. "Will this really work? Surely someone is going to notice!"

"Speak very little like a shy lady, and maybe it will work," Kathleen said. "And, if you have to speak, you had best sound like a woman."

"I'll do my best," Smith said and rolled his eyes at her.

They boarded and found themselves a seat on the main deck amongst the crowd of people who were also hitching a ride on the merchant ship. Smith struggled to sit in the large dress, and he was quite certain he was going to be caught. How was he to explain to these shipmen why he was in a dress if they found him out?

Some of the sailors were looking their way; he could feel their stares. One of the men broke away from the crowd once the ship was moving steadily south towards Kirkston. They had many days left aboard the ship before they would arrive. Were they caught already?

The man smiled at Smith. "Pardon me, Miss, but would the fine lady be interested in a tour of our ship?"

Smith frowned. Kathleen quickly intervened. "I think my fiancée would much rather be here with me."

"Fiancée?" the man questioned and looked at Kathleen. "You look like a mere boy to me. How old are you, lad, to be taking on such a fine woman so soon?"

Kathleen said truthfully, "I am twenty-five."

"Twenty-five?" the man laughed. "You look half that age."

"I have always had a young face," Kathleen said.

The man looked at Smith. "Well, if you change your mind, Miss, I'll be here. Just let me know when you get tired of that boy."

"I think I'll be quite content. Trust me, I am certain my fiancé is much more of a man than you," Smith said, and the man frowned, huffed, and wandered off.

Kathleen giggled slightly. "Me thinks the gentleman fancies my bride-to-be."

"Careful," Smith said. "This lady does not find that very funny at all. Let's just head down to the bunks. The less people I have to interact with the better."

Chapter 15

Smith awoke in the middle of the night; someone had tapped his shoulder. He sat upright in the bunk, and before he could gather his bearings someone threw a hand over his mouth and had gripped one of his arms. Before he knew what was happening, he was standing in the galley. A lantern was lit, so it only took Smith a moment to recognize his assailant as the sailor who had been harassing him earlier that day.

"Let go of my arm!" Smith snapped and yanked his wrist out of the man's hand. Smith was ready to punch the man in the face, but someone else grabbed him from behind.

There were two men behind him as well. "Hello, darling," one of the men said. "I heard you were being rude to my friend here."

"Well, my apologies," Smith said, not quite ready to throw fists and alert them to his secret. The man who had swiped him was strong; he had managed to get him out of the bunks quickly and without anyone noticing. Smith had been half asleep, but he was not sure how much of a difference that made.

"Now," Smith said. "If you gentlemen will excuse me, I am going to head back to my bunk."

The sailor reached out and grabbed his arm, pulling Smith towards him. "Oh, you're not going anywhere –"

"You're out of your damn mind," Smith snarled and threw an elbow into the man's face, breaking his nose.

"You stupid woman!" one of the other men shouted, and Smith felt each of the sailor's companions grab hold of one of his arms.

"That boy needs to make sure he gets this one trained, or she will be a handful," the man gripping Smith's left arm said.

The sailor wiped his bloody nose and gritted his teeth in Smith's direction. "Look at that smirk on her face," the sailor said. He had a clenched fist at his side. "That fiancé of yours is just a weak little boy. I'll show you what a real man is like!"

Smith let out a slight laugh at the thought of this brute ripping away the corset and being met with quite a surprise. "Head back to your bunks, let go of my arms, or I swear I'll –"

"What are you going to do, lass?" the sailor snorted, and his snort was followed by a loud clanging sound right before he collapsed.

Smith smiled to see Kathleen standing over the man while holding a large pan she had picked up from a cabinet in the galley. She pointed the pan in their direction. "Let her go."

The sailor stood up, incredibly wobbly after being beamed in the head. The other two men's grasps loosened slightly, so Smith yanked both arms away and threw both elbows back and into the men's faces. The sailor Kathleen had banged in the head snarled and reached for Smith.

"You're a troublesome little tramp!" he roared, grabbing hold of Smith's wig. Smith cringed, reaching up and gripping the man's hand to prevent the hairpiece from being completely yanked off the top of his head. Kathleen flung the pan into the sailor's head again, and he released Smith and fell to the ground, knocked out cold.

"You little wretch!" one of the other men shouted and ran at Kathleen.

Smith's instinct was to defend her, but it was immediately evident to him that a lot had changed in the past two years. She dodged two quick swings before throwing three punches at the man's face. She then slammed a palm to his throat, right at his Adam's apple, causing him to gag and topple over. The third man managed to grab a hold of Kathleen by her arms and ram her back into the wall of the ship. Smith was certainly not going to stand for that. He came up behind the man, wrapping his arms around the man's throat.

"You're deceitfully strong!" the man shrieked as Smith pulled him back, holding the man in a headlock. Kathleen took the opportunity to punch the man one good time between the eyes, and he fell limp in Smith's arms.

Smith released him, and the man fell to the ground like the other two had done moments ago. Smith stared at

Kathleen. "Where did you learn to fight like that?" he asked.

"Are you all right?" she asked, stepping forward.

He couldn't help but to laugh at the seriousness in Kathleen's question. "Well, sir, I must thank you for coming to this lady's defense," he said and curtsied.

Kathleen's face lost all seriousness, and she laughed to the point that she let out a slight snort. The two of them made their way above deck; there were only a few crewmen about. "I had best speak to the captain," Kathleen said. "Otherwise, those men might try to get after us again. They'll probably be a bit vengeful. That one shipman really seems to fancy you."

"I know, please, don't remind me. And, I swear, Kathleen, you had best never mention that to anyone."

Kathleen reached out and pinched both of his cheeks, shaking his face slightly, "Oh, it is because of that cute face of yours. He could not help himself!"

Smith slapped her hands away. "That's not at all funny. Really, I feel quite ridiculous. I cannot imagine what my crew would think of me right now... my crew... as if I have any right to call them that."

Smith leaned up against the side of the ship, propping his elbows on the side and looking out into the night. Kathleen sighed and did the same, propping her elbows up and nestling in beside him.

"The *Black Dragon* has been a faithful ship during this war. Your friends still man it. You hurt them, Peter. You hurt them badly when you left, oh, but if they could see what all you are doing to return to them!"

"I'm certainly glad they can't see!" Smith said with a slight grin on his face. "I suppose I deserve this humiliation, don't I?"

"Maybe a little," she said and nudged him.

"What will they say when we get there? They will hate me. *I* hate me."

"They have missed you," Kathleen said. "They were angry at first. They were hurt. They are still hurt, but they are your family."

"Are they... it's been two years.? Is everyone still alive?" he asked, and his voice shook slightly. "Two years... a lot can happen in two years, especially in the middle of a war."

Kathleen turned to face him, and he too stood upright, his arms dangling at his side. He felt as though he would cry at the thought. She reached out and touched his shoulder. "The Black Dragons are alive. There have been many close calls, but they watch out for one another in battle like you would not believe."

"And, my uncle and cousin?"

"Alive."

"The Cooks?"

"Also still breathing," she said. "Though many of our friends were ill when I left. Rations have been cut many times. Richard almost...let me just say it has gotten bad around camp. If something does not change soon, we will all perish off in the woods somewhere. John is winning. Desperation brought me to England."

"I am glad you went," Smith said. "Because had you not, and had you not stopped off in Balla, I might still be there. I should have never left. I shouldn't have taken the boy away either. So much happened in such a short period... watching Cannonball and Yang die; my dear mother; losing Nicole, Hethuska, Mrs. Cook, Susan, Tim, and Neela; and then finding out about Pierson... I panicked. It was too much, and I just panicked. Learning about my friend's betrayal just pushed me over the edge."

"It was a lot to take in," Kathleen said. "I will not say you did the right thing, but I will concede and say that I understand. Oh, but do not get me wrong, Smith! I am still a bit furious with you, but I understand. Your friends will too. They may need time, though. It is a deep wound you inflicted on them. But, hear this: I forgive you. I may still be angry, but I forgive you."

"You forgive me for leaving," he said. "But, can you ever forgive me for never telling you how much I love you?"

Kathleen's cheeks appeared red, and she seemed to lose the bout of confidence she had worn since they had left the beach at Balla.

"I love you too, you ninny," she said. Smith came towards her, though he was slightly hesitant after she had nearly beat him on the beach the last time he had dared to move towards her in such a way. She leaned forward too, and their lips met for a moment. Smith felt his chest become warm, his cheeks flush, and his fingers went cold. When he parted and he got a good look at her, he laughed slightly, causing her to tug back in embarrassment. She covered her mouth and looked him in the eye.

"What on Earth are you laughing at, you cad?"

"I have never kissed your lips before," he said. "And, I will admit I have thought about it many, many times. I have imagined it and even dreamed it. Never once did I ever imagine we would be playing the part of crossdressers the first time I kissed you!"

"Oh no!" Kathleen covered her face in humiliation. After a moment, she lowered her hands and lunged forward, wrapping him in a tight hug in the midst of a bit of laughter. "I will never be able to tell anyone of the first time I kissed you without sounding as though we are lunes!"

"How terrible," Smith said, laughing. "It will be our secret, then."

The sun was coming up, so the two of them lowered their voices a bit, not wanting those now on the slightly crowded deck to over hear their conversing. Kathleen was quick to speak to the captain about how inappropriate some of his men had been towards her *fiancée*, and the men were locked away in a holding cell.

As she was returning to Smith who was standing port side, Smith spotted Agatha and Pierson arriving above deck. The three of them met by Smith, all knowing he had a hard time standing in the large dress let alone walking about a moving ship. Pierson gazed out into the water with a big smile on his face.

"Am I going to meet my father since we are going back to Kirkston?" he asked, and Smith froze.

He looked down at Pierson with a saddened expression. After a moment, he knelt down beside the boy. "Pierson, why did you ask me that?"

Pierson seemed embarrassed, as though he wanted to take back the question. After a moment of hesitancy, he spoke. "I'm sorry, Papa… Mr. Smith… but I thought we were going back to Kirkston so that I could meet my real father?"

Smith glanced up at Agatha with a hateful glare. "I did not tell him!" Agatha said quickly. Kathleen shook her head to let him know that she had not either.

"How did you know?" Smith asked.

"I saw the man two years ago at your camp, and now I see him when I look in the mirror. I remember his face, and it is my face," Pierson said. "I'm not an idiot, Papa."

"How long have you known I was not your father? And, why didn't you say anything to me?" Smith asked him.

Pierson looked down at his feet. "I've known since Mama Carissa died. I remember looking in a mirror at her funeral and thinking… *that's not right.*"

"That was a year ago!" Smith shrieked. "Pierson, my boy, why didn't you —"

"Because I wanted it to be you," Pierson said. "Because that's what Mama Courtney wanted. She wanted it to be you." Pierson suddenly had tears in his eyes. "She wanted you to be my father. I never knew her, but she was my mother. I knew you. I knew you from all of those letters she wrote for me. She wanted it to be you so bad! So, I wanted it to be you too. I didn't say anything because I thought we could just keep pretending. But, now we are going back to Kirkston... I thought you were taking me to meet my father. You're not, though? That's not why we're going back? Can we just keep pretending, then?"

Smith pulled the boy into a tight embrace. "We can't, Pierson. We shouldn't. It's not fair to you. It's not fair to your father."

"But, what about you?"

Smith kissed Pierson's forehead. "You do not need to worry about me. And, you had best believe that I will still be there for you, Pierson."

"Yes," Kathleen said and put a hand on Pierson's shoulder. "You're a lucky little boy. It will be like you have two fathers, I'm certain."

Pierson then grinned and pointed a finger at Smith. "Me thinks he looks more like a mother to me."

Smith frowned and popped Pierson's hand out of his face. "Very funny, boy."

Pierson giggled as did Kathleen and Agatha. "I thought so," Pierson said, and Smith managed to chuckle slightly at his own expense.

***

Smith could not help but to notice Agatha's uneasiness as they spotted Kirkston's eastern docks in the distance. The four of them stood by one another, watching the ports grow closer and closer. "Agatha, why are you nervous?" Kathleen questioned. "Smith and I are the ones who should be nervous. If we're caught, we're the ones John will have hanged."

Agatha looked at Kathleen. "I am nervous about going to the rebellion camp, Your Majesty."

"Why?"

Agatha wrung her wrists slightly. "When I lived in Kirkston, I worked at Caldara Castle. I knew His Majesty King Harold, and the man did not care for me."

"What reason would my father have not to like you?" Kathleen asked.

Agatha hesitated to respond. Finally, she said, "I was just a terrible maid."

Smith could sense that something else was amiss, but he chose not to comment. The ship made port, and he could feel his heart racing. Would one of the soldiers realize he was a man? Smith could not imagine being brought to John while in a dress. He would almost prefer the men shoot him there on the docks if he was caught. They got in line to un-board, and Smith could see that the soldiers were quite rigorous in opening up every chest to ensure there were no letters from foreign aids, weapons, or stowaways hiding anywhere. Every person was inspected by soldiers. Their faces were compared to wanted posters. Smith could feel his heart starting to race as they drew closer and closer to the front of the line.

Part III
The Final Sail

Chapter 16

Smith exhaled deeply; a sense of relief washed over him as he took a good look at himself in the mirror above the dresser within his parent's bedroom. He was out of women's garbs at last, and that was an adventure he hoped to never partake in again. The Spaniards at the port had not suspected him for even a moment, and they had traveled south to his childhood home to find rest until they could locate the rebellion camp. Kathleen had said that they had resorted to moving about quite often, so it was likely that the camp had already moved since her departure, though she doubted that it would be too far from where they had been.

He could hardly break his stare; there had not been any Black Dragon uniforms lying about, so he had put on some of his father's clothes that had been hanging in the wardrobe since the man had been killed when Smith was but a boy. The casual tan button up, brown vest, and the matching overcoat was something quite typical of what his father would wear. Although he had only been twelve when his father had passed, Smith remembered the man's face quite well, and it was as though that same man was staring straight back at him. Frankly, if Smith had black hair and blue eyes like his father, he was certain no one would have been able to have told a difference. Smith had gotten his brown hair and emerald green eyes from his uncles on his mother's side, but apart from that, he was most certainly his father's son.

What would you think of me, Father? Smith wondered, and he could not help but to feel that the man would be disappointed with him for choosing to abandon his friends. And, what would his mother have thought?

They were both gone now. He was the last Barons.

He thought of his sisters too; they he had not thought of in a long time. Elizabeth had always been so kind to him as a boy. She had been like a second mother. She would always sing to him, and every year near his birthday she would always work extra hard to buy him something special. His last birthday present from her and his younger sister had been his journal. He had filled up half the journal within a year of receiving it, but he had panicked slightly when he came to the center where the pages were tied in. He had stopped writing in it almost completely – saving it to only write down pivotal events in his life. He had other journals, but the one his sisters had given him was sentimental, and it being the last gift from his sisters he had wanted it to last. His sister Anna had been just a wee little thing when she had died, and the thought made him cringe. She had always followed Elizabeth around – that or their mother. He could picture the little darling running about that house right on Elizabeth's heels.

Smith at last broke his stare. It had been almost too canny. Smith left his parents' bedroom, and right there across the hall he could see Kathleen asleep on his sister's old bed, her feet hanging off at the bottom. Pierson was in Smith's old bed; he too was asleep. It had been a long and trying day. Agatha was nowhere to be seen.

He looked for her in the house, but eventually he found her outside by the old oak tree where his family and Sea were all buried. He cringed slightly as he walked by Cannonball and Yang's graves and the crosses that had been put up for Hethuska and Nicole. "I see you have casted aside your dress," Agatha said as he approached.

"Yes, and I would appreciate *that* not ever coming up once we reach the rebellion," Smith said.

"Too bad," she said. "You made such a pretty lady."

Smith rolled his eyes. He looked at her for a moment, and he could see that she was a bit on edge. "Why did you never tell me you knew the Caldaras?" he asked.

"It was a lifetime ago, and as I told you, they do not care for me," she said. "But, it is time I returned to my home country, and if I can be of use to bringing down a man like John Stevenson, then why not return and go to the rebellion? I am worried, though, that the king and queen will be displeased with my presence."

Smith felt that she was being rather deceitful with him. "There is something more than you just being a terrible maid, I am certain. And, I do not care for this secrecy. If you are so worried, why go with us to the rebellion camp at all?"

"I am not *too* worried. But, if they do become a bother towards me, you will vouch for me, yes?" she asked.

"Of course," Smith said. "You have been very good to me, Agatha."

"And you to me," she said.

Smith looked down at his mother's grave, and he felt a slight sting in his gut. She had been one of the main reasons he had run. After losing his sisters and father and believing that he had lost her for so long only to have her return to him, well, watching her die had been too much. And, she was not just his mother. She was more than just a mother to him. She was a friend – she was brave, strong, and intelligent. Mrs. Barons had taken in each of his friends and treated them as though they were her own children. She had turned a cold man like Jackson White into an outright gentleman. She had held her own in a fight, had attended a university, and she had been on her way to becoming Kirkston's first female physician. To Smith, she was more than a mother – she was his hero, and he had never told her that.

"Kathleen tells me you and your mother were very close," Agatha said.

"For a long time, I believed her to be the only family I had left. Only a few years ago I met my cousins Phillip and Thaddeus and my Uncle Andrew. Phillip was killed within hours of me meeting him, but I still have Andrew and Thaddeus. I abandoned them just like I did my crew. I think my mother would be quite ashamed of me. She loved them all so much, and her son turned his back on people she cared so much for. Yes, I know she would be ashamed. I will try to make amends for that now, but I do not know what my crew will have to say to me."

"If you all were as close as you say you were, then they will forgive you."

Smith smiled. "Thank you," he said. "Now, let's get some rest. Tomorrow is going to be a very busy day."

Chapter 17

Smith felt his hands shaking as they came upon the camp. Surely, Snake and Ace would want to kill him, and the rest of his friends would likely be angry as well? What of Jackson White – Smith had said such cruel things to the man? And, his uncle and cousin? What of the Cooks? He could not even begin to fathom what sort of emotions would be tossed about.

He felt Kathleen hook her arm in his. He smiled, glad to see her in a dress again. Her short, choppy hair reminded him a bit of Sea. Something like that would have once made him very sad, but, instead, it made him laugh. He liked Kathleen's long, flowing hair that she once had, and he was glad to hear her say she wanted it back. It was a strange feeling to have – to have finally let himself move forward. He would always be sad about Sea, but perhaps these past two years had been exactly what he had needed to finally let her go? That, and telling Kathleen he loved her was truly something! He was certain it would end in heartbreak her being the heir and him nothing more than a former pirate, peasant, and now a war deserter, yet, he could not help but to feel relieved now that he had told her.

"They have missed you," Kathleen reminded him.

"Perhaps I should stay back with Pierson for a moment?" Agatha suggested. "There will be a lot of commotion when you arrive at camp..."

Smith nodded. He knew she meant that she was worried someone would want to fight him and that she did not want Pierson to get in the middle of it. "Yes, why don't you two go back to the lake we passed a moment ago? Pierson, why don't you teach Agatha how to skip a rock?"

Pierson seemed incredibly disappointed. "Yes, sir," he said.

Agatha walked with Pierson in the opposite direction. "Was that for Pierson's benefit or for her own?" Kathleen asked. "She is acting strange."

"I am not certain."

They were spotted as soon as they entered into the campsite, and there was a lot of shouting amongst the soldiers. "Princess Kathleen has returned! Someone fetch the king!" one man shouted out excitedly.

"My word, Smith's with her!" another man shouted.

Smith was almost knocked on his back when a young man came at him full speed; for a moment, he thought he was in fact going to be in the middle of a brawl from the mere force of the impact, but the man wrapped his arms around Smith in a tearful fit. "Squirt?" Smith questioned.

"You're a real bastard, you know?" Squirt sobbed.

Smith had hardly recognized him. Two years had passed, and Squirt bore no resemblance of the child Smith had left behind. "I know," Smith said, and he felt a lump form in his throat. He pulled Squirt back into a second embrace.

As more Black Dragon's arrived, Smith could not spit out an apology fast enough. His voice quivered slightly in his attempt, and Squirt held onto him as though he believed that if he let go Smith would disappear again. Yin hugged him around his neck, practically pushing Squirt off him to do so. "You're a devil," Yin mumbled and then pulled away, hardly able to look at his former captain.

Mouth, his stepson Jake, Cassidy, Clara, Knot, and the rest of the Cooks, Blade, Gomda, Stewart, Gwen, and Sky all had similar interactions – cussing at him or yelling at him followed by a rather emotional admission of relief that he had returned. Smith held Knot and Anna's little girl whom he had never met, for Anna had been pregnant when he had left; the two-year-old girls' presence made the amount of time he had been gone seem even longer somehow. Once he put her down, Abigail came up to him and popped him on his cheek before kissing his forehead. Smith frowned to see how thin they had all gotten from malnutrition; Kathleen had said they were low on supplies, but he had not realized how bad it had gotten.

His Uncle Andrew and his cousin Thaddeus came running up to him as well, and Smith felt a pang in his side at the thought of his mother again. His uncle had tears in his eyes. "I'm so glad you're here," he said. "Your mother, she'd want this. She would want us to be together."

Smith smiled and wiped tears away. "I know she would. And, I cannot express how truly sorry I am to all of you that I –"

Smith was interrupted when Jackson White appeared, almost knocking him over as he hurdled himself at him. Jackson squeezed Smith in his arms, and Smith could hear the man starting to sob from the sheer shock of his presence. Smith was a bit surprised at Jackson's reaction; they certainly had not been close, but this man had intended to marry his mother. Smith realized that by leaving, he had likely taken a part of her with him, and it had pained Jackson terribly. "I'm so sorry, Jackson," Smith said in a hushed tone as though he was consoling a child who had taken a tumble. When they pulled apart, Smith could see Jackson's legs shake; the man covered his face in embarrassment. The only other time Smith had ever seen Jackson cry was when his mother, the man's fiancée, had died.

"Smith, I'll leave you to your friends," Kathleen said with a bright smile. "But I must go inform my father of my mission's success." She hurried into camp; Harold and Rachel met her halfway having already been hurrying over to greet them after hearing all of the commotion.

Smith wiped his face dry and took a breath. He shook hands with Maxi; the man gave him another hug and shook his head to let him know he was still disappointed in him but thankful all at once. "I cannot describe how relieved I am," Smith admitted to the small crowd of loved ones who had appeared around them. "I am sorry – truly, truly sorry. I should have never left the way I did – or at all for that matter. I've missed you all." He looked around eagerly for a moment. "Where are Ace and Snake?" he asked, referring to his closest companions.

Sky stepped forward and kissed Smith's cheek. "They are hiding from you, I think. My poor husband ran when you came into camp. He and Ace are both so –"

"Your English..." Smith could not help but to interrupt her despite what a serious topic they had ventured into. "It's flawless."

"It has been two years, Smith," Sky said. "I have learned a lot in two years. English is but one of my newly acquired skills."

Smith frowned and then nodded. Yes, a lot could change in two years. "Snake and Ace?" he asked.

Cassidy answered. "They're by one of the firepits. I could not get Ace to come over here with me anymore than Sky could convince Snake."

"They must hate me," Smith said.

"Hate you?" Mouth spoke up, and Smith turned his head to look the man's way. "Mate, they hate themselves. Please, for the love of God, tell those two poor souls you forgive them for their betrayals, for they are just shadows of their former selves."

"Let me speak to them alone, then," Smith said and left the group. He found them fairly quickly, and the two of them were seated together at a fire that was mostly ash and embers. "Snake... Ace..." Smith spoke, and the two of them looked up at him nervously. Smith felt sick to his stomach. Ace's former jet-black hair was now full of patches of silver, and he had wrinkles around his eyes. Snake looked even worse; he had aged terribly. His hair seemed a bit thinner, and his face was also wrinkled. Only two years had passed, but it looked like his two dearest friends had aged ten. Snake cupped his face into his hands, unwilling to look at Smith for a moment longer.

Ace stood up slowly, and he spoke with a tremendous amount of care in his voice. "Smith, you're back. Why?"

"I should have never left," Smith said. "There are no words to describe how sorry I am for what I have done. I panicked. So much had happened, and I just panicked. That letter, it hurt me, but it was so long ago. I should not have just run. And, I certainly should not have taken the boy from you both!"

He could hear Snake crying; the man was still just sitting on the log by the fire, his hands covering his face. Smith's eyes went from Snake back to Ace. Ace had an almost confused look etched into his sad expression. "You're sorry? We're the ones who –"

"Courtney was the one who was unfaithful," Smith said. "I loved her, and I still do. But, she is not here anymore. I must move on. I forgive you. Both of you. I only hope that you can one day forgive me."

Ace's lip seemed to quiver for a moment, but he prevented himself from crying by letting out a forced laugh – it sounded as though the pain he had been harboring was melting off him through that nervous cackle of his. Ace gave him quick hug around the neck and pulled himself away. "Smith, to think we would not forgive you! You're our best mate. After everything we've been through! I am just thankful *you* say you forgive *me*. I have needed to hear that."

Smith looked down at Snake. "I wish you'd quit that blubbering," Smith said.

Snake at last looked up at him; he seemed to have gotten control of himself, but his face was still a bit shaky, and his eyes were red from his tears. He stood up and looked Smith in the eye. "I wanted to tell you what happened, you know? Then she died, and I just couldn't. I didn't want you to think less of her... or me. And... and... the boy –"

Smith reached out and put his hands on Snake's shoulders. "That was a devilish thing of me to do." Snake embraced him for a moment before pulling back to wipe away the tears that remained on his face. Smith took a breath and looked at them both. "And, now I am especially sorry for this: I know now that I am not Pierson's father." Both of them seemed to become pale from the comment.

"How is it that you know that?" Snake asked.

"Because he looks just like his father," Smith said. "For the past two years I have watched him grow more and more in his father's liking, and I have done my best to ignore it. I can't do that anymore, though."

Before Smith had a chance to say much more, a shouting was heard on the opposite end of camp. It sounded like Kathleen, and he instinctively took off in that direction, Ace and Snake not too far behind him. A small part of him liked having those two behind him, ready to back him up; it felt like old times – like they had sunk back into their former habits already.

Smith arrived before them on the scene, and it was a rather troubling scene at that. The queen was laid out on the ground; she had feinted which was the cause of Kathleen's surprised scream. Agatha was standing there with this smirk on her face that Smith did not care for, and she was standing a few feet from a ghostly pale King Harold. Harold looked like he was moments from joining his wife on the ground.

"Agatha, what did you do?" Smith asked her.

"I just came into camp," she said, and her voice sounded taunting – not at all like the sweet woman he knew.

"Harold?" Smith beckoned, and the man turned to look back at Smith, taking his eyes off Agatha for a moment. The man looked as though he would drop dead where he stood from fright.

"Smith," Harold said, his voice hoarse. "Glad to see you're back." The words seemed almost like they were meant as an effort to keep himself distracted, if only for a moment.

Smith opened his mouth to speak, but before he could ask them what in the world was going on, Agatha was right behind Harold with a dagger to his throat. "Agatha!" Smith roared, and he heard Kathleen shout out in fear from where she was attending to her mother on the ground – the woman just now starting to come to after her surprise.

"Amy, please," Harold said, grabbing hold of the woman's wrist.

"Amy?" Smith questioned. He looked at her with sad eyes. There were men standing around, all with guns pointed in Agatha and Harold's direction. Smith pleaded with her, "Woman, please, don't! Please, they will kill you! Whatever this is about –"

"Tell them what it's about," she hissed into Harold's ear as she gripped onto him, holding the blade against his throat.

Half the camp was gathered around now – the Black Dragon's included. Many of them had their guns drawn, ready to shoot her down if she dared to assassinate the king after all the work they had put into building his army. Smith could not imagine watching Agatha die like this – not after everything they had been through.

"Let go of me," Harold said with gritted teeth.

"You're a corrupt scoundrel, Harry," she snarled.

"Don't be so informal with me when you have a knife to my throat!"

"Tell Smith what you did, and I'll let go right now," she said.

"I buried you," Harold said, sounding almost as confused as the rest of the camp.

"Agatha!" Smith shouted again, and she looked at him, still gripping onto Harold. She looked completely mad. "Please, they will all shoot you. Don't do this. Please, let him go, and we can all talk."

"Do you know this woman, Smith?" Ace asked, his voice rushed and full of worry.

"I met her in Balla. She is my friend," Smith said, staring at her with pained eyes.

"Please," Ace said, speaking calmly in her direction, his pistol drawn. "That man is my father. Please, do not hurt him. We will kill you, and I do not want that."

Agatha stared at Ace for a moment, and then her face seemed to light up, a bit of her insanity leaving her. "Little James Lincoln? No...I never thought..." The madness came right back when Ace dared to get too close. She pulled back, forcing Harold to step back with her. "I just want him to tell the truth," Agatha said. "I'll let your father go as soon as he does."

Smith stared at her in complete disbelief. She held a dagger to Harold's throat with one hand, and upon closer examination he could see that she had a pistol pointed in Harold's back. This was not the woman he thought he knew. "I heard Harold call you *Amy*," Smith said. "You never gave me your real name. Is that it?"

She did not respond to him. She was too focused on Harold. Harold was not budging on whatever it was she wanted, and that was causing her to become angry. Smith watched her eyes become dark, and her fury seemed to intensify from Harold's silence. Just when Smith thought she was ready to pull the trigger and shoot the king in the back, Snake spoke. "I know you," he said, and his voice shook terribly. Snake looked more anxious than even Harold as he stepped away from the crowd of on-lookers and towards Harold and his captor. Tears started to fall down Snake's cheeks.

"You don't know me, boy," she hissed.

"I do," Snake said. "You're Amy Lee – wife of General Robbie Lee. It's me, Mum. It's Johnny."

Chapter 18

Smith stood within the war tent with Ace, King Harold, Queen Rachel, Kathleen, Richard, Snake, and a bound Amy Lee – formerly known to Smith as *Agatha*. Amy stood with her head bowed and her wrists tied in a corner, Snake's arms around her with his head rested on her shoulder. Snake's claim that he was the woman's son had been enough for her to lower her weapons, and the small group now present in the war tent had shooed the crowd of eavesdroppers away so that they could all speak now that the hysteria of the moment had died down.

"Where's Pierson?" Smith asked.

"He is still by the lake skipping rocks," Amy said and then looked straight at Ace. "My word, he looks just like you."

Ace instantly became pale, and his knees seemed to buckle. Smith grabbed onto him. "I hadn't told him yet," Smith said angrily.

Amy frowned. "I'm sorry. That… that was not my place."

Harold rubbed his throat. "Awfully late to be worried about being courteous, Amy."

"I hope you burn in hell," Amy spat back without pause.

"That's enough!" Smith shouted. "Agatha... Amy... Mrs. Lee..." Smith shook his head; he didn't know what to call the woman.

Snake pulled himself away from his mother long enough to look at Smith and ask, "How is it you two came to know one another?"

Smith blushed – not at all sure what he should tell his friend. Amy's face turned red as well, and she did not give Smith a moment to answer. "He hired me as a nanny while in Balla," she said plainly, and it seemed for the time being that she and Smith could both agree to spare Snake the details. Amy reached out and took hold of her son's sleeve to draw his attention back towards her. "What sort of life have you lived? I thought for sure you were dead."

Snake smiled at his mother. "I have lived a good life. I would not wish it had been any different except for it to have had you in it."

"I believe we all deserve an explanation," Smith said as his eyes darted from King Harold to Amy and then back again.

"I'd like one as well!" Harold spat and looked towards Amy. "I buried you! How can this be?"

"You would not have needed to bury me had you not sent John to kill me and my family!" she roared, and Snake took a step back from her.

Snake looked at Harold with a hateful glare. "Is this true?"

Harold took a breath. He looked at Snake sadly. "I would like to think, Snake, that you and I have become friends. So, I will not lie to you any longer. John was the one who pulled the trigger, but I was the one who ordered him to."

"I should kill you," Snake said in a surprisingly calm demeanor. "I knew you had covered it up... but I didn't know you had given the order...Why? Tell me why? You were all friends! You, John, my parents... why?"

Harold was silent. Amy laughed at his discomfort. "*Oh –*" she began.

"You want to start telling secrets, Amy?" Harold snapped, and after a moment of the two glaring at one another, they fell silent. Another long silence passed in the room before Harold finally asked, "Amy, how is it that you are alive?"

"I am alive because of my husband and because of John," she said. "Robbie knew all about the order you gave John because *John* told him. Your men were closing in on us. Robbie begged John to find a way to save me and my son. John negotiated my son's life with you, but you wanted *me* dead. John brought you two bodies, yes? He brought you my husbands, but the woman was just a poor woman my husband killed to save me. John shot her in the face."

"I saw you," Snake said, his voice shaking. "I saw you laid out in the floor of our home!"

"Poison – courtesy of your father," she said. "Robbie and John knew I would never go along with their ridiculous plan to save me. Not if it meant killing an innocent woman. I woke up in a blasted crate; John dumped me off in Balla, and I've been there hiding from the Caldara's ever since." She looked at Snake. "I thought you were dead, Johnny, or I would have never stayed in Balla. John told me you ran and that he could not find you. We both assumed that you were dead... you were so young."

Snake again turned and looked at Harold. "All this time I've been furious with John, and it was you? You made him kill his friends. And, John saved my mother and me!"

"Snake, please, forgive me," Harold said. "There are a lot of things I wish I could take back. I was doing what I thought was best."

Harold's words reignited the anger within Amy. She screamed at him and broke away from her son for a moment to stare him down. "What you thought was best? You had one of your closest friend's murder another just to keep your wife making you a cuckold a secret!"

Queen Rachel let out a horrid shriek, and all three of her children's heads turned in her direction – mouths wide open in shock. "Mother!" Richard cried. "Tell me she is lying! That you did not have an affair?"

"Enough!" Smith shouted and glared at Amy. "That's enough, Amy. Your son has thought you were dead all of these years, and here you are. This should be a happy day. Stop these accusations, please."

Queen Rachel shouted over Smith towards Amy, "I am not the only one who made my husband a cuckold!"

"Rachel, that's enough!" Harold shouted.

Amy huffed. "You know, Rachel, I never really liked you."

"Believe you me that is quite mutual!" the queen snapped.

"Stop it!" Snake shouted. "Stop it – all of you! Whatever is past, leave it there! I don't want to hear it. Nothing will change it. My father is dead, and I went my whole life believing my mother was as well because of whatever all this nonsense is between you three! Let us bury it and forget it, please!" Snake turned to Harold directly, and Smith could see that Snake was borderline hysterical by the shakiness of his eyes. "You say I am your friend, then show me. Let me untie my mother and show me you can leave what is past in the past. I can forgive you, Harold, if you promise me you can forgive her for whatever trespasses there are, please!"

Harold hesitated for a moment, and he responded with a simple nod. Smith noted that Amy did seem to breathe easier once Snake was able to unbind her wrists. She had, after all, attempted to assassinate Harold only moments before; she was lucky the camp had not strung her up in a tree to hang. Snake stared at her. "You too, Mother – what's past is past. You harm Harold, and your harm your sons' friend." Amy nodded, and once her arms were free, she put them around his neck and held him close.

Smith turned to Ace once the tension seemed to be dying down. "Ace, would you like to see Pierson?" he asked.

"Yes," Ace said, sounding weak as he spoke. "Yes, please."

Smith glanced around the room, making eye contact with everyone as though to silently warn them not to get into it with one another while they were gone. He and Ace walked through camp and over to the small lake that Amy had left Pierson by. The boy was skipping rocks as the woman had left him, and the two friends watched at a distance. "I do not believe I can ever make up for the wrong I've done you by taking him," Smith said.

Ace tugged at his shirt collar as though he was being choked. He watched the boy playing by himself, and the man seemed to become even paler than his usual self. "He looks just like me," Ace said. "Like a little me."

"He's going to have your height – and he certainly did not get those broad shoulders from me or from Sea. That pale skin and perfectly black hair is a marking of a Caldara, certainly," Smith said.

"It should have been you," Ace said. "Not me. Not Snake."

"Well, it's not. I'm not the boy's father, and I have pretended to be so for too long now. Pierson knows it, too. He's smart. He figured it out on his own. And, by some miracle, he is not furious with me. I believe I would have been," Smith said as he put his hands in his pockets.

"He was not angry with you because *he* wanted it to be you – for *you* to be his father," Ace said. "Sea wrote about you to him – yes? He must know that Sea wanted you to be his father. I will be such a disappointment."

"He just wants to know you. Go on, and go meet him," Smith said and began to walk away, but Ace grabbed at Smith's arm.

"I do not know what to say to the boy. Does he know... know that his mother intentionally got me intoxicated? That he only exists because Sea wanted some sort of insurance in case my father caught up to us?" Ace questioned.

"I do not believe he knows all that, and it's not necessary," Smith said. "Just go meet your son, Ace."

"Go with me," Ace demanded; he seemed almost fearful. "I do not want to disappoint him after all this time."

Smith nodded, and he smiled slightly. "Ace, you are far from a disappointment." They approach Pierson, and the boy spun around when he heard their footsteps against fallen twigs.

The boy's eyes lit up, and his gaze seemed to completely ignore Smith and focus entirely on Ace. While the notion somewhat pained Smith, he was still glad for Ace. "Pierson," Smith said. "Do you know who this man is?"

Pierson's face seemed to glow as the corners of his lips turned up slowly at first, but soon a large, toothy grin appeared on his face. "I know him," Pierson said. "He is my father."

Smith could hear a heavy exhale from Ace as though the man was fighting off whatever painful or too-joyous of an emotion he was feeling to avoid any embarrassing tears. "My name," Ace began, "is James."

Pierson laughed. "I know that. You're Prince James Lincoln Caldara, but my mama would call you *Ace* in her letters."

"Your mother wrote about me?" Ace asked, sounding almost mortified at what she might have written.

Pierson nodded, a smile still etched on his face. "Oh, yes! She mostly wrote about Papa... I mean, Smith... but she wrote about you and Snake and the other Black Dragons too. She wrote a lot about you and Snake."

Ace nervously questioned, "And, what did your mother's letters say?"

"She said you were a sad person," Pierson said, perfectly summing up the type of young man Ace had been before he had unveiled his identity to his friends – back when Sea had still been alive. "Are you still a sad person?" Pierson asked.

Ace smiled at him, "No, Pierson, not today."

Chapter 19

Smith sat by Jackson at the firepit; the drama of his arrival back at camp was at last starting to wind down. Snake was off somewhere with his mother – no doubt making up for lost time after spending a lifetime apart, and Sky was with them getting to know her mother-in-law. Ace and Cassidy were off somewhere with Pierson on a similar mission of regaining years lost. "Lad," Jackson said as the sun was setting, sounding as though he wanted to have a heartfelt conversation before the campfire became crowded.

Smith glanced to his right where Jackson was seated. "Yes?"

The man fell silent. He seemed quite broken. Clearly, he wanted to say something, but he was having a difficult time forming words. Smith sighed, no doubt in his mind that Jackson wanted to speak about Smith's mother. Smith at last spoke for him. "I should not have left the way I did," Smith said. "It would have broken my mother's heart to see two people she cared deeply for so far apart. Jackson, you were so good to her. I'll admit you and I did not quite see eye to eye for a while, but you are a changed man – I see it. I count you as one of my dearest friends.

After my mother's passing, you were the one who was the better person, not me. You looked to comfort me, and I ran instead of returning the favor, and for that I am sorry."

Jackson looked away from Smith and towards the fire. The man was still quite uncomfortable with sentiment, it seemed. "A lot has changed since you left us."

"I see that," Smith said. "I see that Ace and his family have become closer. That is good."

"Yes – even his cousin Dave seems to be getting along better with him," Jackson said.

"And, I certainly see that Cassidy is still as smitten as ever with Ace. How is she doing? How cruel I was to leave right after that woman lost her daughter!"

"Cassidy is well. Though a few months after you left, Nicole's father joined the rebellion. He had not been at his home on Kevin's Isle during the ambush and had been hiding out on the mainland. When he caught word that Harold was alive, he brought a group with him."

"Nicole's father! That cad came here to help?"

"Yes," Jackson said. "Though speak lightly about him. When the man found out his daughter was dead, he killed himself. Hung himself outside of Ace and Cassidy's tent in the middle of the night."

"My word!" Smith wailed slightly at the thought.

"I never read his suicide note, but according to Ace the man expressed quite an admission of guilt for abandoning Cassidy and Nicole and for the way he had treated them when they met here in Kirkston."

"So much has happened indeed!" Smith shrieked. "And, I was not here for any of my friends. Jackson, would you care to update me?"

"Not sure if there is much more to tell. Clara's illness seems to have gotten better in the past two years but not enough to stop calling her a sickly gal, but Yin always looks out for her. It is good to see those two together, though – after Yang and Nicole dying, they needed one another. Mouth and Abigail, now that Tim and Susan are dead, put all their time into raising Jake, and the boy is becoming an outright gentleman. Squirt and Gwen are lovesick as ever, but I would not say that is much different from the way you left them. Squirt's become quite a capable soldier, I'll say that! My word, he's efficient! You would be proud."

"I imagine that I would be," Smith said.

"Gwen and Stewart are much closer with their sister Gracie now, though Gracie's husband Jamie was killed in battle about a year ago."

Smith lowered his head. "Poor man. Poor Gracie! I did not know. And, what of their sister Helena?"

"My ex-wife and brother are perhaps the only thing at this camp that has not changed. They keep to themselves and occasionally cause trouble, but that is all. I tend to avoid them." Jackson rolled his eyes. "Jeremiah, I will say, has taken on a bit of a leadership role in your absence. He's an ass, but he knows how to fight and how to strategize, so he has sat in on a few tactical meetings with Kyo and the Caldara's."

"Kyo, I have not seen him yet? How are the Mori's?"

"He's here – probably just chasing his daughter around somewhere. His daughter, Saki, she is eleven now. A little devil but a sweet one. She gets into a bit of trouble around camp –nothing serious. Kyo's sister, Chi, well…" Jackson chuckled and pointed towards a grouping of trees where Smith spotted Stewart standing and chatting with the Asian woman; his stance and nervousness said all that Smith needed to know.

"No," Smith said as though he did not believe it.

"Oh, trust me," Jackson said with a laugh. "That one surprised everyone. Apparently, the woman has been smitten with him ever since Kyo held him captive on Akito Berry Island. And, saving her brother's life from John was a plus. The two of them are a fairly recent undertaking, though. I told her to be careful or that she'd wind up as a pastor's wife, and she laughed and said it would be a nice change of pace from being a pirate commodore's sister. Ron and Theresa and their son are healthy and doing well, which is truthfully saying a lot at this camp."

"And, how is Gomda?" Smith asked.

"Doing well for himself. A fine solider. He is adjusting well to life in Kirkston. He and Snake are friends now, I'd say. Not long after you left, he went and found what was left of Hethuska's body and cremated his remains. He and Sky and Snake tossed his ashes into the ocean. Sky said it was so that his ashes might find their way home."

"Gomda is a loyal friend," Smith said. He looked around camp as though seeking more people to ask about. He spotted Maxi and nodded towards the man. "And, the Cooks?"

Jackson seemed sad. "They are better now than they were. I think the loss of Mrs. Cook, Tim, and Susan took a heavy toll on all of them. Especially poor Jimmy. Maxi's wife is pregnant, we believe. She is not entirely certain yet – it is still early, but she is hopeful. I think that makes Maxi nervous after losing his past relations during childbirth. Maxi's son, Tom, he is getting along better with his former gang members. Jimmy Cook, he's not a little boy anymore. He's a wee little man, I'd say. Hannah and Blade are still fond of one another. That's not changed much. And, Anna – "

"Yes!" Smith interrupted. "Knot and Anna, their little girl, I held the beautiful little thing, but I did not catch her name?"

Jackson smiled, but it was a sad smile. "Ellen Jane Storm."

"My mother and Anna's?" Smith questioned, and he felt quite overwhelmed by the gesture. "Why not his own mother?"

Jackson lowered his head. "Said he didn't know his mother's name. He was just a boy when she died. He just knew her as *Mama*. Said he would have liked to have name her after his own mother… in fact, he said he hadn't even realized he didn't know his mother's name until he was holding his little girl. So, says he, he named him after the woman he felt was most like a mother to him. Mrs. Keg, Knot tells me her name was also Jane like Anna's mother, so it was fitting since that woman too had been a motherly type to him. He says the girl bares his birth mother's marital name, Stone, the name of Mrs. Barons, and the name Jane which is both Mrs. Keg's and Mrs. Cook's, so he feels she will be a very blessed little girl with, as he puts it, so many motherly angels looking after her."

Smith stared at him for a moment. "Angels, Jackson? Do you believe in angels now?"

Jackson chuckled. "I don't know, Smith. I suppose I am still where you last left me in regards to where I stand with yours and Stewart's God. Though, if I ever needed any proof of Heaven, I saw it in your mother's eyes. Something still holds me back from true faith, though."

Smith put a hand on Jackson's shoulder. "You have become a rather profound man, you know?"

Jackson laughed and placed his hand on Smith's shoulder as well. "I'll consider that a compliment." Jackson sat upright, glancing off towards where they had last seen Snake and his mother. "The letter we found at my father's home... it was right."

"Yes," Smith said. "Your father knew that Amy was living in Balla."

"But, how?" he questioned.

"Amy was living with the gypsies there," Smith said. "The gypsies by the ports ran in rather unpleasant circles. My best guess is that someone realized who she was and word spread around the criminal community in Balla. Eventually word must have reached your father's inner circles here."

"I suppose that will have to do for an explanation," Jackson said. "With the way Harold and Amy acted when she first arrived, it's a good thing my father never got that letter to Harold. Back then, he probably would have immediately searched for her and had her killed."

"Let's not think on that, mate," Smith said. He still had many questions for Harold and Amy about what happened between the Caldara's and Lee's, but he was not so willing to burden his mind with former scandals at the moment.

Soon the fire was surrounded by people. Smith smiled when Kathleen sat next to him just as the sun disappeared behind the trees. He cringed slightly when, despite her father and many other Caldara's being present, she willfully took him by the hand and began chatting with him as though no time had passed between them. The small crowd around the fire consisted almost entirely of Smith's family and friends; Smith figured those who did not know him had likely retired to their tents. Harold spoke to the group surrounding the fire. "My daughter, bless her, has spoken on behalf of myself and has negotiated with England who promises to send us aid – though how much aid is quite uncertain. It will likely be a rather miniscule number, but hopefully it will be enough to keep us from perishing. In the meantime, we must recollect ourselves and create a new strategy. Smith, though I am quite bitter about you leaving us so abruptly two years ago, I am not so bitter as to be unable to admit that this rebellion had been functioning much more smoothly in your presence than in your absence. That being said, I am not so proud that I cannot turn to you for guidance. If you have any ideas for us, please, we are desperate."

Smith released Kathleen's hand and stood. Everyone he knew seemed to be sitting or standing around that fire: the Caldara's, the two surviving members of the Annihilator's –Jeremiah and Helena, the Black Dragons, the Cooks, the Mori's, the Katch's, and a handful of other loved ones such as Dr. Conal, were all suddenly looking to him. He felt he did not deserve this sort of recognition. "We need to grow our numbers, but the people are giving up on this rebellion. We need to have a show of force grand enough to attract attention but one that will not bring down our own numbers," Smith began. "My suggestion is a brute, sudden surprise attack on one of John's bases – one that is furthest from the others and from the capital. If he has a base near a wooded area that would be best. A location that we can strike fast and flee."

"That's awfully cowardly," Harold said.

Jeremiah White laughed loudly. "It sounds like one of my own attacks."

"Exactly," Smith said. "Like a crew of pirates without their ship. We attack when they're not ready with the sole purpose of making a statement. While I hate to say this, we cannot –"

Jeremiah interrupted again. "You don't want to leave any survivors. No men to tell the tale?"

Smith nodded. "Yes. Make it seem like John's men had time to fight back – make it seem like it was more than just a surprise attack."

"Then sprinkle in some rumors around about our accomplishment," Snake added. "And, we'll get more soldiers if they think we have a chance."

Smith nodded. "Exactly."

Jeremiah White smiled and looked over towards Harold. "If His Majesty would allow it, I think this sounds like something of my taste. Allow me to plan the attack and lead it, and I promise not to disappoint. Let Smith and his Black Dragons come in and do the clean up to make the whole thing look like a battle instead of an ambush. Besides, they won't have the stomach for what I have planned."

Harold nodded somewhat anxiously. "All right. Jeremiah, Smith, let's get to work. Both of you, if you would, meet me in the war tent."

Chapter 20

Smith was not particularly proud of the surprise attack on one of John's bases; the rebellion had slaughtered an entire camp that resided just outside of Caldara City. With a brute like Jeremiah White leading the attack, they had of course left no survivors. Smith and his team had then had the dirty work of attempting to make the attack look more like a battle rather than an ambush, and soon afterwards rumors had spread throughout Kirkston that the rebellion was making a comeback.

Only a few weeks had passed, but new recruits had begun to arrive in packs. Stevenson's men were hell-bent on revenge for their fallen comrades, so the rebellion was once again relocating to avoid any ambushes themselves. After each battle fought, the rebellion tended to head further and further west towards the Kirkston Mountains. "All right!" King Harold announced, "Unload!"

Thank goodness, Smith thought, his back aching him after their long journey. He and Ron Katch got right to work on setting up the war tent so that Harold and the other leaders around camp, Smith included, would have a place to convene later that evening.

"Who are the new recruits?" Ron asked, nodding towards the large crowd of men who had joined them in the midst of their travel west. It was about forty additional soldiers, and they had brought a surplus of supplies – namely, food, which was something the rebellion had been lacking until recently. The rebellion would eat well that night, and Smith was glad for it; his friends were all starting to look sickly after the past two years of fighting.

"They are from Rockwood," Smith said, referring to one of the most densely populated cities in Kirkston right behind the capital and the ports and perhaps the City of St. Dale. "Stevenson has been bringing Rockwood to its knees lately, according to Kathleen. John's latest recruits have all been sent there to stir up the locals like they had done with Caldara City and the port cities. John's just making sure the people of Kirkston know who's in control. Kathleen says the Spanish soldiers hung a few prominent generals and councilmen out that way, so we were bound to get some recruits from there."

"Forty men is not bad for one day of recruiting," Ron said as he helped Smith unroll the tent. "We're bound to get more."

"That is the hope," Smith said and gazed out towards the new group of men. One of the men, a tall, thin fellow, broke away from the group. He was looking to assist with set up of the campsite, and the man soon found his way to a handful of Black Dragons – Mouth, Blade, and Ace were setting up some tents.

Smith watched curiously; he could not hear what was being said across the way, but he could see clearly that the man and Mouth seemed to recognize one another. There was tension, and for a moment he thought to go and check on them, but after a moment of debating he decided against it when he saw Squirt heading over. Squirt, as Jackson had said to Smith a few weeks prior, was a young man now; he seemed ready to break up a fight before it even happened. Smith nodded approvingly as he watched Squirt speak with his brother for a moment, but suddenly Mouth grabbed Squirt's arm, and the two of them walked away from the others to somewhere private.

"What was that about?" he heard Ron ask.

"I'm not sure," Smith said, but he knew whatever it was made him quite uncomfortable.

It was less than fifteen minutes later, just as Ron and Smith were placing a table inside the now pitched war tent, that he spotted Squirt darting across camp and Mouth chasing after him. "What now?" Smith questioned out loud to Ron as the two of them darted out of the war tent to see that Squirt had a pistol drawn and pointed towards the back of the man Smith had seen them speaking to earlier.

"Squirt, stop!" Smith heard Mouth shouting, way too far off to stop Squirt in time.

Smith ran and drove himself into Squirt, tackling him by the waist; they both toppled to the ground just as the gun fired. The man spun around; he had been speaking to some friends, and he grew pale to see that he had almost been shot in the back. Mouth was hovering over Smith and Squirt in an instant, and he kicked the gun right out of Squirt's hands. "Get off me!" Squirt roared and swung up at Smith.

The man looked straight at Mouth and said, "Tommy, I'm sorry."

"Run," Mouth hissed, for Squirt seemed increasingly adamant to get away from them both to kill the man. The man did not hesitate to find a safer place at camp.

Smith took several punches from Squirt before Mouth, Ron, and himself were able to yank Squirt up onto his feet and detain him. "What is the matter with you?" Smith snarled; he could not imagine what had taken place to make Squirt behave in such a way. Squirt was far from violent, and to think he tried to take a man's life with his back turned was disheartening to say the least.

Squirt relaxed, and the three of them felt that they could release him. He stood there sulking for a moment before he glared right at Smith. "Why did you stop me?" he asked, but before Smith could respond he turned towards his brother. "And, you? Why would you help him? I know you must want to shoot him more than I!"

"He was just a child when it happened," Mouth said.

"Tell me what happened, Squirt," Smith said in a firm tone.

Squirt barked back at Smith. "It's none of your business! I don't know why you're even here. What made you want to come back to Kirkston all of a sudden anyways? Go back to Balla! You can't disappear for two years and then start talking to me like you own me!"

Mouth grabbed hold of his brother's arm. "That's enough, Squirt! Don't take it out on Smith." Mouth picked up Squirt's pistol and then made him hand over his dagger and even his pocket knife and sword. "Go finish pitching your tent, and I will be there in a moment. Go on, go!"

Squirt scowled slightly, but he obeyed. Smith watched in disbelief as an almost evil version of the boy he once knew stormed off, kicking over a pot a woman was seated by in his current state of anger. "What happened?" Smith asked yet again. "Who was that man?"

"An old friend," Mouth said as though the word *friend* made him sick to his stomach. "His name's Morris. He recognized me after we started talking for a moment; it took me a while to realize who he was. He asked me for forgiveness."

"Forgiveness from what?" Ron questioned.

Mouth hesitated for a moment, but eventually he replied. "You both know of how my parents died? Three friends of mine told John, back when he was general, that my parents had stolen bread? Squirt was with a neighbor, a nursing woman, at the time. My parents were executed on the spot, and I ran with any money and food I could find. Morris, he was one of the boys who turned my parents in. He was my friend."

Smith was at a loss for words. Smith knew that the same three boys who had turned Mouth's parents in had hunted him down, beat him, stolen his food and money, tied him to a tree, and had force fed him leeches for their own entertainment before leaving him to die. Mouth was terrified of leeches and most sluggish creatures to this day. Had Sea not found Mouth, he would have died from starvation, and Squirt would have died too because the nursing woman had left him, a mere babe, out on the lawn to perish when she found out his parents were dead. "Mouth, should we make him leave? I can speak to Harold —"

"No," Mouth said. "We need soldiers. Besides, Morris seemed pretty upset when he saw me. It… it seemed sincere."

Smith was quite shocked at Mouth's readiness to forgive. Morris, along with the other two former friends of his, were responsible for a lot of turmoil in Mouth. Those were deep, mental scars. Their whole lives Mouth had always been the one to be hesitant to trust new members – Smith included – and it was because of that childhood betrayal he was that way. And, suddenly, when the man responsible stood before him, Mouth had shrugged it off and had stopped his brother from enacting revenge – a revenge Smith could imagine Mouth had thought about from time to time. "Mouth," Smith said with a half-smile. "You are a good person."

A slight chuckle escaped from Mouth, and he thanked Smith. "Just help me watch after Squirt. When I told him who the man was… well, you both saw." He reached out and put a hand on Smith's shoulders. "And, he was just upset. Believe me, Squirt is more than relieved to have you home."

"I'm glad," Smith said.

Mouth dropped his arm. "I'm going to go check on Squirt," he said and began to walk in that direction. Mouth glanced back at Smith and added, "in case you were wondering, Morris was the little asshole who thought the leeches would be funny. The other two just went along with it."

"Leeches?" Ron questioned as Mouth disappeared. "I know what happened, or at least I think I do, but what about leeches?"

197

"I think its best that I not say. But just so you know, I would not dare ever come at Mouth with a worm or a slug or a leech; he'll break your nose."

"He's scared of them?" Ron asked. "What did Morris do to him?"

Smith just shook his head, and the two of them went back to work trying to get the camp put together before sunset.

***

"He honestly tried to shoot that man?" Abigail asked softly as she patted Jake's head; her son, Mouth's stepson, was positively wiped out after the long journey to their new campsite. He had fallen asleep in their tent, and it was likely that the boy would be there for the rest of the night.

"Yes," Mouth whispered back as he watched Abigail coax the restless yet exhausted child into a deeper sleep. After Jake had lost his father and stepmother, Mouth and Abigail had become the primary caregivers for him. When Tim and Susan had died two years prior, Mouth had been worried. Jake was not his son; he had had a son, Ian, but Ian had died long ago. True, Jake could not replace Ian, but Mouth adored Jake. While Mouth was certain he would do anything to bring Jake's true father back, he had grown much closer to him since Tim's passing. *Poor fellow,* Mouth thought as images of Tim and Susan's faces popped into his mind. Yes, he would bring them back if he could, but he did so love that boy as though he was his own. Sometimes it made him sad; had Ian not died, he felt the two half-brothers would have been close.

"That's not like Squirt," Abigail said. "I know that man hurt you when you were a boy, but –"

"You know it's more than that," Mouth said. "He wasn't defending me, Abigail. It's different for Squirt than for the rest of the Black Dragons. Even Gwen, who was just a girl of almost three years, says she can sometimes recall bits and pieces about her parents – she says they're more like dreams than memories, but it is something. Squirt... he was not even a year old. He remembers nothing, and, if I am being honest, I do not speak to him about our parents enough for him to have even gathered a small glimmer of who they were. He has nothing to hold onto, and he has asked me about them so many times in our lives, and I always brush the conversation away. He's angry. And, I think that is my fault for being so closed up about them."

"What are you going to do?" Abigail asked.

"We are a day's ride from Caldara," Mouth said. "My family lived in a small town just outside of the city. I think I will take him to our hometown."

"That's a terrible idea right now!" she snapped, though her voice was still in a whisper.

"When will it ever be a good idea again?" Mouth asked. "We have no idea how much longer this will last, and for all we know next week I could take a bullet to the head during a fight. Squirt should see where he came from. And, I should tell him. I will bring company so that we are safer in our travels. Besides, it is a ghost-town. It is unlikely we will run into people."

"If you insist, do be careful," she said. "John's power has spread to all parts of Kirkston. Do not wear your Black Dragon uniform or anything that might make someone suspect you are part of the rebellion."

Mouth laughed slightly. "Do not be so paranoid, Abigial. Plenty of soldiers have wandered from camp before. My face is more recognizable, sure, but this is not some daring feat. Now, go to sleep. I will go gather some supplies because I intend to take Squirt on our journey first thing tomorrow once I find some willing companions."

Chapter 21

Squirt stood nearby with his arms crossed and a scowl on his face as he watched his brother finish loading up one of the horses. "Where are we even going?" Squirt practically snarled. He was still angry that Mouth had not returned any of his weapons.

"A scouting mission," Kyo Mori said cheerfully as he helped his daughter hop up onto one of the horses. Saki smiled excitedly; she had not been away from camp since the war had first begun. Kyo had not intended to take her with him, but she had started causing a bit of mischief in her boredom that morning, so he had decided not to leave her troublesome self for someone else to watch. For Kyo, this would be a scouting mission, though he was fully aware of Mouth's intent.

Also accompanying them on their journey would be Ron Katch who had volunteered the moment Mouth had told him his plan; after seeing such a kind young man as Squirt react the way he had, Ron was willing to try to do his part to set the normally kind spirit straight again. In addition, a solider named Theodore was attending for some extra man power in the event they ran into trouble.

Once they were away from camp, and in turn far from Morris, Mouth returned Squirt's weapons. During their ride, Kyo, Saki, and Theodore held most of the conversation, for Mouth and Squirt were still a bit aggravated after the incident with Morris the day before. Squirt would ride ahead from time to time just to get some practice on the horse; most of his life had been spent on a ship, so he was not the most skilled rider. The past two years had given him plenty of opportunity to practice horseback riding, but he was nowhere near skilled enough to take a horse into battle just yet. Now seemed like a rather opportune time to attempt to perfect the new skill.

They had left early in the morning, so they arrived at their destination before sunset. Squirt was riding alongside Mouth when they entered into the eerily deserted town. "Where are we?" he asked his brother. "What sort of scouting mission is this? Doesn't look like anyone's lived here in ages."

"Years ago, this used to be a miner's town," Mouth said.

"Miners town?" Squirt questioned.

"The mine was in an underground cavern that was discovered nearly forty years ago," Kyo said. "The town was here less than ten years, though. The workers tore the underground cavern apart in record time, plus there wasn't much there to begin with. The town pulled anything of value out of the caverns, and they kept digging for years without anything else coming up. Eventually the mines collapsed –there's a lake about a mile north of here that formed after the tunnels fell in."

"Interesting," Theodore said. "I had no idea."

"A lot of people didn't," Mouth said. "It was over and done with before half the country knew about it." Mouth pointed to an awkwardly shaped building – the building was only a few yards deep but its length covered over half of what had once been the main road. "An investor threw that building up there as a commune for his workers. They were paid very poorly, but they could live here with their families – renting a room while they worked for him."

"It looks like a piece of shit," Squirt said. "I mean, it's abandoned now, but I can't imagine it was any homier back then."

"It wasn't," Mouth said, and Squirt glanced in his direction.

"Oh?" Squirt questioned. "Have you been here before?"

"Yes," Mouth said. "This was my home, our home, before the Black Dragons." Mouth hopped down off his horse and tied it up. The others followed suit. He looked towards Kyo, Ron, and Theodore, nodding at them in thanks, for they all knew that this was the true reason behind this journey. "Give us a moment," Mouth said and clasped a hand on Squirt's shoulder, leading him away from the group and towards the long building across the main road of the town.

The front door fell in when Mouth attempted to open it, and a whirlwind of dust blew up into their faces. "What are you doing?" Squirt asked.

"Just come with me," Mouth said. Squirt followed. It was just as small and cramped as Mouth remembered. They walked up a creaky staircase to the open rooms on the second floor. The top of the stairwell was awkward; they could either keep going up the stairs or enter a door to the right.

Squirt curiously opened the door, and he glanced into the long room that was simply lined with small beds. Just enough room was left from the foot of the beds and the wall to walk from one end of the room to the other. The room stretched all the way to the end of the building; there were nearly thirty or forty beds. "How many families lived in this building?" Squirt asked.

"The investor employed over a hundred men, and about half of them had families. Come on," Mouth said and pulled Squirt to the third floor. It was no different. They pushed open the door, and again Squirt saw the long room full of beds. They walked a good way, and then Mouth stopped and pointed. "Mom and Dad slept here," he said.

"That bed is hardly big enough for one person," Squirt said.

"They made it work," Mouth said and then pointed at the next bed in the line. "This was my bed. I slept with Morris. His parents slept in that bed there. On the other side of them was our friends Juni and Roman. They were... the other boys you've heard about."

"Where did I sleep?" Squirt asked.

"You were normally in bed with Mom and Dad, or you stayed with the nursing woman across the street. Mom's milk dried up, and she couldn't feed you. This nice rich woman whose husband was part of the investing firm offered to nurse you, so you were there a lot. Her little one was being weaned, so it was comfortable for her to let you nurse. I think it hurt Mom, though. It hurt Dad too that he couldn't provide her with enough to eat to be able to nurse you. Mom was always so skinny – Dad too." Mouth sat down on the bed that had once been his.

"Why did we come here, Mouth?" Squirt asked.

"Because I don't talk about them," Mouth said. "I never talk about them to you. It's not right, and I know that. You ask me questions all the time, and I never give you a real answer. It's no wonder you're so angry. It's not fair to you, and I'm sorry. Squirt, you tried to murder someone. You realize that, right? Morris, he was just a kid. You don't remember – you couldn't possibly remember… remember what it was like to feel so hungry and frightened. I remember what it was like, though. I remember not knowing whether or not there would be enough food to eat. Mother, she couldn't even nurse you. She cried about that all the time, and it would get Dad worked up too. That sort of hunger, Squirt, it can do terrible things to a person. Morris and the others, they were no exception to that. We were friends, yes, and it hurt me. It hurt me something awful. I would like to say that I would not have done the same, but I don't know… maybe I would have. It's been a lifetime since I've been that hungry. So hungry that your stomach swells and you wonder if you're going to make it through the night. What Morris and Juni and Roman did to me, it was wrong. It makes me angry – so angry – to think about it. I thought they were my friends. I never thought they would ever hurt me, but they did. They turned our parents in for the stolen bread for a few gold coins, but I refuse to believe that they did so knowing what John was going to do to them. It was desperation."

Squirt sat quietly as Mouth spoke. He eyed the dusty room, and he could feel a pain in the pit of his stomach. "I just wish I could have known them like you did," Squirt said.

"I know," Mouth said. "And, it can't help that I'm so weary to talk about them. I won't do that anymore, understand? I promise, you can ask me anything. Anything at all, and I promise to tell you."

Squirt was at a loss. He had many questions, but he had never asked one knowing full heartedly that it would be answered. He struggled to pin point something specific he wanted to know, so he asked simply, "What were they like? Mom and Dad, I mean."

Mouth smiled, and words came out like a rushing tide. He painted a beautiful picture of a poor man and woman who both worked painfully hard to keep their children fed. Squirt listened, soaking in every detail about the hard-working father who stayed late at the mines until his fingers bled and the caring mother who would sing them to sleep at night. They sat for many hours talking about their parents, and Squirt lingered on every word as though he intended to memorize every single thing that his brother uttered.

The sun was setting, so the two of them left the building and found Kyo, Saki, Ron, and Theodore waiting for them. Saki was looking incredibly bored, and Squirt chuckled slightly. He uncomfortably thanked the group that had accompanied them on their journey. "Are we done here, then?" Theodore asked with a yawn; he was the only one among them that had essentially been ordered to attend and had not volunteered. Clearly, he saw the trip as an enormous waste of his time.

"Yes," Mouth said. "We will be heading back to camp now."

After breaking momentarily to eat, they headed west back in the direction of the rebellion campsite. They were only back in route for approximately an hour when they were ambushed by Spanish soldiers. A roar of abrupt gunfire frightened their horses, and Theodore fell from his ride. The others drew their weapons, but Mouth and Squirt's horse was shot, so they too toppled down.

Squirt froze up slightly; he counted nearly two dozen men seeping out of the woods behind them.

In an act of desperation, Kyo threw Saki into Theodores arms and shouted, "Flee, I will cover you!" and Kyo began firing towards any man who seemed to lock in on the man carrying his daughter over his shoulder – the girl screaming out for her father to run with them. Out manned and outgunned, the rest were forced to surrender as Theodore made off with Saki.

Kyo, Ron, Mouth, and Squirt were immediately bound and forced onto their knees – their arms behind their backs. The man in charge of the large group of men pointed towards the woods where Theodore had fled and shouted, "Some of you go on and go after them. If you catch them, shoot the little girl in the face. We don't need to have to worry about her."

Kyo's eyes widened, and he angrily attempted to stand, a monstrous wave of vulgarity spewing from his lips. He was immediately struck with the base of a musket and forced back down onto his knees. Squirt glanced over to Kyo, and he could see the man visibly shaking in terror. The Spaniards did not speak to them; they waited, staring off in the direction that Theodore had run off with Saki. Several minutes passed, and they heard a distant gunshot; Kyo screamed and attempted to stand again, but he was immediately knocked down by the soldiers.

The men who had chased after Theodore and Saki arrived back without Theodore. "Well?" the man in charge asked.

"They got away. I think I might have shot the man when he was running, but he kept going. They're long gone," the soldier replied, and Squirt could see Kyo breathe deeply, though he was still a bit shaky after the close call.

The man cussed under his breath, but he turned his attention back on Squirt and the others. "You all are awfully far from your rebel brothers," he said and then laughed, pointing a finger down at Kyo. "Probably should have left this one home. I wouldn't have known who the rest of you were if not for that Asian face. Not a lot of hid kind walking around here. I would have just mistaken you all for travelers if not for him. But, you are Commodore Kyo, sí? Stevenson is going to be pleased to see this."

"I think that one there might be a Black Dragon," one of the soldiers said and pointed at Mouth. "I'm not sure, though. You can only tell so much from a Wanted Poster."

"If so, we struck gold," the leader said. "Load them up. We are taking them to Caldara Castle. When John is done with you, you lot are going to be wishing that you had just stayed home."

Chapter 22

The iron door shut, locking Mouth, Ron, Kyo, and Squirt together in the dark room. The only bit of light was through a small window high up in the cramped chamber. Mouth threw an arm over Squirt and pulled him close; Squirt would never say it, but Mouth knew that his younger sibling was frightened. Mouth watched as Kyo began to pace; the man was worried for his daughter – she had escaped the soldiers, but she was off alone with a man who was frankly a complete stranger. Ron too seemed nervous; he walked about the room, running his fingers against the stone walls as though he thought he could actually find a means of escape.

"Someone went mad in here," Ron said. "Someone scratched the words *Red Dress* all over these walls...it's written in dried blood over there too… it's old… and faded, but it's there."

"Do you think Theodore will be able to get Saki back to camp?" Kyo asked out loud, ignoring what Ron had said.

"I'm certain he did," Mouth said. "Theodore is a good solider; you trusted him with something precious, and I am confident that he will take that seriously and get your daughter back to her aunt."

"You remember what they did to Blade?" Squirt squeaked slightly. "They tortured him for nearly six months, Mouth. He told me some of the things they did. Are they going to do that to us? They hung Yang – they killed him without any trial."

Mouth squeezed Squirt in his arms; he could not be certain what was going to happen to them, and it mortified him that his younger brother was there with him. The men left them alone for nearly half an hour before the iron doors opened. Two recognizable Spaniards entered with a group of armed men behind them. The first smiled at them. He looked directly at Mouth and Squirt and said, "I believe I've already met you two when you helped to swipe Harold and the other Caldara's three years ago." The man's eyes went from Mouth and Squirt over towards where Kyo and Ron were standing. "We have not had the pleasure of meeting just yet. I am Antonio Manrique. This here is my brother, Juan. You two do not know me, but I know you. Commodore Kyo Mori, and I believe, if I am not mistaken, we have the blacksmith for the rebellion, Ron Katch?"

Ron instinctively took a nervous step back when the man spoke his name. Juan laughed. "We know more than you all think, sí?"

"John Stevenson knows a good bit about us," Mouth said. "You don't know a damn thing. Where's John? Is His Majesty too busy to pay a visit to old friends?"

"Don't worry. I am sure John will pay his former pests a visit. For now, though, you three should worry about me," Antonio said and then began to observe each of them closely. He grinned and pointed right at Kyo. "Take that one."

Kyo took several steps back as the armed guards approached him. "Stay away from me," Kyo warned, but the men took hold of him.

"Leave him alone!" Ron snarled and reached towards the men, but he was struck down by the man called Juan. Ron leaped back up, and he managed to deliver a blow against Antonio's jaw.

Antonio roared and knocked Ron back. "Forget the Asian. Grab this man instead." The men threw Kyo to the ground and took hold of Ron.

Mouth and Squirt were pushed towards the back wall as Ron was dragged out of the cell.

"What are you going to do?" Mouth cried out as Ron disappeared from sight.

Antonio looked back over his shoulder as he was leaving. "I believe you should just worry about yourself for now."

The door shut. They could hear the men shuffling with Ron outside. They heard another iron door open, and soon they realized Ron was being dragged into the cell next to theirs. A few minutes passed, and soon they heard their companion screaming. "Leave him alone!" Squirt roared and broke away from his brother. He ran to the side wall and began to bang against the brick. "Ron! Fight them, Ron! Let Ron go! Let him go!"

Mouth and Kyo stood by Squirt, listening to the horrified cries coming from their companion. Kyo placed his hand against the stone above his head and leaned forward, resting his head against the wall and exhaling loudly. He cussed under his breath. Mouth pulled Squirt back and put his hands on his brother's shoulders, looking him in the eye. "Don't listen to it," he whispered. "Pretend it's not happening."

Ron's screaming grew louder. Looking back at the wall, Mouth could see up above Kyo's head a hole – a large chip in the stone wall likely from part of a broken brick being pushed out. He realized there was a reason the men chose these two cells. They wanted them to be able to hear Ron's cries, and it angered Mouth to no end. Suddenly there was silence followed by the shuffling of feet as men left Ron's cell. Their own cell door opened, and Antonio stood in the doorway smiling at them all. He was wiping his bloody hands on a cloth. "Did you three hear all of that? I just want to make my point clear now. We have some questions for you all, and you are going to tell us what we want to know, or what you just heard is going to continue. Your friend passed out, but he's alive. He'll stay that way for now. We want to know how Captain Smith got back into Kirkston – he was spotted during the last battle. We want to know why he left in the first place and what he was doing out of the country. We want to know if Harold has managed to send a request for aid. We want to know what cities Harold is getting his new recruits from. We want to know about battle strategies. Who's in charge at the camp – rankings, the whole lot. Where do you get your supplies? You are going to tell me this and so much more, or you will regret it. I promise you that. It's time we finish this war, and you four are going to help me."

"Go to hell!" Mouth said, and Antonio simply laughed at him.

"Sleep well," Antonio said. "Because tomorrow will be a long day for you all."

***

"Honestly!" John huffed when Antonio continued to hold firm to his rebuttal. "I am in charge, Antonio, or have you forgotten?"

"You are only in charge so long as your plans align with that of Cruz's, and this nonsense you are sputtering my way shows me just how off you," Antonio said, his brother Juan lingering nearby.

They were standing in the war room, and their discussion was getting rather heated. John banged his fists down on the table. "I am only suggesting a tax deduction on people living in the poorer districts. You have raised taxes higher than even King Rylan had ever dared to do, and the people are starving."

"I have raised taxes because we are at war, and we need the funding, or have you forgotten that, John?"

"And, what of rebuilding Kevin's Isle?" John questioned. "Why is that out of line with Cruz's plan?"

"It's a waste of time, energy, and money, John," Antonio explained. "And, you know Cruz has reservations for that place."

"And, removing soldiers from cities that have already complied with our demands?" John asked.

"Until this war is over, the soldiers will remain in their stations to remind the people who's in charge," Antonio declared.

"Your soldiers are murdering people in the streets!" John snarled.

"Only people who are guilty of –"

"No trial – just a bunch of trigger happy lunatics!" John shouted.

"Since when do *you* require a trial for a conviction?" Antonio asked and laughed again.

"You act like I'm not in charge here at all, Antonio!" John snarled.

"Because you're not," a soft yet alarming voice echoed behind them as an old man dressed in Spanish attire entered, walking arm in arm with a nervous looking Maria.

John, Antonio, and Juan all bowed their heads as the man entered. Señor Cruz had just arrived in Kirkston after spending several years in Spain waiting for Antonio to send word that the Caldara's had been wiped out. The man had lost his patience. "Papa, you put John in charge during your absence, yet Antonio and Juan continue to –"

Cruz's head jolted to the side so as to look at his daughter, and his eyes narrowed. She immediately fell silent. He slowly turned his wrinkled old head back to the three men present. "My daughter is right, Antonio. I did put John in charge, but I sent you two to keep Stevenson in check, and you've done that. Yet, Harold and his heir are still running loose in Kirkston killing off my soldiers. You three have proven to be completely incompetent. We must exhaust all options. And, now I hear that you have a handful of captive soldiers in the cells, yes?"

"Yes, Señor Cruz," Antonio said. "The rebellions blacksmith, Ron Katch; Commodore Kyo Mori; and two brothers that are part of the Black Dragons."

"Which Black Dragons are they?" Juan asked.

"The ones who go by Mouth and Squirt," John said.

"Mouth and Squirt," Antonio said with a grin. "John, I think you know exactly what we need to do to get that Mouth fellow to talk."

"Don't," John warned.

"Now, John," Cruz taunted. "I did say to exhaust all options, didn't I?"

"Not that," John said. "Give us time to break them."

"John —"

"Please," John said somewhat breathlessly.

Cruz waved John off, letting out a slight laugh as he did so. "You do not even like the Black Dragon's, John. You think just because —"

"He's a child!" John snapped.

Cruz ignored John's outburst. He looked at Maria and said simply, "leave." Maria gave John a pitiful look before departing the room. Cruz turned his attention back on John. "You know that I am not a patient man, John. I do not care that you're married to my daughter. I do not care that you are the father of my grandchildren. You are expendable. Remember that. From now on, John, we do things my way."

Chapter 23

Smith sat with Ace by the fire; Pierson was attempting to learn the names of his many relatives. With them was Kathleen, Richard, Isabella and her son Jackie, Cassidy, Queen Rachel, and Ace's cousin Dave. Since Smith had arrived back at camp, he had not spent much time with Pierson. Pierson had been spending all of his free time with Ace, and this was truly the first time the child had spoken much with the other Caldara's. He had been incredibly occupied with getting to know his father.

"So," Pierson said as he swayed back and forth in front of the small group who were seated by the fire. "If my Papa is the king's son, does that make me a prince?"

Dave laughed. "I do not know if you could even count your Papa a prince," he said and elbowed Ace in the side.

Ace laughed too. "It is a very long story, Pierson. One that I am certain you will hear."

"I cannot believe how much he looks like you did at that age," Queen Rachel said and waved Pierson over so that she could give him a friendly pat on the shoulder and get a good look at his face.

King Harold came up behind Ace and placed his hands on his shoulders. "He's a handsome boy, son. And, yes, Pierson, you're a prince. Ignore Dave."

Smith watched them all curiously. He had never seen Ace interact with his family so leisurely. Smith could not help but to raise a brow when Ace laughed at his father and patted the man's hand before the king found a seat with them around the fire. Smith sat in silence, listening to them all talk and laugh with one another. Truthfully, Smith was glad. Ace had left the Caldara's when he had been a boy – saying he could not bear the thought of becoming king or being a part of a family who ruled so harshly. Smith knew that John had played a role in Ace's retreat, and he wondered now just how much John had manipulated Ace into leaving. It seemed that Ace had come to terms with it during Smith's absence.

He glanced up and could see Snake and his mother at a safe distance away. The two of them were taking a stroll, and they both had wide smiles on their faces – though they both did everything in their power to not look towards the Caldara's. Snake had told Smith that the woman was completely silent about whatever went on between her and the Caldara's – but clearly there was a lot of hate between them. Smith's gaze went back and forth between Amy, the woman he had once known as *Agatha*, and King Harold. After a moment of doing this, the king noticed, and he was not afraid to address Smith from across the fire in front of everyone. "Do not ask questions you do not want to know the answers to," he said angrily, and Smith dropped his gaze. Harold then cleared his throat and held up a letter. "We have another note that has been recovered from the tree east of Caldara Castle. A note from the Red Dragon."

"He is still sending you all letters?" Smith asked; he had not even thought to ask about the Red Dragon. Two years had change so much. He assumed a spy within the walls would have been caught by John by now.

"He is," Harold said. "Really, he's probably the only reason we've lasted this long, but the letters are less frequent now. It's gotten too dangerous for him."

"What does it say?" Smith asked.

"That the man known as Señor Cruz has arrived. The Red Dragon tells us to be watchful and to behave as though we are paranoid because Cruz will usher in a new wave of cruelty – that even John would not dream of doing the evils Cruz is capable of. I can't say that the letter didn't stir me."

"Have you learned anything about La Cofradía since I've been gone?" Smith asked.

"A little," Ace answered for his father. "They were a militarized group – a gang family –who played a role during the War of Spanish Succession. They were just another group who tried to take over Spain after the House of Habsburg's royal line fell. Thing was, Cruz had zero claim to the throne of Spain. He was just a man with money and men who tried to take over when everything went to hell. He claimed to be a descendant of King Ferdinand, but it was never proven. As you can imagine, he was chased out of town, and he went into hiding for many years. He's just a greedy brute who wants power. He's a wanted man in Spain, so to get power he had to eventually leave his home country. But, the man has followers. Lots of them. Taking over a small country like Kirkston has clearly proven possible with the amount of man power he has. But as to why he has targeted Kirkston we are still uncertain."

"How in the world did John Stevenson get involved? How did he even meet Maria?" Smith questioned. "When we first saw her, I thought she was just his housemaid. Then we found out she was his wife and mother of his child – now children."

"We're not sure how John got involved, but Cruz put John on the throne because he's a familiar face to the Kirkston people. He figured it would prompt less of an outcry than if a stranger from another land came in calling himself king," Harold explained. "According to the Red Dragon, Cruz has been in his hideout in Spain waiting for John to execute the royal line, but he's lost patience now. I'm not sure what we're going to be up against now."

"Help!" a loud cry rang out from behind Smith. The Caldara's all instinctively turned, and Smith could see a man bolting into camp with what appeared to be a young girl in his arms.

When Smith saw who the man was, he jumped up frantically. It was Theodore, the soldier who had gone with Mouth and Squirt to visit the abandoned miner's village. The man had Saki Mori in his arms, and the girl was sobbing. Smith ran to meet them; Chi and Stewart beat him there, and Chi helped Theodore to put Saki down, and she hugged her young niece. "Where's Kyo? Where's my brother?" Chi demanded.

Theodore's face was pale. He started to speak, but his legs wobbled. Smith grabbed hold of the man to keep him standing. "He's been shot," Smith said.

"Where's Kyo?" Chi demanded.

"Stewart," Smith said. "Take Chi and Saki away for a moment so I can get this man some help."

Stewart put his arm around the distraught woman and gently led her and Saki away. Smith helped Theodore waddle in the opposite direction as Dr. Conal ran to meet them from across camp. The man looked like a ghost; Smith imagined that he had lost a lot of blood. When Dr. Conal reached them, the doctors eyes widened slightly at the man's appearance. "Sit down!" he snapped at Theodore, and Smith helped him down. Dr. Conal examined the man's back where he had been shot. He then sat up and leaned forward to look the man in the eye. "When were you shot?"

Theodore's voice was hoarse. "Two… two days ago, I think… I had to… I had to get the girl back home… back home to her aunt…"

Theodore started to slump; it was as though the life had suddenly left him now that his mission to bring the young girl to safety was complete. Smith grabbed hold of the man to keep him from falling over onto his back. "The others?" Smith asked.

"Spanish soldiers got them," he said. "Saki hasn't eaten in two days. She hasn't had… had any water…"

"She's fine now, Theodore," Smith said. "You did good. You saved her. She's safe now." The man nodded and smiled, and he died almost instantly after.

Dr. Conal shook his head. "He lost so much blood. That man must have run for two days straight carrying that girl until he bled out. By the look on his face, he should have been dead hours ago."

"His mission kept him going," Smith said and shook his head. "A good man, and I barely knew him." Smith had not known Theodore personally, but he now respected the man very deeply. Looking up, he could see Abigail and Theresa standing together with their sons at their sides; they both looked ghostly. Smith looked to Dr. Conal to take care of Theodore's body, and the man nodded to let Smith know he would handle things. Smith rose and went to Abigail and Theresa. He did not need to say anything; they had known Theodore had left with their husbands.

"If John lays a hand on my husband or brother-in-law, I will slaughter him," Abigail said, her voice quivering. Jake gripped his mother's hand.

Theresa let loose a loud sob and fell into Smith; he put his arms around her and held his oldest friend for a moment. "I have to go tell Gwen," he said, his heart breaking slightly at the thought of telling that young girl that Squirt had been taken. He doubted they would be able to perform a rescue; the number of soldiers posted around Caldara Castle had only increased in the past two years. He knew the only hope his friends had now lay in the hands of El Dragón Rojo, and Smith was unsure whether or not the stranger helping them would be able to take such a risk.

***

Mouth had not moved from his seat in several hours. He was leaned back against the far wall, his eyes fixated on the iron door. His left arm was broken – he was certain – after receiving his first beating from the soldiers. The men had snapped his elbow. They had been at Caldara for three days; for three day's they had sat and listened to Ron being torture on the other side of the wall, and it had started to drive him mad – especially since Ron never responded to anything they said to him. Then, only a few hours ago – after breaking his arm – the men had taken Squirt. His brother's desperate plea, "Tommy, don't let them take me!" kept ringing in his ear over and over again. He had not been able to do a thing.

"Here," he heard Kyo say; the man was trying to give him some of the stale bread they had at last been given. "Mouth, you have to eat."

Mouth slapped the bread out of Kyo's hand. "I'm not hungry," he said.

Kyo grabbed him by the collar of his shirt as he sat beside him, forcing Mouth to look away from the door. "You haven't eaten in three days. Eat the bread."

"You don't even know me, Commodore," Mouth hissed.

"I know that you and I are in this together," Kyo said. "And, I know you must be as hungry as I am. I know you're in pain – and not just because of your arm. I saw that look in your eye when they took him away. I don't know what they're doing to him, but you can't think about it. That's what they want. They are trying to drive us mad, don't you see? It's why they have us listening to them hurt Ron over and over again. It's why they separated you from your brother. Don't let them win, Mouth. Now, eat, and let me look at your arm."

Mouth ate the bread while Kyo rolled up Mouth's left sleeve. He kept replaying the moment Squirt was taken in his mind. When Squirt had realized the men had come for him, he had gripped onto Mouth. The men had had to peel Squirt's fingers from Mouth's shirt. Squirt's grip had been so tight that it had ripped the hem of Mouth's shirt when they had pulled him back.

Kyo removed his own vest and began to rip it up. He created for Mouth a sort of sling to keep his broken arm still. "They might just wind up ripping the sling off you," Kyo said as he gently placed Mouth's arm into the makeshift sling. "But, for now, it will keep you from moving your arm too much."

"Thank you," Mouth said, though he hardly noticed the pain in his arm. There was still a horrid ringing in his ear that just wouldn't go away.

A loud moan was heard from the cell next to theirs. They both jumped up. "Ron!" Kyo called out. "Mate, are you all right?"

"Ah…." was Ron's reply.

"Ron, please," Mouth said, speaking to the wall. "Say something, mate."

"Ah…." was all they heard from him.

Mouth pressed his forehead against the wall. "Ron, please. Just say something to let me know you're all right."

"Ah…."

Mouth had gotten closer to Ron in recent years. Apart from Smith, the other Black Dragons had never been exceptionally close to the Katch's. They were Smith's old friends from before his Black Dragon days, so apart from that Ron was just their blacksmith. After losing his son, though, Mouth had become close to Ron's young boy, Pete. Because of that, he and Abigail had become better friends to the Katch's than some of the others were, but truthfully Mouth was much more concerned with what Smith would endure if he lost Ron – one of the few things his captain had left of his life from before.

Suddenly the iron door screeched open. Mouth jolted, turning towards the door – hoping that Squirt was being returned mostly unharmed. Instead of his brother, an old Spaniard entered with Antonio, Juan, John, and three soldiers. It was the first time Mouth had seen John since they had arrived at Caldara Castle. He gritted his teeth. "Where's my brother, John?" Mouth hissed.

"You are the one they call *Mouth*, sí?" the old man asked.

"Who are you?" Kyo asked and place a hand on Mouth's shoulder, coaxing him to relax a bit so as not to prompt a beating.

"I am Señor Cruz," he said.

"So, you're John's little puppet master, right?" Mouth spat, and he noted that John, Juan, and Antonio all cringed slightly.

Cruz raised a brow. "And, how is it you know of me, Mouth?"

Mouth laughed. "You have a spy. I'm guessing your little foot soldiers" – Mouth waved his good arm towards John, Juan, and Antonio – "did not tell you about that?"

Cruz grinned at Mouth slightly. "No, they did not. How informative of you." Without a second's hesitation, Cruz gripped his pistol at his side, turned, and shot Juan in the foot. Juan screamed and hoppled over. John and Antonio both flinched as though they expected similar punishments, but they did not run or move from their stances. Cruz returned his gun to his side and pointed at one of the soldiers. "Take Juan out of here. I do not care to listen to him bellowing when I am trying to have a conversation."

One of the soldiers helped Juan to leave. Mouth felt slightly woozy after witnessing Cruz fire on one of his top men so willingly. "Señor Cruz –" Antonio spoke, and the man held up his hand to let Antonio know that this would be a conversation to be had later.

"We'll track down the spy. What other sort of information did this little spy give you?" Cruz asked. Mouth remained silent, but the thought that Squirt was off somewhere being held captive, likely as leverage against him, made him quite hesitant to keep his mouth shut.

"Listen," Antonio hissed in Mouth's direction. "If you two do not give us something worthwhile, we'll send you both to hang. That or we'll keep torturing your friend over there. Or, we'll kill the boy we took."

Mouth cringed, and Cruz laughed. "Antonio, we cannot use... what do they call him... *Squirt* as leverage against his brother."

"And why not?" Antonio asked.

"Because I have already killed him."

Chapter 24

Mouth felt as though all the air had been pulled out of his lungs. He gasped, seemingly choking on air to regain a breath. "You're lying," he managed to say in the midst of hyperventilating.

"I am not," Cruz said. "And, do not try to fool yourself into thinking I did it quickly. He called out for you many times before it was through."

Mouth wanted to lunge at the man – to strike him down where he stood, but he could not move. An intense throbbing started in the forefront of his head. His mouth became dry. If Kyo did not have a hold of his right arm, Mouth was certain he would topple over. "You must be lying," Kyo said. "What good would killing that boy do you?"

"It shows you how serious I am," Cruz said. "I'm going to leave you alone for now – let this all sink in with you. If you think, Mouth, that this is the worst I can do to you, you are wrong. This is only a warning."

Cruz turned, and his company turned with him to leave. Mouth found a slight burst of energy – one fueled by anger – and he lunged. He went for Cruz, but John stopped him. Mouth was willing to kill any of these men now, and he already had a vendetta against John. Mouth, despite his broken arm, quickly overcame the crippled man. The two of them toppled over, and Mouth leaped on top of him, grabbing John by the throat; he squeezed. Kyo certainly wasn't going to stop him, and at first it seemed that Cruz or the others did not appear fazed by what Mouth was doing either. John squirmed and scratched at Mouth's arms; Mouth felt a horrendous pain when John's fist hit him against his break, but he ignored it. Mouth could see fear on John's face as he struggled to peel Mouth's fingers away from his throat with no success. He could feel John's grip becoming weaker, and Mouth knew that John was nearly finished when John's cane collided with the side of his head; Cruz had casually picked up John's fallen cane and took a serious swing.

Mouth fell to his side, and John rolled away from him, taking in a loud, painful sounding gasp followed by several coughs, gags, and eerie wheezes. Antonio laughed slightly as Cruz tossed John's cane down to him. Mouth glanced up from where he lay on the ground to see Antonio yank John up onto his feet like a rag doll. John gripped his cane with one hand and rubbed his throat with the other, still desperately trying to catch his breath.

Cruz looked at Mouth with a menacing eye. "Remember, Mouth, I can do so much worse to you than this. I meant it when I said that." Cruz reached into his shirt and tossed down a blood splattered bandana. "Your brothers," he said as he departed, and John and the others followed.

Mouth remained lying on the ground. He did not want to believe that his brother was dead; he cried at the thought. He screamed and cursed until he was tired and had to lay down on the cold stone floor. Kyo sat near him, unable to find any words of comfort worth sharing.

***

"I do not know if he will be of much help," Harold said as Smith finished writing the letter to the Red Dragon.

"He helped Blade escape," Smith said. "If Mouth and the others are still alive, then maybe he would be able to do the same. I am going to put this in the tree."

"It will take you a few days to get there, and you do so at much risk to yourself," Harold said. "We had two soldiers murdered once while attempting to fetch one of the man's letters. They were killed outside of Caldara City. It's terribly close to the castle, Smith, and you are quite recognizable. John and Cruz have the capital city so scared that even formerly loyal men will turn you in if you are spotted."

"I know," Smith said. "Kyo has been loyal to this cause. It was his idea that got your armies going. Ron is one of my oldest and dearest friends. Mouth, he is family, and Squirt, him too, and he is just a boy. It's not right. If the Red Dragon can help them escape the way he did for Blade, I am not afraid to ask it of him."

There was a soft shouting coming from just outside of the war tent where Harold and Smith had gathered to create a letter for the Red Dragon together. It was Blade and Hannah arguing quietly about something. "Is that the norm now?" Smith asked, for he had only been back in Kirkston for a little over a month now, and this was the third time he had overheard Blade and Hannah spatting about something.

"Not really," Harold said. "It is only recent the way those two have been at each other's throats. I think the Cook girl wants a proposal, and your crewmate is not giving it to her."

Smith shook his head. "What a shame it is you are more knowledgeable of the gossip surrounding my friends than I."

"I have been there for them for the past two years. You have not," Harold said and then immediately appeared to bite his tongue. "That came out much harsher than it was meant to be."

"It was deserved," Smith said. "Though I have been back for over a month now. I do hope everyone drops the grudge sooner than later. I intend to do everything in my power to make this right. I hope you all know this." Smith started to leave, but Harold grabbed him by his arm.

"Do you count me as a friend now, Smith?" Harold asked.

Smith turned back to face the king. It was an odd question – one he never thought he would get from Harold. Smith nodded. "Aye, Sire, I do, though I never thought it would be so. You have earned my respect, and I do hope I can earn yours. When this mess is over, if it is ever over, I do hope I have earned enough of your respect that you could entrust me with something."

"And, what is that?" Harold asked.

"A job, Sire. Working for you in some manner, though I am not certain what. I feel that my life's mission as a Black Dragon is a rather moot point now. I want to help this country in any way that I can – now during the war and in the future when this is finally over. I am not content with twiddling my thumbs when a problem arises amongst my people."

"It sounds like you are asking me to be an advisor," Harold said. "An awfully powerful position for a former rogue."

"I will not ask it of you now. Not until I have proven to you that I am capable of something so important. I love this country. I love the people in it. Perhaps my perspective, Harold, is something your court could use."

"I will consider it," Harold said. "But, I must ask something of you, if you truly count me as a friend."

"Of course."

"I know my daughter fancies you," Harold said. "And, I know she is a strong woman who will do as she pleases. I ask that you keep her honest. Do not tempt one another. I am not asking you to stay away from her, only that you do not –"

"I know what you are asking me," Smith said. "And, I swear to you that this is nothing you should be worried about. I have too much respect for her to behave in such a way. And, even if I did not, I know she respects herself too much to sully her reputation. You have my word."

Harold nodded approvingly as Smith departed the tent. As Smith exited, he saw the Black Dragons, those who remained with them at camp, gathered around a fire. Ace waved him over. "What's all this?" Smith asked as a small glass of liquor was placed in his hands. Though they had all been incredibly distraught and melancholic since Mouth and the others had been taken by John's men, they seemed to be having a small celebration over something.

Yin had pulled out his personal stash of liquor to pour each of his friends a small swig; Smith had not been home too long, but he certainly knew that alcohol was not a common luxury and was something that was definitely not shared around camp. Yin smiled at Smith. "I know we are all mourning right now," he said. "But, I do have something we can drink to, if only for a moment. My wife is pregnant, and I want us to drink to that."

As the others threw back their glasses and offered congratulations to Yin, Smith nearly choked on his drink for he had started to sip before the toast. "Wife?" Smith asked and looked across the firepit at Clara who was smiling happily.

Yin looked Smith's way. "Mate, you've been back for over a month, and you did not know that Clara and I married while you were gone? We have been married for nearly a year. Harold married us."

Smith frowned. There was much he did not know, and it truly sickened him. Jackson had told Smith that they were together, but he had not realized that Jackson had meant that they had married during his absence. "I am happy for you both," Smith said and finished his drink. He immediately walked away as though he felt he should not be part of the small celebratory conversing taking place. Besides, he had a letter to deliver.

***

Mouth was curled up on the ground, his back against the wall. He hadn't slept at all through the night. Kyo was watching him from a few feet away, sitting up on the ground with a saddened expression. "Mouth, talk to me," Kyo said, but Mouth was silent. "We will get through this. Do not let this break you, Mouth. We will have Cruz's head. You will see."

"What do you think we can do?" Mouth snarled and then sat up. A few tears escaped him. "They killed him, Kyo. My brother. I have taken care of that boy his entire life. He was my boy. My child. I want to die. I hope they kill me next." Mouth gripped the blood splattered bandana that Cruz had tossed him the day before; he had known it was true, that his brother was dead, when he had seen his bandana hit the ground beside him.

"The winds may fall the massive oak, but bamboo, bent even to the ground, will spring upright after the passage of a storm," Kyo said.

"What nonsense are you spouting my way?"

Kyo sat in front of Mouth, his legs crossed, and looked at him with almost as much sorrow as Mouth was wearing. "It is an expression that my grandparents used to say to me when I was a boy. It means that even if we feel weak or small or if someone is underestimating us, that we can still spring back up like the bamboo stick. That sometimes even weak or small people can be stronger than those who appear mighty like the oak. This is perhaps the most difficult thing that has ever happened to you, but you will get through this. We will get through this. We cannot let John and Cruz get to us. You have a wife back home at camp. Your stepson too. We must stay strong, Mouth – like the bamboo stick."

"I don't know what the devil a bamboo stick is."

Kyo shook his head. "You still get the point of what I am saying, though, yes?"

"I do," Mouth said, and he thought of Abigail and of Jake. He could not simply fall over and die no matter how much of a relief that would be.

Chapter 25

Smith re-entered camp after having delivered a letter to the hole in the tree east of Caldara Castle that they had been using to communicate with the Red Dragon. He had been gone for several days without incident, and not much had happened at camp since his departure. He returned his horse to the soldier and group of women in charge of keeping up with the steeds, and he was shortly afterwards met by Snake.

Snake clasped his hand on Smith's shoulder and led him away from the horses. "I think you and I need to speak."

"On what?" Smith asked, but he smiled slightly at his friend.

"The way you were after Yin's little announcement the other day," Snake said.

"I had to leave because I had to deliver that letter. You know that," Smith replied.

"You're acting distant with all of us because you feel guilty about leaving," Snake said. "Everyone is flustered over it, yes, but we don't hate you, mate. You were gone for two years. A lot changes in two years. But, it's done. You have to forgive yourself. I forgive you. If you had not left, mate, I never would have known my mother was alive."

"I suppose there is that," Smith said.

"My mother told me about you two," Snake said, and Smith instinctively flinched as though expecting a punch. Snake shook his head and almost laughed at Smith's discomfort. "You did not know who she was. She certainly stressed that to me. I do not think I can be angry at you for taking care of her. But, mate, did you really propose to my mother?"

"You're really not upset with me?" Smith asked.

"I was at first, but I'm not now. I can't be. Smart woman – waited until you left camp to tell me about your... affair...it gave me a few days to cool off before you got back here."

Before Smith could respond, he spotted Blade and Hannah bickering a short distance away. "What is wrong with those two?" Smith asked.

"I don't know. They've been at each other's throats for the past few weeks," Snake said.

"I'm going to go talk to Blade," Smith said.

"That would probably be good. He respects you," Snake said. "Not many would take the sort of abuse he did from Stevenson's men. You do realize Blade did that for you, right?"

"For *me*?"

"For his captain. For his captain's crew. Blade, I dare say even more than me, is entirely loyal to the Black Dragons. To you. He'd do it again." Snake sighed and ran his fingers through his hair, glancing back in Blade and Hannah's direction for a moment. "I think he's starting to torment Hannah. She has been expecting him to speak to Maxi about marrying her ever since Knot married her younger sister, but he has been extremely harsh towards her lately – he loves her, but he has delusion-ed himself into thinking the Black Dragons are still going to be pirating once this is over."

"He can't honestly believe that?" Smith questioned. "With Harold knowing our hideout location and us working with him in such a way, he couldn't possibly think that, could he?"

"I believe he does."

Smith shook his head. "I'm going to go talk to him about Hannah." Snake nodded and departed, allowing Smith to wave Blade down so that they could chat in private.

Blade smile slightly, seemingly eager to get away from Hannah for the time being. "Do you need something, Smith?" Blade asked cheerily.

"A lot has changed since my departure," Smith said. "But there is one thing that is particularly troubling to me."

"And, what is that?"

"You and Hannah," Smith stated. "Though Snake tells me your bickering is only a recent turn of events. What has gotten into you, mate? When I left, you were mad for that girl, and now every time I turn around I am hearing you two whispering harshly to one another. Why don't you just talk to Maxi and ask if you could marry her? I know you want to."

Blade shifted uncomfortably for a moment. "I'm not like Knot," Blade said. "I'm a Black Dragon. I am not ready to leave that behind."

"That was what I was afraid of. Blade, you do not seriously believe that we will continue in the way that we were before all of this, do you?" Smith questioned. "I have been talking to Harold about becoming a staff member in his court. Do you honestly believe that, after everything, we will still be children running around on a ship? Still go pirating in Kirkston waters? Harold is writing us all pardons. He is agreeing to work with us to change Kirkston for the better – that was always the mission, and now we have the king on our side. The mission is still the same, mate, but we are not."

"I spent six months – *six months* – being tortured for this cause! Do you really think I'm that delusional, Smith?" Blade asked, his voice tingling with a hint of rage.

Now, Smith become uncomfortable. He hated being reminded of Blade's torment. "Yes, I am aware, Terrance."

"Stop blaming yourself," Blade said, immediately catching onto what made Smith stir. "I am alive. I have nightmares about it sometimes. Dr. Conal calls them night terrors. Hannah came running into my tent to wake me once during a fit, and I busted her lip. I hate it, but it has gotten better recently. I'd hate to put Hannah through that. I feel like our crew has already put enough harm on the Cook home. Hannah deserves better than me – better than someone who's going to wind up breaking her arm over a nightmare all because she shares a bed with him!"

"I did not know you were dealing with that, mate. I am sorry. Truly sorry, but there is something else, I can tell," Smith said. "What are you holding back from me, Blade?"

"I know it's over – the Black Dragons, I mean. I suppose I am just having a hard time letting go. The war is still going on, and, well –"

Smith interrupted, "Ah. I see. Like Ace, you fear making your woman a widow? Why not tell her that? Offer to marry her after the war as Ace has promised Cassidy? Set the poor girl's heart at ease."

"That's not it," Blade said, and he looked away in a manner that suggested he felt shame.

"Soldiers!" came a call came from a short distance away. One of their scouts came burling into camp. He had spotted some of John's men approaching.

Smith looked at Blade. "We will talk about this another time." Blade nodded, seeming a bit relieved the conversation had ended. After speaking to the scout and hearing about the strong number of men headed in their direction, Smith and Harold agreed the best course of action was to retreat into the mountains and relocate camp. The rebellions numbers had grown, but they were still cautious when confronting larger groupings of John's soldiers. They needed to live to fight another day.

***

Mouth walked slowly beside Antonio, his wrists chained together. Antonio had come to fetch Mouth with two other men who now walked behind them as they headed down the hall. Mouth's shoulders slumped. He was prepared for torture. Frankly, he hoped John's men killed him – the loss of his brother weighed him down in such a way he was not sure if he could ever bounce back.

"Where are you taking me?" Mouth asked.

"Have you seen the Queen's Garden, as it is called?" Antonio asked. "It's beautiful. Generations of queens have, with the help of servants, tended the garden. Queen Rachel's contribution was a lovely collection of vines. Her Majesty, Queen Maria, has added carnations and a number of other plants from her home country."

"Why are you telling me this?"

"Because we are going to the garden, and you asked where we were taking you," Antonio said and clasped his hand on Mouth's shoulder. "I think perhaps you could use some fresh air. Cruz killing your little brother was cruel. Is it so hard to believe that I would reach out and attempt to be kind?"

"Yes," Mouth said plainly.

"Smart man," Antonio said and laughed.

They entered into the garden that aligned the northern walls of Caldara Castle. Mouth was somewhat impressed with the scenery, but it did nothing to relieve his nerves. There was a small set of marble chairs near the entryway; Antonio pointed and instructed Mouth to sit. "Listen to me, dragon," Antonio said. "I am going to tell you this once and once only – we are going to show you something, but I want you to remain quiet. If you shout, if you scream –someone will die today. It will be someone you care about." Mouth cringed slightly. The firmness in Antonio's voice assured Mouth that it was no empty threat. "Do you understand me?" Mouth was too frightened to respond verbally. He nodded. Antonio smiled. "Very good. Now, just wait."

Mouth sat in silence, his chained wrists dangling between his knees. Antonio spoke to his men, the three laughing quietly about something he had said in Spanish. Several minutes passed, and soon he heard John's voice. Antonio tapped Mouth's shoulder and pointed into the garden. Mouth looked up; he spotted John walking rapidly, leaning on his cane as he did so. The man did not seem to notice their presence. John had on a smile that made Mouth a bit uncomfortable. "Robbie! Stop running from me!" John shouted.

Mouth heard other voices – young children laughing. After another moment, he spotted John's young son, Robbie, and another young boy chasing each other around in the garden. "Uncle John!" the other boy called out. "Come play!"

Mouth stirred. He sat upright and gazed across the garden as the young boy playing with Robbie came into full view amongst the rose bushes. Confusion, relief, anger, love, heartbreak, and joy all muddled together within Mouth's heart. It was impossible, and yet there he was. Mouth's voice cracked when he questioned out loud, "Ian?"

Chapter 26

Mouth was forced into a chair across from John within the dining hall. A plate of food was placed in front of him. Two guards stood by the entrance to the hall. They were both quiet, and all that was heard in the room was the occasional clinking of John's silverware as he ate. Mouth felt as though he could not breathe. The array of emotions he was being pulled through was too much for one man to handle.

John glanced up at him after cutting another piece of his steak and plopping it into his mouth. With food still in his mouth, he pointed towards Mouth's plate with his knife and said, "It's better than that stale bread they've been giving you. You ought to try it."

Mouth grabbed the plate and flipped it, sending the mix of vegetables and meat flying across the table and shattering the two plates as they clinked against one another. The two guards were on Mouth in an instance, grabbing hold of him and near ready to beat him. "Easy," John hissed at the men. "Just clean this mess up and leave. I need to speak to him privately."

"Are you certain that is a good idea?" one of the guards asked.

"Clean up the mess and leave," John hissed. "His wrists are chained, his arm is broken, I've got a gun and a sword at my side, and he'd have to fly across this table to get at me faster than I can draw a gun and shoot. I will be fine. Now, go."

The men did as they were told – cleaning up the mess Mouth had made before departing, leaving Mouth alone with John in the dining hall. John picked up his napkin and wiped his face before speaking. "I did not know Antonio was bringing you to the garden. He has a terrible habit of leaving me out of decisions."

"How?" Mouth asked as he tried to keep tears from falling. "I don't understand how this has happened. My son's alive. Have you had him this entire time, John? What have you done to him? I swear, if you've hurt him –"

"He calls me his uncle," John said, and Mouth banged his fist down on the table.

"Don't you be an ass right now!" Mouth screamed and tears started to flow freely down his cheeks. "Don't you toy with me. Not now. Not about this. That was my son. I saw him. That was Ian. How? Just tell me how!"

John nodded and leaned back in his chair. "I thought he was dead too after we got word about the search party finding some clothing of his in the river. Honestly, Mouth, it devastated me – Maria too. Maria blamed herself."

"Good," Mouth snarled. "I hope it kept her up at night!"

John looked annoyed, but he did not address Mouth's taunt. He continued. "It was about a year before the war started. We were doing some recruiting in Balla. That's when I saw the boy, your boy, running around the docks. I knew it was him because, well, he looked just like you. I shouted out, 'Ian!' and he turned around and looked at me. A man was with him, a man named Luke. Apparently, this man, Luke, he was a fisherman visiting Kirkston at the time we all thought your boy had perished. The river pulled Ian onto the northern beaches of Kevin's Isle, and Luke spotted him as the river spit him out into the ocean. He told me he dove over the side of his fishing vessel to save him. He somehow missed the search party, and when he was unable to locate the boy's parents, he took him with him to Balla. If it means anything to you, and I think it must mean something, the man appeared to have taken good care of the boy in the years he had had him."

"So, you just took him?" Mouth questioned.

"It was not hard to convince Luke to give him to me. I had known the boy's name without being introduced. Ian told Luke that he recognized me, but he was not sure who I was, and that also helped to convince the man I knew him. I told Luke that I was the boy's uncle and that I would return him to his parents. The man was sad to see him go, though. It took a good while to convince him to let me take him."

"You have had my son for four years!" Mouth shouted. "All this time my son has been alive, and you have been keeping him from me!"

John calmly leaned forward in his seat. "I took Ian from Luke with the intention of returning him to you if I was ever given the opportunity. We are not exactly friends, Mouth. I was certainly not going to reach out to you about it." John's face softened. "I have become rather attached to him. I did not want to do this, but you've forced my hand."

"Don't," Mouth pleaded, his anger replaced entirely by fear. "Don't hurt him, please. Please, John."

"It is out of my hands now," John said. "You will give us what we want, or Ian will die. And, this time, Mouth, he won't be coming back."

Mouth's body shook. "You kill my brother. Now, you threaten to kill my boy too? If ever I had any doubt that you were truly heartless, I have casted all of that aside now."

"You will give us what we need to help take down Harold and the rest of the rebellion," John said. "Strategies. Plans for attack. Defenses. Names. Locations of your weapons holds. Anything we ask for, or Ian will die. Or worse."

"Worse?"

"You know what they did to Blade. Do not believe that because he is a child that they will not allow him to endure the same torment and make you watch. You are going to help us bring down the rebellion and end this war, or you will watch your boy suffer."

Mouth began to sob. "How can you do this? You realize my wife and her son are at those camps? My friends – my family. You would have a man choose between his babe and nearly a thousand men, women, and children who are counting on him to stay strong? You're a monster, John. If I didn't think it before, I certainly do now."

"I don't want to do this," John said. "I won't have any part in it. I don't have the stomach for it, but Antonio and his men do – and, they will." John rose to his feet. He hobbled on his cane around the table until he was standing over the increasingly hysterical Mouth. John placed his hand on Mouth's shoulder. "I don't want to hurt Ian. I am asking you, Mouth, pleading with you, to just give in."

Mouth forced himself to look up at John. His voice was shaky, but he managed to get through with what he had to say. "I held your son once in my arms, John. I was going to kill him. I was so full of hate that I wanted you to suffer the way I did when I thought I had lost Ian. I could have done it. I'm glad I didn't. Even right now, John. I'm glad I didn't do it. I spared your son once, John. Spare mine."

John took a step back. He wore a somber expression that bothered Mouth. "You spared my son," John said. "I know this. And, I understand why you wanted vengeance. I'm a father... just like you. I can't say that I wouldn't have done the same, but you chose not to. I have not forgotten that, but I have come too far to give up now. I want to end this. Don't you?"

Mouth threw himself onto the floor at John's feet. "Do you want me to beg?" Mouth cried. "I will! John, please, I'm begging you, please, do not make me choose between my son and all of those people fighting for the rebellion. Please, don't do this!" Mouth grabbed hold of John's pants legs. "Please... please... John, please..."

John called for the guards. He placed his hand on Mouth's head. "They have given me until tomorrow to convince you to talk. I do not believe there is anything more I have to say to you. I'll have the guards return you to your cell. If you do not comply, if you do not agree to help us, your son will die tomorrow. Ask yourself if your rebellion is worth such a loss."

"Please, John, don't do this," Mouth pleaded as the guards appeared, hovering over him. John pushed Mouth off him; the men each gripped one of Mouth's arms and pulled him to his feet. A shooting pain erupted up his broken arm, but he ignored it to the best of his abilities. "Let me see him. I want to see my son, please."

"That's not going to happen, Mouth," John said and nodded at the guards. "Take him back to his cell. Let this moment fester with him."

"John, you're going to burn for this!" Mouth screamed as the men dragged him out of the room. "He's just a child, John! I could have killed your boy, John! I could have! Don't let them hurt, Ian, please! Don't let them hurt him!"

The men dragged Mouth across the castle, eventually throwing him into the cell he had been sharing with Kyo. Kyo jumped to his feet as Mouth landed flat on his back, and the guards closed the iron door. Mouth screamed and sobbed as Kyo made his way over to him. "What did they do, Mouth?" Kyo asked.

Mouth shook violently. "My son's alive. My son's alive, and they're going to kill him!"

***

Mouth sat on the ground, his back against the cell wall. It was the middle of the night, but he certainly was not going to be able to sleep with the haunting promise that his son, his child, was going to be tortured the next morning. Kyo was pacing, and it was starting to make Mouth a bit nervous. "You'll give in," Kyo said at last.

"I know," Mouth said, his voice raspy.

"I know I would if it was my daughter," Kyo said. "They'll hurt him, and you'll tell them anything they ask for."

"I know," Mouth said again. "The moment they took us, I was prepared to die. I was prepared to watch them torture my brother when they first grabbed us, but they killed him. It's war, so I had prepared myself for what I thought was the worst. It's what we signed up for, but this... I can't do it, Kyo."

Kyo stopped pacing. "My daughter is at that campsite, you know. My sister. Your wife. Your stepson. Your friends. King Harold – the royals. I don't know what information they will get from you, but what will you do if what you say results in the deaths of all of them?"

"I do not know," Mouth said. "But, it's Ian. Abigail would want me to save him if I could... even if it meant her dying. I won't be able to remain silent. I know I won't."

"I know. Which is why you need to be dead when they come to get you tomorrow," Kyo said.

"Excuse me?"

"What if I killed you?" Kyo asked, but he made no advancement towards him. In fact, the man would not make eye contact with Mouth. "If you're dead, you cannot talk. If you're dead, they have no reason to hurt your boy. I don't know him – no sense in trying to get me to talk by hurting the child. They will come tomorrow and see you dead and think I'm a heartless rogue who will kill a companion to keep his mission safe."

"What if they kill my boy anyways?" Mouth asked – completely unmoved by Kyo's suggestion.

"If they do, then that means they planned to kill him whether you talked or not. This way, your boy has a chance. I'm not really giving you a choice, though, Mouth. You realize that already though, don't you?" Kyo questioned.

"Do you see me running?" Mouth asked and looked up at Kyo. "If I give them what they need, your sister and daughter are dead. And, I *will* give them what they need, Kyo. It is probably a long shot, but perhaps that is the only way my son will be safe. Kill me. Do it."

"I'm sorry," Kyo said and lunged at Mouth before Mouth could resist. He gripped Mouth around the throat and squeezed, but Mouth did not move even after he began to choke and suffocate underneath Kyo's tight grasp.

The iron door opened, and a dark figure stood in the archway. "Stop!" the voice called out. "Señors, I am here to help! Release him! I am El Dragón Rojo!"

Kyo glanced up and upon seeing that the shadowy figure was alone, released Mouth. Mouth gasped for air. He coughed for a moment, desperately trying to catch his breath. When he could at least speak, he looked at the figure wearing the masquerade mask and a woman's mourning veil. "Why hide your face if you are a friend?" Mouth asked.

The figure took a step away from the entryway, ignoring Mouth's question. "Ron's cell is opened. Help him, and then go to the royal chambers. Your boy is there. Take the passageway to the stables. You must go quickly while John and Maria are in the war room. I will meet you in the stables." The figured dipped away, scurrying out of the prison chambers.

Kyo helped Mouth stand. "El Dragón Rojo is a woman," Kyo said.

"I agree," Mouth responded. "I could tell in her voice."

"But, Blade said he was certain El Dragón Rojo was a man," Kyo reminded him as the two of them slipped out of the cell, both eagerly pretending that Mouth had not almost voluntarily allowed himself to be strangled to death by Kyo.

"It seems we are dealing with more than one person. Perhaps there is an entire resistance within the walls of Caldara Castle?" Kyo suggested and hesitated before entering into Ron's chamber. They had listened to him scream for many nights, so they were not sure what they were about to come upon.

Mouth entered first, and he rushed to Ron who was lying flat on the cold, hard ground. Ron's legs had been sawn off and branded – the men had calloused the wound to prevent him from bleeding out. Mouth touched Ron's shoulders, and the man opened his eyes. "Ron, it's all right, we're going to get out of here," Mouth assured Ron as the man began to weep in his relief. Mouth looked up at Kyo. "You're going to have to carry him. I can't with my broken arm."

Kyo paused a moment before kneeling down beside Ron; he helped the man sit up. "God, help him!" Kyo cried.

"That's why you weren't speaking, eh, mate?" Kyo looked at Mouth. "Look at him. They cut out his tongue."

"Ron, I'm so sorry," Mouth said and fought back tears. "We don't have time to hesitate right now. Grab him, Kyo. We have to go – *now*."

"Easy, mate," Kyo said and wrapped his arms around Ron's waist. "I've got you."

They hurried through the castle hallways; the Red Dragon had timed their escape perfectly. Mouth had been to the castle enough times to lead them straight to the royal chambers, and they rushed inside. He looked around, and, as promised, he spotted Ian curled up on a couch with Robbie. Kyo sat Ron down on the bed in the room to rest his back for a moment. Ron's eyes drooped; the man seemed half dead.

Mouth knelt down beside the couch, and he took a moment to stare at the sleeping child that was his son. His hand shook as he reached out and gently touched his shoulder; he had not held his son in over five years, and he felt himself starting to tear up. Ian's little eyes blinked open, and he jolted back in surprise. Mouth frowned, knowing that Ian likely did not even recognize him. "Ian," Mouth said in a calm voice.

"Who are you?" Ian asked, his voice quivering slightly.

Robbie stirred beside him. The boy sat up, and when he saw Mouth he became incredibly frightened; Mouth could not blame Robbie. He had almost killed him once. "Madre!" Robbie screamed, and he grabbed Ian by his arm as though he intended to pull him away.

A door that led to an adjoining room flung open, and Maria stood in the doorway in her nightgown. The Red Dragon, it seemed, had been incorrect in his assumption that neither of the Stevenson's were present in the royal chambers. Her eyes scanned the room, and Mouth could see she looked frightened. "¡Robbie, ven aqui!" she snapped.

Robbie leaped off the couch and ran around it to his mother. When Ian attempted to do the same, Mouth instinctually grabbed him by the arm, and the boy bit him. "Ah!" Mouth called out and yanked his hand away as Ian ran to Maria's side.

"Aunt Maria!" Ian called out and ran to her and grabbed Maria by the leg. "¿Aunt Maria, quién es ese? Who is that?"

Mouth remained still; he was certain there must be guards near, and a simple shout from Maria would likely result in them being dragged back to the chambers and beaten. Kyo and Ron were both painfully silent behind him near the bed. Mouth stood, his eyes fixated on Maria as he waited to see what she would do. There was hesitation in her eyes. He could tell she wanted to scream for help, but instead she looked down at Ian and patted his head. "Él es tu padre, Ian. Your father. Go with him, now."

Ian looked terribly confused, and Robbie's hateful retort did not help. "¡Tu padre es un hombre malo!"

Mouth watched his son grip Maria even tighter. "No, Robbie," Maria said. "He is not. Ian, go with your father. He has been looking for you for a very long time. Go, now, before your Uncle John gets back."

Ian hesitated, but Maria gently coaxed him off her leg, and he went to Mouth. Mouth took his son into his arms, but he did not have time to even allow the sense of relief the moment should have granted him to be felt. They needed to go. He looked at Maria with sad eyes as they all backed up towards the closet with the secret chamber that would lead them to the stables. "Thank you," he said to her.

"It is my fault he was taken from you," she said. "Now, go."

Mouth walked through the chambers behind Kyo who was carrying a barely conscious Ron. Mouth held Ian with his good arm, and the boy was staring at him. "I remember you," Ian whispered to him as though it was a secret.

"What do you remember?" Mouth whispered back.

"I remember you taking me swimming in the river by the big ship," Ian said, referring to the base of the waterfall near where the *Black Dragon* once made bay.

Mouth smiled. "You remember that, Ian?"

"Yes," he said. "I remember."

"Well," Mouth said. "Maybe I can take you swimming again very soon."

They reached the end of the long tunnel, and they climbed out of the cabinet that led into the royal stables. A wagon was set up and ready to go for them, and they were greeted by the Red Dragon, dressed in the same attire they had seen the figure wearing only a short while ago. "The driver will take you out of here," the Red Dragon said, though Mouth raised a brow slightly at the sound of the person's voice. Earlier he had been sure the figure had been a woman, but now he was not certain.

"Remove your mask," Mouth said. "If you are our friend there is no need for secrets."

"I assure you, I am a friend," the Red Dragon pointed towards the wagon. "You know your driver."

Mouth turned, and the Red Dragon used the opportunity to climb into the cabinet and leave them. Someone was seated up front, ready to steer the wagon out of the courtyard beyond the castle walls. "Who's there?" Kyo called for the driver to reveal himself.

Squirt stepped down from the front of the wagon. "We have to go now," he said, and Mouth nearly fell over to see his brother standing before him. Kyo hurried to help Ron into the back of the wagon as Mouth attempted to put his arm around his brother. Squirt pushed him off, but he smiled. "We don't have time for that. The Red Dragon said the guards will be back at the gates in only a few minutes, and they will see that the gates have been opened. We must go – *now*." Squirt then looked at the child Mouth was holding, and Squirt could hardly move in his shock. "Ian?"

"Both of you get in the back of the bloody wagon!" Kyo snarled as he climbed up front. "I will drive us since you two seem to have completely lost your wits. Glad to see you're all right, lad, but we do not have time for this!"

Mouth and Squirt did as they were told, and Kyo steered them away. As promised by the Red Dragon, the guards were nowhere in sight. Kyo drove the wagon as quickly as he could without drawing attention. Because it was the dead of night, they drove straight through Caldara City and turned due west. "We must head further south and then redirect back towards the mountains to avoid groupings of soldiers," Squirt said. "That's what the Red Dragon told me. The rebellion is somewhere in the mountains now. We must be cautious to avoid being caught again."

Mouth sat with his son in his lap and his brother at his side. Ron lay flat on his back, staring up at the ceiling of the wagon. "Ron," Mouth said to him, and the man turned his head to the side. "I want you to know that I am here for you, mate. Whatever you need, I will help you."

Ron attempted to speak, but he was completely unintelligible without the use of his tongue. "Eh-weh-ah," he repeated several times, and after a moment Squirt questioned, "Theresa?" and Ron nodded. "What about Theresa?" Squirt asked. Ron pointed toward his eyes, shook his head, and then waved his hand across his mouth and motioned towards his legs. "I do not understand," Squirt said.

Mouth frowned as he pieced together Ron's movements. "You do not want her to see you like this," Mouth said, and Ron nodded. Ron then pressed two of his fingers against his temple and twitched his thumb as though to imitate the shooting of a gun. "There is no way we are giving you a gun so that you can do that," Mouth said, and a few tears started to stream down Ron's cheeks. "Your wife loves you. She is going to want you home, mate. She's going to be sad when she sees what they've done to you, I'm sure, but I know that woman would prefer you like this than to not have you home with her at all."

"Did my Uncle John hurt you like that?" Ian piped up suddenly; he had been incredibly quite the entire ride thus far.

Squirt cringed. "He calls *him* his uncle?"

Mouth motioned for Squirt not to say anything more. Mouth put a hand on Ian's head. "John did not hurt Ron, but he let men hurt him."

"I'm sorry they hurt you," Ian said. Ian looked at Squirt; Squirt's face was bruised. "Are you my Uncle Jacob?" Ian asked.

Squirt smiled. "Do you remember me, Ian?"

"Yes, I think so," Ian said, and his face lit up suddenly. "Are we going to go see my Mama? I remember her, I do!"

Mouth wrapped his good arm around his boy and pulled him close. "Yes, we're going to go see her. We're heading there right now, Ian. And, oh, how much she has missed you!" Mouth exhaled heavily and kissed the boys head. He then looked at Squirt with sad eyes. "Cruz told me he killed you."

"He beat my face," Squirt said. "But that is all. Took my bandana though, old cad."

"No doubt they were planning on using you against Mouth later," Kyo snarled from the front of the wagon.

Mouth did not want to think about that. Somehow, they had made it out alive – all of them. That was all that mattered, and he was at last bringing his son home.

Chapter 27

Smith was half asleep in his tent when his cousin Thaddeus popped his head in; the boy came tumbling inside and leaped onto Smith, scaring him out of his wits awake. "Wake up!" Thaddeus roared. "Cousin Peter, your friends are alive! Mouth, Squirt, Ron, and Kyo… and a little boy they are calling *Ian*."

Smith sat up quickly. "Ian? What do you mean, Thaddeus?"

"Mouth has a little boy with him; he says it is his son, Ian," Thaddeus said, reaching and grabbing Smith's wrist.

"Ian is dead," Smith said as he followed Thaddeus out of the tent. "Where is Mouth? He's safe? And Squirt and Ron? And Kyo?"

"Yes, they're all here!" Thaddeus squealed.

Smith followed Thaddeus to the far end of the campsite where up ahead he could see a crowd forming. He could hear Abigail sobbing loudly, and as she came into view Smith instantly recognized the child she was holding.

"Ian," Smith said under his breath. Mouth stood by her, one arm wrapped around them both – his other arm wrapped up in a makeshift sling. Smith felt his throat tighten. The other Black Dragons were already standing around, all looking just as confused and overjoyed as Smith felt. "Mouth?" Smith called, and the man looked up to him with tears in his eyes.

Mouth turned his attention to Smith for only a moment and addressed all of his friends who were all standing nearby. "John had him. He was going to kill him, but the Red Dragon helped us escape." Mouth rested his head on his wife's shoulder.

Ian looked over in Smith's direction. "I remember you," the little eight-year-old boy said, but he turned his attention back to his mother and father and buried his face into them immediately.

"Where's Ron?" Smith asked.

Squirt approached Smith, pulling his captain into a tight hug. "He is with his wife in the back of our wagon. He's hurt, Smith. *Really* bad."

Smith thanked Squirt for his warning and hurried over to the wagon. He looked into the back, and he saw Ron lain out in the base of the wagon with Theresa on her knees beside him, kissing his face and sobbing. Smith saw that his friend's legs had been severed from his body, and it filled him with rage. "Ron," Smith spoke, and Ron's head lifted up. The man's eyes glossed over. "Oh, Ron, I'm so sorry this happened to you," Smith said. "This isn't right. I involved you in this war. I shouldn't have ever –"

Ron waved his hand, letting him know to stop talking, but the man did not speak for himself. Theresa looked to Smith. "They cut out his tongue," she said and wiped tears from her cheeks.

Smith felt a pang in his side. "I don't know what to say," Smith admitted, and Ron reached a hand out to him. Smith climbed into the wagon and grabbed Ron's hand. Smith was angry. John and his combatants had taken enough from him. He wanted this to be over, but he feared that it was just beginning.

***

"There is a storm coming," John muttered as a few raindrops fell around him; the thick, dark clouds overhead spoke volumes and made his words unnecessary.

Out of fear, Maria had alerted John and Antonio about Mouth and the others escape. She had even admitted to waiting to alert them until she felt they had gained enough ground so as to save Mouth's son, Ian. For that, Cruz had dragged Maria, Robbie, and even young Amy to their new base. John could not be certain, but he felt as though the man was using his own daughter as hostage against him – making sure that he performed exactly as expected. They had managed to follow Mouth and the others at a safe distance, and now they had the latest location of Harold's rebellion. Maria sat with their children in the royal carriage in the midst of the crowd of soldiers not far from where John stood speaking with Antonio, Juan, and Señor Cruz.

"Then close the door," Cruz said and slammed the carriage door shut to keep his daughter and grandchildren from getting soaked in the rain.

"You know that's not what I meant," John said. "I mean that we should wait to attack the camp."

"You're out of your mind," Antonio retorted. "This needs to end now."

"We don't even know how many men are there," John said. "This is suicide."

Cruz laughed. "We know he couldn't possibly have over three hundred. We know that they are all weak from having to run and relocate time and time again. They can't keep this up forever. It's time to finish this, John. You will lead the attack. Kirkston will see that you are strong, and they will follow you."

"I'm just your puppet," John snarled. "I know what this is, Cruz. When the war is over, when Harold is dead, then what? I know I'm expendable to you."

"You are my daughter's husband. How cold-hearted do you think I am? Kirkston needs to have a Kirkston man on the throne to keep them reassured. You and I know who is really in charge, though, sí?"

"Sí," John said, practically spitting the word out of his mouth. "What are you going to do if the rebellion flees into the mountains? They will have higher ground. They might slaughter your men."

"It is only one troop," Cruz said. "If that is the sacrifice that we must make to scatter them into the mountains, then so be it. There is another troop on its way to finish off what this troop starts."

"You are going to sacrifice these men?" John questioned.

"Whatever is necessary. Three years, John. Three years is a long time for Harold to hide in such a small country. It is an embarrassment. He knows he has lost. The people of Kirkston, they have accepted their new rulers. He is running out of steam. Your men should have finished them off two years ago during the attack at the waterfall. Now, we have them. Antonio, you and John will lead this assault – though I recommend you lead from the back lines. It is going to be a blood bath. I am returning to Caldara Castle where it is safe."

"And, your daughter and grandchildren?" John asked.

"Let them see the horrors of war," Cruz said with a smile. "It is good for the soul. They stay here at base, though. A somewhat safe distance away with a guard – have the carriage brought into the woods a good way off. I do hope to see you all again soon… alive. Kill Harold, boys, for I am done playing games."

John stood by Antonio and Juan as Señor Cruz rode off with his entourage on a horse. Juan laughed as the man disappeared in the distance and the rain started falling harder. "John is so afraid of him."

"So are you," John said and smacked Juan's injured foot Cruz had shot with his cane, causing the man to nearly topple over in pain. Juan growled in response, near ready to jump John and kill him – Antonio warned him to play nice. John called for a guard to escort the carriage to a safer location, threatening the man with his life if he let harm come to Maria or to one of the children.

John went with Antonio, and without giving John warning, the Manrique brother ordered the soldiers onward.

***

The attack came just as the storm unleashed its monstrous fury, the rain pouring down with little mercy. Smith managed to mount a horse, but he knew it would not do any good; Harold screamed an order for the rebellion to flee into the mountains where they would have higher ground. A fury rose up inside of Smith: there were innocent women and children at this camp, but that had not stopped John's men from launching the attack.

The rain beat down against his face; Smith had no way of knowing who was safe, who had already been shot, or who was fighting to allow others to escape. He worked to get to higher ground. They had been moving further into the mountains for weeks, but now it seemed that this was their one and only means of escape. John knew what he was doing; the rebellion would become separated in the mountains, and with the number of soldiers John had swarming in on them, his men would easily pick them off. The only chance the rebellion had was if they got to higher ground in a hurry, but with the amount of rain and wind it was doubtful they would be able to fire accurately towards the oncoming slaughter of Spaniards.

Smith ditched his horse, knowing the poor beast would not be able to make the climb; he set it free and began stumbling over rocks and mud in the opposite direction his horse was headed. Nearby he spotted Kathleen, and as a clap of thunder struck down nearby, igniting a tree, her horse threw her. "Kathleen!" Smith wailed and ran towards her, bullets and wind zipping by him as he did so. He helped her to her feet, and she seemed to have a sprained ankle.

"Leave me," she hissed.

"You're out of your mind," he retorted, and he had to practically drag her up the mountain, though she did her best to assist.

A group of three men began closing in on them, clearly having spotted a Caldara. By some miracle, a shooter overhead provided the backup they needed by firing down – killing all three men in a flurry of quick, impressive shots. Squinting through the rain, Smith spotted Blade running and slipping down towards them and tossing aside his now useless gun. "I've got you, Kathleen," Blade said and each of the two men allowed her to throw an arm over their shoulder. Between the two of them, they were able to rush Kathleen further up the mountain and out of the line of heavy fire.

"Thanks for that, mate," Smith said, and just as they thought they would make it out of harm's way, the ground began to shake.

"What's happening?" Blade called out over the powerful, incessant booming of the storm.

Kathleen let out a horrified scream, but it was muffled by a sudden explosion of thunder. The light from the lightning gave way, and up ahead Smith could see a flood of mud and rock and broken trees clambering down towards the rebellion and John's attacking men. "Mudslide!" Smith shrieked, but his words meant very little. There was no time to escape. "Hold onto each other!" he ordered, and the three of them gripped together as the ground came out from under their feet.

Chapter 28

The unforgiving mudslide was followed by several aftershock tremors, and by the time the land settled the entire rebellion along with John's army was either buried, fleeing, or dead. The rain continued to pour down hard, and each man, woman, and child who had survived the initial act of nature scurried to find a safe haven in the event of another catastrophe. There were no longer sounds of gunfire – just horrified screams from both sides of the fight all desperately trying to locate shelter before more mud, rock, and trees could bury them.

Squirt and Gwen opted to run down the mountain rather than up. It was a dangerous and risky choice, for if they did not get far enough away before another mudslide, they were sure to be buried; plus, they had a difficult time finding their way down in the dark. They passed by dead soldiers, and behind them they could hear additional screams as another pile of mud and rock came crashing down on those who were too slow to escape their muddy prisons. The young couple reached the tree line at the base of the mountains just in time; they hurried deeper into the woods, and they stopped to catch their breathes under a large oak. They were both covered in mud, and Gwenyfar had a terrible gash from a small stone down her right arm. Squirt pulled her into a tight embrace and kissed her several times. "Are you all right? Your arm looks awful. Does it hurt?"

"I'm all right; I'm all right," she assured him. "It's not as bad as it looks."

They heard the sound of boots sloshing in the mud nearby, and Gwen was first to draw her sword. "Help," a soft cry echoed around them. A bolt of lightning struck and lit up the sky and tree line around them, and they saw Richard attempting to pull his wife and child from the mud.

Squirt and Gwen hurried to them, and Gwen took the crying child into her arms while Squirt helped Richard pull Isabella free from the mud. The family had just barely escaped. "We have to help," Richard said, glancing over his shoulder towards the mucky mess. "John's men are freeing themselves, and they have the man power to take out anyone who wasn't killed by the mudslide."

Richard looked directly at Squirt and Gwen. "One of you, please, get Isabella and Jackie out of here. I need one of you to cover me while I search for survivors."

Squirt responded, "Gwen, you go with Isabella, and –"

Gwen put her hand on Squirt's chest. "You and I both know I am a better shot than you. I'm Richard's best chance if he is going to go darting into the line of fire."

Squirt's heart sank. "If you think I'm going to let you go –"

Gwen kissed his cheek. "You don't *let* me do anything. Now, go. Get Isabella and Jackie to safety."

The group anxiously began to part ways. Squirt called out over the storm after Gwen, "When this is over, Gwenyfar, I want to marry you!"

Gwen glanced back over her shoulder towards them, and Squirt smiled at her. She laughed. "Are you asking me, Jacob?"

"Yes."

"Good!" she shouted. "I will see you when the storm clears."

***

Ace and King Harold pulled Knot from the thick mud and then quickly began their ascension towards a cave that Harold had spotted only moments before the mud had piled down on top of them. Knot was sobbing loudly as Cassidy, Clara, and the queen worked to wipe the thick slosh from their friend who had nearly perished. "Ellen Jane! Anna!" Knot screamed over the storm, but he did not get a reply.

"Stay down," Ace warned. "You're hurt." His own eyes darted about the altered landscape. "Pierson! Pierson!" Ace felt Cassidy touch his arm, and he turned to look at her just as a bolt of lightning lit up the sky. "He was right beside me," Ace said, his voice shaking. "Then he was just gone!"

Harold spoke over them. "We have to keep moving. If we stay down low, one of John's men will surely take us out."

Ace and Harold each took one of Knot's arms, throwing an arm over their shoulder to walk him up the steep incline. "I don't see Kathleen or Richard," Queen Rachel said, her voice just as shaky as her sons had been.

They heard gunfire, but the darkness shielded whoever was firing and whoever was being fired upon.They heard a soft cry nearby. "Help…"

"Hannah?" Knot called, recognizing his sister-in-law's voice. "Someone help her!"

Cassidy and Queen Rachel turned on their heels. "Pierson!" Cassidy cried out, and Ace turned his head to see Pierson sitting by Hannah whose legs were trapped under heavy mud and bits of rock. The women rushed to unbury Hannah, and Ace breathed a sigh of relief as his son hurried to his side and hugged his leg. The group continued their climb towards the cave.

As they were making their way into the cave's entrance, a shadowy figure lunged towards them. Ace heard Cassidy cry out in fear, for the figure had a hold of her. Another bolt of lightning struck, illuminating the cave, revealing a fear-stricken Blade holding a dagger in their direction. The man breathed and released his dagger that he had held towards Cassidy. "Thank God," Blade said, and his eyes lit up to see Hannah and Knot.

"Are you alone?" Ace asked.

"No," Blade said and averted their attention towards two figures sitting down at the back of the cave. "Smith and Kathleen are with me."

"Kathleen!" Queen Rachel hurried to her daughter.

Ace and Harold helped Knot to sit. Knot was still quite hysterical. "Have any of you seen Anna or Ellen Jane?" he asked. "My wife and daughter – they were not with me when John's troop arrived!"

"I'm sorry, mate," Smith said as he rose from his seat. "It seems we may have to wait for this storm to clear before we get answers. The ground is too unsteady to move out."

**

Richard met up with Kyo and Chi who had already gathered a good number of survivors; they led them from the mudslide, making their way around John's remaining forces. The goal was to fight another day. Much to Richard's pleasure, a number of familiar faces were among the group fleeing the mountains – heading north through the woods. Mouth and his sons and wife, Anna and her daughter, Smith's uncle and his young son Thaddeus, Yin, Maxi and his family apart from Hannah, Dr. Conal, Stewart, and many others he had come to know from the three years the rebellion had been active. Unfortunately, there were many he did not see, and he hoped that his missing loved ones had escaped through another route. His father and mother, his sister, Smith, Hannah Cook, Blade, Knot, the Irish sisters, his brother and his brother's son, Snake and his wife, the Katch's, and the White's were all unaccounted for.

"Wait! Oh, God, please, wait!" a familiar voice called out behind.

"Hold fast!" Richard called out over the sobbing crowd. He had heard his wife's voice. He looked to Kyo

Mori. "Continue leading this group onward, and I will catch up."

Kyo nodded and encouraged the group to press on despite the many loved ones and soldiers that were still missing. Richard hurried to the back of the group, and not too far back he spotted his wife flailing her arm. He took a horse, one of the few horses his group had managed to get a hold of, and walked it towards her. "Isabella, I thought you were with Squirt!"

"I'm right here," Squirt said, surprising him a bit; it was frightfully dark out. Squirt was holding Jackie in his arms.

Sitting on the ground near them was Theresa and Ron Katch along with their son Pete. It did not take much for Richard to deduce that Isabella and Squirt had come across the couple while fleeing. With Ron's injuries, it would have been impossible to get them all to safety had Richard not come with the horse, and obviously Theresa had not been inclined to leave her husband to perish at the hand of enemy soldiers. "I'm here," Richard promised. "Squirt, give Jackie to Isabella and help me get Ron up onto the horse. We can still catch up with Kyo and the others." He reached out and touched Squirt's shoulder. "Gwen is safe. She's with Kyo leading the escape. Your brother and his family are there as well."

"Thank you," Squirt said and passed Jackie to the boy's mother.

"Thank you, thank you, thank you," Theresa muttered, knowing the easy answer would have certainly been to leave them behind.

"Climb up there with him, Theresa," Richard said, seeing the woman's exhaustion on her face. He knew she must have dragged her husband a good distance to safety. "Let's go," Richard said, passing Pete up to his parents as he said this. They pressed onward.

***

John gritted his teeth as he watched half of his soldiers get swept away by the mudslide. Many more were crushed by falling rocks. A part of him was praying that Antonio and Juan were buried with the others, but he knew he was not that lucky. John had been leading the flank, and he and a few around him had managed to completely miss the dangerous flood of debris. "Look for survivors, and kill any that aren't with us," John hissed, and the small group with him pressed on as the storm continued to weigh down on them.

As for him, John attempted to trudge through the mud and to avoid any additional avalanches that were coming in wave-like aftershocks. The storm was maddening, and John knew that his men were in trouble just as much as the rebellion. His men had taken the blunt of the mudslide as most of the rebellion had already travelled out of the path and up the mountain when it had occurred. Coming here had been a mistake, and he had known it all along if only Señor Cruz had listened.

A nearby moan jolted him, and he drew his gun and shot at the rebellion soldier attempting to pull himself from the mud. *Good*, John thought when he realized his pistol still worked after all of the rain and mud. He was certain many were probably weaponless apart from knives and swords after so much slush had come their way.

John made his way upward to get away from the dangerous terrain below – quite a difficult feat with his bum leg, and suddenly he spotted a familiar face – and he was in pain. John's stomach churned. "Johnny?" he questioned, and he suddenly felt someone swing a stick into his gut with such force that it felt like the flimsy piece of wood had been an iron pole. John fell onto his back, and he saw the little American Indian girl staring back at him. "*You,*" he snarled.

"Stay away from us," she snarled right back – this time in a much clearer dialect from the last time he had spoken to her.

John raised his hands above his head. "I'll stay down," he said, knowing he did not have it in him to shoot Snake's wife in front of him. Glancing over, he could see Snake lying down amongst some of the larger fallen stones. John shouted over the whipping wind, "Is he all right?"

"No," she called back and after much hesitation, she reached her hand down to John. "If you care for him at all, please, help me."

John took her by the hand, and she pulled him to his feet. His cane was useless in the mud, so he abandoned it. Snake was moaning. "Don't tell me those rocks are on top of him?" John shouted, squinting through the pouring rain.

"No, but they hit him," Sky responded. "His leg is broken, I think."

John knelt down beside Snake. "Son, we're going to get you out of this muck."

271

Snake frowned, and the unpleasant look the younger man was giving him did not go unnoticed. Nevertheless, John and Sky worked tirelessly to free him. "My leg…" Snake groaned. "I think it's broken."

"There's no question," Sky said, the rain beating down on them as she spoke. "We need to get out of this storm."

John pointed upward towards a cave. "There," he said, and they each threw one of Snake's arms over their shoulders. It took them much effort, but soon they made their way to the cave's entrance. Each stepped caused John tremendous pain in his bum leg, but he was determined to get his godson out of harm's way.

John could just barely make out the shadowy figures of men and women towards the back of the cave, and he was certain he was walking right into a group of his enemies. He would do it to get Snake to safety, though. "Who's there!" a voice called out, and John knew it was Smith's.

"Help me!" Sky called out. "Snake's leg is broken!"

A shadowy figure stepped forward, and John reached for his pistol. Smith had caused him enough trouble, and now here he was presenting himself for slaughter. Killing Smith in front of Snake was not ideal to him, but John had let Smith get away one too many times. And, now that he was back in Kirkston his leadership was strengthening the rebellion in ways that were not fitting with John's plans. He raised his pistol, and as he fired a second figure bolted near Smith.

Lightning struck outside, and John could see for a moment Blade gripping his gut in surprise. Snake yanked away from John. "Who fired?" someone called out in horror, and in the confusion, John slipped back towards the entrance of the cave. It was too dark for them to grab hold of him or to even know who was responsible – though he was certain that Snake knew.

"Blade! Blade!" John could hear several of them shouting. He slipped away, and a pang of guilt gripped him.

Chapter 29

"I need a light!" Smith screamed at the top of his lungs. "Someone get me a light!" He grabbed hold of Blade and helped him down to the ground; he could hear his friend gasping and gurgling.

Ace had a bit of flint, and all he had on him that was dry enough to light was an old piece of parchment from his coat. The bit of light did little to help apart from revealing the look of death on their friend's face. "Hold on, mate," Smith said, pressing his hand against Blade's stomach in an attempt to slow down the bleeding. "Why did you do that? You pushed me out of the way! Who was that? Why did they shoot?"

From the small flicker of light Ace had managed to provide them with, Smith could see Sky helping Snake to sit. Snake's eyes were wide, and his expression was one of complete hate. "Stevenson!" Snake roared. "It was Stevenson! Where did he go? I'll kill him!"

"He's going to bleed out," Ace said and wiped tears from his eyes.

"No, no he's not!" Smith declared, but the haunting look in Blade's eyes was undeniable.

"Garret...Hannah," Blade said, his voice raspy.

"Help me to him!" Knot demanded, and Hannah took his arm and led him to Blade's side.

Knot collapsed near Blade's head across from Smith, and Smith could see streaks of tears washing away the mud that covered Knot's face. "Daddy," Pierson's little voice cried out in fear, and from the corner of his eye, Smith saw Ace lift the boy up and step away from them to stand with the king, queen, and Cassidy.

Hannah fell to her knees beside Knot and reached for Blade's hand, gripping it tight. "Don't. Don't you dare," she said and began to cry.

A bit of blood began to drip from Blade's mouth. "Hannah," Blade gagged.

Smith clasped the back of Blade's neck to keep his friends head off the ground. He felt his throat tighten. "Where did John go?" Smith snarled.

"He's gone," Harold said as the rain continued to beat down outside.

Another bolt of lightning lit up the cave, and Smith could see clearly that Knot, Hannah, and himself were all covered in Blade's blood. The bit of fire Ace had lit against the parchment had already dwindled. Another lighting strike, and Smith saw that Blade's hand was pressed firmly against Hannah's stomach. "I'm so sorry, Hannah," he said, his words followed by a slight burbling sound.

Blade's shaky hand left her stomach for a moment. "Harold!" Blade called out. "Marry Hannah and me now!"

Harold seemed a bit shaken by this, but he hurried over and knelt down by Blade's head. The king did not hesitate. "Hannah Cook, do you take Terrance Simon?"

"Yes."

"And, Terrance Simon, do you take Hannah Cook?"

"Yes," Blade said weakly.

Harold again spoke quickly, "Hannah and Terrance have joined together in holy wedlock. Because they have exchanged these words before God and these witnesses, have pledged their commitment to one another, and have declared the same by joining hands, I now pronounce that they are husband and wife. Those whom God hath joined together, let no one separate. Kiss your bride, Terrance."

Hannah leaned down and tearfully kissed Blade's lips. Blade's head turned towards Knot. The rain had begun to lightened up outside, and a bit of sunlight trickled into the cave. "You take care of her and my child," Blade said.

"Of course, mate," Knot said, his hand gripping Blade's shoulder.

"You should have just let John shoot me!" Smith exclaimed. "Don't die, Terrance. Not like this. Why would you do this for me?"

Blade smiled. "Even after everything, Smith, you are still my captain."

***

The sky became clear, and Jackson could see where he had wound up in the midst of the maddening storm. He found himself on a large ledge overlooking a dense wooded area. He was not even entirely sure how he had managed to climb up onto the large ledge, but he had been thankful that it was steady. All around him was difficult climbing area, but he spotted a path not too far off. He began to stumble and climb over rocks when he spotted Helena, of all people, attempting to pull herself from mud.

He sighed, knowing he wasn't going to leave her to fend for herself. "Helena, are you hurt?" he asked as he approached.

"I don't think so," she griped. "Get me out of here, would you? My boots are stuck."

He bent down and helped to dig her legs out of the thick mud. Looking towards the edge of the cliff, he realized just how lucky she was that the bit of mud that had captured her had not continued to slide her much further. He helped to pull her to her feet, and she took a moment to kick her legs a bit to rid herself of additional mud.

"Where is everyone?" she asked.

"I have no idea," Jackson said. "But, our rendevu point is not far from here. We just have to get off this mountain."

"Help!" Jeremiah's voice called. "Helena, are you there?"

"Jeremiah?" Helena called out.

Jackson frowned; it sounded as though his brother's voice was coming from over the side of the cliff. They hurried over, and they spotted Jeremiah coated in mud gripping onto some loose rock and muck. "Help me!" he called up. "I'm slipping, help!"

They could not even see the bottom of the drop from the thick trees, but Jackson was certain it would be a deadly fall. Jackson hurried to lay on his stomach and reach down for Jeremiah. The man gripped onto Jackson's wrists. Just as he did, part of the cliff crumbled. "Ah!" Jackson cried out as he too began to slip. Jeremiah lost his footing, and so Jackson became the only thing keeping him from tumbling down.

"Don't drop me!" Jeremiah's eyes widened. Jackson gripped him tighter; Jeremiah swayed, making it all the more difficult to hold on.

Jackson began to feel strained, and he felt himself sliding through the mud on his stomach towards the edge of the cliff. After everything the two of them had been through, Jackson was not so certain he was willing to fall to his death for his brother. "Oh, let go of him, Jackson," Helena suddenly sang.

"What!" Jackson called out. "Help me pull him up, you stupid woman!"

"Why?" Helena laughed.

"Helena!" Jeremiah cried. "Help me!"

Helena was suddenly knelt down by Jackson, and he felt her touch his shoulders. "Come on, Jackson. Think about it. He's to blame for everything bad that has ever happened to you. Let him fall."

"He's your husband, you wench!" Jackson screamed. "Help me pull him up; I can't do it myself!"

Helena stood, and Jackson felt her foot press against his elbow. She was sliding him close to the edge as he lay on his stomach, reaching down for his elder brother. "Helena, stop it!" Jackson screamed, and he could see true terror in Jeremiah's eyes. Their fingers were slipping as they gripped one another, the mud on their hands making it too difficult to grip one another.

"Jackson, do you remember why I left you?" Helena asked. When he did not respond, she answered for him. "Because you were weak. I cheated on you, and you did nothing. Well here he is, Jackson. The man I left you for, and you're trying to pull him up? Show me you're not weak, and I'll take you back."

"I don't want you back," Jackson said between breaths as his breathing had become deep in his physical strain.

"Your lovely Ellen is dead," Helena said. "And, she has been for a long time. I know you want a real woman, Jackson. I know you."

He met his brother's eyes for a moment. "She'll push us both off this cliff," Jeremiah said, and he suddenly released his grip on Jackson entirely.

"Jeremiah!" Jackson cried out and held on tight.

"You're both so pathetic," Helena scowled. "I'm done with you both."

Jackson felt her boot press into his shoulder, and he continued to slide towards the edge. Then the rocks crumbled yet again. He heard his brother scream as they all fell forward a bit, and Jeremiah's grabbed hold of Jackson in fear. The ground broke away at Helena's feet while

Jackson was able to keep from tumbling to his doom by pinning his knee against a sturdy stone.

Jeremiah swung by Jackson's arm and rammed into the cliff wall, but Jackson held on. He heard Helena scream, and she disappeared beneath the trees below. "Climb up me before I drop you!" Jackson shouted, and his brother struggled to pull himself up.

Jackson pulled with every bit of strength he had left, and soon the two of them collapsed on the ledge after scooting away from its unsteady edge. Jeremiah clenched his chest, and his breathing grew raspy in his state of shock. "You saved me," Jeremiah said.

"I did," Jackson retorted, but he did not dare look Jeremiah in the eye. For the past two and a half years they had fought alongside one another for Harold's rebellion, but they had not ever spoken to one another unless it had been necessary. They acted like strangers.

Jeremiah's eyes drifted towards the edge of the cliff. "Do you think…"

"I don't know. We best go down there and check," Jackson said. "No sense in leaving her down there if she's alive."

They did not utter a word to one another as they made their way down a path, having to climb a good bit in order to reach the bottom of the ledge where Jeremiah had dangled moments ago.

When they reached the bottom of the cliff, they saw a mangled Helena. Jeremiah exhaled loudly and looked away. "I'm sorry, Jeremiah," Jackson said.

"She tried to kill us," Jeremiah said.

"She did," Jackson said.

"I dreamed this," he said. "I dreamed that this would happen. About three years ago, I dreamed that she made you push me off the side of the *Annihilator*."

"Well, you probably have always known what kind of person she was," Jackson said. "Jeremiah, please, do not tell Stewart or Gwen about this. Not Gracie either. They don't need to know."

"Their sister was a raving lunatic; I think they knew that already," Jeremiah hissed.

"Please," Jackson said and eyed his brother with a harsh gaze. "Jeremiah, do not tell them what she tried to do."

Jeremiah crossed his arms. "If you insist."

"For what it's worth, Jeremiah, I am glad you are all right," Jackson said.

Jeremiah's shoulder slumped, and he turned his body away from Helena. "Jackson, thank you." He looked Jackson in the eye. "After all I've done to you, I cannot believe you did not just let me drop when she started pushing you down too."

Jackson shook his head. "A few years ago, I might would have let you drop. That Stewart is always lecturing me on forgiveness and on sin. Maybe some of it actually stuck with me."

"Forgiveness?" Jeremiah questioned. "Are you saying you have forgiven me for stealing your lunatic wife from you?"

"Yes," Jackson said. "That was perhaps the easiest thing to forgive. Your betrayal was one of the best things that ever happened to me. I'm thankful I found the Black Dragons."

"Forgiveness. Thankfulness. You are starting to sound like a Christian!" Jeremiah said, and Jackson snorted slightly.

Jackson smiled as a realization hit him. "You... you tried to let go," Jackson said. "So that I wouldn't fall. Jerry, I —"

"Don't call me that," Jeremiah said, turning around and pointing towards the woods. "We should head to the clearing. No doubt that's where Harold's people will be assembling." Jackson nodded in agreement and allowed Jeremiah to lead. Jeremiah walked slowly, and he turned his head towards Jackson. "Should we have just left her like that?" he asked.

"I'm certain Harold will send someone to negotiate with John's men so that we can all safely retrieve our dead. We will return for her," Jackson said.

Jeremiah nodded. He paused for a moment before asking, "You say our affair was the easiest thing to forgive. What was the hardest?"

Jackson frowned, but he answered truthfully. "That day you left me with father to go live in Caldara," he said.

Jeremiah would not look directly at Jackson. "Not helping Father dispose of Mother? Not all of those beatings I gave you as boys?"

"You did all of that out of fear of our father," Jackson said. "I never hated you for any of that even as a boy. When you just left me there with that man, well, that one hurt."

"I am sorry, Jackson," Jeremiah said and stopped walking. He spoke with his head hanging low in shame. "Ever since we joined the rebellion, I have wanted to tell you how sorry I am."

"You have been part of the rebellion for over two years," Jackson said. "What has held you back until now?"

"Helena," Jeremiah said. "I thought if I got close with you that she would leave me. She's always been such a hateful woman, and she could hold a grudge like no one else I knew. She hated you."

Jackson shook his head in disagreement. "Helena didn't hate me. That woman has never felt a thing in her life. Not love. Not hate. Something was wrong with her, and I think you know it. I certainly saw it. I would see it in her eyes – the way she drew pleasure from others pain was unnatural and wrong. Love. Hate. Helena, I don't believe had the capability to feel such emotions. Jeremiah, are you crying?"

"No!" Jeremiah snarled and looked up. His eyes were a bit red and watery, but he certainly had not been crying.

"Just making sure," Jackson said. "You loved her?"

"I did," he said. "But you are right. She has never felt anything in her life. Certainly not affection! What kind of person am I to have felt anything towards a woman so cruel? And, you want me to lie to her siblings and pretend she was some sort of saint?"

"I never said that," Jackson said. "They know what she was, but they need hope that she could have been different. As for you, do not worry yourself about your feelings of love. At least you could have those feelings. You are not Helena. Not even John Stevenson is Helena. Jeremiah, you have become a leader here in this camp. To think you of all people are serving alongside the king! You are a good, fair leader too. I am proud of you and what you have become."

A slight smile appeared on Jeremiah's face, but it was quickly replaced with woe as they continued their walk. "It seems that you and I are the last of the Annihilators, brother."

"No, Jeremiah," Jackson said. "I am not an Annihilator. I am not anything those men stood for. I haven't been for a long time. And, you know what? Neither are you. The last Annihilator is dead. She's gone."

The two brothers entered into the small clearing where, as predicted, Harold's people were gathering. Jackson and Jeremiah were both spotted by Stewart who came rushing up to them. He placed hands on Jackson's shoulders. "Good to see you made it out of that madness, Jackson!" Stewart said and then glanced in Jeremiah's direction. "My sister?" he asked.

"I am sorry, Stewart," Jeremiah said. "But, your sister is dead."

Jackson was not quite sure how Stewart would react; the woman had always been a monster to him. The young man had tears in his eyes. "Dead?" he asked. "How? Was it the rockslide? Was she shot?"

Jackson lied. "She died trying to help us off a ledge. The ledge crumbled away, and she fell. She died trying to save her husband."

Jackson could feel Jeremiah's stare, but he ignored it and put an arm around Stewart. After a moment, Stewart pulled away and took a deep breath. He glanced over at Jeremiah again. "I am sorry for your loss," Stewart said.

"And yours," Jeremiah said.

"She really was trying to save you?" Stewart asked.

"Yes," Jeremiah said. "Then the ground crumbled beneath her feet."

Stewart nodded as though he believed it. "I should go tell Gracie and Gwen." And, he left them.

"So, not only are you lying, but now that she-devil is a hero?" Jeremiah questioned.

"He needed to hear that," Jackson said. "He needs to believe there was good in her."

More of Harold's soldiers started to appear, and Jackson nodded approvingly as people he knew whom he had come to care for arrived. In the distance, emerging from the trees, Jackson saw King Harold approaching with a group of familiar faces behind him – all of them red-eyed and incredibly distraught. He spotted Snake, an arm over Sky's shoulder as he walked on a broken leg. Behind Snake and Sky were Ace, Smith, Cassidy, and young Pierson carrying a limp body – each holding a limb. Jackson's stomach dropped, and he could hear a number of cries from those who had already arrived as they spotted whose body was being brought in. "Blade," Jackson said under his breath, and he felt his throat tighten. Jeremiah placed a hand on Jackson's shoulder.

Chapter 30

Blade's was the first body brought into the clearing. Currently, Richard was negotiating terms with some of John's soldiers for a ceasefire so that both sides could collect their dead and tend to their injured. Smith sat by Blade; his friends, the Black Dragons, had all gathered around. Everyone was silent, their eyes fixated on the lifeless corpse.

"Smith," Harold's voice called out a short distance away, and Smith rose from his seat –giving Knot a reassuring pat on the back before he departed from the group.

Richard and Harold both had sad eyes as Smith approached. Smith could see that Harold was truly disturbed by Blade's death almost as much as the Black Dragons themselves. Clearly his relation with Smith's former crewmembers had changed drastically during his absence. "Did you manage to convince those lunes to ceasefire?" Smith asked.

"He did," Harold said. "Richard and Jeremiah are going to head up a team to fetch the bodies of our dead. I'm putting Kyo and some Skull Island Gang members in charge of keeping watch over the clean-up crew. Kathleen and I will lead the rest of the rebellion to our rendezvous point down south to pitch a new camp."

"What do you need me to do?" Smith asked.

Harold glanced back at the Black Dragons. "I need as many bodies as I can right now, but I know it would mean a lot to your crew if Blade was buried with the rest of your fallen team."

"Are you granting me leave to go bury a body many miles from here?" Smith questioned.

"Yes," Harold said. "Take one horse and carriage to transport it. You may bring Knot with you… let your uncle and Jackson come as well so they can act as support in the event of an ambush, but that is all."

"I believe that Hannah would want to go as well," Smith said.

"You will be marching through or around territories heavily controlled by La Cofradía. Blade meant enough to me for me to deny such a request. Ms. Hannah will be safer coming with us to our new camp whether she likes it or not. Give her a moment to bid her husband farewell, and then you all need to leave now. I expect your party to regroup with us in three days' time."

"That will not give us much time," Smith said.

"Make it happen," Harold said and stepped away to go speak with Kathleen about leading the group south.

Richard nodded approvingly at his father's decision. He reached out and touched Smith's shoulder, looking at him through a saddened expression. "Blade was the most loyal man I have ever had the pleasure of knowing. After he was held captive by Stevenson for those six months…well, I knew then what kind of man he was. My father tells me he married Hannah and Blade while he was dying?"

"Hannah is pregnant," Smith said, and Richard instinctually glanced over to where Maxi Cook was standing.

"Is Maxi aware?" Richard asked.

"No, I don't believe so," Smith said. "And, he does not need to know just yet. Not until Hannah wishes to tell him, I don't think."

Richard nodded in agreement, and then he went to gather the necessary men to complete the task he had been assigned. Smith took a breath and headed back towards his friends. They glanced in his direction as he approached. "Knot," Smith said. "You, Jackson, Uncle Bartholomew, and Thaddeus – you all will come with me to our family's burial plot to lay Blade down. The rest of you will go with Kathleen and Harold to the new camp."

Hannah glanced up from where she was seated by Blade's head. "I will go with you."

"No," Smith said. "Harold's forbidden it."

"Since when does the great Captain Smith listen to Harold?" Hannah sneered. "We were married. I should be at my husband's funeral!"

"Blade would want you where you would be safest, and that will not be with us," Smith insisted.

"That's not fair, Smith," Snake said from the ground as Dr. Conal was attempting to create for him a brace for his leg.

"I did not say it was fair," Smith retorted. "But, I agree with Harold. I'd do my fallen comrade a disservice bringing you through those territories. You will go with Harold to the rendezvous point. I'll give you all a moment to say goodbye, but then we are leaving. Jackson, come with me and help me prepare a carriage to transport Blade."

***

Smith, Bartholomew, Thaddeus, Jackson, and Knot had only made it a short distance when one of the wheels of the wagon came loose from the rough terrain, and they were forced to stop to repair it. "We're close to a pond," Smith said, grabbing hold of their canteens. "Might as well refill these before we begin our journey east."

"Go ahead," Bartholomew said. "Jackson and I will work on the wheel."

Thaddeus and Knot both found themselves a seat outside of the wagon. Smith took a moment to observe Knot before departing the group; the man was distraught. Knot and Blade had practically been brothers. They had not had time to gather clean clothes before their departure, so they each had their friends dried blood still coated on their shirts and trousers. Smith took the canteens with him through the woods, checking and rechecking to make sure his pistol and sword were both at his side. They were still considerably close to where the rockslide and surprise attack by John's men had taken place. Though Richard had negotiated a ceasefire, Smith could not be too careful.

As Smith was refilling the canteens, he spotted a large coach-style wagon hidden amongst the tree-line. He found himself a hiding spot; the coach Smith recognized as one of the old Caldara travelling wagons. He assumed it was now owned by John and his men. The door to the carriage opened, and he saw Maria step out. She spoke in Spanish to whomever was inside. Then he saw that she had only her children with her. The girl she carried, and the young boy, Robbie, was whom she had been speaking to. He kept a close eye, glancing around in all directions. They were alone.

He thought of Blade – how John had struck him down so cruelly, and he became angry. Smith drew his pistol, and he marched towards the coach. It would be so easy to approach her as she was distracted by her children. He pictured John's face as he arrived back at the carriage to find his wife dead, and it satisfied Smith in a way he did not think was possible for himself, but he was so full of hurt that the bloodlust drew him in closer. He even contemplated shooting the children as well – so unlike his usual temperament.

Just as Smith had approached the carriage and the woman spun around with wide eyes, spotting him, he felt a pistol touch the back of his neck. Maria practically threw her daughter to her son and slammed the door to the coach shut, standing her ground and guarding the coach with her body. She still seemed afraid, but based on the pistol pointed to the back of his neck Smith was almost certain a rescuer had arrived.

"Drop it, Smith," a familiar voice commanded.

Smith still gripped his pistol with it pointed in Maria's direction. He glanced over his shoulder only to see

Knot standing there with his own gun pointed at his neck. "What are you doing?" Smith snarled.

"Put your gun away, or I will end you," Knot swore.

"How does a man with one leg sneak up on me?" Smith snapped, but he did not lower his gun.

"Put your gun away!" Knot shouted.

Smith gritted his teeth and lowered his gun, but he did not put it in its holster. "Shoot her yourself then," Smith said.

"No," Knot said. "You and I are going back with the others. You dog, were you really going to shoot an unarmed woman in front of her children?"

"Please, leave us," Maria pleaded, and Smith spun his head in her direction.

"Your husband just gunned down one of my friends," Smith said.

"That is not my crime," she said and then tapped the side of the coach. "Nor theirs."

"Smith, we need to leave before someone spots us," Knot said. "No doubt the dictator's wife has guards around here somewhere."

"You're telling me you don't want to get back at John?" Smith questioned. "Blade was your best friend."

"Of course, I do, but I don't want to turn into John in the process," Knot said. "And, I don't want you to either. There is a ceasefire right now; it won't take but a single shot to alarm both sides. Let's go – now!"

Smith glared in Maria's direction, but he followed Knot back through the woods. They made quick time even with Knot's handicap. Smith returned his gun to its holster. He breathed deeply. "Thank you," he muttered to Knot.

"For what?" Knot asked, his voice still seething.

"For not letting me do something I would regret," Smith said. "It should have been me, Knot. Not Blade."

"Be worthy of that sacrifice," Knot said, and he seemed done with the matter as he chunked his crutches into the back of their carriage.

***

Bartholomew watched his nephew and his friend down the last of the alcohol they had managed to find in his sister's home. They had just finished burying Blade in the former garden near the rest of the fallen Black Dragons. He never thought he would see a day when Jackson was the soberest Black Dragon around; Jackson had not had an ounce to drink.

"Papa," Thaddeus nudged him and pointed towards some wild flowers growing a short distance from the river. "Can I put those on Aunt Ellen's grave?"

Bartholomew nodded, and his son hurried off. Jackson wandered over to him; the sun was starting to set in the distance. The two of them stood side by side watching Smith and Knot who were both sitting in the dirt by Blade's fresh grave. During Smith's two-year absence, Bartholomew had developed a somewhat friendship with Jackson. His sister had cared enough about this rogue to wish to marry him, and she had always been a good judge of character. In that time, Bartholomew had learned of some of Jackson's more redeeming qualities. He was certainly no William Barons; in fact, the two men his sister had loved in her life could not be more different, but Jackson was a good man in Bartholomew's eyes.

"They're both real tore up about this one," Jackson said.

"I imagine so," Bartholomew said. "Blade was practically Knot's brother. And, the man threw himself in between my nephew and a bullet."

"Cannonball also died keeping Smith out of trouble during this war," Jackson said. "It's weighing on his conscience now, I think."

"What are they talking about over there?" Bartholomew asked.

"Blade, of course," Jackson said. "A bit about Ms. Hannah too."

"What is that poor woman going to do?" Bartholomew asked.

"Apparently, Hannah wishes to come be a servant in Knot and her younger sister's household when this is all over," Jackson said. "That's what she asked Knot before we headed out this way, at least. Harold married them before Blade passed on, so perhaps her brother will not be too cruel to her about the pregnancy. The Cook's, though they come from pompous circles, have always been a bit more openminded. I'm just not sure how much more open mindedness Maxi can handle."

"I see," Bartholomew said. "I hate that my nephew ran off the way he did. I hardly knew him, but I still wish I could have been there for him when my sister died the way she did. He did not give me the chance."

"Well, I suppose you could now," Jackson said. "I think both of us are going to have to each take a drunk to handle for the night. You take your nephew and try to sober him up, and I'll take Knot."

"Smith would prefer to have to deal with you, I'm sure," Bartholomew said. "He does not know me from Adam. You're practically his father."

"I would not go that far," Jackson said.

"I saw the way you looked at him when he first came back to camp," Bartholomew said. "He was your prodigal son returned."

"Funny," Jackson said. "I think Smith's father often thought of me in that light. Very well. I'll take Smith. You can drag the one-legged drunk inside."

Bartholomew nodded. "Perhaps I did not think this arrangement through entirely."

While Thaddeus spent the last bit of twilight burning off his youthful energy finding flowers for all of the graves, Bartholomew and Jackson dragged Smith and Knot indoors. "We'll throw the drunks into the girl's old room," Jackson said. "You and your boy can take the master, and I will sleep in the living room."

Bartholomew nodded in agreement, and he managed to convince Knot to curl up in what had once been his niece's bed. From what he had been told by his sister, Elizabeth would take the largest bed, Smith the smaller, and the niece he had never known would often sleep in the window seal of this small room. He sighed at the thought. Things were supposed to have gone quite differently. They were going to send their family money to help them, but William and the girls had been killed, his sister had been arrested, and Smith had wound up joining a pirate crew, so Bartholomew and the rest of his family had lost all contact with Ellen Barons and her family. He could not help but to wonder if the rest of the family had just stayed behind in Kirkston if Smith's life would have turned out differently.

Jackson got Smith into his old childhood bed, and the man's feet hung off the bottom. "Easy there, lad," Jackson said to him. "You've had more than you can handle."

Smith insisted he was fine, but he fell asleep before he could finish his argument. Jackson smiled slightly as he threw a small sheet over Smith, shaking his head a bit. "What are you smiling about?" Bartholomew asked.

"Just that I'm having to tuck a grown man into bed," Jackson said.

The two of them slipped out of the room and into the hall in time to see Thaddeus dragging his feet inside. "Go wash those muddy hands of yours in the river," Bartholomew said, and Thaddeus hurried back out in obedience. "Are you certain you are all right sleeping on that small couch?"

"I'll survive," Jackson assured him.

Once Thaddeus returned, Bartholomew dragged his son to the back room so that they could attempt to get some rest.

***

Jackson could not sleep. He found himself pacing in the small living area, occasionally glancing in on Smith and Knot to make sure the drunken fellows hadn't fallen from their beds. Eventually, he lit a few candles he had found lying around. There was dust all around the place. Mrs. Barons home had not had a visitor since Cannonball had died there two years before. Since then, they had buried Yang and Mrs. Barons and now Blade on the property as well. They had hung up crosses for Hethuska and Nicole too.

It was not at all the happy home it had once been. He could still remember all the times he had come here with the Black Dragons to enjoy a fine meal prepared by the woman he had come to love, and it saddened him to see so much dust. He still thought of Ellen Barons often. A little over two years ago, he had lost her.

Helena's maddening display in the mountains had him on edge. He would not have taken up her offer for even a second to come back to her – especially not at the expense of his brother's life. Mrs. Barons, his beloved Ellen, had changed his heart. But a deeper change was stirring inside of Jackson. Perhaps it was the loss of Ellen that had caused him to start actually listening to Stewart when he spoke of God? Jackson needed to believe in the God that Mrs. Barons loved – the God that she had sworn time and time again who loved him as well.

He was not an educated man. In fact, he was far from it, but he had learned to read fairly well from Stewart. He managed to find a copy of *My Daughter's Solider* sitting in the living room – the book that Ellen's father had written about her and her husband, William. Jackson had read it before, but he had not been as fluent of a reader the last time he had picked up the book. This time he read it with a clear, more educated mind. He smiled at first, but soon he began to weep and wish that Smith and Knot had not been so greedy with the only bit of alcohol they had found.

Jackson missed her, and being back here was almost too much for him. Back in the very home where William Barons had taken him in when his own father had abused him. This home where he had once held Smith as a baby and had once watched the man's older sister run around in her little dresses. This home where he had first kissed Ellen. There was no peace in Kirkston like that – not anymore.

His mind went back to God. It was the strangest sensation – one he had been having quite often lately, but there was an intensity behind it now that burned him. He wanted to pray. He had never prayed before, and it almost frightened him. Would praying be an admission of belief? Would God strike him down for finally praying now? No, God was just too much for him just yet.

If God is in Heaven, he wondered, *and Stewart says I can speak to God through prayer –then could I not speak to someone else who is in Heaven? Would they hear me through my prayer too?*

The thought intrigued him. He knelt down on the floor by the couch. No, that would not do. Too uncomfortable. He sat back up on the couch. He was not sure whether to press his palms together or to sit with his hands open. He crossed his arms as though to intentionally show off his reluctance. Until the words left his mouth, he was not even sure who it was he was hoping to speak to.

"William," he mumbled, and almost instantly a few tears escaped from his closed eyes. "You were the first person other than my own mother to ever show me you loved me. You were the closest thing to a father I ever had. When Ellen and I became engaged, I felt strange. I loved her so much, William. I did. But, a part of me is glad she never had the chance to marry me. You deserve to have all of her. Not me. I never deserved a woman like that. I could never have taken your place, and I never wanted to. I loved you both. Ellen…if you can hear me, I hope you know that. I hope you know how much I loved you. I will never love anyone like that again. I want you both to know I'm going to watch after your boy…boy! He's a man now, isn't he? And, he's such a good man. He's heartbroken for his friends, but I want you both to know I will be there for him. I won't ever leave him. I promise." Jackson took a breath. "Blade… if you're there listening too… we're all going to look after Hannah and your child. There's been so much death. I'll make it my mission, Blade. I'll do whatever I can to make sure… to make sure you are the last Black Dragon we bury…" Jackson leaned back slightly and tightened his chest. He squeezed his eyes shut tighter as well. He didn't want to address Him directly, but he could truly feel something tugging at his chest as though He was there. "God," he said, and the word felt as though it pulled his very breath from his lungs. "I don't want anyone else to die in this war. Please, help us end this war! I can't bear it anymore, God! Please listen to me! I know you're there. I believe it now! Please, listen to me!"

"Jackson," Bartholomew's voice broke Jackson off from what he was sure was about to be himself becoming a blubbering fool. He was thankful.

Jackson opened his eyes, and he saw Bartholomew standing in the light of the candles half asleep. "How much of that did you hear?" Jackson asked.

Bartholomew came and sat down in the empty chair by the couch. He had on a serious gaze. "All of it," Bartholomew said. "And, I'm glad."

Jackson wiped tears away. "You're glad you walked in on me making a fool of myself?"

"I do not think you are a fool," Bartholomew said. He sighed. "I miss her too, Jackson. I wish my family had never left Kirkston. Perhaps things would have been different? Then again, how different would they be? Perhaps Ellen would have never met you then… and, I think that would have been a shame."

"Your sister would have been much better off had Will not ever been killed," Jackson said.

"Perhaps," Bartholomew said. "But, we will never know that, will we? She loved you. I know she did. Now, what is this I heard you blubbering about my former brother-in-law?"

"William took me in briefly as a boy," Jackson said.

"Yes, you told me about that," Bartholomew said. "Ellen told me she had thought of you as a little leech back then."

Jackson smirked. "She was right about me. I *was* a little leech."

"But you grew up," Bartholomew said. "And, now you are a man. A man praying to God, no less."

Jackson shifted uncomfortably. "Yes, I suppose."

"Have you ever prayed to God before, Jackson?" Bartholomew asked.

"No," he said. "I was not sure what to say."

"Whatever you felt called to say," Bartholomew said. "He listens. And, He answers prayers. Not always in a way you might hope, but He will answer them in His perfect timing."

"I assume you are a Christian," Jackson said.

"You assume correctly," Bartholomew said. "My son, Phillip, he was like Stewart –fancied himself to become a man of God. He wanted to preach. There was much talk of God in our household."

Jackson nodded. "I think I believe at last."

"You think?" Bartholomew questioned.

"No," Jackson said. "I do. I don't… I don't want to be like this anymore. I want what Stewart has. What you must have too. I want to be with God the day I die. I want to change. *Walk in the light,* as Stewart calls it."

Bartholomew smiled. "Stewart has been sowing seeds with you for some time. I can imagine he will be thrilled if I reap this crop for him!" Bartholomew jumped up happily and sat down on the couch by Jackson.

Jackson felt Bartholomew's arm go around him and grasp his shoulder. His other hand grabbed one of Jackson's wrists. "What are you doing?" Jackson asked.

"I wish to pray with you," Bartholomew said. "Let us make you an official Christian tonight."

"It is far too cold out tonight for you to go baptizing me in the river!" Jackson argued.

Bartholomew laughed. "No, Jackson. That symbol of rebirth is just a symbol. You can be baptized later at camp – that should be public! This, this is personal. This is for you, friend. Close your eyes, and we will pray together." Jackson closed his eyes, and he felt himself fighting back tears as Bartholomew prayed over him. "Father, bless this man for seeing the light and goodness that you offer! God, we come to you as lowly sinners seeking redemption through the blood of your son, Jesus Christ. We believe in the saving grace you offer, and tonight Jackson accepts it wholeheartedly. Thank you, Heavenly Father, for the seeds young Stewart has spent a lifetime sowing in this man. God, I ask that You strengthen Jackson's heart. Make him strong. Let him be evidence of your saving grace. Wash him in your son's blood and let him rise up a new man cleansed by Christ's sacrifice! It is in Jesus's holy and righteous name that we pray to You, Amen!"

If there was no peace anywhere else in that war-torn country that night, it was most surely found in the heart of the former pirate captain, Jackson White.

Chapter 31

Maxi Cook, along with the rest of the surviving rebellion soldiers, had arrived at the new campsite less than a day before. He now stood facing his two surviving sisters, Hannah and Anna, as Hannah nervously told him of her pregnancy and how Harold had quickly married her to Blade as he had lay dying. His brother Jimmy, his wife Jenny, and his son Tom sat nearby, eavesdropping, by one of the few fires the camp had managed to get started up in their brief time in the wooded area southeast of the mountains.

"You and Blade..." Maxi's voice failed him. He was angry, but his face remained solemn and unmoving.

"I beg you not to speak ill of him right now," Anna said on behalf of her elder sister. "She has only just lost him a day ago, Maxi. Scorn her now if you must; she can handle that, but don't speak ill of Terrance, please."

Maxi felt himself shaking, but he obeyed Anna's one request not to curse Blade's name —no doubt it had been something Hannah had expressed concern about to Anna prior to this conversation. "I have failed you," Maxi said at last. "All of you. Our grandparents were right about me. I am my father's son. The son of a peasant fool who had no idea how to raise people of their circles!"

"Father was a good man, and so are you," Hannah said.

"Am I? I let Susan marry a blind old fool with a bastard child from a previous engagement – and they're dead now! I married Anna off to a crippled former pirate! And... now, Hannah, you are pregnant with a dead man's child! That you would dare disrespect me by lying with that man...you are a little –"

Before the swear could leave his lips, a fierce slap was delivered across his cheek. And, there was Cassidy. She had seemed to appear out of air. "Say it, and I'll gut you," Cassidy said fiercely. "It's done," she said. "You will have a new niece or nephew. Be thankful that Blade's dying request was to marry your sister to try to right the shame he put on your house. That was for you – not for himself, you realize? Now, you can tell all your pompous acquaintances that Hannah is a widow instead of a pregnant embarrassment. That will help you save face, won't it? But, that will do nothing to help Hannah. Your reputation is saved, fool."

Maxi's face turned red. He had not thought of this. "You really think Blade had Harold marry them so quickly for *my* benefit?"

"What good will it do Hannah?" Cassidy questioned. "Widows are not popular trophies in your circles any more than a shamed woman."

Hannah lowered her head. "It is to my benefit too, I think," she said. "I wanted it."

"Of course, it was, dear," Cassidy said reassuringly and placed a hand on her shoulder. She then pointed a finger at Maxi. "Act like she's shamed you, and everyone will whisper. Act like your sister is a poor, sad widow, and Blade has managed to salvage the poor woman's name. This is the world we live in. I won't let you embarrass her, your own sister, Maxi. This will be hard enough on her not having Terrance by her side. Do not make her feel like she does not have her brother either."

Maxi's shoulders slumped. "Of course," he said weakly and stepped forward, placing his hands on each of Hannah's shoulders. "I love you, Hannah. And, I loved Terrance, too. Perhaps if this war ends quickly, we could find you a husband before –"

"No," Hannah pleaded. "I do not want a husband. I have one, and he is dead."

"What then do you want, little sister? Tell me," Maxi said.

Hannah leaned towards Anna and gripped her sister's hand. "What my sister's husband was kind enough to offer. To be a servant in their household when this war is over. He wants to be a father to my child in place of Terrance. He promised Terrance as much – that he would take care of me and our child. Would you permit me to work as my younger sister's servant?"

"Is that what you really want, Hannah?" Maxi asked, and she nodded. "Then that is what we will do."

At this point Jenny, Jimmy, and Tom rose from their seats by the fire and joined the family. Jenny took Hannah's face into her hands and kissed her forehead.

"That child will be well loved, you know this?" Jenny assured her.

Tom nodded. "Amen!" he said. "Though no doubt it'll be a little rascal between yourself and my good man, Blade, but the rascal we'll love nonetheless."

Hannah smiled ever so slightly at Tom. "Oh, I should assume so," she said.

Jimmy scrunched up his nose a bit. "So… you're going to go live with Anna when this is over? That's just awful as now it will just be myself, Tom, and Jenny! How positively boring!"

"Don't forget you'll have another little person about our house before too long, Jimmy," Jenny said and touched her stomach that now had only a slight curve to it. "Oh, how awful this war has been to this family. We've lost so many! But, between little Ellen Jane and these two little ones on the way, our family has much to feel blessed about!"

"Yes," Tom said, smiling. "Hannah, I love that child of yours already. Yours too, Jenny."

Maxi smiled. "I do love you all," Maxi said and then looked at Cassidy. "Thank you," he said to her, and she nodded.

Hannah reached out and grabbed Cassidy by her wrist. "Cassidy, could I have a word?"

***

Cassidy walked off with Hannah, not quite sure what the young woman wanted to talk about. A part of her thought that perhaps she had some questions about pregnancy. It was not as though Cassidy had not done that several times before. "What do you need, sweet girl?" she asked.

"To thank you," Hannah said. "My brother has been through a lot. This war has taken everything from us. Our mother. Susan. Tim. Our home. He carries the weight of the world on his shoulders, and I feared that learning what I did would be what would finally send him over the edge."

"Do not ever be ashamed of your child," Cassidy said firmly. "Get excited. A happy pregnancy is a healthy one. Terrance is gone, and that makes me very sad, but you have the Black Dragons, and you have your family. That child will be loved."

"Thank you, Cassidy," Hannah said. "This war has been difficult on you too, I know."

"It took Nicole from me," she said. "My daughter was everything to me. You will know this soon enough."

Hannah nodded. "I already feel such love for something I cannot even see. Might I ask you something quite personal, Cassidy?" Cassidy nodded somewhat reluctantly. Hannah continued, "You had four other children apart from Nicole... have you ever thought about reaching out and attempting to locate them?"

"Every day," Cassidy said. "Though only three of those children survived. I had one die on me. But, yes. I wish I could. I have no idea what happened to them. I do not have the resources to find them, though. It pains me knowing they are out there and that I never had the chance to know them."

"Perhaps after the war –"

"I do not wish to give myself false hope," Cassidy said. "It would mean the world to me to see them, but that is a fantasy. I am blessed to have known my first daughter. I just wish that she had been with me longer." Cassidy placed a hand on Hannah's cheek. "Thank you for your concern, though."

Cassidy left Hannah, but her heart was heavy. Her dreariness did not go unnoticed by Ace, so she revealed to him what was bothering her. He expressed his concern for her heartache on never having met her surviving children, but Cassidy assured him she would push through it. She always did. She always had to.

***

When Jackson and the others at last arrived back at camp, his first instinct was to find Stewart. All of the Black Dragon's were exceptionally glum, himself included, because of Blade, but there was still a certain lightness to Jackson's step that was unfitting for a man in mourning. His heart, though aching for Blade, was fuller somehow. Was this really God?

He believed, and it was a strange feeling. It was an overwhelming sense of joy even in the midst of a great tragedy, and he wanted to understand it. Stewart, he found near Chi – the two of them close together by a fire. By the glossiness of Stewart's eyes, Jackson was almost certain that they had been speaking about the tremendous losses they had just experienced in the mountains. Chi nudged Stewart, and the young man glanced up in Jackson's direction.

"Jackson!" Stewart said, sounding relieved. "You all have returned."

"Yes," Jackson said, and he could tell that Stewart knew something was different. He had this quizzical look about him as though he was trying to determine whether or not Jackson had cut his hair different or had grown contrarily somehow. "It was a rather emotional journey," he said. "Chi, would you mind if Stewart and I had a private word?"

Chi nodded and rose to her feet. She too looked at him with the same curious gaze. "Are you all right, Jackson? You seem a bit off," she said.

"Yes, thank you," he said before she politely departed.

"She's right; you do seem off," Stewart said as Jackson sat himself down beside the fire.

Jackson smiled at Stewart. "I'm quite different since you last saw me," he said.

"What, a few days ago?" Stewart questioned in a tone that suggested he found the idea humorous.

"Stewart, I did it," Jackson said. "I spoke to God. I prayed, Stewart. I asked Him to forgive me. I asked Him to guide me. To help me. To make me better. I believe, Stewart. I believe in God, and I want to spend the rest of my life doing His will above my own."

There was a moments hesitation from the young man. He opened his mouth as though he intended to speak, but he closed it again as his eyes had begun to water. After a deep breath, he at last spoke, "You… you have converted? You have accepted the Lord?"

"I have," Jackson said, and he felt himself becoming somewhat worked up because of Stewart's reaction.

Stewart took another deep breath, and with one hand he wiped his eyes before looking at Jackson again. "I've prayed for this... prayed for it since I was a boy...prayed for you, Jackson..."

"I know you have, lad," Jackson said. "Thank God for you! What boy... what person... would befriend the man who murdered his own parents? Would pray for the man who beat him? Would love him? Would hope that he would come to God to save his soul? I can think of no one else but you, Stewart. Thank you, lad. Thank you."

"It was not my doing, Jackson," Stewart said, now crying freely to the point of a nervous laughter. He gripped Jackson's shoulder. "My brother in Christ! I never thought I'd see the day! Thanks be to God!"

Jackson exhaled several times to keep himself from getting as emotional as his younger counterpart. The amount of love and forgiveness this young man had shown him time and time again was almost too much to understand, and to think there was a God who knew his sins (even greater than Stewart knew) who was willing to forgive him and to call him His child – well, that was more than he could have ever hoped for.

Chapter 32

Several Weeks Later

"It looks good, Ron," Smith said, admiring the first thing his friend had created as a blacksmith since losing his legs and tongue.

Ron smiled. Smith could tell his friend was proud of his creation. Theresa sat near him wiping tears from her eyes. The piece he had created was awe-inspiring. "You did so wonderful, Ron," Theresa said. "Peter, do you really think something like this is going to work?"

"The people need to see her," Smith said. "Not Harold. Her. Theresa, go get Harold, if you would."

Theresa stood and hurried out of the war tent. She returned shortly with King Harold, and his eyes glistened when he saw the golden chest-plate that Ron had formed so carefully. "I am having second thoughts," Harold said.

Ron mumbled something, and he used his hands to speak to Theresa for a translation. Gomda had been teaching him and Theresa to sign, but he was still amateurish at it. Theresa smiled and translated. "He says you would be a terrible father if you were not having second thoughts but that this is going to work."

This was no regular military chest-plate that Ron had created. Only shortly after arriving back at camp after burying Blade did Smith have a revelation: people were not fighting for Harold. Much like himself, they were fighting for his heir. Harold was getting a bit old, after all. The thought was to put Kathleen out on the battle field – a small battle that likely would not cause the heir harm but would showcase her in a public place in action. Show people that their heir was ready to win this war at all costs. Show Kirkston that Kathleen was leading. Perhaps it would gain them more allies to help to finally push John and his men out of Kirkston?

Smith had been specific in what he had told Ron to create. Not a basic chest-plate but one dipped in gold to show off her royal status and to help her to stand out to ensure that all would take note of her. That would be dangerous as that would mean John's men would spot her more easily, but she would be protected at all costs. Finally, the chest-plate was not to hide her feminine physique but rather to accent it. They were making a statement. The rebellion was fighting for this woman, and this woman was going to be fierce. Ron had added red, blue, and green rubies up and down the side – a fashionable statement that made the chest plate resemble the popular jewelry piece, the golden bangle, of Kirkston women.

"What is she to do, wear this over one of her dresses? She cannot ride into battle in a dress, can she?" Harold questioned.

"We're going to put her in one of Helena's outfits," Smith said, and Harold nearly feinted. Helena had had quite a reputation for her attire. She wore men's pants that she had sewn up the legs herself to appear tighter – more like riding wear. And, her tops were lacey and feminine but loose like men's clothing. "One of her more conservative ones," Smith assured him. "She will look like a soldier, and she will wear her crown into battle."

"I am going to die from shock of all of this!" Harold exclaimed. "We are intentionally drawing attention to her!"

"One battle," Smith said. "And, you best believe that I would take a bullet for your daughter if it came down to it. If all goes according to plan, the next fight is going to be just outside of Caldara City. There will be a multitude of civilians who will witness this. Word will spread fast that your daughter is leading this rebellion and that she is ready to finish this war."

Harold nodded. "If this is how it must be. It's time we got the support that we needed. This is not my army anymore. It is Kathleen's."

***

Kathleen sat anxiously on her horse, sword in hand. It would be a very simple mission. A grouping of John's foot soldiers had breached their agreed upon safe-zone outside of Caldara City because they knew the rebellion would not act. It was less than twenty soldiers, and Kathleen would be leading a small group of horsemen to chase them off with close to double the numbers and gun power. It was just a show of power, and in doing so right outside of the city was bound to attract attention.

Most of her companions were Black Dragons. Smith was on horseback right beside her. "Snake is going to be sorry he missed this," Smith said. With his leg still broken, Snake had been left behind at camp.

"This chest-plate is uncomfortable," Kathleen said.

"It's a chest-plate. It's not meant to be comfortable," Smith said and then whispered. "And, I don't want to hear a word out of you after having me wear a corset on a sea journey."

She laughed. "I suppose that's true." She tapped the top of the chest-plate that covered her breasts. "But, remind me why it is so form fitting? I don't believe I should be making a fashion statement."

"Hiding that you are a woman is not the goal," Smith said. "In fact, our intentions are quite contrary to that. The first female heir of Kirkston needs to make a statement today. That she is not going to back down. That she is going to fight for her crown and that she can do so regardless of her sex. Many have not come to fight for our side yet because they fear you."

"Fear me?"

"Fear what you cannot do," Smith said. "Some fools think John's dictator state might be a better alternative than an unmarried queen. We will inspire a nation today."

Kathleen nodded, and she spun her horse around to face her soldiers. "This battle will be won quickly!" she called out, and the men cheered and drew swords. "But, do not enter the battlefield with your defenses down simply because we have the numbers. We will fight, and we will show La Cofradía that we will not surrender our nation to them! No more games! We move our lines forward today!"

Kathleen pulled on her horse's reins, and she gave the signal to her men to move in. They sprung from the trees on horseback towards the clearing just outside Caldara City. John's men scattered; they were ill-prepared, and as predicted the fight was won in minutes and without injury to Kathleen's soldiers. It was an easy battle for her first victory leading the charge, but it was the first of many more to come.

They took four prisoners, two men escaped into the city, and the rest fell to their onslaught of bullets. The incident had caused quite a bit of noise, and she could see a crowd emerging from the city. Smith smiled approvingly, and Kathleen rode with him beside her to the crowd. There were perhaps fifteen people in the small group – mostly men, but a handful of women and children. Kathleen could feel a bit of blood on her cheekbone, but Smith told her not to wipe it off just yet.

"Princess Kathleen?" one of the men from the crowd greeted her.

"Aye," she said.

"You led this charge?" he asked in awe.

"I did," she responded. "I realize it may seem bleak now, but the Caldara's will take back our crown. I will pry it off Stevenson's head myself if I must! We need more soldiers if we are to take back the capital, and even more to take back Caldara Castle where Stevenson is stationed."

There was a small girl in the crowd staring up at Kathleen with twinkling eyes. "Did you truly lead this troop, Princess Kathleen?" the little one asked.

"Yes," Kathleen said. "I wish for you all to deliver a message to my people who are trapped in Caldara City under Stevenson's marshal law."

"Yes, Your Majesty," the man who had first addressed them said.

"Resist," Kathleen said. "Resist – band together. Come and fight! I will not have my people be made slaves to Stevenson. I will cut off that devil's head! We seek more soldiers so that we may end this! Come to the rebellion. We will make our presence known and be a thorn in Stevenson's side until I am sitting on *my* throne!"

Kathleen pulled the reins of her horse, and she returned to her soldiers. Smith smiled and followed closely behind.

***

"You need to take it easy, Snake," Smith said as he walked alongside his friend who was attempting to move much faster than his crutches would allow.

"It's an awful break," Snake moaned. "But, Dr. Conal says it's healing."

"Don't put any weight on it," Smith warned.

"Not yet, but soon," Snake countered.

"Your wife will beat you if she sees you moving around like this," Smith said and laughed.

"She'll beat you for letting me," Snake retorted. "Why are we meeting so far outside of camp?"

"Our war tent does not provide the privacy we need to discuss strategy," Smith said. "Not anymore now that it has a giant hole in the side." The tent that had acted as the rebellions war room had been one of the many items damaged during the rock slide in the mountains many weeks before. "Harold says he found a good place to meet in the woods."

They arrived shortly after everyone else, and Smith nodded approvingly at Harold's location. It was on a hill, but the hill was covered in trees. They could look down on the camp, but no one would see them from below. "Good," he said under his breath, and he laughed to himself to see that a large stump was being used as a table. Harold was lying out a map on the makeshift table as they arrived.

Jeremiah, Jackson, Kyo, Richard, Ace, and Kathleen were among those present. Jeremiah, Jackson, and Kyo had all essentially become their battle strategists, and they were good at it. Richard and Ace acted as advisors mostly regarding public opinion and the well-being of the soldiers. Smith and Snake had unofficially become generals, and that put Harold and Kathleen on top as their leaders of the rebellion as a whole.

Kathleen's golden chest-plate sat at the edge of the clearing, propped against a tree. She wore Helena's old clothes – always ready for battle now. As Smith and Snake approached, she could hear Jeremiah jesting with Kathleen about wearing his deceased wife's clothing. "You look lovelier than Helena ever did," he said.

"I am not dressed to amuse," Kathleen said harshly. "Your former wife does not have my respect, so I hope you know that this is not me honoring her in some way. You and Jackson told Stewart and the others that she tried to save you and perished, and I do not believe it for a moment."

Jackson turned a bit pale. "What makes you say this?"

"Because I've spent the last several years alongside that creature," Kathleen said. "And, she was no hero. She was wicked and cruel, but there is one thing she did manage to get right."

"And, what is that?" Ace asked his sister curiously.

"She was unapologetically woman!" Kathleen exclaimed. "No shame. And, she was a leader too… though she cared very little about those she led. I intend do what is best for my people, but I will not apologize if that means shredding my woman's garments to fling swords!"

"Fierce," Kyo said proudly. "I like it."

"She's like Helena with a soul," Jeremiah taunted, and Kathleen pulled her dagger from her belt and pointed it in his face

"Compare me to her again, and we will lose a strategist!" she warned, and Jeremiah held up both hands.

"Of course not, Your Majesty," he said.

"That's my girl," Harold said under his breath. "Now, we need to get started. John's men have moved additional forces to outside of Caldara City after our little display a few days ago. This thankfully means other cities are a bit freer from his soldiers, so I believe we could try to obtain additional soldiers most anywhere but the capital."

"Taking back the capital city is impossible right now anyways," Kyo said. "Soldiers have that place on lockdown."

"The people there need our help, though," Richard argued. "Soldiers killed eight civilians yesterday, according to my sources, after a dispute regarding a man wearing red and black – the soldier said he looked like he was wishing to support the Black Dragons."

"Madness!" Smith exclaimed.

"That's only the half of it," Kyo hissed. "They shot three men because they looked a bit Asian, so they thought they might be Silver Queen's! Only ones on my crew who are Asian are my sister and myself, but that didn't stop John's soldiers from making the assumption."

"Richard, I hear your concern," Jeremiah said. "But we simply do not have the numbers. Even if our numbers doubled, taking on the soldiers at Caldara City is not an option right now."

Richard nodded, disappointed.

Snake suddenly jolted. "Ladies!" he exclaimed, and Kathleen chuckled.

"I beg your pardon?" Jeremiah snarled.

"Look!" Snake pointed towards the camp.

An enormous crowd a short distance away from camp was marching through the woods towards the rebellion. "Ladies?" Jeremiah questioned as he observed the crowd of women waving several Kirkston blue flags. There were nearly a hundred of them, and many were dragging horses and supply carts.

"I think this meeting needs to be temporarily adjourned," Kathleen said.

They came down the hill, Snake falling a bit behind, and they met the crowd before they could enter the camp. "Ladies," Harold addressed the crowd. "How is it you all managed to find our camp?"

"Scouts," one woman said plainly.

"And, what brings you all here?" Harold asked.

A pale, tall woman stepped forward. She wore an elegant dress, and a young boy who looked similar to her stood at her side. "Your Majesty," she said to him with a slight curtsy.

"Mrs. Oden?" Harold questioned.

Smith nudged Richard. Richard whispered, "She's of a noble family within the capital."

"Yes, Your Majesty," she said. "We come to bring the rebellion supplies and soldiers."

"Soldiers?" Harold asked, glancing around the crowd that consisted almost entirely of women and frightfully young boys.

"Are you referring to yourselves?" Kathleen asked.

"Aye, Your Majesty," Mrs. Oden said. "My husband would not fight for the rebellion. Said that was the duty of a peasant. Well, he was shot yesterday by one of Stevenson's soldiers when he asked the scoundrel to leave our property. Seems those men do not care what our status was before the takeover. Most of these women behind me have lost their husbands and sons already as they have fought alongside the rebellion."

"I am terribly sorry for your losses," Harold said.

Mrs. Oden's young son spoke. "My father said to fight a war was a poor man's game. That men of our status need only help fund them. He is dead now, and I have been told that you, Princes Kathleen, have yourself fought in this war now. Who am I but the son of a cowardly noble that I would dare let my kingdom's princess fight without first offering myself? We want to fight. All of us, and we come bearing any weapons that we were able to sneak out of Caldara City."

Harold looked at Kathleen anxiously. "What say you?" he asked his daughter.

Kathleen nodded. "Let them fight if they can handle a gun and a sword. If not, we will have experienced soldiers teach them. If they are unable to learn quickly, the rebellion can use them somewhere other than the battle field. Let them into camp."

Chapter 33

The rebellion continued to grow. The people of Kirkston had become tired of their oppression under John's dictatorship, and people were flocking to the rebellion campsite. They had had several more battles since Kathleen's first display with her golden chest-plate, and she continued to lead many of them with great success. John's men were being crippled at every turn, and Señor Cruz was not pleased.

John felt himself becoming anxious. He and Maria had hidden themselves away in the royal chamber, their children quietly playing in the floor as they whispered to one another. "Look up at me," he said firmly. She did, and he could see a dark bruise around her eye. "Who?" he asked.

"Mi padre," she said.

"Why?"

"I dared to speak up for you when he was questioning your leadership," she said.

"This is getting out of hand," John said. "Someone painted an emblem of a golden chest-plate on the exterior wall of the castle. The people of Kirkston are not afraid of us anymore. It is only a matter of time. I told your father that we could not conquer Kirkston this way! We needed to show these people that we could be better leaders than Harold – not crush them for questioning our authority!"

"Papa will have your head," she said. "If your soldiers lose another battle, he'll announce himself as ruler and have you hung publicly."

"I am surprised he has not done so already!" John exclaimed.

The door to their room flung open, and Señor Cruz entered with Antonio and Juan behind him – the later still walking with a limp. Cruz did not look pleased. "I put you in charge of training soldiers and generals," Señor Cruz began. "And, now we are losing to armies that are halfway made up of women!"

"What is it you would have me do, sir?" John asked. "I have done all I can. I asked you not to strike so fiercely upon the people of Kirkston. I warned you that this would happen – that the people would eventually resist. We came as conquerors; they were already hesitant towards us. But, now –"

"It's not our forces that have stirred things – it is theirs!" Cruz exclaimed. "This ridiculous charade Harold is having his daughter put on is affecting their numbers. If his armies continue to grow like this…"

"*Her* armies," John said. "From what my men tell me, Harold has relinquished control to his heir."

"That is nonsense," Cruz said. "She is just a pretty chess piece meant to protect its king. This is a game Harold is playing."

"Maybe," Maria said. "But it is working."

Cruz glared in his daughter's direction. "Which is why we are going to act now. John, I want a small team who can go in and assassinate Harold and his darling heir. The rebellion is far too large now to hide their location, so instead of sending an army in after them I want to send a small group of men with a target."

"Consider it done," John said.

"No," Cruz said, holding up his hand. "Do not get ahead of yourself. I have already chosen the team. You will lead it up."

"Me?" John questioned. "I can barely walk with my bad leg, and I'm nearly blind."

"My men do not know Harold and Kathleen personally. We must ensure we accomplish this quickly and quietly without alerting the rebellion. You will help with the assassination, or I will have your head."

"Papa, please," Maria started to beg, but Cruz held up his hand to her to let her know he was not in the mood to argue.

"Antonio and Juan will accompany you, and I have already selected ten of my best men to come along for assistance," Cruz said. "You will steak out the camp, learn their movements, and you will kill Harold and Kathleen. If you can take out anymore Caldara's without being spotted, that would be a step in the right direction. You are not to take prisoners. There will not be a public hanging – too many have escaped thanks to our secret traitor already. You execute them on the spot. Do you understand me?"

"Yes, Señor Cruz," John said. "And, when do you wish for us to leave on this mission?"

"Tomorrow morning," he said. "At dawn."

"Aye, señor," John, Antonio, and Juan said in unison.

Cruz turned on his heels and departed, and Antonio and Juan followed. "Papa, are you leaving then?" Robbie asked from the floor where he had been playing.

John sighed. "Yes, I am sorry, Robbie. You will take care of Mamá and Amy for me?"

Robbie smiled. "Yes, sir."

"But, I do not need to leave until tomorrow," John said and rested his cane against a chair where he then sat. "Until then, you three have my undivided attention." His wife and children smiled in his direction.

**

John, Antonio, Juan, and the others had remained hidden in the woods near the rebellion camp for the past four days studying everyone's movements. Now, it was dark, but they did not light a fire despite the cool breeze. They could not risk being spotted by any rebellion scouts. The group of ten soldiers Cruz had sent with them were asleep, so it was just John and his two least favorite Spaniards sitting up discussing strategy in the dark.

"Our choices are to either sneak into camp at night or wait until their next little war meeting on that hill just outside of their camp they keep going to," Antonio said.

"And, unless they are all deep in conversation, it is likely that they will spot us if we try to make our way up the hill. They will signal an alert to their camp, and we'll all get slaughtered that way."

"Then let me go in, and I will slice their throats in their sleep," Juan said, always the brave and foolish one.

"The royals are all in the center of that enormous camp," John said. "If you want to get yourself killed snooping around, be my guest."

"Hilltop it is, then," Juan said, sounding disappointed.

"That still does not solve our problem," Antonio said. "We cannot sneak up on them from there."

"No," John said. "But, we could be there waiting for them. It's a long walk from their campsite to their little meeting spot. If we head there tonight, it's likely they'll break for their morning meeting."

Antonio smiled. "King Harold, Prince James, Prince Richard, and Princess Kathleen," he said. "That's all but the queen herself and one of Harold's nephews. Cruz would be pleased if we managed to take out four Caldara's."

"And, don't forget – Smith, Jeremiah, Jackson, and Kyo are among them. They are high priority as well," Juan said. "Plus, your blasted godson, John."

"You know my condition there," John hissed.

"We know," Antonio snapped. "No harm to little Johnny. He's on crutches – probably from that rockslide,

I'm sure. He won't be difficult to contain. You're lucky Cruz allows that."

"He promised me no harm will come to Johnny, and I expect you two to stay true to that," John said.

"Yes, John, we know," Antonio said with an eye roll. "We do this tomorrow morning, then."

"Yes," John said. "Tomorrow morning, and we will end them."

***

Smith stood just outside of camp early in the morning. He stood at the base of the hill waiting for the others to discuss strategy. He was up and ready too early, but that was quite intentional on his part. Kathleen arrived, and he saw that she had ditched Helena's former get-up for her own pair of riding trousers, a man's shirt, and a loose-fitting corset she wore overtop the shirt. He knew as soon as the war was over she would return to her lovely royal garbs, but a part of him liked seeing this side of her. He found it charming that she still wore her little tiara on top of her head even though she was practically dressed as a man.

"You look precious," he mocked her.

"Funny," she said, crossing her arms.

"Are… are those *my* boots?" Smith asked.

"Maybe," she said. "Can't march around this nasty campsite in my slippers, now can I? I had to shove stockings in the toes to make them fit, though."

"You little thief," he said.

"I have spent most of my time in these past three years with pirates and rogues and soldiers," she said. "Theft, no. They were merely *tactfully acquired.*"

"So, that's what they call stealing around here," Smith said and came near her. He grabbed her wrist and pulled her to him, giving her a kiss. There was a new, exciting feeling each time he kissed her. They had certainly been careful not to kiss in front of anyone lest it get back to Harold, but that morning he felt a little freer.

"You are in a feisty mood this morning," she said, draping her arms over his shoulders.

"I sense an upcoming victory," he said.

"We've had a few of those lately," she said. "The rebellion is growing stronger every day."

"John's men did not know what to do when half of our front lines were a bunch of women," Smith said. "I was not entirely sure what I wanted to accomplish with that golden chest-plate of yours, but I suppose that this was it."

She held his hands and kissed his nose, and he laughed at her. "Ah-hem," they heard Harold grunt from behind them, and they jumped apart. Harold frowned, but he surprisingly did not say anything. "We have a meeting to get to this morning, aye?" he asked.

"Yes, Your Majesty," Smith said.

Richard arrived next followed by Ace and Snake, still on crutches. They waited several minutes, but it seemed that Jeremiah, Jackson, and Kyo had either slept in or had completely forgotten about their morning meeting all together. "Where are those rogues?" Harold asked.

"Richard, go fetch those fools, and we will meet you at the hilltop."

"Yes, sir," Richard said and scurried back into camp.

"Takes me forever to get up that hill anyway," Snake said. "You could not have picked somewhere better to meet, could you?"

"Sorry, Snake," Harold said as they all began their walk up the hill. "It is private, and we can oversee the camp from there. It is the best we have for now."

As soon as they reached the top of the hill, they spotted men. Smith went for his pistol only to realize he had arrived unarmed. It seemed that only Kathleen and Snake had arrived armed, but they came bearing only swords, and Snake struggled to get to his with the crutches.

"Put it down, princesa," the man named Juan sang as several men stepped forward, surrounding them.

Kathleen gripped her sword tight, but there were simply too many guns on them for her to even try to make a move. Smith's heart raced. Would Richard be able to see that they were in distress and get help, or would he simply walk up the hill and into these men's clutches as well? "Scream, and we shoot every one of you now," the man named Antonio said as he and John stepped into the center of the circle that had formed. "Hands on your heads, go on," Antonio insisted.

They were all separated, though Smith did wind up being nearest to Kathleen. A gun was held to each of their backs. "How do you want to do this, John?" Juan asked.

"Quickly," John said. "Hang the girl first, and then shoot the others in the back of their heads – apart from my godson."

"You best stop acting like we have any relation," Snake warned, and one of the men detaining him kicked one of his crutches from under his arm. Snake fell down to his side, unable to bear the weight on his broken leg.

"Harm him again, and I'll shoot you myself!" John shouted at the soldier who held up both hands defensively, smirking in John's direction.

One of the men were already tying up a noose. Smith clenched his fists. There was no way he was going to let that noose get around Kathleen's neck. "Why hang me?" Kathleen asked as though she did not fear it. "Why not just shoot me and get it over with like what you plan to do with the others, John?"

John raised a brow. "You sure have gotten… *vocal*, haven't you?"

"Come shoot me yourself, you coward," she taunted. "Be a man and do your own dirty work."

John started to speak, but Antonio stepped between them and trotted over to her. He looked her up and down and laughed. "Big words coming from such a little girl," he said. "Harold, you have let your daughter turn into a crossdresser! Do those clothes make you feel tough, chiquita?"

Kathleen head butted him. Smith bit his bottom lip to keep from chuckling. *That's my girl*, he thought proudly as Antonio fell flat on his back in surprise, his nose busted and bleeding. The men standing by her grabbed hold of Kathleen's arms to keep her still.

John laughed louder than anyone. "Shut up, John!" Antonio shouted as he scurried back to his feet. He wiped his nose and looked at his hand; the man looked furious.

"Oh, lighten up, Antonio," John said. "She got you pretty good there, didn't she?"

"Golpearla haste ella muera," Antonio ordered the men lingering by Kathleen.

"No!" John snapped. "We don't have time for you to play games, Antonio!"

"I did not stutter!" Antonio shouted and pushed John with two sturdy arms, knocking John down to the ground. "Now!"

Smith was not certain what order had been given, but the men hesitated. "She's a lady," one of them said.

"Now!" Antonio ordered, and the men turned on her like dogs.

As soon as they tossed her to the ground, Smith moved. He swung his fists, but he did not manage to make contact with anyone before he was tackled. "Him too!" Antonio shouted, pointing down at Smith, and they turned on him as well.

He felt the bottom of the men's boots as they made contact with his back, legs, arms, and face. What was worse was the sound he heard each time one of the men did the same to Kathleen. "John, stop!" Smith could hear Harold pleading. "That's my daughter, John! Call them off! Please, stop!"

Smith felt one boot strike his temple, and he became dizzy. He wrapped his arms around his head to protect himself from anymore strikes like that. "John, stop this!" Ace screamed, and for a moment Smith saw Ace attempting to pull away while three men held him back. "Help! Someone help!" Ace shouted, doing whatever he could to escape but to no avail.

John sat on the ground where he had landed after Antonio had pushed him unmoving until Juan offered a hand and pulled him to his feet. "John, make them stop, please!" Smith heard Snake scream as he was coming closer to blacking out.

"Antonio, that's enough!" John roared. "Detener, now!"

Smith gasped when the men stepped away from him, but he remained curled up on his side for a moment. He tried to sit up, but he could not. The men yanked him up by his arms and forced him to his feet, but he dangled in their grasps. Smith turned his head, glancing over to see that the men were doing the same with Kathleen.

"Just shoot all of them, and let's go," John said. "Surely someone at the camp has heard all of this shouting by now."

Antonio huffed. "We have time. We will be able to see them coming from here." He walked up to Kathleen who attempted to stand by her own accord, two men still holding her arms back. Antonio struck her across the face, and Smith forced himself to stand upright despite the pain.

"Stop," Smith said, hardly able to recognize his own wheezing voice.

"John, please!" Harold shouted from the opposite end of the small clearing near the stump they had been using as a table. "We were friends once. Don't let him hurt my daughter like this!"

"She's not even crying!" Antonio said with an eye roll. "The woman is just glaring at me! Tough little devil!"

"Frankly, Antonio, I agree with Harold," John said, crossing his arms. "Enough is enough. Be done with it so that we can go."

Antonio stepped away from Kathleen, this time marching up to John. "You are so slow to get into the mess of things, John. It's time you earned your place alongside Juan and me again." Antonio pointed his thumb over his shoulder in Smith's direction. "I know you have been itching to get rid of that one." Antonio pulled a dagger from his sheath and handed it to John, and then he placed a hand on John's shoulder and marched him up to Smith. "Show me you are not afraid to get your hands dirty, and we will finish the rest off quickly. Who better to help get you back into the swing of things than this young man here?"

Antonio turned to face Smith and punched him in the gut three times while two men continued to hold him defenseless. Smith lost his breath, and he wheezed slightly with the last punch, kneading over in pain. "Stop it!" Snake shouted from where he was now pinned down on the ground by one man. "John, don't hurt Smith, please!"

John stepped forward, gripping Antonio's dagger with his left hand. He switched his cane and dagger so that he might hold the large knife with his good arm. He pointed the knife in Smith's face. "And, here I thought,

Smith, that we were destined to do this back and forth forever," John said wickedly.

Smith looked over in Kathleen's direction. He saw no way out of this. He could still hear Ace tussling with the group of what was now four men attempting to hold him back. Even if Ace set himself free, they would just shoot him down. Richard was still far off. It seemed that no one was coming to their aid otherwise Juan, who seemingly had taken over as watchman, would have warned them. So, Smith just looked at Kathleen. She looked beaten and bruised, but he took time to memorize her face.

John dropped his cane and reached out to grip Smith's shoulder. He placed the tip of the dagger against Smith's left cheek. Smith looked away from Kathleen and instead glared at John. "One of us was probably bound to kill the other eventually, eh, John?" Smith said, accepting his fate.

"Eventually," John said and leaned forward, his lips near Smith's ear. Smith almost could not hear John over the pleading of his friends. "If you can, help my Maria and my children. Get them away from these people. That's all I ask."

"What?" Smith questioned, but there was little time to process John's odd whisper.

John spun around in a manner that was surely difficult on his bad leg. He thrust his dagger into Antonio's gut and pushed the man back, taking three quick lunges with the man until they found themselves in the center of the circle that their men had formed. Antonio gagged, and John took one step back as the man fell.

"Antonio!" Juan shrieked in surprise.

John held up his hands in surrender, but that mattered very little to the stunned men who all open-fired in their confusion in John's direction. Smith managed to slip out of the grasps of the men who had been detaining him, but he knew he would be able to do little to fight them off. It did not matter – they fled. Ace managed to grab a gun off one of the men who had released him in order to shoot at John, and he fired on any of the soldiers who had dared to remain behind instead of fleeing with Juan and the others.

Four of La Cofradía's men went down by the woods, and Antonio and John remained laying in the clearing.

They had survived the encounter. Smith sat on his knees, staring a few yards away where John lay flat on his back unmoving, attempting to piece together what had just taken place.

Chapter 34

Smith fell to his hands and knees, and he looked to his left where Kathleen was in a similar position. "Kathleen?" he beckoned, and she crawled to him quickly and broke down in tears. She had been incredibly brave, but he imagined she was in just as much pain – if not more – than himself, and that saddened him.

They sat in the dirt by one another, and he kissed her – relieved that he still had her and not caring who saw. "Smith, are you all right?" she asked pitifully. She touched his left cheek where John's dagger had actually managed to cut him before he had turned on his own men.

Ace came bolting to them, and he slid into the dirt right next to them and had his arms around them both in an instant. He kissed his sisters head and kissed Smith's forehead as well. "We need to take you both to Dr. Conal right now," he said with tears in his eyes. He looked at Kathleen. "I thought I lost you."

Harold was right behind him after pausing to toss Snake his crutches. He fell to his knees and took Kathleen's face into his hands. Smith had never seen the great Kind

Harold blubber like such a fool. "Are you all right?" he sobbed and kissed his daughter's bruised face. "My little girl, they broke your pretty nose… what hurts? Is anything else broken?"

Kathleen nudged him slightly. "I'm a bit stunned to be sure," she admitted.

Snake stood over them as it was far too difficult for the man to get up and down, so Smith demanded Ace to help him to his feet. Smith reached out and put his hands on Snake's shoulders once Ace had him upright. "Are you all right?" Smith asked.

"Me? You ask me *that* after what I just saw?" Snake exclaimed and wiped tears from his eyes as well. "I… I really thought that this was finally it. That John was finally going to kill you all right in front of me!" Snake glanced over his shoulder where Antonio and John still lay perfectly still in the grass. Snake covered his mouth and looked away. "Oh… John! That fool!"

"Oh, gracious!" Kathleen cried from where she was still seated on the ground. "He moved! John moved! He's alive!"

"What!" Snake wailed just as Richard, Jeremiah, Jackson, and Kyo were arriving with a surplus of armed men behind them – all obviously having heard the shots. "Help me, Ace, help me to him!" Snake begged, and Ace did without question. Ace helped Snake down onto the ground at John's side. "He… he's breathing. Looks like he's been shot at least twice…" Snake looked back at Harold with desperate eyes. "He… he saved us!"

Smith felt Jackson's hands on him suddenly. "My boy, what happened to you!"

"Kathleen and I need help walking back into camp," Smith said.

"I've got you," Harold said to his daughter and helped her to her feet, and she winced as he did so.

Jackson allowed Smith to throw his arm over his shoulder. "John..." They could hear Snake mumbling. "Please, Smith... Harold... don't leave him out here to die like this."

"We're not going to, Snake," Harold said. "I would not do it to Señor Cruz himself let alone John Stevenson." He looked to Jeremiah and Kyo. "Hurry and go fetch a stretcher."

Kyo huffed. "I'll make sure he has a good fall on the way back down if you make me carry that man into our camp!"

"That's an order!" Kathleen snarled at him in a raspy voice caused by her throat having been hit at least once. "We don't leave men to die in the woods like dogs. Not even *that* scoundrel. You heard my father!"

"Um..." Kyo stammered. "Aye, madam."

Kyo and Jeremiah both ran off and returned promptly to help rush the unconscious John Stevenson into the rebellion campsite.

***

They had strung up what had once been the war tent and then propped some blankets over its tears for some privacy. Smith sat on a wooden stool at the foot of the small cot that John now lay in. Snake sat at John's side staring at him while Sky stood over him, a hand on his shoulder. Dr.

Conal finished tying up the last of John's bandages and then pulled a blanket over the man to hide the bloody mess.

"It won't be long now," Dr. Conal said. He had pulled two bullets from John's chest, and a third had lodged itself too deep in his back for Dr. Conal to even make an effort. "I gave him some medicine that should help with the pain, but that's all I can do."

"You've done more than what his people would have done for one of us," Snake said. "After what all he put you through at that camp of his, I imagine caring for him has been troublesome for you."

"I am not going to stand here and lie to you, Snake. There is a dark part of me that is quite satisfied to see him like this," Dr. Conal said. "But I imagine you yourself feel incredibly conflicted."

"I do," Snake admitted. "How can I care for someone I hate?"

The flaps to the tent opened, and Snake's mother, Amy, stepped in. Her eyes went straight to John, and she shuttered. "So, it's true; he's really here." She came and stood next to Sky, kneeling down for a moment to kiss Snake's forehead.

"You came to bid him farewell?" Smith asked.

"We went through a lot together in our youth," Amy said. "He killed my husband. He shipped me off to Balla. And, he separated me from my son. But, that cannot make me forget all those years running around Caldara with him and Robbie." She looked at Snake. "Your father loved this man. They were as close as brothers."

"I know," Snake said. "And, he saved your life."

"Yes," she said. "Poisoned me to do it, but he did it. I thought John showed up at our doors to help us make an escape from Harold. At the time, I knew nothing of his and your father's plan to hide me away and to trick Harold into believing I was dead."

The tent's flaps opened again. King Harold, Queen Rachel, Ace, Kathleen, Richard, and Harold's nephew entered together. It seemed the Caldara's had also come to bid John farewell. "It is getting a bit crowded in here," Dr. Conal said. "And, truth be told, I do not want to be present if the man wakes up."

"You think he will?" Harold asked.

"Possibly with the pain medicine," Dr. Conal said. "But, either way, he won't be with us much longer." Dr. Conal departed.

"Tell me something," Smith said, looking to Harold. "You've known John most his life. I saw the scarring on his chest when Dr. Conal was patching him up… what was that?"

Harold turned a bit pale. "The letters?" he asked.

"Yes," Smith said. "Someone sliced into his skin; it looked like a rather old scar. I could not read what it said, though, as his chest was covered in blood when I noticed it."

"*Peasant*," Amy said. "It reads *peasant*."

"How did that come about?" Ace asked.

Harold and Amy exchanged glances. The two of them still did not get along very well, but they accepted one another's presence at camp for Snake's benefit. Harold answered, "A very cruel prison worker at Caldara Castle did that to him. When we were boys, Robbie, myself, John, and another friend of ours got ourselves into some trouble with my father."

Ace raised a brow. "Your friend Frederick you've mentioned?"

Amy looked down. "Oh, that is a name I have not heard in a long time." She looked near tears, so Sky reached out and took her mother-in-law's hand.

"Yes," Harold said. "Father… he instructed his prison guards to roughen up my friends. None of them cared for John; he got the blunt of it all."

"Why the word *peasant*?" Ace asked.

"John's parents were hung for treason when he was just a boy," Amy said. "Robbie's parents more or less adopted him – unofficially, and he came with them when they moved to Caldara Castle. John's inheritance was taken from him by the crown – retributions for his parent's crimes. He was not born into the peasantry, but if not for the Lee's he certainly would have wound up there. It was a cruel taunt some of the castle staff would throw John's way as a boy." Amy then glanced at Harold. "He was not the only one, though, was he?"

"John and I became friends," Harold insisted. "Don't try to insinuate I was cruel to him as boys."

"No, just after *that* night, right, Harry?" Amy hissed.

"I'll come over there and strangle you myself," Queen Rachel warned.

Snake stood up abruptly, silencing everyone in the tent. "What happened? Go on! Say it! We've all been tip-toeing around it. What was it, Harold? What happened that made you give John the order to kill my parents? After everything we've been through, I think I deserve some honesty."

Harold hesitated, but Rachel nudged him and nodded with a sad expression. Harold was still a bit shaken – unable to form the words himself. Amy crossed her arms in annoyance. "Rachel went to bed with Robbie the night of Harold's coronation," Amy hissed.

Rachel shrieked in anger. "Oh! You devil! And, where were you but up in the royal chambers with Harold!"

"Mother!" Kathleen cried. "Father, what madness is this!"

The older generation in the room all seemed to turn a shade of red. Smith bit his bottom lip. He was not normally one to get the giggles during a moment of discomfort, but they were daring to burst through. He pointed to Ace and let loose a chuckle. "Your father went to bed with" –he pointed to Snake – "your mother. And, your father went to bed with" –he pointed back to Ace – "your mother."

"Oye!" was all Ace could muster, doing his best to avoid looking in Snake's direction.

Amy did not find Smith's comment amusing. "Honestly, Peter, if you want to make everyone uncomfortable, why don't we discuss our time in Balla?"

"Ah!" Smith sat upright. "No, I am quite all right."

"So that's it then?" Snake asked, completely ignoring the side comment his mother had made. "My father is dead, my mother and I separated, and I spent my life an orphaned pirate all because *you* wanted to cover up a royal scandal!" Snake rose as he shouted this, pointing a finger in Harold's direction.

Harold gazed in Snake's direction with sad eyes. "Yes, Snake. That is exactly it."

"You're a monster," Snake said to Harold.

"Snake, please," Harold said. "If I could take it back, I would. Snake, I hope you know, that I value your friendship. I have been afraid to tell you what happened –"

"I am sure!" Snake shouted.

"King Rylan found out about it," Amy said as though she intended to suddenly come to Harold's defense. "He did not really leave Harold much of a choice."

Snake slammed himself back down into his seat. "You turned John into a monster, Harold," Snake said. "You involved him in something he should never have been involved in. You ordered him to kill his best mate and his wife – and me, too, yes? Because John had to convince you to spare me, am I right?"

"We had an arrangement," Harold said. "John was going to adopt you after he fulfilled the order." He paused and then looked at Kathleen before turning his gaze down to his feet in shame. "Robbie and Amy went on the run quickly, but I knew John would be able to get close to them. I told him if he took out the order that I would spare you, but that was not good enough for him."

"Tell them," Rachel said and then touched Kathleen's shoulder as though this somehow involved her.

"John wanted to make sure you would have a good life," Harold said. "We were already plotting to take your parents from you. He agreed to fulfill the order if we arranged yours and Kathleen's marriage. And, that was when I announced Kathleen as my heir ahead of Richard...so that you would one day become king. Ace had already run off at this time, so everyone was expecting Richard as the next logical heir."

"I did not know that," Amy said under her breath.

"It was my way of somehow making amends for the order," Harold said. "You knew my father, Amy. If I did not act, he would take it as a sign of weakness and come up with something far worse. I thought if I somehow looked after Johnny... Snake... that it would make up for what I was about to have John do. John agreed. I did not know he had plotted with Robbie to ensure your safety, Amy. But, then Snake ran off, and John never found him. But, I had already made it public that Kathleen was to be heir, and John was irate that our deal could not be fulfilled. I made John general, and in doing so we would fulfill a long-standing tradition."

"And, you arranged mine and Stevenson's marriage," Kathleen said with disgust. "I am appalled!" she exclaimed and slapped her mother's hand away. "I suppose I always thought... that by making me your heir you were trying to start a movement. Trying to help women! But, the whole movement was just a sick cover-up for yours and mother's unfaithfulness to one another!"

Smith stood; he wanted to hurry over and put his arms around Kathleen as she appeared rather distraught, but the tent was too crowded to get around to her. "Everything you all ever told us were just lies," Richard said. "I suppose I should be used to it by now, but you manage to shock me every time, Father!"

"Richard, I am truly sorry," Harold said.

"For what?" Snake snarled from his seat. "For having my father killed? For your affair? For lying to Richard and Kathleen?"

"Sweetheart," Amy started to reach to touch his arm, but he jolted.

"You too, woman!" Snake shouted. "Do you realize what all you have put us through?"

"A man cannot die in peace?" a weak, shrill voice sent a shiver up everyone's spine.

Smith fell back into his seat at the foot of John's deathbed. All heads turned in the dying man's direction as John attempted to blink his eyes open. He coughed weakly. His eyes seemed to adjust, and Smith was certain that John saw him first. Smith instinctually frowned, and John turned his head so he would not have to look at him. "Amy!" John wailed as soon as his eyes fell on the woman. The man's eyes grew wide, and he looked sickly. "I thought..." John gasped for air.

"I know," Amy said, and she took Snake's seat next to John and grabbed one of John's hands. "I told the inn-keep in Balla to tell you I killed myself," she said. "I know you saved me, John, but I hated you so much. I just wanted to get away from you. I'm sorry."

His one good eye watered. "I'm dying," he acknowledged.

"Yes," Harold said, and John turned his head in Harold and Rachel's direction. "But, you saved us, John. All of us."

"Harry," John said. "Rachel... I don't want to hate you anymore."

"I know, Johnny," Harold said and knelt down at John's bedside for a moment. "Us either. I can forgive you, old mate, if you can forgive me."

"I've done so many things, Harry," John said and glanced over Harold's shoulders towards Ace, Kathleen, and Richard. "I've tried to kill your children. To kill you."

Ace placed a hand on both Kathleen and Richard's shoulder. "What kind of people would we be not to offer a dying man forgiveness?" Ace questioned. "Even you, Stevenson."

John then smirked slightly. "I don't suppose I can get a dying kiss from my old fiancé, could I?" he teased, though his voice was shrill and weak.

"Not even if you begged, you old fool," Kathleen said, but her voice was soft with him.

"I tried," he said and adjusted himself a bit more upright, and Smith could see a horrid look of pain cross over the man's face when he did so, and John let out a wretched cry of agony.

"Stay down, John," Harold said.

John rested his head, but he glanced towards his feet at Smith. Smith cringed to have John look at him with that confused stare. "My mind can reason these fool's presence, but why are you here, Smitty?"

"Well, John, I've known you so long, it's like we're old pals," Smith said, though his frustration he could not hide. "And, you did… well… you're dying, John. And, you saving me is what got you in this position, isn't it?"

"All the back and forth between us over the years," John said and took an agonizing breath. "I suppose you finally won, Smith. I'm glad… because I have been rooting for you the entire time." John closed his eyes, and for a moment they thought he was gone. But, he was merely resting. He opened them up again, and he looked back at Smith. "Cruz is out of reserves," John began. "He has nearly forty men stationed on the northern road leading up to Caldara Castle, but there are more stationed just within the walls that probably double the size of your rebellion. But, he's getting desperate. Continue hitting him hard, and he'll send those men out to fight." John spoke quickly, knowing he did not have much time.

Smith was taken back by the sudden influx of information. He snagged a quill and piece of parchment from the small table Dr. Conal had been using as a desk and began writing down all of what John had for them. The man was not holding back. Smith stared down at the piece of parchment as he took notes on all John had to offer. He had nearly run out of ink when he heard Snake mutter, "Smith."

Smith glanced up, and he could see how pale John had become. The man could hardly keep his eyes open. "That's enough, John," Smith said. "Thank you."

Each of John's breaths seemed to be a struggle now. "You remember my request I made on the hill?" John asked, his eyes fighting to stay open.

"I do," Smith said. "And, I promise, we will try to protect your wife and your children."

John's head then turned, and he looked only at Snake. "I am so sorry," John said, and the man seemed to want to weep when he said it but was simply too tired to do so.

Snake took his seat back from his mother and scooted it closer to the head of John's cot. He took John's hands. "I know," Snake said. "John, you loved me even when I hated you."

Smith watched Snake carefully. The man seemed so tormented and conflicted. John had somehow managed to become someone that Snake both loved and despised in a single breath.

The next moments happened quickly. John seemed to find a comfortable position, resting his head to the side so that he could look directly at Snake. There was this slight look of joy on John's face. "Your father would be so proud of you." The words came out of John's mouth in a raspy whisper.

"After today," said Snake. "He would be proud of you as well, John."

Three final breaths and this bizarre look of pure, unadulterated satisfaction crossed over the man's face, and then that was it.

John Stevenson was dead.

Chapter 35

In sacrificing himself for Smith and delivering them vital information on his deathbed, the end of the life of John Stevenson did not feel as satisfying as some of the Black Dragons had hoped. It was late, and it seemed that they had all instinctually gathered around a firepit while the rest of the rebellion headed to tents and sleeping berths.

Smith sat himself by Snake on a log. On the other side of Snake was Sky, and she held her husband's hand. Ace sat near Cassidy and Pierson, occasionally helping himself to whatever was in his flask. On the ground in front of him was Mouth, attempting to get Ace to handover the flask; Abigail sat curled up beside Mouth with her two sons, Jake and Ian, each boy fighting for a place in her lap through gentle nudging. Ian, the poor lad, had spent a good bit of the evening in tears over "Uncle John," and he rather quickly fell asleep curled up with his mother and half brother from the exhaustion the news had brought the poor child.

Yin and Clara sat close on the opposite side of the fire on a small log not quite big enough for the both of them, but they silently made it work. On the longest log by them sat Knot, his wife and daughter asleep in a tent with Hannah not too far off. Next to Knot were Gomda and Jackson. Stewart and Gwen sat in front of Jackson, warming their feet by the fire, and Squirt sat near Gwen casually holing her hand.

All were silent, mulling in the unsatisfying vengeance against John they had all hoped for. The pain he had caused was still there. It had not vanished with him, and he had left this world by a heroic act. It was difficult to hold onto hate when someone attempted to redeem themselves so valiantly as to sacrifice his own life for his enemy.

"So, what now?" Mouth muttered from where he sat, his question filling the void of silence.

"We keep fighting," Smith said. "We put an end to this war and put Harold and Kathleen back on their throne."

"This whole time I presumed we were fighting John," Ace said. "Now… he is gone, and I feel like we are… missing something."

"Clearly, John was not as involved in all of this as we had initially suspected," Yin said.

"The Red Dragon did say in one of his messages that John was just a figure head," Smith said.

Snake sat up suddenly. "You do not suppose that John was the Red Dragon?"

"We will know soon enough," Smith said. "I sent a messenger to place a letter in the tree by the palace. If we do not receive a response, then it seems our inside man is dead."

"I just don't understand why John would throw everything away for you, Smith," Stewart said. "I am relieved he did, but why?"

"I do not know. It seems we know less about Stevenson than we thought. He begged me that we would try to get Maria and his children away from the Cruz's. The Red Dragon told us that Maria was their leader's daughter, but John seemed sincerely worried that something is going to happen to her now."

"Almost sounds like John and Maria's roles in this have been somewhat involuntary," Cassidy suggested.

Knot practically growled in response. "I buried my best mate less than a month ago. If John was a mere prisoner by chance, there was no need to try to kill Smith then and in turn wind up killing Blade."

"John did help Smith pull Cannonball from that ditch before he died two years ago," Yin said. "And… he made sure Smith had the key to the iron cage where they placed my brother's body so that we could bury him. He even had Yang write me a farewell letter and placed it on his person."

"John is the one who had your brother hanged in the first place!" Gwen jeered.

"This situation is far more complicated than I could have ever imagined," Smith said. He heard footsteps behind him, and he turned to see King Harold escorting his wife and Amy Lee over to the fire. It was a rare site to see Amy near the royals without them bickering, let alone with her arm hooked around Harold's. "Come to join us?" Smith asked. He made room so that Amy could sit by her son.

Ace sat himself on the ground by Mouth so that his mother could have a seat on the log by Cassidy; Harold joined his son on the ground. "You all are speaking about John?" Harold asked.

"Aye," Ace said. "Just trying to understand." Ace glanced across the fire in Smith's direction. "Mrs. Lee, have you been weeping?"

Amy looked down. "Perhaps a bit. The John I knew died long ago, though."

"I would not be so sure," Harold said. "He showed a bit of his old self today."

"When did he become the version of John that we all know?" Smith asked.

"I do not know exactly," Harold said. "But, I am certain I am to blame. I saw a change in him, but I refused to acknowledge it. He was my friend once. The only friend from my boyhood whom I still had. I would not accept what he was becoming. I couldn't. I was so blind to it that he almost killed Kathleen aboard the first *Black Dragon* and came close to poisoning Richard. He shot Ace right in front of me. Until that moment, I still counted him as a friend because I just could not believe that the boy I knew had become such a devil."

"I think it was after his fiancé was killed by General Gregory," Queen Rachel said. "He was different after that."

Harold sighed. "I think me having him execute Robbie was what did it. I was cruel enough to sentence my own friend to death, but to have John execute a man he called his brother… Robbie was no more to blame than the rest of us about what happened. He was a good man, and I had John kill him all because I was afraid of my father's judgment. Robbie deserved better than –"

Amy cut him off. "My husband, may he rest in peace, is not entirely innocent in creating the monster that John became, and you know it."

"What did my father do?" Snake asked.

Amy frowned. "Robbie was still a young general when his parents were killed by some robbers. He was almost killed himself. It was a family of four; they were fairly notorious in the region at the time for robbing carts, but they had never hurt anyone before. Robbie's father had drawn a weapon, and one of the boys panicked. Robbie would have used up all of Kirston's resources trying to find those bandits. Harold's father felt that Robbie had grown obsessed, so he ordered Robbie to put someone else in charge of finding the bandits."

"John?" Snake asked.

"Yes, and what's worse is Robbie ordered John to torture those people when he found them," Amy said. "The Lee's had taken John in when he was only twelve. They were practically his parents. Robbie should have chosen someone else, but Robbie wanted someone who would take it just as personally as he would. You don't just give someone that sort of power and then sick them on a family who were just trying to get by. I think if Robbie had known how far John would take it, he would have chosen someone else for the task. But, after that day, he just started to falter."

"It's not that John enjoyed it," Harold said. "Maybe in the moment he did, but he was shaken afterwards."

"How bad was it, really?" Ace asked.

"Awful," Harold said. "John had his chance at revenge for Robbie's parents, and he took it. It was as though he had lost his parents all over again, and Robbie gave him the order to torture those people when he found them. The town the family lived in was in such an uproar about what John did to those people that my father threw John in prison for a week to pacify them."

"And, John?" Snake questioned.

"Shaken," Amy said. "He regretted what he did. I think it would not have affected him so much if not for the little girl."

"Little girl?" Smith questioned.

"Yes," Harold said. "John beat the bandits all to death in their home, and when it was all over he found a little girl hiding under a chair. Witnessed John slaughter her whole family. He gave her to some friends of the family. John had nightmares about that little girl's face… why are you all so shaken?"

Smith lowered his head. "Because we have heard this story before. You all are talking about Sea." Smith instinctually looked across the fire at Pierson. The child's eyes were hazy and full of rage.

"Son?" Ace beckoned and went to touch Pierson's shoulder, but the boy jerked away.

Pierson's hateful gaze fell on Amy. "It is no secret I had hoped Smith to be my father. How glad I am he is not, or he might have stayed in Balla with you and me instead of bringing me here to Ace – we were almost a family. How disgusting of me it would have been to call you *mother*! You, the widow of the man who ordered my grandparents to be beaten to death! My mother witnessed that! It was the start of her short, miserable life! Thank God I did not turn out to be a Barons if it had meant calling you *mother*!"

Smith felt a little heartbroken to hear Pierson say he was relieved to not be a Barons, though he knew the attack was directed at Amy.

"Pierson!" Snake scorned. "She is not responsible for her deceased husband's choice; do not be so cruel."

Now Pierson looked at Snake with the same hateful eyes. "How much worse would it have been to learn I was a Lee! To learn my Father's father was behind my mother being orphaned so young!" Snake frowned, but he did not respond.

"Pierson, that is quite enough!" Ace snapped and reached to grab Pierson by his arm, but Pierson jumped up from his seat. His angry glare went back and forth between Ace and Harold. "Oh, but how much grander is it to be a Caldara? My grandfather –" he pointed an accusing finger at Harold – "you ordered the death of my mother! John pulled the trigger but by your order!" Pierson had tears in his eyes now. "A Barons, a Lee, a Caldara – none of you suit me! I would call myself a Livingston for my mother, but she was an adulteress wench! And, she abandoned me!"

"Do not speak so poorly about your mother," Ace warned from where he sat.

"Nothing I said was untrue," he said. "And, you know it, Ace!"

Ace frowned. Pierson had never called him anything but *Papa*. "I know you are disappointed with me," Ace said. "You wished Smith to be your father."

"No," he snarled. "I might have once, but only because of my mother's letters. I'm glad Smith was not my father! He is the reason I never knew my mother!"

"What a ludicrous thing to say," Ace said, refusing to shout back at the young lad who had become irate.

"It's all his fault!" Pierson shouted. "My mother abandoned me because she would rather have been with him than me! She was afraid he would have left her when he found out about me, so she abandoned me!" Pierson looked directly at Smith.

Smith felt truly wounded. "I loved your mother," Smith said.

"Then you loved a selfish devil-woman! She loved you more than me! I hate you!" Pierson stepped forward and spit right in Smith's face.

Ace jumped up, and he scooped Pierson clear off the ground in a violent snatch. He kept a calm look about him as he dragged the screaming child off and out of sight. Smith wiped his face and started to stand, but Amy grabbed his wrist. "Let Ace handle him. It's not your place. He is upset. His mother is a sensitive topic for him. We should all take note of that for the future."

Smith sat down, and he hoped that Ace was not being too harsh on the boy. Pierson had put on quite a display, but who could blame him? He had not asked for any of this. "That boy loves you, Smith," Snake said. "This is just a lot for him to handle. Sea did abandon him, his adopted family died off, he finally meets you only to learn you are not his father, and then he gets dragged into the middle of a war."

"You boys do not even realize why the boy is really upset, do you?" Jackson said, and Snake and Smith glanced up. "He almost lost all three of you today. Ace, Smith, Snake. If John had not done what he did... it would be like Pierson was burying his father three times over today! Not to mention his grandfather and his Aunt Kathleen. I did the same sort of thing as a boy – it's why I distanced myself from William Barons. You can only lose so many people, especially that young, before you become too afraid to get close to anyone."

Smith nodded. He stretched his sore back and took a moment to look at all of friends. "I am tired of losing people too. It is time we end this."

***

Pierson felt himself scooped up by his father, and he was taken back by how aggressively the man was handling him. Perhaps spitting in Smith's face had been a step too far. Up until now, Pierson had never given Ace much of a reason to enact any form of discipline, so Pierson was not quite sure what to expect.

The boy was angry, but he was not exactly sure why. True, his life had so suddenly been turned upside down when his mother's cousin had become ill. But, these people had all been so kind to him. Smith especially.

And, upon arriving back in Kirkston, Ace had been eager to win his affection. "Put me down!" Pierson screamed. A part of him wished he would stop squirming and being so resistant, but he had already acted out. It would be far too embarrassing to admit he had been wrong simply because he was afraid of getting a whooping.

Once they were a considerable distance away, Ace put him down. He did not say anything. He just glared down at him in such a way that it made Pierson's stomach drop. He had not realized how frightening his father could appear. He was a tall, well-built man with a pale face and dark hair that hung down in his eyes, casting a shadow over the man's disappointed gaze. "I'm not sorry," Pierson said bravely, but he lost his voice halfway through the declaration.

Ace did not raise his voice, but his tone expressed his anger and disappointment. "Smith took a beating today – a bad one. He doesn't need you treating him like that. The man probably has cracked ribs, and you made him jolt back trying to avoid your spit. You *will* apologize." The finality of his tone made Pierson nod in agreement. "Look at me," Ace said to him when he dared to break eye contact. "You will apologize to Snake and to Mrs. Lee. That woman was very good to you and did not deserve those harsh words. And, you will apologize to my father as well. Do you hear me?"

"Yes, sir," Pierson said.

"Now, tell me what is bothering you," Ace said.

Pierson looked down. "I'm scared."

"I'm not going to leave you, Pierson," Ace said.

"You don't know that," he said. "You could die tomorrow."

"You are right," Ace said. "But, that is no reason to push me away. You have learned a hard lesson very early, haven't you?" Ace knelt down by him so that he was at Pierson's eye level. "I love you so much, Pierson. And, your mother I know loved you too. I know it must have hurt her to leave you behind. She certainly had selfish reasons for doing it, but I know it was for you too. What life would you have had with her? Before your cousin grew sick, did you not have a good life?"

Pierson's cheeks grew red. "I did."

"And, your mother knew that you would with her family," Ace said. "And, when this war is over and my homeland is safe again, I want to give you a good life. I do not want you to feel afraid. I want to give you a home where you feel safe and loved. Tell me, son, what do you think of Miss Cassidy?"

Pierson smiled. "I like her, Papa."

"Good. Because when this is over, I am going to marry that woman. Then we will buy a home. I will get an honest job. We will be a family."

Pierson felt warm. He hugged his father, but when he pulled away he felt sad. "Papa, what about Cassidy?"

"What do you mean?"

"She is so sad, Papa," Pierson said. "Her daughter is dead, but she has other children too, right?"

"That is true," Ace said. "But, that is something I do not want you to worry about."

"It just makes me sad. My mother gave me up. Cassidy gave up some of her children too, but she is so sad about it. Do you think my mother ever missed me like that?"

"I am certain of it," Ace said and glanced up to see that his friends were slowly parting ways to turn in for the night. "Go do what I asked of you and apologize."

"Yes, sir," Pierson said and hurried off towards the fire. He ran into Harold first, and Ace watched approvingly from a distance. Harold kissed the top of Pierson's head and then headed over to Ace while the boy made his rounds, taking his time especially with Smith.

"I half expected the boy to come back with a bloody nose after that display," Harold said with little sincerity.

Ace chuckled a bit. "You have little faith in me as a father then?"

"You had a terrible example to follow, I'm afraid," Harold admitted.

"You were not so awful," Ace said and laughed. He then became serious. "After all I have put you through, Father, I am ashamed to ask a favor of you."

Harold looked at Ace with the most genuine of expressions. "Anything."

"When we return your throne to you, I ask that I be permitted to make use of your resources to aid me in locating Cassidy's children she was forced to surrender," Ace said.

"If that is what you wish," Harold said. "I know you intend to marry that woman. Do you really wish to make yourself responsible for her bastard children?"

"She already loves mine," Ace said. "And, if her other children are of any resemblance to Nicole, I will cherish them."

"You have my word then, son. We will find them."

Chapter 36

Young Robbie Lee had just finished singing his little sister to sleep. He took a key to the door and locked her within the bedroom, making sure he was the only one able to enter. He was a young child, but he was old enough to know that the death of his father could very well put the two of them in danger.

"Your marriage to John was never sanctified to begin with!" he heard his grandfather's voice snarl down the hall. He could hear his mother sobbing.

Robbie hid himself behind a curtain in the darkened hallway and listened. "Papa, don't make me do this, please," he heard his mother say.

"Juan and the priest are in the throne room waiting for us," his grandfather snarled. "Shy away from this, and those little creatures you call children will join their father in purgatory."

"They are your grandchildren!"

"They are nothing but the causes of a falsified marriage I never approved of! I own this nation now! You think I would ever hand it over to *Robbie*? You and Juan will give me the son I never had, otherwise you are useless to me. Get to the throne room, or I will end them both tonight." Robbie peered out from behind the curtain and watched his mother exit the room and head down the hall.

His grandfather exited after his mother had disappeared from view, and Robbie stepped out from his hiding place. "Abuelo," Robbie said, and the old man jumped.

"Ah, Robbie, you should be in bed, my boy," the old man said.

"Diablo," Robbie said. "My father is not even buried yet, and you are forcing my mother to –"

The man put a hand on Robbie's shoulder, and the boy froze. "You have your father's mouth. I loved your father once. Counted him as my friend, but he betrayed me when he ran off with my child. He is lucky he lived as long as he did. You want to be angry, that's fine. But, do not be angry at me, nieto. Your father died today a traitor. He stabbed Antonio. Did that to save an enemy, why? Because of his damn godson, that's why! The one they call *Snake*. He couldn't go through with the task I assigned him because of his love for that boy! Your father is dead because he loved his godson more than you."

Robbie yanked his shoulder away, and he saw his grandfather smirk with the satisfaction of shaking him. "That's not true."

"You know it is, Robbie. Your father did not even care enough to teach you to be a man."

"He did so!" Robbie declared.

"Then what would a man do now?" his grandfather asked. "Your father is dead because of Johnny Lee. What would a man do now? What are you going to do, hombrecito?"

"I will kill Snake!" Robbie shouted. "Cruz blood runs through my veins whether you care to admit it or not. I am my mother's first born. I will show you that I am worthy of your inheritance. I will kill the man my father dared to love enough to die for."

The old man smiled. "Perhaps I was wrong about my little Protestant grandson?"

"If I kill Snake, will you release my mother from Juan?"

"Your mother is getting married tonight," Cruz said. "God does not tolerate divorce."

"Then after I kill Snake, I will kill Juan so she can be free," Robbie said.

Cruz then laughed, but it was a pleasant laughter – one riddled with amusement. "You think you can kill those men? Tell you what, boy. If you manage to kill Snake, swear to the Catholic faith, and take my name, I will kill Juan myself, make you my heir, and I will never force your mother to marry another man."

"I will do it!" Robbie shouted.

"I am sure," Cruz said doubtfully and headed to the throne room, somewhat intrigued by the wager he had made with his grandson.

***

Smith breathed deeply. He had with him his most trusted rogues. Commodore Kyo Mori, Kyo's sister Chi, and Jeremiah White. They had been chosen to accompany him on this task for two simple reasons: they were all excellent shots with a musket, and they were not the type to hesitate to end a man's life. To keep them in check were his closest companions: Snake, Ace, and Kathleen.

A large Catholic Cathedral outside of the city of St. Dale was still under construction, and it had been called as a meeting place between Smith and the notorious Señor Cruz of La Cofradía de Cruz. A message had been sent to the rebellion camp by means of an unarmed soldier demanding a meeting between Cruz and either Harold or Smith.

Smith stood a good distance from the partially built cathedral. Chi and Kathleen had been sent out to search the surrounding area to ensure that this was not some sort of trap. The two women arrived just as Smith was starting to grow anxious. "Well?" Ace asked, helping his sister down from her horse.

"He has brought only three men to protect him just as his message stated," Chi said. "And, those men you can see from here posted outside of the cathedral."

"Hard to believe Cruz called this meeting just to retrieve John and Antonio's bodies," Snake said, wringing his wrists as he leaned on the cane that he now carried.

Smith nodded, recalling the subject matter of the message. "Snake, Kathleen, and Jeremiah. You three man the bodies and stay hidden. The rest of you will act as my guards."

Smith departed from their hiding place with Ace and the Mori's on his heels, all heavily armed. They approached the building, and Cruz's guards flinched nervously. "He is inside?" Smith asked.

"You must enter unarmed," one of the men said.

"He is unarmed," Ace snarled. "And, we trust that Cruz is as well?"

"He is," the man said, so Smith entered.

Only after confirming that no one apart from Cruz was present inside did his friends agree to remain outside. A bitter looking old man sat in the empty room at a small table where he was enjoying some wine and a bit of red meat. Smith sat in the empty chair across from him, and he stared blankly at the man.

"About time I met the great Captain Smith," Cruz said. "You have been a thorn in my side for some time now. I've had the pleasure of meeting only a handful of your men. The brothers they call Mouth and Squirt – a lively lad. Commodore Kyo. And, of course, your little blacksmith; my men did a number on him. But, let's not talk about that. What I want to know is what is so special about you that my man would die for you and betray me?"

"Your man, John, merely turned from his wicked ways in his last act," Smith said. "There is nothing special about me."

"You think we are wicked?" Cruz lowered his glass and looked at Smith with a hateful gaze. "You are all Protestant devils who –"

"Is that what this is? Some sort of religious conquest? You think you are doing the will of God by overthrowing a Protestant king and tormenting his people?"

"Catholics once faced persecution in Kirston under the rein of King Kevin. Perhaps I believed it was the turn of you Protestants," he said. "It is not merely religion that drives me."

"Power, then?"

"I am a descendant of King Ferdinand of Spain," Cruz declared. "I have always meant to rule."

"Not according to the current rulers of Spain," Smith said. "Seems to be some disagreement about your lineage. You tried conquering Spain once, but your followers were crushed and tried for treason. So, instead you turn your eyes on a smaller nation you felt you could conquer? Why Kirkston?"

Cruz laughed. "I have hinted it already."

"The persecutions that took place under Kevin? Is that why you had your men destroy the island named for him so harshly rather than just attacking the reserves? Because you harbor a one-hundred-year-old grudge?"

"My ancestors came to Kirkston to escape a political threat only to be met with death and persecution here under King Kevin's dreaded Akito poison he was using to wipe out the influx of Catholicism. My family, those who still lived, fled back home to Spain and have been living in the dark ever since – building a resistance for generations."

"And, you got greedy and impatient. Decided to try to take on the Spanish government before you were ready, so instead you turned your eyes on the country who refused to welcome your ancestors in their time of need. Nearly a century of hate passed down, I see."

Cruz nodded and then took a sip of wine. He then poured Smith a glass and pushed it in front of him. "But, we are not here to talk about that sort of thing, are we?"

"Why are we here, Cruz?" Smith asked.

Cruz took a bite of his dinner and another swig of wine. "Just to fulfill a silly request of my daughter. She wants her husband to have a proper burial in the royal cemetery. I suppose he was technically a Kirkston king for a few years. I come here only to discuss the return of his body so that my daughter can grieve properly – and the body of Antonio for his brother, Juan."

"How noble of you," Smith said with a trace of sarcasm in his tone. "So, your daughter and her children are well?"

"Young Amy has just begun to notice her father's absence, I believe. She is just a little thing. Robbie is angry as one would expect from such a lively boy."

"And, Maria?" Smith asked.

"Unhappy at best. She does not care for her new husband, but that concerns me little. What business is this to you anyhow?"

"New husband?" Smith questioned. "John has been dead less than two days."

"Maria is my only living child. I need a proper heir, and right now Robbie does not suit my needs. Juan and Maria will produce for me a proper Spanish lad."

Smith took a swig of the wine. "You have turned your own daughter into a plaything for that miscreant before her husband could even be buried."

"Awfully concerned for my daughter, aren't we? Tell me, did John have you swear some sort of oath? Answer me not; I do not care. Am I permitted access to John's body for my daughter or not?"

"Yes," Smith said. "But, in exchange for John and Antonio, we insist you grant us a five-day ceasefire."

Cruz grinned. "Are your troops being crippled, Captain?"

"Far from it," Smith insisted. "But, our people need rest as do yours."

"I can agree to the ceasefire," Cruz said. "You have brought the bodies?"

"We have," Smith said.

"Then we are done here," Cruz said. "Tell your men to enjoy these next five days, Smith, because when the ceasefire ends, I will rain fire down on your camp."

"We will take you, Cruz," Smith threatened as he stood. "Kathleen will lead us to victory."

"You put too much faith in that woman."

"I put all of my faith in that woman. She is fierce, and now she knows it. And, she will lead us and bring you to your demise."

Cruz stood and swigged the rest of his wine. "We will see." He walked around the table and bypassed Smith, leading the way down the aisle.

They exited, and Smith could see a standoff had formed between his men and Cruz's. "Arms down," Cruz said. "We have negotiated a five-day ceasefire. Behave."

"Aye," Smith said, and he watched as Ace and the Mori's lowered their weapons as Cruz's men did the same.

"Señor, Esta un Caldara," one of the men said, nodding in Ace's direction.

"I am aware," Cruz said. "But, I am a man of my word. The ceasefire starts now." Cruz looked at Chi with an upturned nose. "This is why your rebellion is sure to fall. This little woman is no soldier."

Chi sneered in his direction. "I am Chi. My name means *blood*. Care to learn why?"

Cruz chuckled as though he found her aggression comical at best. "The Mori's?" he asked. "I thought I recognized you, Kyo. Care to return to Caldara Castle with me? I have your room reserved in the prison chambers."

"I'll end you," Kyo warned.

"There are not many yellow men here in Kirkston," Cruz said. "I know my Kirkston history, but it seems you have failed yours, Mr. Mori. My ancestors owe yours a debt for the discovery of the Akito poison cure. It is only a matter of time before the Protestant heathens turn on your family again in an attempt to make rid of the rest of you Japanese primitives. It's why your family turned to piracy in the first place, yes? Your kind will never be fully welcomed here, but if you and your people swear your loyalty to me, I can give you sanctuary."

"I am not trapped in the past, and neither is Kirkston," Kyo said. "I prefer to fight for Harold and Her

Majesty, Kathleen. They have at least never called me a primitive because my father was Japanese! Have you not been paying attention these past three years? Rogues, Japanese pirates, noblemen, Africans, and now women too are all taking up arms against you. You can hardly threaten me into believing that a win for Her Majesty would mean persecution because of my ancestry! What a foolish thought! I have already spent time with your people being tortured and spat on while being called *the Asian*. I am respected by Smith and his comrades. Do not test me."

Cruz merely huffed in response to Kyo's rant. "Just show us where the bodies are so that I can be on my way. My daughter has been abysmal about fetching John's corpse to bury, and I would like to put this troublesome venture behind me."

Smith called for Snake, and Snake and the others came toting John and Antonio, both dead men wrapped in cloths. Smith could tell Snake walked with pain in his leg; the leg had healed, but it would never be quite right again which was why he now always carried either a cane or a crutch. Cruz grimaced at the sight of Kathleen. "Had I known you were bringing her, I might would not have agreed to a ceasefire," said Cruz.

"Ceasefire?" Kathleen questioned as she walked behind Jeremiah and Snake who were lying the stretcher out they had used to carry John. "And, here I was hoping to put a bullet in that man's head." They then dragged Antonio behind and plopped him down by John.

"So, you are the pretty little princess causing me so much headache," Cruz snarled in her direction. "Your head will roll by the end of this."

"Take John and Antonio and be on your way," Ace roared.

"Of course," Cruz said. The man's eyes lingered on Snake for a moment as his men carried John and Antonio to a nearby carriage. He looked at the cane Snake now carried. "In his last moments, did John even tell you?" Cruz asked as he began ascending into the back of the carriage.

"What are you talking about?" Snake jeered.

Cruz laughed, and as he shut the carriage door behind him he called out, "That he was your father, you fool!"

Chapter 37

Cruz and his men hurried off immediately after he had shouted his claim out of the carriage and laughed in a mocking tone. Smith turned to look at Snake, and the man seemed almost ghostlike. The very thought of what Cruz had said, that John could have possibly been Snake's father, seemed to have sent tremors through him.

"Snake?" Smith beckoned, and he watched his friend grip his shirt collar as though it was choking him.

"Cruz is only attempting to get in your head, mate," Ace said.

It was a ridiculous notion to Smith. Snake bore no resemblance to John, but then again, he had no idea what Robbie Lee had looked like. Many who knew Robbie Lee had often commented that Snake looked just like him. "Snake, mate, are you well?" Kyo asked.

"Of course, he's not!" Chi jeered, and she seemed the only one who had not become frozen in place from the comment. She stepped to Snake and hooked arms with him, forcing him out of the daze he was in. "You need to sit down. You look like you are going to fall out."

"All these years... John would have said something," Snake declared. "John has tried to snatch me up so many times – why not just tell me he was my father? He always called me his godson. If it were true, then it would make sense to just tell me if he wanted me so desperately, yes? Cruz is lying to me!"

"Sit down," Chi insisted, leading him to a stump.

Snake sat, and Smith could see his friends entire body shake. His hands in particular seemed possessed with the shivers. Snake's breathing became so heavy that it appeared as though the man was struggling for each breath. "I am a Lee," Snake said firmly, and his voice cracked slightly. He fought off an onset of tears by replacing them with a look of anger and fury. "I need to speak with my mother." A slight greenish haze appeared on Snake's cheeks as though the man was going to be physically sick from this potential revelation. "Surely my mother did not bed both John and Harold!"

"It does appear that there were a number of strange relationships in our parent's youth," Kathleen said, and Smith nudged her with his elbow angrily to let her know it was not her place. She crossed her arms. "I do not know what to make of what Cruz said, but denying the possibility would be absurd, Smith."

"I met Robbie Lee as a boy," Ace said. "And, you are his son. You favor him."

"Aye," Kyo said. "As did I. You favor him, Snake. This is a cruel jest is all it is."

"I need to speak with my mother," Snake said. He took a few deep breaths, and he wrung his neck as though he could not breathe at all.

"Then let's go," Smith said. "No sense in waiting around here. We need to let the camp know that we have negotiated a ceasefire."

***

When they drew near to camp, Snake took off on his horse. Smith hurried close behind, leaving the others in the dust. Snake dismounted his horse carelessly and nearly fell thanks to his bad leg, and the man did not tie up the beast. Smith dismounted with a bit more care and called for Squirt who was nearby, requesting he take care of the horses for him. Squirt looked at Smith with these knowing eyes. "Is Snake all right?" Squirt asked.

"I do not know," Smith said, handing over the reins to Squirt before hurrying after his friend.

He caught up to Snake near where a group of women were broiling some stew, Amy Lee among them. She clearly saw the madness in her son's eyes, and she hurried to meet them both away from ear shot of the particularly gossipy group she had been standing with. "Johnny, what ails you?" she asked her son.

"Was John Stevenson my father?" Snake asked as Smith caught up to them.

"Not wasting anytime there, I see," Smith muttered, a bit breathlessly from his sprint.

"Ah!" Amy shrieked as though the idea disgusted her. "What makes you ask me such a thing!"

"Cruz," Snake said. "He claims that John was my father. What say you?"

"What say I?" she said, looking as though she could feint. "I say that I am your mother!"

"I did not ask whether or not you were my mother," Snake said. "I want to know about John! Is that man my father?"

"I tell you truthfully that until my foolish evening with Harold, I was never with another man apart from Robbie Lee!" she again shrieked and appeared almost dizzy. "Everyone says how much you look like Robbie."

Smith stared at Amy. He had lived with that woman for quite some time, and he knew her well enough that he could sense extreme uneasiness in her. "Amy, what are you keeping from your boy?" Smith asked.

"Robbie and I are your parents," Amy said to Snake as though she was chastising him. Her defensiveness did nothing to convince Smith that she was being entirely truthful.

"Tell that man the truth!" Queen Rachel hollered as she and Harold came marching up on the scene – both appearing somewhat anxious about the confrontation.

Snake reached up and gripped the top of his head as though he intended to rip every bit of hair from his scalp. "What truth!" he screamed. "What truth!"

Smith could see they were now attracting a crowd; Sky was among them looking quite flustered by her husband's behavior. Without much warning Amy spun in Queen Rachel's direction and attacked the woman's face with her fingernails. "Ah! You mad woman!" Harold hollered, throwing himself between the two women. Harold received several scratches and punches from Amy for his attempt to intervene, but Snake eventually yanked his mother back by her arm.

"Tell me!" Snake screamed, and when he did Amy burst into tears.

"I am your mother!" she cried. "And, Robbie Lee – "

"Is dead," Harold said. "Your husband's feelings do not matter now. He wants to know. Tell him!" Harold then turned to his wife, cupping her scratched up face in his hands to check the extent of the damage Amy had managed to inflict during her state of lunacy.

Snake took several breaths. Smith placed a reassuring hand on his friend's shoulder, and when Snake was calm, he brushed it away and nodded a thank you in Smith's direction. Amy was now openly weeping as Snake gently placed a hand on either of her arms. "You are my mother," Snake said. "But I deserve the truth, don't I?"

Sky stood a safe distance back, and Smith could tell the poor woman desperately wanted to fix whatever this was but was unsure of what circumstance had led to this uncomfortable moment for her husband. Amy wiped her tears. "Robbie and I wanted children. We tried to conceive, but we struggled," she said. "When we did manage to conceive, I could not hold onto them. I lost six babies when I was just barely pregnant with each of them! My seventh I carried until I delivered a stillborn! That was around the same time John lost his fiancé after General Gregory killed her; she had been in labor with his child when Gregory harmed her. John cut you out of her and saved you. He gave you to me to nurse as I had just lost a little one myself. Robbie called you Little Johnny, and then John told us to give you the name Lee. He knew how much we wanted children, and losing his fiancé in that way…"

Snake now had tears rolling down his cheeks. He suddenly looked in Harold's direction. "You knew. You knew this whole time!"

"You are a Lee!" Harold shouted in Snake's direction. "You have been since the day you were born. Robbie loved you. Robbie *died* for you."

"And, now, so has John! He did not sacrifice himself for Smith; you all know that was for me," Snake said. "How can a man have two fathers and barely know either of them?" Snake turned, hooking arms with Sky to go and find some privacy with her as his comfort.

"Snake," Smith started to speak, but Snake stopped him.

"I believe I just need a moment, mate," Snake said, and he and Sky left.

Smith looked at Amy. He still cared about her deeply, and she looked like a complete mess. A mere shell of a person. "Amy, Snake loves you," Smith assured her.

"I have brought nothing but trouble to this camp," she said. She glanced in Rachel's direction. "I am sorry." Rachel nodded in Amy's direction, rubbing one of her scratched up cheeks.

Smith turned and left Harold, Rachel, and Amy standing together, but he spoke over his shoulder at them as he walked away. "You three have caused that man more heartache than you could ever repay."

Kathleen, Ace, Kyo, Chi, and Jeremiah all stood at the outskirts of camp as they tied up their horses. "What happened?" Ace asked. "Is John Snake's father?"

"Yes and no," Smith said. "I think that is something he should tell you if he feels you need to know."

Ace nodded, seeming somewhat disappointed. Kathleen sighed. "Poor Snake," she said and took Smith by the hand. "Is he up for company, do you think?"

"Not now," Smith said, and she nodded. He put his arms around Kathleen and rested his head on her shoulder. The news of Snake's lineage and unusual birth was almost too much for Smith to take in. He could not even imagine how Snake felt on the matter.

***

It seemed that several ships made use of the five-day ceasefire. As soon as word spread through Kirkston, help arrived. British ships treaded along the southwest coast of Kirkston not but two miles from the rebellion's current hideaway. Kathleen, Smith, Harold, Ace, Rachel, and Richard all met the men as they arrived on shore in small cockboats.

Kathleen was dressed in her warrior attire – the golden chest plate in particular she had become known for. A man in military garbs approached, and he had with him a letter. "For Her Majesty, Princess Kathleen," he said.

Kathleen thanked the man and took the letter. She smiled. "I see Melusine has done me right. You come here as our aid?" she asked as she read the letter to herself.

"We are here," the man said. "But parliament only granted the woman a thousand men."

"A thousand men!" Harold exclaimed with excitement. "That will give as an advantage for the first time in this war."

"I am glad His Majesty is pleased," the soldier said. "I am General Joseph Earlsworth, and I am happy to offer my men as assistance to the allies of Great Britain. Our Virginian brothers are just behind us."

"Virginian brothers?" Kathleen questioned.

"My word, they came?" Richard asked.

"Who?" Smith beckoned.

"While Kathleen was in England, Snake managed to smuggle a letter out to the American colonies requesting aid," Harold said.

"Aid from the Americas?" Smith asked.

"They came to England first," Joseph said. "They were unwilling to risk sailing in Krikston waters with their small numbers, but they come with four hundred men."

Harold's face lit up. "We gained fourteen hundred men today!" he exclaimed.

"Aye," Joseph said. "Your allies have finally woken up, and if you ask me, sir, it is about damn time."

"Three years of us struggling," Richard griped.

"Easy, son," Rachel warned.

"He is right to be upset, madam," Joseph said. "George hesitated because he thought he could strike a deal with John that would be beneficial to them in regards to reopening Kirkston as an additional route along the slave trade that Harold had dismembered. But, he has since changed his mind in this regard. I hear we will be fighting alongside Africans and pirates while here?"

"And women," Kathleen said. "A third of our camp are female soldiers."

Joseph squirmed slightly, but then he smiled as he looked at Kathleen. "You are a symbol of great hope here, Your Majesty. Who am I to judge someone who could rally troops in the way you have in these past weeks?"

Two ships dropped anchor behind the ships the English had arrived in, and they were loud and rowdy. "Americans," Joseph moaned.

The Europeans unloaded first, but as the American colonists made bay they bolted onto the shores like a group of hooligan miscreants. Smith laughed. "I believe they will fit right in at our camp," he joked.

A young man with dark hair and a reddish tent to his skin came running up, his eyes full of excitement. While he dressed like a colonist, Smith could tell he was one of the natives of that land. "Boy, where is your captain and general?" General Joseph asked.

"A bit behind me," he said and looked at the Caldara's. He bowed politely. "I am seeking a gentleman by the name of Snake?"

"And, you are?" Smith asked.

"You may call me Degataga – or Edward. Whichever is easiest for you," the young man said with a laugh.

"Degataga it is," Smith said, smiling slightly. "How is it you know Snake?"

"Oh, I don't, not personally," Degataga said, grinning in Smith's direction. "But, I have a letter for him from a mutual acquaintance. Charles."

Smith beamed. He knew the name. "Ah! Yes, I think Snake would be eager to read that letter."

"Charles?" Ace asked. "The translator who helped Snake in the colonies?"

"Aye!" Degataga exclaimed with excitement. "When Charles heard that Governor Spotswood was looking for soldiers to send to your aid, Charles insisted I bring this to your friend." Degataga held up the letter excitedly. "That Spotswood fellow has a liking for Snake. He paid for this venture himself, you know? Hired every one of the Americans onboard."

"Snake did make quite a mark in Virginia," Ace said.

"Snake, Gomad, Tom, and Sky I'm sure will be eager to read that letter," Kathleen said.

"There was another Charles mentioned... Hethuska?" Degataga asked.

Smith frowned. "I'm afraid that this war took him."

"I see," Degataga said, looking quite saddened by this. "My deepest sympathies. Charles will be most shaken by that news when it reaches him. He spoke highly of each of them to me."

Harold cleared his throat, putting an end to the excited American's conversation with Smith. He turned to Joseph. "Tell your men that you may begin setting up camp here, and we will bring our troops southward," Harold said.

"Of course," Joseph said.

"I will stay to offer assistance," Richard said.

"Much thanks," Joseph said and shook Richard's hand.

"If my commander permits it, might I venture with you lot to your camp?" Degataga asked. "I am anxious to meet these fellows my good friend has told me so much about."

They agreed to it, and Degataga accompanied them. Smith smiled at Kathleen as the rest of the party headed back north to their camping grounds. "You did this," he told her, glancing over his shoulder at the vast numbers arriving on shore.

"Snake brought many of those men," she said.

"You brought a thousand. Snake's four hundred would not have come if George was not now supporting our fight," Smith said. "Do not belittle this accomplishment, Kathleen. You have won this war."

"Until my father sits on that throne again, do not count it won," Kathleen said. "Not until Cruz is tried and hung."

Chapter 38

Snake had been hiding out in his tent for nearly two days, and Sky had sat by him for much of it. His mother had come to visit to check in on his well-being often, and he each time had reassured her of his love for her. She had held him, nursed him, and loved him until they had been separated in his youth. Amy Lee was his mother, but that did not deter his emotional drainage and curiosity about the woman who had carried him in her womb.

He was lying on his back, staring up at the ceiling of the cramped tent while Sky sewed. She was learning this new task with much commitment, and she was just awful at it – but she was convinced she would be able to improve with careful study. "I think it is time you left your hideaway," she said, not looking up from her tedious work.

Snake turned his head slightly. "But, in my hideaway, no one asks me questions or looks at me as though I am something to be pitied."

"My darling, you truly are something to be pitied if you think hiding out in this tent will change that," she said and put down her needle and thread to look at him. "John

Stevenson was many things. But he loved you. As did Robbie Lee."

"The part that bothers me most is perhaps that John chose to never tell me," Snake said. "He had many opportunities over the years."

"And, what then?" Sky asked. "What would you have done if he had told you?"

Snake pondered this, but he had no resolution. "I think I still would have hated him. I would have called him a liar. I think if my own mother had confirmed it, then I would not believe it now."

"Then perhaps that is your answer," she said. "John loved you enough to keep it to himself. He knew after everything that you resented him, and to tell you that the man you loved as a father was not as such would have only hurt you. He did not wish to put doubt in your head and make you question what you knew and torment yourself."

Snake sat up slowly. "I suppose that is as good of an excuse as any. How could I not have known, though? To not have seen it? Everyone always told me I looked like my father. Like Robbie Lee. Why then –"

"Your true mother was Robbie Lee's half-sister," Sky said.

Snake raised a brow. "And, you know this how?"

"I asked your mother once she had managed to calm herself down," Sky said. "I asked about the woman. It seems it is difficult for her to talk to you about her, but when she spoke to me, she spoke about the woman like they had been close. The girl, on her mother's side, was also a distant cousin of your mothers. Amy tells me they shared a trait —"

"Their eyes," Snake said. "Everyone always said I had my mother's eyes." He frowned. "I *do* have my mother's eyes...just not Amy Lee's. Did my mother tell you her name?"

"Margarette," Sky said. "I know that she was Robbie's older sister, a result of a premarital affair before your grandfather wedded Robbie's mother. Amy tells me Robbie became close to Margarette and introduced her to John when they were older. Margarette's mother was akin to Amy's mother. So that would explain why —"

"Why I look like the Lee's," Snake said. "Because of my birthmother; she was kin to both my mother and father. She died the day I was born. I never knew her... perhaps now I know how Squirt has often felt. I want to know about Margarette, but I am afraid to ask my mother and break her heart."

"Give her time," Sky said. "Rekindle that bond first. Amy has wept for you for years, it is clear. You were her boy, and the fact that you came from Margarette and John did not change her motherly affections for you. She was so relieved to see you alive like only a mother could be. Let her become secure in your relationship before you ask her too many questions."

"I will do just that," Snake said. "When did you become so wise?"

"One of us has to be," she teased. Snake pulled her into a kiss and sat himself more upright. "Are you feeling well now, husband?" she asked.

"I think so," he said.

"You are over your shock?" she asked.

"As well as I could be," he said. "I just do not wish to deal with my friends."

"I have already threatened Mouth to not pester you," she said.

Snake laughed. "You are good to me, woman."

"Since you are no longer flustered, you should know then, that you are going to be a father," she said, and Snake's heart jumped.

"You are with child!" he exclaimed with an enormous grin. "How long have you known?"

"I realized it while you were escorting Smith on his meeting with Cruz, and I intended to tell you upon your return."

"And, then I came bursting into camp like a lune," he said. "Forgive me, Mapiya. That joyous news must have been eating you alive, but you waited until I was sane to hear it. Does anyone else know?"

"Hannah Cook," Sky said. "She was having a spell over Blade, and I was comforting her. She is frightened over her pregnancy, so I informed her so that she would know we would go through it together. I did swear her to secrecy until I could tell you."

"It is Hannah Cook," Snake said and laughed. "No doubt she told Anna. Anna would tell Knot. Knot would tell Yin, and Yin would likely tell Mouth."

Sky blushed. "Oh dear," she said. "Husband, it is possible the entire camp already knows if it managed to get to Mouth."

Snake kissed her forehead. "It is all right. At least it is good news they are sharing about us! I think we should leave the tent. I have been in hiding long enough."

As though the man had sensed it, Gomda poked his head in. "Pardon, friends!" he exclaimed. "But, a letter has arrived for us from the America's!"

Snake and Sky followed Gomda out, and Snake was immediately bombarded by a feisty young man with a dark complexion calling himself Degataga. "A pleasure to finally meet you, sir!" he said, shaking Snake's hand so fiercely that Snake thought he would rip his arm from his socket.

"Do I know you?" Snake asked, pulling his hand away.

Gomda and Tom Cook both laughed as they were standing nearby.

"No, but I know much about you. How you took on Blackbeard and saved my cousin many a times on your journey!" Degataga said.

"And, who is your cousin?"

"Charles, of course!" Degataga exclaimed. "Though he goes by Mojag now."

Snake beamed. "A cousin, you say?" Snake asked and hugged the man as though he had been greeted by Charles himself. "How is he? Has he been spending much time with his mother's tribe?"

Degataga pulled a letter from his coat pocket. "Here. He has written you all a letter, and when he heard I was taking part in this exhibition he insisted I deliver it to you myself the moment we arrived in Kirkston."

Snake ripped open the letter and read it aloud to Tom, Gomda, and Sky.

To my dear friends Snake, Sky, Gomda, Hethuska, and Tom,

I do hope this letter finds you well! When I heard of Governor Spotswood recruiting men for your war, I must say, I was greatly tempted to come along just so I could see my rogue companions once more! But, I could not. I am sad to say that there is great conflict on the horizon between my father's fellow colonists and my mother's people, and there are very few translators left who can act as a peacekeeper between them. My duty has kept me here.

I have been amongst my mother's people ever since your departure, and I feel truly at home here. My relatives have been most gracious and loving and kind. I have grown particularly close with my grandmother whom I did not even know I had! She has many daughters who remind me so much of my mother. Snake, I must thank you especially, for if I had never met you, I fear I would still be dancing about in costumes!

You may be pleased to hear that I have worked hard at remedying my relationship with my father and stepmother also. They were very displeased with my decision to live amongst my mother's people at first, but it seems they have grown used to the idea. Elizabeth even dined with an aunt of mine here in the tribe! Bless them, and bless you as well, dear friend!

I have enclosed my father's addressing information, and he assures me he would see to it that any correspondence between us is taken directly to my tribe. Please do write soon, all of you! Stay safe and stay vigilant, my friends.

Yours Truly,

Mojag

Once he was finished reading the letter, Snake felt a sort of happiness in his chest he had not felt in a few days. He had become quite fond of the lad, Charles, and he had known it would be unlikely that he would ever see him again. Snake felt as though he would cherish the letter the boy had written him.

"Thank you for delivering this letter to us, Degataga," Snake said, hugging the young man again. "I must hear all about your travels!"

Degataga grinned ear to ear, seeming quite glad to have been inducted in Snake's little entourage.

Snake glanced out over camp, and he could feel many eyes lingering in his direction. He took a deep breath; it was time to face everyone again after hiding out for nearly two days. They were still at war. He would need to put matters concerning John behind him as much as it pained him to do so.

***

"Well, I'll be," Smith said as he retrieved a letter from within the tree east of Caldara Castle.

"There's a letter in there?" Snake asked. "Surely not! John was the Red Dragon, yes?"

"That's what I thought," Smith said as he handed his only companion for this journey the envelope. "But it seems we still have our inside man."

"This could play greatly to our advantage," Snake said. "After what he did, Cruz probably believes that it had been John as well."

"But... who then is this mysterious partner of ours?" Smith questioned.

"I do not know, but let's see what he has for us," Snake said, tearing open the letter. "He has given us soldier's locations as well as their regular schedule – where they are posted in Caldara City and at what time."

Smith smiled. "Good. Because it's time we took back the capital."

"And then... Caldara Castle," Snake said.

"Perhaps if we are wise we can do one last assault with our increased numbers to take back the city," Smith said and grinned. "This war will be over soon, and Cruz knows it."

"I hope he tries to fight," Snake said. "I will be on the front lines when we break through the walls of Caldara Castle."

"You can barely walk, mate," Smith said, concerned.

"It doesn't matter," Snake said. "I will fight to take back Kirkston until the very end."

The two of them hopped up on their horses and began their long journey back to camp. "So, I hear you are to be a father?" Smith asked.

Snake chuckled. "I am. And, I assume you heard that from Mouth?"

"Stewart, actually. The man was positively giddy," Smith said. "Though he heard it from Mouth."

"Of course," Snake said. "I am thrilled. Perhaps a bit rattled with everything surrounding John and Robbie. I have not exactly had the most outstanding examples of fathers."

"They both loved you," Smith said. "That you can take from them both – even John. How are you holding up on that regard?"

"Still shaken," Snake admitted. "It's John. He has been the source of so much pain for me and my friends. Honestly, after hearing Harold's involvement, I had half a mind to walk out of his camp. But, it is clear we are not fighting for Harold anymore."

"Kathleen herself is a bit... how did you put it... rattled," Smith said. "Learning about Harold and Rachel's affairs and that her being named heir was merely a cover for that madness. I suppose she had always been told her father saw something special in her or that her father cared about women... she is questioning everything now."

"It is sick," Snake declared, gripping the reins of his horse. "The Caldara's and the Lee's had a filthy amount of secrets that have been uncovered due to this war, but they are only human, I suppose."

"Yes, I suppose so," Smith said. "Kathleen has more than proven herself, though. Richard himself says he is grateful the crown never fell to him. Says his sister is a natural leader and that he'd follow her to his death if asked."

"Yes, he has gotten awfully loyal after he tried to kill her."

"Pardon!" Smith exclaimed.

Snake chuckled slightly. "That's right. You were not here during that, now were you? You missed a lot, mate."

Smith lowered his head. "I know."

"You too are only human," Snake said. "You are here now. That is what matters. And, now this war is nearly over. What then for you, Smith?"

"I do not know," he said.

"You do, but you are afraid to ask for what it is you want," Snake said.

Smith rolled his eyes. "I will not even try to deny it anymore. I am in love with that woman, but I am just a pirate."

"Just a pirate!" Snake exclaimed. "Mate, you are a fool. Even Harold would not demean you by saying you are *just* a pirate. You are a soldier. A leader in his army. A general like myself!"

"A former peasant," Smith said.

"Your mother was a Wilks – you have noble blood," Snake countered.

"That matters very little now," Smith said. "I could never live up to the expectations for a man worthy of her."

"I think you could be," Snake said.

Smith smiled slightly. "Thank you, mate, but I am not so certain. Now, let us hurry. We need to get back to camp before the ceasefire ends so that we can be prepared for our assault."

Chapter 39

Smith gripped the wheel of the *Black Dragon*, and he exhaled deeply. There were five other ships following them close behind as they approached Kirkston's eastern docks. They would be hitting Cruz's ships hard during a time recommended by the Red Dragon when there would be few men onboard.

He wished that he had more of his mates with him on this mission, but they would rendezvous at Caldara Castle if all went well. Jackson White was present, and Smith felt glad to have him along with Stewart and Gwen. Knot was at his rightful place in the crow's nest. Smith had also gotten Mouth, Abigail, and Squirt. The rest of his ship was full of random miscreants: Africans, Europeans, and a handful of Americans and Kirkston soldiers both men and women. The rest of his friends were divided amongst two other attacking parties.

King Harold as well as Smith's Uncle Bartholomew were also aboard the *Black Dragon*, and they stood by Smith at the helm. Harold seemed a bit distracted as he gazed out into the water. Bartholomew stood closer by, and he clasped his nephew on the shoulder. "This could be over today. Finally," he said.

"One way or another, yes," Smith said, and he gazed at his uncle through sad eyes. "Uncle, when it is over... if we win this thing... I pray that you will remain here in Kirkston."

"I have no intentions of returning to Balla, Peter," he said.

"I know I hurt you and Thaddeus after I left, and I –"

"Speak no more of it, Peter," Bartholomew said. "We've forgiven you. My boy wants to be close to his cousin, and I want to get to know my nephew. Let us make it through today, my boy, and you and I will do whatever it takes from this day forth to mend our kinship."

"I would like that very much," Smith said, and he smiled.

Bartholomew excused himself, making his way down to the other soldiers who were waiting on deck. "Is this your first time actively fighting in this war?" Smith asked the nervous looking king, drawing Harold's attention away from the water.

"Yes," Harold said. "And, I am honored to fight alongside you, Smith."

"Have you at least been training?" Smith asked.

"Very funny," Harold said. "I am well trained with a gun as well as a sword."

"Why do I doubt that?" Smith asked, and Harold rolled his eyes. The man looked nothing like the indifferent king he had once known. Harold was dressed in casual clothing dirtied from their use. He wore no crown; instead he wore a belt that held all his weapons along with mud-covered boots.

"This is it," Harold said rather ominously.

"Anxious?"

"Very much so," Harold said. "I will die if I must in order to put my daughter on that throne, but I worry about her."

Kathleen was leading the northern assault along with Snake; they would attack the northern docks by ship, using the *Silver Queen* as their flag ship. They would likely be the first to reach Caldara Castle.

"She is capable," Smith said simply.

Leading the third assault would be Richard and Ace, and they would be entering into Caldara City from the west as Smith and his crew made their way into the capital from the east after attacking the docks. "I am aware," Harold said. "She is my daughter."

"Tell me, Harold, did you truly only give that wonderful woman the crown to cover up an affair?" Smith asked.

Harold sighed. "It had a lot to do with it, but I had contemplated it long before John and I made our deal."

"Really?" Smith asked.

"Her mother very much inspired that thought," Harold said. "Though my father was quick to cover it up, Rachel is not exactly a noble or really anyone from a family my father would have considered for me had he been more informed on the matter. My dear wife lost her father young, and her family suffered greatly. She has told me many stories of their struggles trying to live off small jobs her brother managed to gather. *If only I could have worked*, she would say. I thought this was not right, and I thought perhaps giving Kathleen the crown would improve conditions for the women of Kirkston."

"Why have you not spoken to Kathleen of this? She has felt saddened about learning of yours and John's deal," Smith said.

"I suppose it is a conversation we should have," Harold said. "My daughter is my inspiration. She should hear that, but after hearing about mine and John's deal I thought perhaps she would think I was lying. I should tell her, though."

Smith nodded in agreement, and then he called out his orders. His men alerted the other ships in the fleet, and they open fired on the unsuspecting men at the coast. The military vessels that Cruz had brought with him to Kirkston were bombarded by cannon fire. The desperate men at port were only able to get one of their ships turned in a manner to return fire. The flag ship, the *Black Dragon*, took a good bit of the heat, but they were salvaged by one of their fellow ships. Cruz's soldiers managed to get the one ship out into sea, and they rammed straight into the *Black Dragon* in a last-ditch effort to take down at least one enemy vessel.

"Board them!" Smith ordered, and soon his rogues, Harold included, were flinging themselves onto the dock of the enemy ship. It would take several minutes before one of their accompanying ships could pull up right alongside Cruz's for aid, but the men and women aboard the *Black*

Dragon were doing a fine job at overtaking them on their own.

"Oye! Captain!" Knot shouted from his lookout.

"Eh?" Smith called back.

"Harold and his nephew are cornered!" Knot called, prepping his long gun to shoot down at the enemy ship from his position.

Smith called to Squirt who was working defense at the ropes of their ship, and Squirt hurried to Smith at the helm. "Man the ship, boy, and keep it steady," was Smith's order, and Squirt took on the role with extreme enthusiasm – gripping the wheel with a menacing grin as though he knew that the stars had aligned just right to give him the opportunity to captain the ship he knew so well.

Smith then darted to the edge of the ship and threw himself onto the enemy vessel, calling for several defensive fighters to follow. Knot managed to take out two of the men surrounding Harold and his nephew, but by the time Smith and his assault had reached them young Dave had already taken a sword to the chest for his king. Harold responded mercilessly, and a part of Smith was impressed to see the king going toe to toe with excellent swordsmen. The king held a pistol in his free hand, and he fired at will on the man who had stabbed his nephew.

"On your left," Harold called to Smith, and Smith spun in time to prevent a man from shooting him right in the back.

Smith shot the man attempting to take him on, and then he held out his sword as additional men made their way towards himself and Harold. The ship shook violently as one of the other ships in the rebellions fleet rammed up against the starboard side. These men knew they were beaten, and they at last threw down their arms. By the time they surrendered, the rebellion had lost five soldiers, and there were only seven Spaniards still standing. Harold ordered these men's immediate execution, no doubt out of anger for his nephew who was now lying out on the deck of the ship.

Harold hurried to Dave's side, and he called out for someone to tend to him as he was still breathing. Smith's uncle, who had picked up a good bit of medical training from Mrs. Barons before her death as well as a bit from Dr. Conal, was the first to hurry to the young man's aid. There was no time to mourn or to remain with Dave; they put more medically efficient men in charge of the young Caldara and the other injured soldiers as they pulled the ships into port. They removed the flag of Cruz at the docks and replaced it with the Kirkston flag. Again, there was little time to waste. They had brought horses on this venture, carried by the ship in the back of the fleet. They unloaded them quickly and began their march to Caldara City.

As they reached the city, Smith grinned to see men were already fleeing from the west where Ace and Richard were leading an assault. *Fleeing right to us*, Smith thought with amusement. He gripped his horse's reins, and he glanced at Harold who was seated on his own horse beside him. The man had a bit of dried blood on his face, and he was covered in filth. He bore little resemblance to the elegant king Smith had once known, and Smith was glad for it.

***

Ace breathed deeply as the sun peeked over the horizon. He and a third of the rebellion were stationed amongst the trees just west of Caldara City. "It's time to wake up the men who dared set foot in our city's capital," Richard said to him.

"They are going to be surprised," Ace said. "My greatest worry is for the citizens."

"We sent out word warning people to remain indoors this morning," Richard said. "But, to finally chase the soldiers out of the city, this is necessary. We may lose some civilians in the process." Richard took a nervous breath. "I am surprised they put me in charge of one of these attacks."

"You are ready," Ace assured him. "And, I'm honored to fight alongside you, little brother."

Richard smiled, and Ace could see a sincere warm nature in his younger brother. This is perhaps what Richard had always wanted from him. Acknowledgement. His affection. Ace was only sorry it took a war for him to truly grow close to his family. As one of the few Black Dragons with any family left, he felt truly grateful. And, they had all proved themselves to him in these past three years to be more than the corrupt Caldara's he had once believed them to be. "What will you do first when this is over, Ace?" Richard asked.

"I am going to marry Cassidy," he said. "I hope that our father will grant me a position of some sort so that I might earn an honest living for her and Pierson."

"You are a good man, Ace," Richard said.

"And, you? What will you do?" Ace asked.

"I will kiss my wife and son," Richard said and looked back towards the group of soldiers who were climbing aboard their horses – Isabella and Cassidy were among them. "Isabella insisted on coming today. Says she hasn't fought once in this war, and she is an experienced soldier."

"How will she ride and bear a sword with only one arm?" Ace asked.

"I have asked myself how she will do many things, but she always proves me to be foolish for thinking she cannot," Richard said. "I did not even ask this time because I knew she would prove me to be paranoid."

Richard climbed onto his horse, and Ace did the same. Richard called out to his soldiers. "Today we end this!" His soldiers cheered.

Richard led the assault. He and nearly four hundred soldiers bombarded the capital city from the west, sending unprepared Cruz soldiers fleeing to the east. Ace smiled, knowing that by now Harold and Smith would be meeting the more cowardly soldiers in an open field outside of the city.

The battle within Caldara City lasted several hours, and many citizens came outside of their homes bearing weapons when they realized this fight could actually be won. Blood was spilled in the streets, but it was almost entirely the blood of the enemy. The two groups rendezvoused just north of Caldara City once they had taken the city under their control. Ace, drenched in sweat and blood, shook hands with his father and embraced him, glad to see he had made it out of the attack at the docks.

They looked to the north where an orangish smoke was burning at Caldara Castle. Smith smiled and looked to Ace and Richard. "Looks like your sister has taken the northern ports."

"Aye," Harold said. "Now we just need to take back our castle!"

Chapter 40

Snake looked at Kathleen with a bit of awe. She looked like a warrior goddess among mortal men. He and Kathleen had led the assault against the northern docks, a considerably small effort compared to what Smith and Harold had dealt with that morning along the eastern docks, the main port in the country. Kathleen had a significantly larger fleet despite having less ships to deal with at the northern port, so they had taken the men out without losing a single soldier and with virtually no serious injuries. The reason for her larger fleet, however, was so that she could lead the initial assault on the palace grounds.

As expected, Cruz had brought most of his men to Caldara Castle during the ceasefire. He had likely heard of British ships being spotted nearby, so the man had gone on the defensive. Thus far that day, Kathleen and her family had greatly outnumbered Cruz's men, but once they reached the castle walls, they would be much more evenly matched.

"You did well, Your Majesty," Snake said formerly to Kathleen.

"It's not over yet," she said and called across the way to Sky. "Set the fire."

"Aye, Madam," Sky said and hollered at Gomda and Degataga for assistance. Using a special breed of weeds Degataga had been able to concoct a mixture that would cause an orangish tented smoke – their signal to the other troops that they were ready to begin their assault and to hurry to their defense.

Kathleen looked in Snake's direction, down at his cane in particular. "You should stay behind and man the ships," she said.

"I have no intentions of sitting this fight out, Kathleen," Snake said. "I know I am injured, but I will not sit back and do nothing. Not today."

"You've done your duty," Kathleen said. "Stay with the ships."

"I cannot," Snake said.

"Then stay at my side then," Kathleen said.

"You should not go into battle having to protect me, Your Majesty," Snake said. "Besides, I have a very particular mission in mind."

"You are going after Maria and her children?" Kathleen asked.

"Those are my intentions. I know I would surely lose in an on-foot battle in this condition," Snake said. "So, I am hoping to sneak in and find their location before harm can come to them."

"Then be careful, friend," Kathleen said. "You can travel with a search party up until you pass the throne room, but after that you will be on your own."

"I understand," Snake agreed, for Kathleen needed all the man power she could get to overtake the northern wall.

They began their short march up the hill, and they took on fire from Cruz's men who were stationed at the top of the exterior wall, but with the numbers they brought Cruz's men eventually fled within the castle itself, leaving the wall defenseless. The invasion of Caldara Castle had begun.

***

Snake swept through the palace as quickly as he could with his bad leg. There was much cheering, shouting, and general cries of horror from both ends. This was quite a battle to be won, but Snake could not fight. He knew if he was forced to do hand to hand combat with only a single shot left in his side arm that he would perish, so he crept on carefully. He had intentionally not worn his Black Dragon uniform because it would make him too easily distinguished.

Snake made use of the secret tunnels he had learned of over the years to sneak about the palace grounds until he could reach the secondary level where most of the bedchambers were. He suspected that Maria, and very likely Cruz, were somewhere hidden on this most interior part of the castle. He slid out of one of the tunnels and soon found himself in the hall. He heard a brutish man's voice around the corner, and he recognized it as Juan's.

"Your father told me to keep you inside, so stay inside, you vile creature!" Juan roared, and Snake heard Juan strike someone. A feint cry echoed down the hall, and he was almost certain it was Maria.

"I am going, you brute!" Maria shouted, sounding as though Juan's strike had brought her to tears.

Snake peered around the corner to see Juan shoving Maria into the royal chambers. Juan stood outside the door armed. No one else seemed to be protecting Maria during the assault on the castle – no doubt Cruz had most everyone surrounding wherever it was that he was stationed.

After checking that his pistol was ready to fire, Snake took several deep breaths. He could not afford to miss. In one swift motion that pained his leg, Snake threw himself around the corner and took two steps forward before firing on Juan. The man fell, and Snake sighed in relief. *Now I really need to move,* Snake thought. His plan was to retrieve Maria and the little ones and then lead them through the tunnel in the royal bedroom that went directly to the stables – an area where Harold and Richard's parties likely already had full control over. And, he needed to do so before the shot he had fired attracted any attention.

Snake hurried to the door, flinging it open to see Maria sitting huddled together with her children. The look of relief on the woman's face saddened him. To think she was more relieved to see a face of her enemy than that of those she had lived with! John had been right to beg for their protection.

Maria rose, looking past him. "Did you kill Juan?" she asked.

Snake closed the door behind him. "It was necessary."

"Bless you," she said and came to him as though they were old friends. The woman's arms wrapped around his neck, and she kissed his cheeks. There were tears in her eyes. "Please, get me out of here, Johnny!"

"Get the little girl. We need to move quickly. Robbie can walk on his own accord," Snake said, leaning on his cane.

"You're injured?" Maria asked as she scrambled to pick up the little toddler. Robbie's hateful glare went unnoticed by Snake in his hurry.

"Yes, but I can walk with the cane just fine," Snake said. Snake opened the door to the closet. "Let's go." Maria went through, holding her daughter. Robbie did not budge. "Boy, did you hear me? We must get you to safety," Snake said, staring back at the boy who had now backed himself into a corner.

"Robbie, come with us now!" Maria shouted from within the closet.

Robbie said nothing. "I will get him," Snake said, hurrying to the boy – thinking that he was merely fear-stricken. He stood over Robbie, and he offered a friendly smile. "Lad, it's me. You remember me, yes? You need to come with me so that we can get you somewhere safe."

Robbie still did not budge. Snake bent down, prepared to throw the child over his shoulder if he had to despite his bum leg, and when he did, he was greeted by a blade in the eye. Snake fell away, landing on his back. He could still feel the small dagger within his socket as he let out a horrid scream. "What have you done!" he could just barely make out Maria's voice. "Where did you get that dagger!" Snake reached up to his face with shaky hands, but by now Maria was knelt over him. She grabbed his wrists. "Do not touch it! Let me help you!" she shrieked.

For a moment, everything went dark as blood seeped into his good eye. "I'm blind!" Snake hollered in horror.

He felt Maria touch his face, and he felt her laying a sheet around his face. "Do not move," she told him, and she slid the small dagger out of his eye. It was the worst feeling Snake had ever experienced – worse than when the blade had gone in. Maria pressed the ripped sheet against his wound and cradled him in her arms. "Robbie, how could you? Why would you do this?"

"Let him die!" Snake heard Robbie shout. "Let him die so Abuelo will let you go!"

"Your abuelo told you to do this? He's a devil! Your father loved this man! How could you, Robbie?" Maria sobbed as she continued to put pressure on Snake's wound. "Forgive me, Johnny, but I do not know what else I can do to help you!"

Snake drifted in and out of consciousness. His sight in his one eye did return to him. He caught bits and pieces of the conversation between Maria and Robbie. "My father loved him more than me," Robbie would say. "Let him have a glass eye like Papa! He already has a bum leg like him!"

"How could you? How could you?" was Maria's repeated sob, though much of their conversation had now drifted into Spanish, and Snake could make little sense of it.

He could occasionally hear little Amy crying out from all of the commotion. The next of what happened Snake only remembered in bits and pieces. Smith's voice pleading with him. Mouth, Smith, and another man he could not identify lifting him up. Maria screaming to help him and to hurry. He remembered the pain of Dr. Conal doing something to his injury that sent him right back into a state of unconsciousness.

When at last Snake awakened, feeling significantly better but incredibly dizzy, his wife was at his side and he was lying on the dirt ground within the royal stables. "Sky!" he exclaimed with relief, and she knelt down and kissed him.

"Smith! He is awake!" Sky called out in sobs, and Smith came darting into the stables with a face full of relief and horror.

"What happened?" Snake asked as Sky helped him to slowly sit up.

Smith smiled. "We won, mate. We've taken back the castle. It's over. It's finally over."

***

Smith kissed Snake's forehead, and when his friend demanded to stand he assisted him. "That face of yours is a mess," Smith said.

"Is it that awful?" Snake asked.

"Just be glad you're bandaged up," Smith said and embraced his friend once he was standing. "You're going to be stuck wearing a patch like Yin… or a glass eye like John."

"Patch," Snake said. "I think the cane is homage enough to Stevenson. Is Maria all right?"

"I think she is a bit stunned is all," Smith said. "She is with the rest of the prisoners along with her children."

"Take me to them," Snake said. "I'd like to try to make sense of what just happened to me. My eye aches… I do hope Dr. Conal has more medication he can give me."

"I'm certain he does," Smith said.

Smith and Sky walked on either side of Snake, helping him to keep his balance as he had lost a lot of blood. They entered the courtyard where several men and a select few women were being held at gunpoint while soldiers put them in chains. There were perhaps two dozen who had been taken captive rather than killed – Cruz was among them standing with a smirk on his face.

Kathleen and Harold stood amongst the enormous crowd. People were cheering as Harold stepped forward to address the growing crowd of spectators and soldiers. "Today we have our freedom," Harold said. "These scoundrels will see a day in court with a fair trial, the wish of my daughter, since they were among the few who put down their arms and surrendered."

Maria screeched. "You give this man a trial?" She waved her hands in her father's direction.

Cruz shook his head as though his daughter's outburst was an embarrassment. "I appreciate the sentiment. You Caldara's are not such heathens as I first expected to treat an enemy with such respect," Cruz said.

Young Robbie was viciously sobbing at his mother's feet, and Smith's heart went out to the lad. When they had brought Snake down to the courtyard in a desperate attempt to save him, the boy had broken down into near hysterics over what he had done. Snake spoke up for the Stevenson's. "What of Maria?" he asked.

"She too will face a trial," Kathleen said and then addressed Maria directly. "Surrender your children over to someone, or they will remain with you in prison."

Maria's eyes darted in Snake's direction. "Oh, mercy, please."

"Maria, I will take them," Snake assured her. Robbie continued to sob as he took his sister from his mother and walked her over to Snake and Sky. Sky lifted up the little girl from Robbie and patted the boy on the head. Smith took pity on Robbie and patted the boys head as well.

"Have this group taken to the prison cells," Harold ordered a handful of soldiers. "We need to prepare to address the people of Kirkston – to let them know they are free again!"

The small but growing crowd cheered, and as the group of prisoners were turned to head to the castles prison, Maria broke from her march. She had with her the dagger her son had used to harm Snake, and she thrust it into her father's throat. Two soldiers grabbed her, pulling her back and one drew his gun. Harold shouted for the man not to shoot, and thankfully the order came before Maria could be put down in front of her little ones.

Robbie's cries became louder, and frankly the entire court was stunned. "No trial for him!" Maria roared and

412

held up her bloody hands in surrender as the soldiers checked her for any additional weapons. The men took the time to check everyone over again since Maria had clearly been overlooked.

"Get them out of here, and someone clean up that man's body!" Kathleen shouted, waving her hand in Cruz's direction. The man was dead without question. She turned and looked to Snake and Sky. "Take the children to the royal chambers. There's no sense in subjecting them to this."

"Aye, Your Majesty," Snake said. He and Sky left with the children, the young boy still sobbing loudly as they exited.

Smith remained in the courtyard. There was much excitement. Local citizens who had not been a part of the rebellion but who had fought to take back the city in this final battle were flooding the gates – all cheering for Harold and for Kathleen.

"We did it," Smith breathed and looked to Kathleen who was crossing through the crowd to him.

She embraced him. "Thank you," she said to him. "I do not know if without you this would have been possible."

"Without you, Your Majesty, I *know* it would not have been."

Smith thought to kiss her, but before he could bring the thought to prurition, Harold called out to him. "Smith! A word, please!"

"Of course, sir," Smith said and followed Harold inside to the castle's war room.

Once they were inside the large but empty war room, Harold fell into a seat like a man who was truly experiencing exhaust. "Sit," he said and wiped sweat from his brow.

Smith sat by him, and he chuckled. "Harold, you look like a warrior king!"

"I am covered in filth," Harold said and laughed. "I look more like a rogue than you, pirate."

"A pirate I am no more, sir," Smith said. "And, I do hope you plan to stay true on your promise of pardons."

"It will be my first official act to grant the *Black Dragons* and the rest of my hired rogues full pardons," Harold promised.

Smith smiled. "Thank you, Your Majesty."

Harold smirked. "It's just you and me, Smith. Harry is just fine."

"I hardly ever thought I would be calling you by a nickname," Smith said.

"Aye," Harold said. "Life is funny that way. I wish to ask your opinions on a few things I finally am able to ponder without my thoughts clouded by war tactics." Harold stretched, and there was a slight sparkle in the man's eye. "More so than anyone else, the *Black Dragons* have made this war turn in our favor. I have plans for Jeremiah and Kyo and his men as well, but we will not go into that just yet. I wish to talk about your friends."

"Aye," Smith said.

"Knot has expressed interest in helping to rebuild Kevin's Isle to its former glory. I wish to put him, Mouth,

Abigail, and the Cook's in charge of this venture. It will come with a grand pay, and I will put them in charge of the local government there."

"Government!" Smith exclaimed. "Knot and Mouth and Abigial?"

"You think they are not suitable?"

"I believe they are suitable, I am just surprised to hear it come from your mouth," Smith said.

"Abigail's son Jake should be with the Cook family as well as with Abigail, and they have all expressed a desire for this. I wish to grant Maxi a loan to help his family restart their shipping business on the island as well. But as far as Knot, Mouth, and Abigail, I want them to run Kevin's Isle. It will ensure a bright future for their children, and I am certain this will please them. What say you?"

"A fine gesture, Your Majesty!" Smith could hardly contain himself. It was an enormous responsibility, but it was an honest career – something those family men certainly needed and desired.

"So, you vouch for them?"

"Absolutely!"

"Good. Squirt will act as his brother's attendant until he can gather experience, and when he is older, I will put him in charge of any pop-up towns in Kevin's Isle so that he can be with his brother. I suspect a wedding between himself and Gwen is not far off, so I will offer her the same to work under Mouth and Knot. Gwen wishes to be an honest working lady, and I intend to make it doable for her. As far as Stewart, I am going to see to it that I send that man to school to properly educate himself as a preacher. Kathleen wants us to open an orphanage in Caldara City as one of her first acts as queen, and I want Stewart to lead that venture. I will ensure that he will be able to spend most of his time on Kevin's Isle with his sister, but his work will take him to the main land often. Knowing him, though, he will be very satisfied doing the work of God."

"An orphanage, sir?" Smith asked.

"Kirkston does not have one," Harold said and then looked at Smith with sad eyes. "And, let's be honest, a repeat of yours and your friends childhoods is not desirable. Our government should aid the country's orphans – not toss them out in the street and hope for the best. We'll have another crew of Black Dragons on our hands if we don't start doing something."

"Harry, I do not know what to say," Smith said. "I believe Stewart would be more than thrilled to follow in his father's footsteps – and to run an orphanage would be desirable for him. The man loves children and often quotes Christ's love for little ones. An orphanage! Our country needs that... after what happened to my friends..."

"Kathleen has already named the building, and we have not even struck ground," Harold said with a slight laugh. "It will be her first project as queen, and it suits her."

"What name has she chosen for our country's first orphanage?" Smith asked.

"Livingston and Barons Home for Orphaned Children," Harold said, and Smith felt a lump form in his throat.

"That is a true honor to me and to Sea," Smith said. His heart was now racing. He had only expected pardons for his friends – not this!

"Clara seems content on being a housewife to Yin," Harold continued. "But, if she changes her mind, I can find a position that will need to be filled in this New Kirkston that will satisfy her. Yin has proven to be quite the intellect, but it is his heart that I am fond of. I believe he should become an advisor on my daughter's court once she is coronated as queen. I also plan to make Cassidy our first woman advisor – also to my daughter's court when it is established. I'll ensure they both receive some additional education, of course, while they are in waiting for my daughter to succeed to the crown. In the meantime, I will give Yin an advancement for his future position so that he and Clara can get settled in near Caldara City."

Smith now felt his eyes beginning to water. "Bless you, sir."

"Ron and Theresa I will move here to Caldara Castle. I intend to put Theresa in charge of the library – though she too will require much more education. Ron I wish to have train my blacksmiths, and I will provide for the man's retirement myself as I know he will not be able to work. Their son will receive training here at Caldara Castle wherever Ron and Theresa feel that he is called."

He has thought of Ron and Theresa too! Smith felt his lip shaking. This was so unexpected. He could not even speak now. Harold continued. "Snake I believe will be a fitting head general – and one far better than either of his father's. Snake and Sky will remain here at Caldara Castle in the general's quarters. As for my son, Ace, he will be my courts viceroy alongside his brother Richard – they will act as their sister's top advisors for her court as well. They proved to be true champions of the people during the war, and they work well with their sister."

Tears now fell from Smith's eyes. "Harry, you are too good to us. When we signed up to help you, we only thought you would offer us pardons."

"You did not do this for the pardons, Smith. You did this out of the kindness of your heart, and that is something I can never repay. My family owes the Black Dragons their lives. My nephew is well, I hear. Dave will survive his wounds. My wife and my children are alive because you all came to our rescue and offered us sanctuary." Harold reached out and touched Smith's shoulder. He laughed at him slightly. "Pull yourself together, my boy!"

Smith laughed, but his tears would not stop. "Aye, I will try, sir."

"I almost forgot about Mr. Jackson!" Harold exclaimed.

"You have thought of him too, sir!"

"Of course," Harold said. "I intend to make him a personal steward to Kirkston's future king to serve under my daughter and more specifically to her husband. I cannot think of a better man more suited to keep you in check, Smith."

"Pardon?"

"I have already spoken with my daughter," Harold said. "I believe by now I have learned not to be presumptuous with her relationships."

Smith's hand went to his chest, and he inhaled deeply. "Sir?" he questioned. He knew what Harold was getting at, but he just could not believe it.

"There are... conditions, of course. She is a future queen, friend. I will need you to educate yourself, take courses here at Caldara on our laws, I need you to –"

Smith practically lept into Harold's lap, wrapping his arms around the man's neck – nearly knocking him out of his chair. "I will do whatever you ask of me," Smith said, though he was not sure Harold could even understand the words with how ridiculous his excited cry had become.

"Get off me," Harold said with a sound that sounded almost like a chuckle but was more of an annoyed grunt.

Smith pulled away and instinctually went to the ground, kneeling before his king – an act he never thought he would feel drawn to do. "I adore her," Smith said. "And, I am honored that you believe I could be suitable for your daughter."

"Not just her," Harold said. "But, for Kirkston. I cannot think of a man better suited to take my place."

Smith rose to his feet and wiped his eyes, getting a hold of his breath that had escaped his lungs at this incredible news. "Harold, this is almost too much for me."

"I intend to speak to the people of Kirkston shortly at Caldara City," Harold said. "You, my sons, Snake, Jeremiah, Jackson, and Kyo will be knighted by myself and Kathleen for your leadership in this war. Normally something like this would be done in the throne room, but I want all of Kirkston to see and know their heroes – especially you. I want them to see it as we will be announcing your betrothment to my daughter in a few weeks' time once the dust settles." Harold stood and placed a hand on his shoulder. "I told Kathleen I would speak to you immediately after this mess was settled today. No doubt she is waiting to see you. Go."

Smith turned to bolt out the door, but as soon as he opened it Kathleen was standing there. She lept forward and wrapped her arms around his throat and kissed him.

"Kathleen, it is time to address our people," Harold said. "Smith, do gather your friends whom I intend to knight publicly today."

"Yes, of course," Smith said and hurried to locate Ace, Richard, Snake, Jeremiah, Jackson, and Kyo.

Within the hour Smith was kneeling before King Harold as a sword was placed on either shoulder. He knelt by Snake and Ace, the rest lined up along Ace's left. *Sir Peter,* Smith thought to himself with a bit of humor in his chest as Harold knighted him in front of the enormous crowd of relieved citizens. He was not permitted to announce the engagement to his friends yet, but they would know in due time. From the inescapable grin and the sensation of walking on air, he almost felt that they suspected that Harold had made such an arrangement. Once they had all been knighted, Harold announced them as the saviors of Kirkston and stated that in the evening there would be a celebration open to the public on the castle grounds.

And, indeed there was! Dancing, singing, drinking, and general merriment surrounded Caldara Castle that evening. The country was free, but it was more than that. Smith stood near the interior castle wall that evening watching the king of Kirkston mingle with peasants who had fought in the final battle with nothing but weapons they could find – utensils raided from a blacksmith shop, and Harold held up a glass to these men as he heard their individual tales – laughter radiating off him. African men and women danced with nobility like they were truly brethren. The princess of Kirkston, sweet Kathleen, curtsied to the former pirate Commodore Kyo and gladly took up the man's offer for a friendly dance. Black Dragons and the only surviving *Annihilator*, Jeremiah White, sang loudly and drunkenly together. The American rogues and the British military leaders laughed together over their victory alongside Sky and Gomda, former victims of their leader's choices. Members of the Skull Island gang clasped Tom Cook's shoulder, calling him a brave soldier and admirable man. Smith soaked in the moment, for he doubted he would ever see a day like this again: Kirkston united on the last heel of war! It was over, and they were all free once more.

Epilogue

Five Months Later

"To His Majesty, *Prince* Peter – husband to Kirkston's first future queen!" Snake hollered, holding up his large glass and causing the room of rogues to erupt in cheer and unnecessary banging of their fists against the formal dining table.

Smith felt Kathleen reach and grab his hand, and he felt his heart bounce joyously to see her in her lovely wedding attire. He looked out across the table, a formal luncheon Harold had insisted upon just for Smith. The wedding feasting and celebrating would likely continue for days, but this was a private gathering while the rest of the guests continued their celebrating within the courtyard.

Smith sat at the head of the table next to Kathleen, hardly feeling suitable for such a position in the royal dining hall. To his right, his best mate Snake and his family: his mother, Sky, Robbie, and little Amy who was being held by her namesake. Sky's belly was incredibly round now, and they all were anxious for the new one's arrival. Next was Ace and Cassidy with Pierson and young redheaded boy named Connar – Cassidy's bastard boy whom Ace had in recent weeks adopted. Connar was but one of three they were searching for, but it was a start; his father and stepmother had died during a great famine, and he had come willingly to Kirkston to join his birth mother and her family. The boy was near Pierson's age, so the two lads had become instant brothers. This warmed Smith's heart.

Next to Pierson was Mouth, Abigail, Jake, and Ian. Abigail's stomach too had a slight curve; the couple had at last with the return of Ian become more intimate as they had once been, and so their family would continue to grow undoubtedly. Squirt and Gwen sat near Mouth's family; they had recently married and were living with Mouth and Abigial on Kevin's Isle.

The next group was Knot's dear family. Anna and their growing daughter Ellen Jane sat close together. Hannah had accompanied them to this private dining experience, and she had in her arms a little girl – Blade's daughter whom she had named Terrance after her father. Smith recalled visiting them on Kevin's Isle after the little girl's birth and learning the girls name was Terrance; Hannah had giggled and said, "Oh, I will call the little thing Terrie. Such a sweet name for a little angel!"

Yin and Clara had their hands full with their newly born fraternal twins – Michael and Nicole, named for Yin's brother and Clara's niece. Already the gathering of friends had dubbed the twins Little Yin and Yang. Across the table from Mouth and his family was Stewart and, oddly enough, Chi Mori who had just recently become engaged to the future preacher. Gomda and Jackson sat together, the odd men out of this group, and they laughed and pestered one another like old friends.

The former Black Dragons and their families – all honest men and women now sitting at the formal dining table on their former captain's wedding day. "Tell me, Harry," Smith said with a grin. "For what reason have you gathered us separate from the rest of the wedding guests?"

"I have a gift to present to my new son-in-law," Harold said with a smile. "And, I need you all to sneak out with me for a bit to avoid the soiree outside until the coronation ceremony this evening."

Smith's stomach flipped a bit. He had been anxious enough about the wedding day, but then Harold had planned their coronation ceremony on the same evening! Smith was almost convinced that Harold was trying to kill him with anxiety. Ms. Melusine had been invited to the wedding and coronation, and she had been Smith's first interaction with a diplomat from England. It was all a bit much for one day.

Richard, Isabella, and young Jackie entered the dining hall. "Father, we are ready," Richard said.

"Excellent." Harold rose. "There are carriages waiting out back for us all. For our expecting mothers, I have reserved our finest carriages for you and your families."

Smith laughed. "What sort of gift have you gotten me, Harry, that we must transport the entirety of my former crew and their families?"

Kathleen giggled. "Let Father have his fun, Peter. He is about to retire this evening and will have nothing to entertain himself with but to pester us for the rest of his days."

"Oye!" Harold exclaimed. "Are you mocking me, daughter?"

"Absolutely," she said.

They headed out a back exit, all bundling up in their coats as it was terribly cold out. Smith spied a few castle guards waiting with Queen Rachel who appeared to be in on the fun. The massive group slipped away from the castle as the celebration continued without them. They rode through Caldara City. In the distance Smith could just barely make out the Cathedral that Cruz's men had built – its highest tower sticking out over the distant tree tops. Smith had requested the Cathedral be left standing, and Harold had obliged. Cruz, though clearly a raving lunatic, had gotten one thing right, Smith felt. Kirkston should have never oppressed their Catholic brethren under the rein of King Kevin. So, despite the country not having a bishop, Smith wanted to ensure a message of religious tolerance between the predominately protestant nation with any living within their borders who practiced the Catholic faith. Soon the Cathedral disappeared in the distance, and Smith began to wonder how far the royals were taking them into the city.

Soon the cluster of carriages arrived at a large, empty lot that was the future home of Livingston and Barons Home for Orphaned Children. Not much had been completed apart from some very basic construction of exterior walls.

Harold stood at the front of the group as everyone unloaded from their carriages. In the courtyard of the orphanage, a large sheet was draped over what Smith could only assume to be a statue of sorts. "What is this?" Smith asked, and he felt Kathleen squeeze his hand in excitement. Obviously, the woman knew of what it was Harold was positively giddy to reveal to them all. Smith looked to Ace, but the man shrugged to ensure him that he was not in on his family's little plot.

Once they were all gathered together in the courtyard, Queen Rachel, King Harold, Kathleen, and Richard each grabbed hold of the bottom of the fabric and yanked on the sheet, unveiling a large statue that would overlook the orphanages courtyard where the children would one day play. The dark marble statue depicted seven individuals standing together.

Towards the back, facing forward, was Cannonball, clear as day even though the marble could not depict his Irish hair and skin. That tall, thin man grinned back at Smith as though he was reassuring him, "I'm all right," and he stood with one foot propped up on a cannonball – homage to his nickname. Beside Cannonball and in the middle of the back row was Smith's own mother, her nose in a book and a doctor's satchel at her side, a pleasant smile on that woman's face. Next on the back row, sweet Nicole with her hands on her hips and that same smirk on her face they had all grown to love. The second row moving forward was Blade, knelt in front of Cannonball and Mrs. Barons with a serious yet childlike look about him, his swords drawn as though he was prepared to leap into battle. Beside him was Yang – resting up on one knee with his arms crossed and a half smile that made him look only slightly mischievous. Beside Yang on the end of the second row was Hethuska, a serious gaze like the man often wore was depicted – beads and feathers in his hair just how he would always wear them. And, finally, all on her own on that front row, was a young Sea – her legs dangling off the side of the base of the monument. Her arms propped up behind her as she leaned back and appeared to almost be laughing – her hair choppy and seeming almost to sway slightly to the imaginary wind.

Smith was at a loss for words. "Read the plaque, darling," Kathleen said, pulling Smith by his hand so that he could read the inscription that rested in front of the resemblance of Sea. He read it out loud for the entire group to hear:

"Sacrifice"

David "Cannonball" Steele, Ellen Barons, Nicole Dain

Terrance "Blade" Simon, Michael "Yang" Hill, Hethuska,

Courtney "Sea" Livingston

For The Heroes Who Gave Everything For The Country That Granted Them Nothing

We Are Forever In Their Debt

They Are Forever In Our Hearts

When Smith finished reading, he had to look away to collect himself. He wiped a tear and stood upright, glancing back at his friends who all had similar emotional reactions to the small monument Harold had petitioned. Smith looked to the royal family: Rachel, Harold, Kathleen, and Richard – what a gift this was! After a moment, Smith was at last able to speak. "I never dreamed that my friends and my mother would be honored in such a way. Bless you."

"They will be read about in the history books," Harold said. "Children will sing songs about them. The official unveiling of the statue takes place tomorrow, but I wished for you all to see it first. The bottom of the stand the statue sits on is still a work in progress."

Smith glanced down at the stand where names were still being carved into its side. Names like Neela's or even simple foot soldiers who had lost their lives in the war were also being honored by Harold with the unveiling of this statue.

"Thank you for this," Smith said. "It is beautiful. Truly beautiful."

They stood about in silence, admiring the piece of artwork. Many of the former Black Dragons came up closer for a more personal look. Some, like Yin, reached out and touched the image of their loved ones with shaky hands. Jackson fixated his stare on Mrs. Barons, and he lowered his head and smiled while a tear escaped him. Pierson reached out and touched the image of his mother on her cheek and then stepped back with a quizzical and proud look about him. While Sky was wiping her tears over the image of her brother, Snake took a step forward on his cane and nodded approvingly at each of the images – running his fingers across the name *John Stevenson* that had been placed on the stand as a fallen member of the rebel army. The gesture of adding John's name to the memorial alongside people like Neela or even Smith's cousin Phillip brought tears to young Robbie's eyes. Snake's eyes lingered again on the statues, and he spoke with a voice that cracked as tears drizzled out from under his eyepatch. "It is strange, but I feel like we are all together. I do not know when it will be like this again." The man wiped his face.

Smith smiled at his best mate. "We are not children on a pirate ship anymore, mate."

"I know," Snake said. "I just meant I feel like I need to savor this moment."

They were all silent again. No more dinners at Mrs. Barons home. No more late nights out on the ship. No more secret hideaways or far away adventures. No more sword fights. No more dragging Mouth out of Benny's Inn after he had had one too many. But, that was well with Smith's soul. His friends had found their places, and he had found his. It was far from what he had expected, but he was all right with that. He knew he would see these people again; they were his family. They meant the world to him. They simply lived their own lives now, and that was a good thing.

Smith embraced each of the Caldara's – his new family. He thanked them somewhat pitifully while trying to conceal the emotions this gift had brought forth. Kathleen hooked his arm, and eventually they were all able to begin walking out of the courtyard.

"Christmas at Mrs. Barons," Ace said suddenly as the group had arrived back at the carriages. The snow was just beginning to fall around them as Ace reached his hand out, a small snowflake landing on his opened palm. "Every year we would have Christmas at Mrs. Barons. That was our tradition – one of the few we had before the war interrupted us. Would it be so hard that we set aside one day? I do not want to lose this, mates."

"Aye!" Mouth shrieked and grabbed hold of Ace in a violent manner. "If the Caldara's are hosting and providing grog, you know I am happy to bring my family to celebrate a holiday!"

"Aye!" many of them called, and Smith laughed as he and Kathleen both said, "Aye."

**

"I'm sorry, you know?" Sea said as she sat in the corner of the royal chambers. Smith was sitting up in bed – his queen lying beside him fast asleep. He remained under the blankets as he had been undressed.

"I know," Smith said, hardly sure why he was responding; he was well aware that this was a mere dream. "Pierson is a good boy, Sea. I am sorry you died before you could have met him."

"I am sorry he was not yours," she said.

"I am not," Smith said. "Learning he wasn't was just what I needed to finally let go of you."

"Have you truly forgotten me, Peter?" she asked, but she did not sound angry.

"Forget? Never," he said. "Moving on – absolutely."

"Good," she said. "It is time for that."

"I still love you," Smith said. "But…"

"Not the way you love her," Sea said for him. "That's all right. You loved her long before you ever loved me – back when you were just a peasant boy washing his clothes outside the palace walls. You loved her then. You always have. I am glad you finally found one another again."

"I miss you," Smith said.

"And, I you," she said. "Fair winds, Captain."

"Fair winds, Sea."

There was a sense of finality to the farewell.

Smith awoke suddenly to the sound of knocking. "I will kill whoever that is," he moaned as he blinked his eyes open to see Kathleen still sleeping like a sweet angel beside him. No longer his princess – but his darling queen. Her wedding dress was tossed to the floor in a corner. Her hair was in his face, so he brushed it away slightly. That was the last dream he would ever have of Sea, and he knew it then that she would no longer plague him. True, he would think of her from time to time, but his heart only had room for Kathleen.

"Someone's knocking," Kathleen said softly, not opening her eyes.

Smith kissed her lips and felt himself almost swoon. She still did not open her eyes; the poor woman had likely had too much wine, and they had been up quite late. "Sleep," Smith told her. "I will take care of this."

Smith threw on some trousers and a shirt, checked to ensure that Kathleen was well covered, and then headed to answer the door of the royal chambers. He cracked the door open and saw Snake staring back at him. "I will put a knife to your gut," Smith said.

"King Peter," Snake said with an awkward nod. "His Former Majesty Harold needs you. I need you – *now*."

"I know I have responsibilities, mate, but of all mornings for you to come knocking on my door so early why the morning after my wedding night?" Smith snapped.

"Is that Snake out there?" Kathleen's voice called. "Tell him I'm going to kill him later."

"Smith, it's important," Snake said.

Smith sighed. "Give me a moment to get properly dressed." Smith closed the door in his friends face and finished adorning himself in proper attire.

"Come back to bed," Kathleen said. "Leave him out in the hall." She had her face partially buried in a pillow to emphasize her exhaustion.

"I can't do that to him. I'll be back soon," Smith promised and kissed her head.

Kathleen sat upright and yawned. "Hold on, let me get dressed. Make the dead man who woke us wait a bit longer." She stood up, and Smith felt himself blush as she dressed herself. It hardly seemed real knowing that he was married to this woman.

He glanced out onto their balcony – a beautiful sunrise. He smiled. "How lovely," Kathleen said as she gazed out the balcony window with him. "We will enjoy many more of those together."

"Yes, we will," Smith said.

The two of them followed Snake out into the hall, and the man limped off on his cane. "You know who you look like hobbling around like that?" Smith taunted.

"Say it, and I'll murder you," Snake said.

"You're passing on the glass eye, I assume?" Smith said.

"I will not get a glass eye, you ass," Snake said. "I forgot how cranky you are in the morning."

"Leave him alone, Peter," Kathleen said and nudged Smith slightly for being so cruel to his friend.

They entered Harold and Rachel's bed chamber. Ace was there as well. They had a large chest they had opened and set in the middle of the room. "What is all of this?" Kathleen asked.

"Maria told us where she and John had kept some of their belongings hidden from the Cruz's in one of the secret passages her father was unaware of," Harold said. "There are journals dating all the way back to John's childhood – letters too. Even the ones that were exchanged between Robbie and himself regarding their plot to save Amy when I had ordered her execution."

"It seems we have the entire tale of the making of the monster here before us," Rachel said, wiping tears from her eyes. "We've been piecing it together all morning."

"Incredible," Smith said. "What have you found?"

"It was him," Snake said, handing Smith a handful of notes written in Smith's own hand. "Maria was helping him – that's why the letters kept coming and why we were uncertain if our friend was a man or woman – because there were two of them."

Smith held the letters in his hands, and frankly he could hardly believe it. John had been helping them from the beginning. What did this mean? Why would John sacrifice so much for them? Was it all for Snake, or was there more to this tale? "Unbelievable," Smith said. "It was him this entire time. John Stevenson was the Red Dragon."

Characters

Black Dragon's Past and Present

Peter "Smith" Barons – Captain of the *Black Dragon*, war deserter, and a generally conflicted individual whose actions are driven by a deeply broken heart

Courtney "Sea" Livingston – Deceased, former captain of the *Black Dragon*. She is also the former love interest of Smith and keeper of many dark secrets

Johnny "Snake" Lee – Second member to join the Black Dragons. He is Smith's closest friend and first mate aboard the *Black Dragon*. Snake takes on a general-like role in the rebellion, paying homage to his father

Mapiya "Sky" Lee – A young native girl from the American colonies who was rescued by Snake, now his wife

Hethuska – Sky's elder brother

Gomda – Sky's former fiancé

Mathew "Yin" Hill – He and his twin brother were the third and fourth members of the crew. Yin has a scar over the left side of his face as well as an eyepatch after one of

John's men shot him in the face many years ago. Yin is now having to cope with the loss of his brother and closest friend

Michael "Yang" Hill – He and his twin brother were the third and fourth members of the crew. He allowed himself to become a prisoner of war to keep his brother out of harm's way, and as a result he was hanged in the capital. Deceased

Tommy "Mouth" Staff – He and his younger brother were the fifth and sixth members of the crew. Mouth finds it difficult to trust people after being betrayed by some of his closest friends as a child, but this is something he has learned to cope with. His greatest remorse comes from the loss of his son, Ian

Jacob "Squirt" Staff – He and his elder brother were the fifth and sixth members of the crew. Squirt was a mere infant when he joined the crew, but he is now a young man and is ready to give his heart to Gwen, another member of the crew

Abigail Proctor-Staff – She is married to Mouth and is often underestimated by her enemies for being a woman, but she has proven herself to her crew countless times. She was originally engaged to Prince Richard and has a lovechild with former general Tim Valley. The loss of her second son Ian hurt her to the point that she has difficulty being intimate with her husband

Ian – Mouth and Abigail's young son who drowned in a river; a body has never been found

Jake – Abigail and Tim Valley's illegitimate lovechild

David "Cannonball" Steele – He was the seventh member of the Black Dragons. He's the only original member not born in Kirkston as an Irishman. He earned his nickname because he knew a lot about weaponry on ships; he lost his father and older brother, Thomas, in a shipwreck caused by Stevenson when he was younger. He was particularly close with Yin and Yang prior to sacrificing himself for Smith during the war. Deceased

Terrance "Blade" Simon – He and Knot were the eighth and ninth members of the Black Dragons. The two of them stuck together after their parent's deaths, and until recently Blade had harbored a heavy guilt for his involvement in the deaths of Knot's parents. Blade is in love with Hannah Cook, but his absolute commitment to the crew prevents him from leaving for her

Garret "Knot" Storm – He and Blade were the eighth and ninth members of the Black Dragons. A year younger than Blade, he had always looked up to him as though he was an older brother. He lost his leg during a shipping accident, making it easier for him to retire as Knot was the first to quit the crew, marrying Anna Cook and moving to Kevin's Isle to earn an honest living

James "Ace" Lincoln Caldara – He was the tenth member of the Black Dragons and the last to join the crew before Smith. He has in recent years become more open with his teammates, but he harbors a secret from Smith. For Ace, the war has been a blessing in disguise as he is able to mend broken bonds with his family

Stewart Clifton – He and his sister joined the Black Dragon's after Stewart was abandoned by his former pirate captain. A former Annihilator. He has become close friends with Mouth since joining the crew as well as his former abuser, Jackson. He aspires to become a preacher one day like his father

Gwenyfar "Gwen" Clifton – Stewart's younger sister and one of the Black Dragon's fiercest fighters. She and Squirt have developed a romantic relationship

Jackson White – The former captain of the *Annihilator* who has fallen madly in love with Ellen Barons. He has a fatherly relationship with Smith. In recent days, mostly thanks to Stewart and Mrs. Barons, Jackson has begun to question matters of faith

Cassidy Dain – One of the former Irish stowaways who became a functioning member of the Black Dragons. She is the love interest of Ace and is greatly burdened after having been forced to give up some of her children in her youth

Clara Dain – Cassidy's younger sister who was born with a serious asthmatic condition. Love interest of Yin and a former love interest of both Cannonball and Yang

Nicole Dain – Cassidy's daughter and her only child she managed to not have taken from her. Nicole is a bright young teen who has developed a father-daughter relationship with Ace

Smith's Family

William Barons – Deceased father of Smith; he was shot by John Stevenson on Smith's twelfth birthday and was a fatherly figure to Jackson White for a brief period of time

Elizabeth and Anna Barons – Deceased sisters of Smith; both girls burned to death in a fire set by Stevenson

Ellen Barons – Smith's mother and motherly figure to all of the Black Dragons; she is on her way to becoming the first female physician in Kirkston

Andrew Wilks – Smith's uncle and one of Ellen Barons' long-lost brothers. He is a weapons specialist and desperately seeks a relationship with his nephew

Phillip Wilks – Deceased cousin of Smith's and son of Andrew Wilks; he was shot to death by one of the invading Spaniards before the war

Thaddeus Wilks – Smith's young cousin; Andrew's youngest son

The Royals

King Harold and Queen Rachel – They are the rulers of Kirkston and parents to Black Dragon member Ace. The two of them are harboring a number of secrets from their new allies regarding royal scandals of the past

Princess Kathleen – The princess of Kirkston and heir to the throne. Her friendship with the Black Dragon's is what made it possible for her family to survive the initial invasion, and now she works diligently to abide by her duties as future queen

Prince Richard – The prince of Kirkston and twin brother of Kathleen. He enjoys the freedom that comes with not being the heir, but he is beginning to question why he was never given the opportunity. Richard is now missing an ear after being shot in the head during the war

Isabella White-Caldara – A former illegal soldier and amputee who escaped a hanging by lying about a pregnancy while living in England. She is now the wife of Prince Richard and younger sister to Jeremiah and Jackson White

Jackie Caldara – The young son of Prince Richard and Isabella

Dave – The son of one of Harold's deceased sisters

General Alex Ashley – Current acting head general of Kirkston and former fiancé to Princess Kathleen

The Cooks

Mrs. Jane Cook – The mother of the Cook children

Maxi Cook Junior -The oldest of the Cook children who took over the family estate after the death of Maxi Cook Senior. He struggles deeply with social expectations as a member of the wealthy class, and at this point his main goal is to try to hold his family together

Tom Cook – The former leader of the Skull Island gang and illegitimate son of Maxi Cook Junior. Previously an enemy of the Black Dragons, Tom now works alongside the crew to fight to put the Caldara's back in power

Evan Cook – Deceased, legitimate son of Maxi Cook Junior; killed by Gwen in a self-defense incident. He was meant to be the heir to the Cook fortune prior to his death

Jenny Cook – Wife and former servant to Maxi Cook Junior

Susan Cook-Valley – The eldest of the Cook daughters and younger sister to Maxi. Wife to Tom Cook

Tim Valley – He was once a stable boy turned general of Kirkston, but now after being blinded by John Stevenson, Tim finds himself as the husband of Susan and a member of the Cook household. He has a childhood friendship with Ace as well as a past love interest with Mouth's wife, Abigail, and is the father of Jake

James Valley – Deceased; the young son of Susan and Tim who was born without the use of his legs due to an injury after a pregnant Susan was knocked over by John Stevenson. He was named after Ace, and he passed away during the night due to complications from his injury

Hannah Cook-Simon – Another one of the Cook children. Hannah has deeply fallen for Black Dragon member Blade

Terrance "Terrie" Simon – Hannah and Blade's daughter, named for her father

Anna Cook-Storm – Another one of the Cook children and wife to Black Dragon member, Knot

Ellen Jane Storm – Knot and Anna's young daughter. Knot says she is named for all of his mother's: *Ellen* Barons; *Jane* is both Mrs. Keg's first name and the name of Anna's mother – Knot never knew his mother's name as she died very young and he knew her as only "Mama" but his daughter carries the woman's married name, *Storm*

Jimmy Cook – The youngest of the Cook children

La Cofradía

John Stevenson – The former general of Kirkston who has somehow become acquainted with the brotherhood of invading Spaniards. However, John is beginning to express doubt in his own cause

Maria Stevenson – The wife of John Stevenson and daughter to Señor Cruz

Robbie Stevenson – The son of John and Maria Stevenson

Amy Stevenson – The young daughter of John and Maria Stevenson

Antonio Manrique – A Spanish man working for La Cofradía directly under Cruz. He happily displays his control over John despite John being labelled as king

Juan Manrique – Antonio's brother whose morals are questionable

Señor Cruz – The true leader of La Cofradía, a cult like organization created over generations of his family's hatred for Spain and Kirkston. He believes himself to be the rightful ruler of Spain, but he has instead turned his attention on Kirkston because of a revengeful attitude towards the country's monarchs

Buddy – Jeremiah White's former slave/crewmate who betrayed the rebellion to work for Cruz

Friends, Family, Allies, and Former Combatants

Ron Katch – A childhood friend of Smith's who took over Mr. Anderson's blacksmith shop; Ron and his family have now joined the rebellion

Theresa Katch – A childhood friend of Smith's and wife to Ron

Pete Katch – The young son of Ron and Theresa Katch. He was named after Smith

Dr. Scott Conal – The good doctor friend of the Black Dragons

Benny – Deceased owner and operator of the former *Benny's Inn* on Skull Island where the Black Dragon's would often gather in their youth. He is one of the few people who knew all of Sea's secrets. He was killed for harboring fugitives from La Cofradía

Kyo Mori – Commodore of the *Silver Queen* fleet. He once won Stewart and the *Black Dragon* in a card game until both were stolen back by the Black Dragons. His parents and wife were killed by John Stevenson, and it was Kyo's idea to pull together pirates and criminals to help fight for the Caldara's

Chi Mori – Kyo's sister and one of the captains of his fleet; she has fancied Stewart ever since he came to Akito Berry Island

Saki Mori – Kyo's young daughter

Helena White – Jackson's ex-wife and current wife to his brother Jeremiah; she helped Jeremiah lead a mutiny against Jackson. Helena is Stewart and Gwen's eldest sister, and it has become clear that Helena suffers from some sort of psychological disturbance

Jeremiah White – Jackson's older brother who led the mutiny against him. He has now become a leader within the Caldara's rebellion

Charles – A professional translator and the son of an American colonist and native woman who befriended Snake during his and Sky's journey to Virginia

Agatha – A gypsy woman originally from Kirkston whom Smith befriends in Balla, but she is hiding her true identity from Smith

Pierson – Sea's illegitimate son who was raised by her cousin, Carissa. The identity of Pierson's father is uncertain

Carissa Livingston – Sea's cousin from the country of Balla who took on the role of Pierson's adopted mother

Gracie Freeman – Stewart and Gwen's sister who abandoned them to live aboard the *Annihilator*

Jamie Freeman – Husband to Gracie Freeman

General Robbie and Amy Lee – presumably deceased parents of Snake

Melusine Von Der Schulenbur – The Duchess of Kendal and Munster; she is who Kathleen goes to in order to be granted aid from Europe. She is also King George's mistress nicknamed "The Maypole" for her tall stature

Eric Senior – A barkeep outside of London whom Kathleen meets; his wife advises Kathleen to speak to Melusine to request aid

Eric Junior – The son of the barkeep, Eric Senior

Mark – A fisherman Smith offers a business deal to during his stay in Balla

Morris – A childhood friend of Mouth's who is one of three boys (Morris, **Juni**, **Roman**) who betrayed Mouth's parents for bread, resulting in their deaths. Morris was the boy who force fed Mouth leeches as a child, but now Morris is a soldier in the rebellion's army

Mrs. Oden – A noble woman who leads a group of female civilians and young boys to fight for the Caldara's rebellion

Degataga – A cousin of Charles who arrives in Kirkston with American soldiers to help fight the Cruz's

Connar – One of Cassidy's long lost children whom the Caldara's work to reunite with her

Michael and Nicole Hill – Fraternal twins born to Yin and Clara, named after Yin's brother Yang and Clara's niece who lost their lives during the war

Long before the *Black Dragon* ever set sail, a twelve-year-old boy from Kevin's Isle made his way to Caldara Castle to attend his parents hanging – never expecting he would be invited to stay. Witness the story that created the monster who became the silent hero of Kathleen's Rebellion, The Red Dragon.

Follow John Stevenson as he comes to live with the Lee's at Caldara Castle where he works his way from humble servant to the country's head general – eventually becoming the conqueror of Kirkston.

Made in the USA
Columbia, SC
04 May 2019